# Blood of the Phoenix

Bonnie

Copyright

This book is a work of fiction. Names, characters, places, dialogue and incidents either are the product of the author's imagination or are used fictitiously, and any resemblance to actual events, locales, or persons, living or dead, is entirely coincidental.

Copyright ©2017 by Bonnie Humbarger Lamer

All rights reserved.

No part of this text may be reproduced, transmitted, down-loaded, decompiled, reverse engineered, scanned or distributed in any printed or electronic form without the express written permission of the copyright holder.

ISBN-13: 978-1977680570

ISBN-10: 1977680577

# Other Titles by Bonnie Lamer

## The Witch Fairy Series:

True of Blood

Blood Prophecy

Blood Lines

Shadow Blood

Blood of Half Gods

Blood of Destiny

Blood of Dragons

Blood of Egypt

Blood of Retribution

Blood of the Exiled

Doppelganger Blood

Blood of Centaurs

Blood of Sirens

Elf Blood

Blood and Spirits

Demon Blood

True of Blood: Kallen's Tale

Blood Prophecy: Kallen's Tale

Blood Lines: Kallen's Tale

Shadow Blood: Kallen's Tale

Blood of Half Gods: Kallen's Tale

Blood of Destiny: Kallen's Tale

Blood of Dragon's: Kallen's Tale

Blood of Egypt: Kallen's Tale

Blood of Retribution: Kallen's Tale

Blood of the Exiled: Kallen's Tale

Blood of Centaurs: Kallen's Tale

Blood of Sirens: Kallen's Tale

Elf Blood: Kallen's Tale

**The Eliana Brennan Series:**

Essence of Ra

Exposed

Homeland

Sutekh

**The Secrets of the Djinn Series:**

Marked

Bound

Unchained

I love to hear from fans! Contact me on Facebook at http://www.facebook.com/pages/Bonnie-Lamer-Author/129829463748061

*For my ever patient fans. Sorry this one took so long.*

# 1 Chapter

"I have had a vision."

These words from Isla are surprising. She rarely tells anyone about her visions. Even more surprising? Her need to share this with us at three o'clock in the morning. Shielding my eyes from the explosion of light she let loose in our bedroom, I mumble, "Huh?" I am not at my best at three o'clock in the morning.

Kallen is even less coherent with a mumbled, "Mmm?" I feel no movement from his side of the bed, so he may not even be awake. Despite the blinding light unleashed upon us.

"The Phoenix is going to refuse to die."

Peeking out from under my arm, I ask, "Are you sleep walking? Because you are making no sense."

Next to me, Kallen sits up and rubs his eyes. He was awake, after all. "Grandmother, that is impossible." I guess her words make more sense to him than they do to me.

Maybe I should take this conversation a little more seriously. Opening both eyes, exposing dual retinas to everlasting damage, I ask, "You have a pet Phoenix you haven't mentioned until now? And why do you want him dead?" Even to my sleep addled brain that is awfully cruel.

The scowl directed my way is a clear indication that Isla is annoyed by my questions. "The Phoenix is not a pet."

Joining Kallen in a sitting position, I stretch my arms over my head in an effort to wake up. "I still don't understand why you want the Phoenix to die." Under my breath, I whisper to Kallen, "Are we talking about a bird?"

"Sort of," he replies. "The Phoenix can take many forms, but when it dies, it does die as a bird."

"That's not confusing at all," I grumble. Turning my attention back to Isla, I ask, "Why do we want the Phoenix to die?"

"If the Phoenix does not complete her life cycle, the universe will be consumed by Cosmic Fire."

"You're back to making no sense again," I inform Isla. "I may only have a basic understanding of astrophysics, but that just doesn't add up. The sun is nowhere near ready to go supernova." Not to mention, our sun would not affect the entire universe. Just our small portion of it.

"It will not be the sun that burns, it will be the Phoenix," Kallen says, getting out of bed. "Fueled by energy usurped from the sun."

Now I am even more confused. "I thought the whole point of a Phoenix is to burst into flames and then be reborn to symbolize the eternal life cycle of death and rebirth. I have never heard that it could steal energy from the sun to kill us all."

Kallen holds a hand out to help me out of bed in a clear signal that we will not be going back to sleep anytime soon. "It is more than symbolism, but you are correct. The Phoenix must die before it can be reborn. If it does not, the flames that are meant to continue the cycle of life and death will continue to intensify until not even the universe can contain them."

I give him my hand, but he does not have my confidence yet. "You're telling me that one creature has the power to end the universe simply by refusing to die? And how is it even possible to refuse to die?"

The sound of a crying baby moving closer to us proves to be too much of a distraction for Isla to respond to me, regardless of Phoenixes and the threat of cosmic demise. She steps into the hall and says softly, "I apologize for waking the child. It could not be helped."

"It is fine, I am growing accustomed to only two hours of sleep at a time," Kegan grumbles. "I assume there is an emergency to be dealt with?" He is in the doorway now, and Keelan is cradled against his chest. Kegan is bouncing him gently, and his little tears begin to ebb.

Isla holds her arms out for her great-grandchild. "Let me see him," she insists.

Kegan hands his son over. "Feel free to change him," he tells her. The 'you are the one who woke him up, after all' is implied in his tone.

Isla narrows her eyes at him, but does not chastise Kegan in front of his son. Instead, she tells him what she told Kallen and me a few minutes ago. "I have had a vision. The Phoenix is going to refuse to die."

Kegan's eyes grow round. "You must be mistaken," he declares. Apparently, everyone but me understands the significance of this. I should probably get up to speed. A good start would be believing what Kallen told me a moment ago. It's just so hard to swallow, though. A bird is going to destroy the universe? Really? Who dreams these things up?

"I have had the same vision every night for a week," Isla informs him.

My mouth drops open. "Wait, a week? Then why wake us up at *three in the morning* to tell us about it?" I gripe, growing more annoyed by the second. She could have told us earlier at dinner, or waited until breakfast.

Isla narrows her eyes at my chastisement. "Because the previous visions were vague. This one clearly showed me the end. It is imperative that you act now."

"The end?" I ask, needing clarification. I have found through unwanted experience that it is best to never assume things. Though, I suspect I do know what she is going to say. It's what she always says in situations like this. Or, at least, some variation of it.

"The end of the universe." Yup, that was what I thought she would say.

Putting my hands on my hips, I demand, "What am I supposed to do about it? Am I supposed to track the Phoenix down and kill it? I'm not going to do that. One, I'm not a hunter, and two, I don't kill other beings."

"The Phoenix cannot be killed," Kallen tells me. "She must choose to die and be resurrected."

I am getting a headache. "So, I'm supposed to talk her into being suicidal?" I snark. This situation is growing more unbelievable by the second.

"You will travel to the Cowan realm and enlist the help of your friends," Isla insists out of the blue. Almost as if she has ignored everything I have said in the last two minutes. Wait, I believe she has.

Frowning, I ask, "Which friends?" I don't have a lot of friends in the Cowan realm, but still, I want to be perfectly clear who she means.

"The friend who possesses the essence of Ra within her. He was intimately associated with the Phoenix in the past, even taking on the responsibility of guarding her ashes. He may be able to talk some sense into her."

Hmm, call upon Eliana to ask her to try to talk some sense into Ra's old girlfriend? That won't be awkward for any of us. "As much as I would like to see Eliana again, is it really necessary to drag her into this?"

Kallen touches my arm. "If Grandmother is correct and the Phoenix is refusing to complete her cycle, we will all perish. I know that you want to believe the cosmos are guided only by science, but Xandra, you know enough of the universe to know that simply is not true. The universe is a combination of science and magic." After a brief pause to let that sink in, he continues, "Think of the many religions in the Cowan realm. All of them have a Phoenix legend in their earliest forms. In all of nature, the cycle of life and death is perpetual. While there is science behind it, because there must be order in the universe for us to survive, there is also magic. Consider her a failsafe, if you will. She is closely associated with the power of the sun, and she draws on this power to perpetuate the life cycle. For whatever reason, the responsibility of maintaining balance, meaning the power to perpetuate life and the power of ultimate destruction, was given to the Phoenix."

"Isn't that a bit too much responsibility for one being?" I grumble, still not entirely convinced this is all true.

"It is, but he is correct, my dear granddaughter," Lailah's singsong voice rings in my ear.

I whip my head to the side to find my grandmother in all her Angel glory and perfection standing next to me. I smile and give her a big hug, careful not to bend any of the feathers on her wings. "Grandma, I've missed you!"

"I have missed you, as well," she says, kissing my cheek. "You really should spend more time among the Angels," she chastises lightly. Turning her attention to Keelan, she smiles and sighs, "What a precious child." She moves closer and takes him from Isla's frozen arms. Touching his smooth, still cheek softly, she says, "It broke my heart to use him as a tool to fight the Demons."

"He wasn't harmed," I remind her, even though I still have traces of guilt lingering in me over the whole thing, too. Someday, he is going to learn about it. What will he think of me then?

Lailah smiles. "No, he was not harmed. He will grow to be strong and fierce, this Fairy. His destiny is that of greatness." She glances up at me and winks. "Of course, that is all I can say about it."

I roll my eyes. "Of course, you would not be an Angel if you did not speak cryptically. It's the law, isn't it?"

Lailah laughs. "As a matter of fact, yes."

"So, you're here to tell me that Isla is right, and I really do need to go talk this Phoenix into killing herself?" That comes out ruder than I meant, but Grandma isn't bothered by it.

"It is not quite that simple."

"It never is," I mutter. Realizing I am taking my annoyance out on her, I smile sheepishly and ask, "Can you simplify it for me?"

Lailah's smile remains warm and understanding. "I will try. Like the Angels and the minor deities, the Phoenix is immortal. The difference is, she must walk among the mortal beings of the universe forever. She lives as they do. She travels from realm to realm and lives many lifetimes in one."

I can't help it. Words slip out of my mouth. "That sounds tedious."

"It can be. But the Phoenix has never minded. She loves being free to wander, free to take on new identities, new lives."

Frowning, I ask, "Then why is she suddenly bent on destroying the universe?"

With a heavy sigh, Lailah admits, "We do not know."

"Then how do you know she is going to refuse to die?" I ask.

"She said so right before she disappeared."

I guess that is pretty good evidence. "Could she just be teasing you?" I ask hopefully. Yes, it would be in poor taste, but I would rather the Phoenix have a terrible sense of humor than be bent on destroying the universe.

"The Phoenix may not lie. She is bound by the truth of existence and carries within her a spark from the Flames of Truth."

"Um, the stuff the Demons were created from?" I groan. I really do not want to fight Demons again.

Understanding where my thought process has gone, Lailah shakes her head. "Demons were created from the ash. The Phoenix was not created from these flames, nor the ash as the Demons were. But, the flame that allows her to die and be reborn is from the Flames of Truth."

"Got it," I mumble, hoping there really is a difference between the Phoenix and the Demons. I am not yet convinced. After all, both seem to want to end the universe.

Lifting her hand from Keelan's cheek, Lailah rests it on mine. "Find the Phoenix. Discover what has caused her to defy her destiny and help her see this is not the way."

I open my mouth to argue that I am not the best diplomat in the world when her first sentence sinks into my brain. "Wait, what do you mean 'find her?'"

Lailah is suddenly consumed with the need to adore Keelan again. Without looking at me, she says, "As

Kallen said, the Phoenix can take many forms. We have lost track of her."

My jaw just became unhinged. I am going to have a nasty bruise from it hitting the floor. Pushing my jaw back into place with my finger, it still takes me a moment to find words. Finally, I go with, "The Angels don't know where she is, but I am supposed to find her?"

Lailah glances up from Keelan and gives me an encouraging smile. "Yes."

I am not encouraged. Another thought hits me. "You all believe that Ra will be able to figure out what form she is in right now and where she is." That's why I need Eliana.

With a nod, Lailah confirms I am right. "In Heliopolis, Ra stored for the Phoenix the ashes of her previous resurrections. There are wards in place that only he may see through. We believe there are clues there which will help you find her."

"If you believe that, why don't the Angels go?" Not that I don't want to help, but it would be faster if they searched for clues themselves seeing as they know so much more about the Phoenix than I do.

"Because we do not know where it is."

So, there is no choice but to include Eliana in this. Ra is apparently the only one who knows the secret location of the Phoenix's hideout. I hate to do it. I know Eliana's life has gotten very complicated now that she works for the government. But, I doubt she will mind too much. I assume she would like the universe to continue to exist just as much as the rest of us. "Fine," I grumble.

Lailah leans over and gives me a kiss on the cheek. "Someday, you will be rewarded for all of your sacrifices."

I cannot help but scowl. "Unless the reward comes in the form of no more universe threatening incidents, I'm not really looking for compensation."

"Which makes you perfect for the destiny set out for you," Lailah replies sweetly. I try not to roll my eyes. Smiling down at Keelan, she gives his forehead a final kiss. "Good bye, little warrior." She hands him to me. I assume because it would be hard to put him back into Isla's arms since the Fairies are frozen in time at the moment.

Situating Keelan in my arms, I give my grandmother a wry smile. "Thanks for the information."

"I do what I can to help you." With a wink, Lailah disappears and I am back in Fairy time.

It is not often that Isla is startled, but suddenly finding her great-grandson missing from her arms does the trick. Her eyes immediately zero in on me. "Who was here?" she demands. She may have been startled, she is not stupid.

## 2 CHAPTER

"Lailah," I respond, handing the now very calm Keelan back to her. A benefit of having the Angel of Love hold him, I imagine. But, as much as I love the little guy, he stinks and I don't want to be stuck changing his diaper because I am the last one to hold him. Selfish, yes. Am I okay with that? Definitely.

"What cryptic information did your grandmother bring this time?" Kallen asks.

Ignoring his snide tone, I tell him, "She was actually very helpful. Well, sort of," I amend. Glancing at Isla, I complain, "You didn't tell me that no one knows where the Phoenix is, not even the Angels."

Kallen scowls. "The Angels have lost track of the Phoenix? That is unprecedented."

"So I gathered," I grumble. "Which is part of why we need to enlist Eliana's help. Ra might have a clue somewhere in his temple, or whatever he built for the Phoenix, as to where she is currently hiding."

Turning to Isla, Kallen asks, "Is there anything else we should know before we depart for the Cowan realm?"

"I suggest you bring your friend here once you have enlisted her help. We can formulate a plan together," Isla says.

Surprised, I ask incredulously, "You want us to bring Cowans here?" I use the plural because there is no way Eliana is coming without Josh.

Isla gives me a wry smile. "It is the Witches who keep magic from the Cowans, not other supernatural beings. While that may be a good idea considering the current state of that realm, your friend is fairly well-versed in the existence of magic and in our existence."

"Good point," I agree sheepishly.

"We can be ready to leave in a few minutes," Kallen tells Isla. He glances down at himself. "We should at least be presentable when we go to them."

I suspect that he means me more than him. His sleep tossed black hair and wrinkled t-shirt only make him look more gorgeous. He also put jeans on over his boxers before getting out of bed. My long hair needs a serious brushing to get out the sleep induced snarls, and my pajamas are not exactly what I want to wear when traveling from realm to realm. "Give us five minutes," I say, heading back into our bedroom.

"Do hurry," Isla insists.

Kallen follows me, closing our bedroom door behind him. Before I can reach the dresser where I keep my brush, he wraps his arms around my waist and nuzzles my neck. Leaning into him, I groan, "I don't think we have time for this."

"Probably not," he agrees. Still, he turns me in his arms and kisses me passionately. When we finally come up for air, he says with a sexy grin, "I have no idea when we can do that again. I was not going to give up the chance."

"I like the way you think," I purr, leaning up and kissing him again.

We are interrupted by a loud pounding on the door. "Grandmother suggests you hurry," Kegan calls in a mocking voice. Was he listening outside our room? I scowl at the door and my annoying cousin-in-law. Isla must have taken Keelan to change him if Kegan is willing to make so much noise.

"We're coming!" I call back snarkily before Kallen can say what is on the tip of his tongue. Just in case Keelan is still within hearing range. I don't want to scar his little psyche. My gorgeous husband narrows his eyes in my direction for cutting him off, but he doesn't say anything.

Reluctantly leaving Kallen's arms, I move to our dresser. I run a quick brush through my hair getting most of the snarls out. Opening a drawer, I pull out a pair of jeans and start to reach for a sweater but stop. Over my shoulder, I ask Kallen, "Any idea what season it is in the Cowan realm?" Since time moves differently between realms, we are not always on the same season schedule.

"Fall, I believe," he tells me. As he speaks, he magically trades his wrinkled t-shirt for a black pullover sweater. The jeans he put on when he crawled out of bed stay.

I am going to wear real clothes, not magic ones. One less thing for Kallen to worry about if we run into trouble. I pull out a lavender sweater to go with my jeans. Once I am dressed, I turn to Kallen. "Ready?"

Pulling me gently into his arms again, Kallen studies me. "The question is, are you ready? The universe is always demanding more and more from you."

I shrug in an effort toward nonchalance. "That's what I was created to do."

Kallen chuckles. "Here I thought you were created to be worshipped by me."

Wrapping my arms around his neck, I pull him in for another kiss. "I was created for that, too," I murmur against his lips.

Another loud knock on the door causes us to pull apart. "Does he think being a father will save him from being punched?" Kallen asks, not at all kidding.

A giggle escapes me as we pull apart. "If so, I suspect he is about to learn how wrong he is." Proving me right, Kallen strides to the door, opens it, and proceeds to punch his cousin hard in the arm. At least he checked to make sure Kegan wasn't holding Keelan before he hit him.

Rubbing his arm and laughing, Kegan insists, "I was just doing as Grandmother asked."

I raise a brow. "Quite the dutiful grandson. Was this in exchange for getting out of changing your son?"

Kegan's grin is shameless. "Pester my cousin or change a dirty diaper? Is there really a choice there?"

"What is going on?" a sleepy Alita asks from their bedroom door. "I checked on Keelan in the nursery and Isla is changing him."

"Your husband is too busy being a wanker to attend to his duties," Kallen informs her.

Rolling her eyes, Alita yawns and says, "You can explain in the morning. I am going back to bed." Being the practical new mother who needs her sleep that she is, she closes the door and does just that. Good for her. I wonder, though, if my curiosity will be tempered as much as hers when I am a mother. I doubt it.

"Come on," I say, grabbing Kallen's hand and pulling him toward the stairs. "The sooner we convince Eliana to help, the sooner we can get back here and make a plan to find the Phoenix." Though, I doubt Eliana will need much convincing after she hears about the end of the universe thing. Even if the universe wasn't in danger, I know I can always count on her for help.

At the bottom of the stairs, we turn toward the terrace. Isla prefers that I do not open passageways inside the house. We trudge down the terrace steps and onto the beach where a cool breeze makes me glad I am wearing a sweater. I debate for a moment where I should open the passageway on the other side. I've been admonished by the Witches for opening passageways out in the open of the Cowan realm because of satellite imagery. Humans may lack magic, but they make up for it in technology. I worry about it less when going back to our house in the Colorado mountains because of all the trees. But, going to a city I should be more cautious. Not just because of satellites. I would scare the hell out of normal people if they saw me doing this.

Glancing up at Kallen, I say wryly, "I hope Eliana doesn't mind the intrusion." I try to avoid opening passageways in houses in general because, outside of the numerous possibilities of things that could go wrong, it is rude to just barge in. But this time, I don't think I have a choice. I reach out and tear the fabric of the realms.

# 3 CHAPTER

An amusing scene unfolds before us. Three couples are peacefully watching a movie and eating popcorn. As the passageway opens, one of those bowls of popcorn crashes to the floor. Someone other than the popcorn dropper gasps loudly. Someone else growls, "What the hell?!" This same person reaches for a sidearm at his waist. He doesn't find it. I'm glad he doesn't. I mean, who wears a sidearm while watching a movie? That would be ridiculous. It also would have been pointless to aim one at us since either Kallen or I would have simply gotten rid of it with magic, or blocked the bullet if he managed to fire it first.

The responses from the other three in the room are quite the opposite of those first ones. Jadyn leaps up, a grin covering her face. "Xandra!"

Eliana and Josh also rise, smiles in place on their faces, as well. "I hope that's fixable, otherwise it's going to be awfully drafty in here come winter," Josh teases, knowing full well that the tear between realms is not permanent.

Eliana elbows him before saying, "Hurry up and come through so I can give you a hug!"

"You know these people?" the large man who had reached for an imaginary side arm demands. He is seriously regretting not having his gun with him. The defensive stance he takes tells me that he is still willing to take us on in a physical fight if need be. Kallen stiffens next to me, already disliking the guy, and more than ready to meet him in a fight. The scent of testosterone is now flooding the night air.

Josh notices this, as well. He turns to his friend and orders, "Stand down. Trust me, this is not a fight you would win."

Without changing his stance, the guy demands again, "Who the hell are these people?"

With a raised brow, I say to an amused Jadyn, "He's charming."

Deciding to ignore the large man's question, Kallen and I walk through the passageway, and I close it behind us. The big guy's eyes are going to pop out of his head if he doesn't at least blink or something. I would feel sorry for putting him in such a state of shock if he wasn't being such a jerk about it. Obviously, we're not a threat or Eliana would already be battling me. Something we would both like to avoid. Though, I suspect it would be one heck of a battle.

Jadyn shrugs. "He's human, what can I say?" The guy scowls down at the Skin Walker, but she ignores him. "So, what brings you to this realm? I doubt this is a social visit."

"This realm?" a voice says behind us.

I turn to find the other couple in the room still staring at us in shock. It finally dawns on me who they must be. Eliana and Josh's best friends. Pasting a warm smile on my lips despite the reason we are here, I say, "Sam and Jenna, right? Eliana told us all about you."

"Um, yeah," the guy says, holding his hand out to first me and then Kallen. He has also figured out our identities. "I take it you're Xandra and Kallen."

"In the flesh," I acknowledge, wondering just how much Eliana has told them about us. Considering she trusts them with all of her secrets, I suspect a lot. Which is fine with me. I trust Eliana's judgement.

"Good guess since we only have one friend who can tear holes between realms," Josh teases, confirming that they shared information about Kallen and me.

"Is someone going to tell me what's going on here?" the other guy demands, growing more agitated by the second. He is starting to make me believe that humans can self-combust from anxiety. One more thing happening that he doesn't understand and his guts are going to be plastered on the walls, I'm certain of it. I wonder if Kallen's restoration magic could put him back together? Probably not. I don't think it works on people. I am starting to feel a little guilty about causing the guy so much stress and vow to be nice to him. As long as he doesn't try to become violent. I have not forgotten that his first reaction was to reach for a gun that he must usually carry.

Josh steps forward and finally makes introductions. "Alonzo, these are our friends, Xandra and Kallen. This is Alonzo. We work with him."

When I opened the passageway, I didn't think about the fact that Eliana and Josh may have people here who wouldn't know about us. I guess opening a passage directly into the living room wasn't a great idea, either. Maybe the kitchen would have been better. Then again, we do most of our entertaining in the kitchen back home.

A hall closet, maybe? I'm not sure I could be that accurate with my ability. Clearing my head of locations, I hold my hand out to Alonzo and say in a massive understatement, "Sorry about surprising you like that." Around him, I mouth a sincerer apology to Eliana for putting her in such an awkward position with her coworker.

"Don't worry about it," Eliana tells me. "All of our team at Homeland know about me. Alonzo can keep a secret."

"He won't have to for long because he's about to have a coronary," Sam snickers. Jenna elbows him in the side and the large man glowers in his direction. Sam doesn't seem to care. I am going to assume there is some tension between the two guys that I don't want to know about.

"What the hell are you and what was that?" Alonzo presses, waving his hand in the air toward the spot where the passageway was a moment before.

"She is one of the most powerful beings in the universe and my wife. Therefore, you should watch your tone when addressing her," Kallen growls. He has definitely taken a dislike to the guy.

Alonzo takes a step forward. "I already know one of the most powerful beings in the universe, so I'm not intimidated by the likes of either of you."

Kallen takes a step forward, as well. And so do Eliana and I. Stepping between the two, we create a powerful bridge that they would have to cross to get to each other. Eliana turns to her friend and says, "Look, I know your training is kicking in because you think they are a threat, but really, Alonzo, you need to stand down. Josh was not kidding when he said that this is a fight you cannot win." With a surreptitious glance in my husband's direction, she continues, "Kallen spoke of Xandra's strength, but he left out the part that he is an extremely powerful Fairy who could lay you out without ever making contact with you. You wouldn't even feel it coming."

Alonzo takes a moment to absorb her words before asking, "He's a what?"

Jadyn smiles up at the large man. "There are more beings in the universe than Witches and Skin Walkers, remember. Many more. And Eliana is right. Kallen is not one to mess with."

Growing tired of the testosterone choking the life out of the oxygen in the room, Jenna takes charge. "Alonzo, sit down and be quiet. Jadyn was right. This can't just be a social call, and the rest of us would like to know what is going on. You can get caught up on the magic part of it all later." Alonzo opens his mouth to argue, but thinks better of it when the petite human glares at him. Instead, he crosses his arms over his chest and presses his lips firmly together. He does not sit down, though. Good for him for holding his ground. I try hard not to smile at his obstinacy.

I like Jenna. She may be small, but she makes up for it with strength of character. "Thank you," I say to her with a grateful smile.

"Not that we aren't glad to see you, but why are you here?" Josh asks.

With a jerk of his head toward Alonzo, Kallen asks, "Are you certain we can speak freely in front of him?" I'm pretty sure a growl escapes from Alonzo's throat, but he doesn't say anything.

Josh nods. "He's fine. He's just new to all of this."

"I am in the room," Alonzo grumbles. Still, the big man finally moves back to the couch and takes a seat as he tries to wrap his head around what is happening. Jadyn joins him and pats his knee affectionately. Hmm, I wonder what is going on there?

"I'll grab a couple of chairs from the dining room," Sam says, turning to leave the room.

"Oh, that's okay," I tell him just as Kallen uses magic to create chairs for him and me.

Once again, the large man's eyes are going to bug out of his head. Maybe I should get Kallen to make him some protective goggles so when it happens, we won't have to crawl around on the floor looking for his eyeballs. "How did you do that?" Alonzo demands.

Eliana laughs. "Their magic is a little different than mine," she says by way of explanation, and she returns to her own seat.

After everyone is settled back into their spots, I jump right in. "There's a situation." Okay, I didn't jump right in. I sort of waded in up to my toes. It's just so rude to ruin date night with a 'the universe is about to end' scenario. I feel bad.

Eliana isn't fooled by my hedging. She knows what kind of 'situations' I find myself in. With a groan, she says, "Please tell me it's not Archangels again."

There's a snort from Alonzo's direction. "Archangels?"

"Shh," Jadyn admonishes. Alonzo glowers at her but doesn't say anything else.

Ignoring him, I continue. "No, not this time. This time it has to do with the Phoenix."

"The bird?" Jenna asks.

Since I know hardly anything about the Phoenix, I decide I am not the best one to explain all of this. I give my gorgeous husband a pleading look, wanting him to stop glowering at Alonzo and finish the explanation for me. Which he does. Focusing his attention on the whole group now, he says, "The Phoenix only takes the form of a bird when she dies." I expect another snort from Alonzo until I remember that he is sitting next to a Skin Walker. Shapeshifting probably isn't a new concept for him. "The rest of the time, the Phoenix takes on the form of whatever beings she is living among at the time. She travels the universe, jumping from realm to realm with each rebirth. Her only function is to ensure eternal life."

"Her own eternal life?" Eliana asks.

Kallen shakes his head. "No." He pauses, considering how best to explain the next part. Finally, he just lays it all out. "The Phoenix represents the life cycle of the universe. She is the personification of death and rebirth both metaphysically and physically. If she does not complete the cycle of life and death every five hundred of her years, she creates an imbalance in the order of the universe." Okay, he doesn't want to jump right into the whole 'the Phoenix is about to end the universe' thing either. Man, are we cowards or what? Or, we just don't want to face the reality of the universe ending. I'm going with that explanation.

"Let me guess, she is refusing to complete the cycle," Sam says. For humans, he and Jenna are taking all of this rather calmly. Then again, they are Eliana's best friends for a reason. They accept her for who she is and aren't weirded out by it.

"What does that mean for the universe?" Josh asks, assuming his friend is correct. Which he is.

Glancing around the room, I decide to stop being a coward and just blurt it all out. "If the Phoenix refuses to die, which she is, she will be consumed by the Cosmic Fire she carries within her. It will expand until the entire universe is engulfed and destroyed."

I expect denials from Alonzo, or snorts of disbelief. I do not expect him to start laughing. Loudly. "Good one," he says.

Kallen scowls at him. "Good what?"

"Good joke, man. This is great. The whole dramatic entrance, the little show of magic, all to play an elaborate end of the world prank."

Eliana gives her friend a worried look. "Um, Alonzo, I don't think they're joking."

I shake my head. "We're not."

Falling back on the same argument I did earlier, Alonzo says, "Look, I don't know if you have science where you come from, but the universe does not depend on a bird for its survival. Unless all the suns and stars decide to go supernova all at the same time, which is impossible, we're going to be just fine. At least for a few billion more years or so."

I give him a wry smile. "That's what I thought, too. And just so you know, I grew up in Colorado."

This surprises and confuses him. "I thought you supposedly just came from another realm?"

Nodding, I confirm, "We did. I moved to the Fae realm after meeting Kallen. I didn't have to hide my magic or my ghost parents there. Plus, my biological father is King of the Fairies, and I need to take over for him some day." With a grimace, I add, "I'm supposed to take over for my grandfather, who is King of the Witches here, but that is much less appealing. Honestly, since the Angels decided that my destiny is to bring harmony to the universe, finding the time to be Queen of either is going to be pretty tough."

Kallen reaches over and takes my hand in his. Out of the corner of his mouth, he says, "My love, you are rambling a little." He is clearly amused both by my rambling and the confusion spreading over Alonzo's face.

"Yes, I suppose I am," I admit. I also shouldn't be giving out too much information about myself or the Witches to a stranger. I know Eliana has been careful to keep most of the Witches' secrets from everyone to help keep them safe. To Alonzo, I say, "Sorry, I'm used to spending time with other supernatural beings, and they all tend to know who I am. I don't usually have to explain myself." Maybe I could write up a little bio to hand out in these situations to keep me from saying too much.

"Xandra has quite the reputation in the supernatural world," Jadyn confirms.

"So, back to this Phoenix thing," Sam says, more interested in the end of the universe than in my supernatural reputation. "I'm kind of with Alonzo on this." He is clearly not happy about being on the same side of an argument with the guy, but he continues, "The science part doesn't make sense."

"Do I make sense?" Eliana asks.

Josh smiles and says, "You make perfect sense." Love shines from his eyes when he speaks to Eliana. It's really sweet. But, his words didn't help her argument.

Rolling her eyes but smiling back at him, Eliana presses her point. "I mean, my existence doesn't make sense." Turning to her friends, she says, "I don't know all the details of this yet, but I know enough about how things work to know that magic and science are intertwined in ways that sometimes defy explanation. If Xandra and Kallen say that this Phoenix woman can destroy the universe, we should believe them."

I grin across the room at her. "Thank you for the vote of confidence."

Eliana shrugs and admits, "I still kind of wish you were wrong, though."

Nodding in agreement, I say, "Me, too."

Growing sober as a thought hits her, Eliana narrows her eyes and asks, "You aren't here to ask me to help you kill the Phoenix, are you?"

With a shake of my head, I say, "I asked the same thing when Kallen's grandmother first told me about it. I flat out refused to do it if that was what she wanted." I can appreciate the relief that washes over Eliana's face, as I felt the same way during my conversation with Isla. Neither of us are killers.

Kallen also reassures Eliana. "The Phoenix cannot be killed. The only way she can die is if she chooses to do so."

"What can we do to help, then?" Josh asks.

Now things are going to get a little awkward. More awkward than telling them a bird is going to end the universe. "Apparently, Ra and the Phoenix had some sort of…relationship." A bit of color rushes to Eliana's cheeks, and mine, but I push on. "He had a temple or something dedicated to saving her ashes. The Angels believe there may be a clue there as to where to find the Phoenix."

"Wait, the Phoenix is missing?" Jenna gasps.

I nod. "No one can find her. Not even the Angels," I say with a grimace.

Alonzo is not content to remain silent any longer. "I thought Angels knew everything. How is it they lost someone?"

"There is only one truly omniscient Angel," Kallen informs him. He does not add that he is currently Fallen and that he lives with us. We can only pile so much on the guy before his head really does explode. I do not want to spend my night scrubbing brains off the walls. Technically, Kallen would use magic to scrub them off because I would be way too grossed out to help, but still. It's the principal of the thing.

"Okay, then why doesn't he tell you where this Phoenix is?" Alonzo demands.

"I'm afraid it doesn't work that way. He's not allowed to share his omniscience," I explain. "It would be detrimental to free will. We have to find the Phoenix on our own, even if that means the universe ending before we do." It is what it is. Not that it makes it any less annoying that Raziel keeps his information to himself. I understand why he does, though. "So, we're hoping Ra can help."

Turning his attention to his friend, Alonzo says to Eliana almost accusingly, "I thought you couldn't just ask the gods inside you questions?" Hmm, I'm starting to dislike the guy as much as Kallen does.

"I can't," she admits. "But, if Ra knows anything, he'll find a way to communicate it with me. I'm sure of it."

"In the meantime, we were hoping you would come back to the Fae realm with us so we can try to come up with a plan," I tell her. "Kallen's grandmother is much more knowledgeable about all of this than we are."

Eliana and Josh pass a look back and forth, and my hope that they will come with us begins to fade. Turning her attention back to me, Eliana says, "We want to help, but it will be hard to just leave. We would have to make arrangements with our boss."

That's right, their jobs are a little different than mine. "Do you think your boss will mind?" After all, they will be helping to save the universe. That seems like a reasonable excuse for taking time off to me.

Alonzo snorts. "Mind? She's going to demand that she be allowed to come with you."

I glance at him in horror. "Seriously?"

He nods. "Oh, yeah. Just you wait and see."

"This is not a sightseeing trip," Kallen grumbles.

"No, but Liza is determined to learn as much about the supernatural as she can," Josh sighs. "Especially since she was recently cursed."

"Cursed?" I ask in surprise. "Is she okay?"

Eliana nods. "She's fine now. We had a recent run in with some Witches."

Frowning at Jadyn, I complain, "You told me about the Witches working for the ancient god, but you didn't tell me that their boss was cursed."

Jadyn shrugs. "I didn't want to worry you since it all turned out okay."

"Next time, worry me," I grumble. Jadyn is my eyes and ears with the Witches. She helps me make sure that my grandfather is not getting too old to keep things under control. He hasn't been doing the best job of that since Grandma left him and returned to being an Angel. Not that I blame her. They had a sham marriage after my mother left them. My grandfather is pretty weak in the character department, which he proved during that whole incident and after.

Seeing the concern on my face, Eliana assures me, "She really is fine."

Pulling a cell phone from his pocket, Josh sighs in resignation. "We should get this over with. I assume you want to get back to your realm as soon as possible." When Kallen and I both nod, he pulls up his boss's number and holds the phone to his ear.

Funny, human technology is becoming odd to me. I forget how convenient things such as telephones are when I am in other realms. I admit, I still miss television and movies, too. Fortunately, Kallen and I find other ways to occupy our time.

"Liza, we have a situation. How soon can you get to our house?" Josh asks into his phone. "Okay, see you then." Ringing off, he announces to the rest of us, "Twenty minutes."

More than a little surprised, I ask, "She didn't want to know what is going on?" My curiosity would be eating away at me the entire drive over here.

Josh shrugs. "She would rather hear about it in person." Okay, I can appreciate that.

"Maybe you could show us some of your magic while we wait," Sam encourages, ignoring the elbow to his ribs from Jenna.

Out of the corner of her mouth, Jenna reminds him, "Just like Eliana, they are not a circus act."

I really do like her. I like Sam, too, and I can't blame him for being curious. I can tease him, though. So, I do show him some magic. I take his voice away. Which he realizes when he opens his mouth to argue with Jenna. His lips move, but no sound comes out.

Eliana and Josh laugh. They've seen this trick from me before. "Can you keep him that way?" Josh asks.

Missing the joke, Alonzo scowls. "What are you talking about?"

"Xandra took Sam's voice away," Eliana explains.

"Right," the large man snorts.

Apparently, he wants his voice taken away, too. Which I do. "What was that?" I ask, then laugh when he tries to respond but can't. Even Kallen's lips rise a little.

"Did you say a spell or something under your breath?" Jenna asks, staring curiously at Sam's mouth. "I didn't hear anything. I didn't when Kallen made the chairs, either."

"Unlike Witches, Fairies do not need spells to work most magic," Kallen explains.

Her eyes lighting with curiosity, Jenna exclaims, "Really?"

"Really," I confirm.

"Why is it different?" she asks.

Amused by her curiosity, I say, "I don't know if I can give you an exact reason for that. Kallen once explained to me that it has to do with how magic is pulled. Fairies do it internally, and Witches do it externally. That's the best I can do explanation wise."

Satisfied with that answer, Jenna forgets her admonishment to Sam a moment ago and asks, "What other kind of magic can you do?"

Jadyn chuckles. "That list is too long to enumerate. Suffice it to say, if these two want to do something, it is pretty safe to assume that they can."

"I wouldn't go that far," I complain, growing embarrassed by the attention to our power.

"Remember, I have seen you in action," Jadyn counters with a grin. Yes, she has. Both in this realm, and when my doppelganger was causing trouble and I confronted her in the Fairy realm.

Recognizing my growing discomfort like only another supernatural enigma could, Eliana changes the subject. "Would you guys like something to drink while we wait? We have cola, coffee, juice."

Grateful, I tell her, "I would love a cola, please." When Kallen gives me a questioning look, I remind him, "You've had one before. You liked it." Well, didn't that comment make me feel like an old married couple. Actually, I kind of like the feeling.

Nodding even though I don't believe he remembers having a cola before, he says, "I will have one, too, please."

"Um, you will eventually give Sam his voice back, right?" Jenna reminds me.

Oops, I forgot. "Done," I tell her.

"Thanks," Sam says dryly, but I don't think he means it. I give Alonzo his voice back, too, but he doesn't say anything. I doubt I will get even an insincere thanks from him. I am going to assume that the guy grows on you, because Eliana seems like a really good judge of character. I don't believe she would purposely hang out with jerks.

"So, other than this Phoenix thing, what's been new with you?" Josh asks, trying to spark a new conversation while we wait.

"Well," I glance around the room, debating what to say. I decide to be vague. "Since Egypt, I've been introduced to a lot more new and interesting beings."

Returning with our cola's, Eliana says, "Jadyn filled us in on a little of it. She said you met your doppelganger from another universe."

"Yeah, she was a real treat," I mutter under my breath.

This interests Alonzo. Sitting forward on the couch, he asks, "Are you saying the multiverse theory is real?"

I nod. "It is."

"Who else have you met?" Jenna asks, eager to learn more.

I glance at Kallen and he gives me a little shrug as if to say, 'why not?' Okay, if Jenna really wants to know, I'll tell her. "After the whole doppelganger thing, we helped the Centaurs and the Sasquatch end their feuding; we ended the reign of the Sirens; we were tricked into babysitting the Elf Queen's baby, which actually turned out to be her consciousness inside her child's body in a twisted scheme to trust our loyalties; we found my parents' bodies, and with the help of the ancient Greek gods who felt badly because one of them played a nasty prank on us, we put my parents' spirits back inside them; and most recently, we fought Demons." Pausing, I give Alonzo a sheepish smile. "I can see how that would all sound unbelievable to you."

With a sigh, he says, "Actually, I'm starting to believe you. I've seen enough crazy stuff with Eliana that I really shouldn't doubt anything anymore." Since my internal lie detector isn't going off, he must be telling the truth. I guess the shock of our surprise visit is starting to wear off.

"There's the Alonzo we know and love," Eliana says with a fond smile, convincing me even more that his behavior tonight must not be his usual.

"Speak for yourself," Sam mutters under his breath. I am definitely going to have to ask Eliana later what the deal is with him and Alonzo.

"Yes, here I am," Alonzo says with a cocky grin and a wink in Jadyn's direction. I do not have to ask what the deal is there. Alonzo is obviously interested. Jadyn just rolls her eyes and doesn't respond. I can see in her expression that he is wearing her down, though. It won't be long before the two of them are dating if they aren't already.

Jenna and Sam ask a few more questions about what I said, but Eliana's boss must live much closer than she said. Or she drove really, really fast. Only ten minutes pass before she is knocking on the door. Josh lets her in, and her eyes immediately zero in on Kallen and me.

"Who are they?" she demands.

With a tolerant smile, Eliana says, "Liza, I would like to introduce you to some friends of ours. This is Xandra and Kallen."

"Nice to meet you," Liza says tightly, obviously reserving any real judgement on the matter until she knows more about us and why we're here. Turning back to Eliana and Josh, she asks curtly, "What do they know?"

Josh chuckles. "A lot more than we do."

Liza is not amused. "What does that mean?"

"It means you should probably sit down," Alonzo informs her.

Scowling in annoyance, Liza does scan the room for a place to sit. I suspect she has had too many surprises from Eliana to underestimate the effect of learning more about the supernatural world will have on her. Not to mention, she was recently cursed. I am still annoyed with Jadyn for not telling me about that. I would have come earlier and checked on her. From afar, of course.

Next to me, Kallen rises from his chair. "Please, sit here," he says politely.

Glancing nervously in my direction, Liza squares her shoulders and bolsters her courage. She sits down next to me. Geez, I'm not that scary looking. I did get most of the snarls out of my hair before coming here. Giving Liza the once over, I can't help noticing that she is visibly armed. Humans do tend to feel safer with their guns, even when they would prove to be totally useless in a given situation. Like this one.

Liza seems to have the same deficiency in regards to patience as I do. "Okay, I'm sitting. What is going on?"

Eliana and Josh exchange a look, obviously debating who is going to speak first. Josh ends up taking the lead.

"We need a leave of absence. We need to help an old friend with a situation."

Not being stupid, Liza easily determines that I am that old friend. "Help with what?" she asks me, bypassing her employees in her quest for immediate knowledge.

Having no clue what Josh and Eliana want her to know, I defer to them. "I'll let Eliana explain."

Giving Alonzo a wry look, Liza asks, "Is she afraid this is all above my pay grade?"

Alonzo chuckles. "I think this is above all of our paygrades."

Not encouraged, Liza turns back to Eliana. "Explain." Not the most personable, is she? She kind of reminds me of Isla.

To my great surprise, Eliana tells her boss everything that Kallen and I told her about the Phoenix. I am even more surprised when Liza accepts it all as fact, unlike Alonzo who struggled to believe any of it at first. Bringing her attention back to me, Liza asks, "What if Ra refuses to help?"

That was not the question I expected. "Why would he do that?" I ask.

Liza shrugs. "From working with Eliana these past months, I have learned that the gods within her strongly encourage the 'figure it out for yourself' approach."

"I don't believe that Ra wants the universe to end, though," Josh points out. "When the time is right, I believe he will step up in this situation." He looks to Eliana for support in his claim.

The best she can do is offer a half smile. "He has not stirred within me yet, but I think you are right. He will do what he can to help us."

Slapping her hands on her thighs, Liza stands. "When do we leave?"

Another chuckle from Alonzo. "I told you."

"Yes, you did," I sigh.

"Do you expect me to sit idly by while the universe is in danger?" Liza demands. She does a lot of demanding.

"It is not that," Kallen begins. "But honestly, there is probably very little assistance a Co…a human can offer."

Squaring her shoulders again, Liza declares, "That does not mean I shouldn't try." I give her credit, she is brave. Or, just very, very curious about the supernatural and other realms. Probably both.

Glancing helplessly at Eliana, I say, "It's up to you who comes along. It's not like anyone who comes could ever find their way back to the Fairy realm, or any other." I emphasize this last part for Liza's benefit. I have only known her for a few minutes, but I would already not be surprised if she tried.

"Really?" Jenna asks eagerly. "Does that mean that Sam and I could come?"

I know that if she was my friend, it would be impossible to say no to the eager, and guileless, look in Jenna's eyes. She is curious, but there is no hidden agenda behind her curiosity as I suspect there is with Liza. But, again, I defer to Eliana. "That is up to Eliana and Josh," I say as kindly as possible. I watch in amusement as she turns those hopeful eyes to her friends.

As I suspected, Eliana cannot say no to Jenna. "Of course you can come. If anyone deserves to, it's you." From what I understand, Jenna and Sam have been faithful friends since learning of Eliana's inner gods.

Liza clears her throat and gives Eliana a pointed look. "Remember, I am the one who determines if you get a leave of absence or not."

Not liking the underlying threat in her voice, I snark, "I could always move them to the Fairy realm permanently." The horror on Liza's face is almost comical.

Hoping to avoid an argument spiraling out of control between us, Josh asks, "How would you explain your absence?"

From her expression, this is something Liza has obviously not thought about. "I would come up with something."

"Not anything your superiors would buy," Alonzo counters. I wonder if he is just being helpful, or if he is angling for a spot on the away team for himself. He hasn't asked yet, but I know the question is waiting to jump off his tongue.

Liza is quiet for a long time, and we wait somewhat patiently for her decision. At least, everyone else waits somewhat patiently. Me? I am going crazy waiting for someone else to make a decision about what we can or cannot do. Wow, this would drive me insane. I'm feeling pretty fortunate right now that I don't have a boss.

I guess technically, I do. Dagda and Isla could be considered my bosses. Though, I still tend to do my own thing even if they disagree. Hmm, that might not say good things about my ability to work well with others.

Finally, Liza opens her mouth to speak. Then, she closes it. And she opens it again. This time, words actually come out of it. "Take Alonzo with you."

Out of the corner of my eye, I see a particularly smug grin forming on the large man's face. On the other side of me, a deep scowl is forming on my husband's face. Out of all the people in the room, Alonzo is the one Kallen least wants to take with us. This should be fun.

Josh doesn't miss the displeasure covering Kallen's face, either. With a quick glance at his coworker, he asks Liza, "Not that I am necessarily opposed to the idea, but why? It will only put him in danger." He sends a glance toward Jenna and Sam. He is not as keen as Eliana to bring them along, either.

"Honestly, I believe he is less likely to leave out important details when you file your report upon your return," Liza says frankly. Ouch. She just insinuated that Eliana and Josh would lie to her. Okay, they probably would if it meant keeping important magical secrets from the government. After all, they haven't shared my grandfather's name with her, or any other information that could have the government going after the Witches – either to stop them or to use them.

"As important as you may believe that to be," Kallen growls. "Our concern is saving the universe, not babysitting a Cowan so he can report back to you."

Liza turns assessing eyes toward my gorgeous husband. I admit, a twinge of jealousy hits me when apparent admiration flashes through her peepers. The coldness in her voice takes away any concern of mine that she's hot for my husband, though. "What did you call him?"

It takes me a moment to realize that she thinks Kallen just insulted Alonzo. An explanation is in order before this spirals into a major misunderstanding. "Cowan is simply the supernatural world's name for people from this realm. It's a neutral term," I add, just so there's no confusion over whether or not the term is derogatory in nature.

Liza looks to Jadyn for confirmation. The latter nods. "It's true. No racial or ethnic slurs involved. Since most supernatural beings are humanoid, they don't refer to people from here as humans, but Cowans."

Appeased, Liza relaxes. Then it dawns on her what Jadyn just said. Eyes wide, Liza says, "*Most* are humanoid?"

Jadyn shrugs. "There are notable exceptions." Like Dragons and dinosaurs. It still amazes me there is a realm of just dinosaurs. Maybe that's what happened to all the dinosaurs from here. They simply crossed over. That would certainly blow all of Cowan scientists minds, and theories. A little giggle escapes me at the thought, and I get a couple of strange looks from around the room. I ignore them.

Fortunately, Alonzo takes the spotlight off me. He is still offended by Kallen's comment. "I do not need a babysitter," he snarls.

In a rare instance, I get to lay a calming hand on Kallen. It's usually the other way around. I'll gloat about this to him later. "You have no idea what's waiting out there in other realms," I tell Alonzo. "We have no idea where we will have to go to find the Phoenix, or what beings we may encounter. I understand that you have had a lot of training in this realm, but do you know how far away from a Dragon you have to be to avoid getting burned by their fire? Or how to fight a Centaur or a Sasquatch? Could you defend yourself against Elf glamour? Trust me, wherever we go, you would need babysitting." I don't miss the smirk on Kallen's face as I finish my little speech. Alonzo's mocha colored skin turns a deep red.

"Are you saying Josh knows all these things?" Liza counters.

Josh holds his hands up, palms out. "Hey, don't drag me into this. I know perfectly well that I wouldn't stand a chance against these beings without Eliana." The love in his eyes when he looks Eliana's way makes me smile. He in no way resents her power.

"Regardless, I need to come up with a reason for your sudden departure, which I believe gives me a say in this matter. Taking Alonzo with you gives this more of a 'mission' feel instead of you going off on your own. You know what could happen if those above me thought you simply disappeared," Liza says pointedly.

Did she just threaten my friends? I believe she did. The world has righted itself and it's back to Kallen's hand trying to send calming messages my way. Too late. I find it impossible to remain calm when someone threatens one of my friends.

I didn't realize I am now standing until Kallen, Eliana and Josh all stand, as well. "Xandra," Eliana begins.

I cut her off by putting my hand up, palm out. Rounding on Liza, I say in a frosty voice, "You seem to be under the impression that you can threaten my friends and their families." I assume the underlying threat was what would happen to Eliana and Josh's families if the government thought they disappeared.

Liza rises from her chair. "I am not personally making any threats. But, we all work for the government. I cannot control what they do if they think there is a problem in our division."

"Then maybe I should give you some motivation to make sure they don't find out," I growl.

"Xandra, what are you going to do?" Eliana asks, true concern in her voice.

Registering this, Liza finally has a healthy dose of fear in her eyes. "I guess the threats are on your side now," she sneers.

I shake my head. "I don't threaten." Before anyone in the room can react, I reach out and touch Liza's arm. Then, I teleport us out of the house, satellites be damned.

# 4 Chapter

"Kallen and I came here once," I muse, glancing around at the familiar terrain. "We were trying to find the Fallen Archangel Raguel, or Ray, as he prefers to be called."

Liza is now grasping my arm. Hard. I will likely have a hand shaped bruise on my skin. I don't blame her. She was not expecting to suddenly be standing on top of a large rock in Ireland. "Where are we?" she demands. Still with the demanding. You'd think she'd get a clue that she's not really in a position to demand anything at the moment.

"On top of the Wishing Stone on Tory Island," I inform her. It's not as bitterly cold as it was the last time I was here, but it's not exactly warm, either. My sweater just isn't cutting it, so we won't stay here long.

"How did we get here?"

"I teleported us."

"Impossible," Liza declares, scanning the area. I believe she is trying to determine if this is all an illusion.

With a wry smile, I say, "You haven't even begun to touch the edges of impossible yet. Trust me." With a shrug, I say, "If Ireland isn't your thing, how about Egypt? I'll show you where I first met Eliana." With that, we are suddenly in Giza on the far side of the pyramids. I didn't want to run the risk of appearing in a crowd. I'm still worried about that whole teleporting inside someone else thing. I know it's not very likely, but why take the chance?

Dropping my arm, Liza whirls around trying to get her bearings. She almost trips in the sand and I reach out an arm to steady her. I'm not sure she even notices. Her eyes are kind of crazy, and I'm not certain what all is registering in her mind right now besides confusion and fear. "How are you doing this?"

"Just one of my many gifts," I say with a pleasant smile.

Liza does not believe any of my actions are pleasant. She proves this by pulling out her gun. "Take me back," she demands.

With a scowl, I ask, "Do you ever ask nicely for things?"

"Not when I've been kidnapped," she snarls.

I wave her accusation off. "I just borrowed you for a minute. Trust me, I don't want to keep you."

"I will shoot you."

"Try," I say with a shrug.

Liza levels her gun at my heart. "I'm not kidding."

"Neither am I," I inform her. "In fact, I'll help you out." Using magic, I reach out and press her finger against the trigger. Liza's eyes go wide when a bullet leaves the chamber and hurtles toward me. Her eyes go even wider when the bullet hits my invisible wall of magic and drops harmlessly to the ground.

"You can deflect bullets like Eliana can," she says in awe. A sudden realization hits her, and she takes a step back almost tripping again. "You also have the power of influence over people. You forced me to pull the trigger even though I was trying not to do it."

I roll my eyes. "That wasn't the power of influence. That was me literally pushing your finger against the trigger with magic."

Nonplussed, Liza says, "But, you weren't touching me."

"That's the beauty of magic. I don't need to be touching you," I explain.

Aghast, she says, "You could start wars that way."

I nod. "I could. And there are some magical beings who would do that. Which is why the passages to this realm are closed off to some of the other realms." Like Fairies. Not all Fairies would do that, but enough that it could decimate the human population. I keep this tidbit of knowledge to myself.

Fear is sinking bone deep into the woman in front of me. "What is keeping them from reopening these passageways?" Liza asks.

I shrug and try not to sound too conceited when I say, "My family and me." To put it in terms that she will understand, I add, "So, if you want to exchange threats back and forth, I have plenty of them in my arsenal." Not that I ever would open the passageways for the bad guys.

She had lowered her weapon after it discharged, but Liza finally puts it back in its holster as she realizes how utterly useless it is right now. "You are implying that I don't really have a say in all of this. Nor do the people I work for."

I shake my head. "Implying isn't a strong enough word." With a frustrated sigh, I continue. "Look, I don't want to threaten you or anyone else in this realm. I grew up here. I love this realm. All I want is for you to realize that there are bigger things at stake here than your government. I understand that this puts you in a terrible spot, and you'll probably have to lie. But, if you don't, you may not have to worry about it at all. There simply won't be a universe anymore."

Liza studies me for a long time in the growing light of dawn in the Egyptian desert. "How do I know you are telling the truth? How do I know you aren't really here to start war or hurt people?"

"How do you know Eliana is telling the truth when she says she isn't going to do that?" I counter.

"She has earned my trust."

"Then let me do the same thing."

Liza's eyebrows hit her hairline. "You say that after kidnapping me?"

"Borrowing you," I counter with a grin.

Glancing around again, Liza says, "We really should get back. I am on foreign land without my passport." So, she finally believes this isn't all some elaborate illusion. I wonder if the giant pyramids in the distance convinced her.

I roll my eyes. "Out of all the things to worry about right now, that should be pretty low on your list."

Liza narrows her eyes. "Remember, I need to live here long after you go back to wherever it is you live."

"Good point," I acknowledge.

With a heavy sigh, Liza says, "I will find some reason to give my superiors about their absence. It won't be easy coming up with something they will believe, though."

"You'll figure something out. And thank you," I add with a sincere smile and hold my hand out to her. After a moment, Liza puts hers hand in it. In a blink, we are back in Eliana's living room.

# 5 CHAPTER

"That is amazing!" Jenna exclaims when we reappear. "Where did you go?" Someone obviously filled her in on my ability to teleport.

"Ireland and Egypt," I admit a bit sheepishly. That may have been overkill. But, I did have to prove my point.

"The Wishing Stone?" Kallen asks with a fond smile.

I nod. "It made me miss Ray. I should visit him soon." As Grandma pointed out, I haven't made a casual trip to Angel time in a while. I should visit my friends and family from time to time when I don't have an emergency and need to try to pry information out of them.

"Who is Ray?" Sam asks.

"The Archangel of Harmony and Order," I tell him.

"And he goes by Ray?" Sam asks in surprise.

I laugh. "His real name is Raguel. Ray is the name he uses when he Falls."

"Got it," Sam says, though I'm not sure he really understands. Shaking his head, he adds, "I thought Eliana had some powerful friends."

Interrupting our chatter, Liza announces, "Alonzo, you will be staying here." Ignoring the argument Alonzo opens his mouth to rage, she cuts him off and turns to Jadyn. "I would appreciate it if you stayed, as well. In case we need any assistance of the supernatural kind while Eliana is gone."

The disappointment runs deep in Jadyn's eyes. She wanted to help hunt for the Phoenix. Still, she nods. "Fine."

Alonzo is less gracious about it. Glaring at me, he growls, "What did you threaten her with?"

"I told her I'd turn you all into toads," I say sweetly. Jenna giggles and Eliana bites back a laugh. Sam and Josh laugh outright. Even Kallen smirks a little.

Instead of getting mad at my snark, Alonzo asks with the tiniest trace of fear in his voice, "Could you?"

"Yes," Kallen lies. I try not to laugh myself now. Who knows, maybe there is a spell to actually turn people into toads and I just don't know about it.

"Do we still get to come?" Sam asks. He is ready to argue his and Jenna's case if anyone says no.

Eliana looks to me for guidance even though she already said yes earlier. Now that Alonzo and Jadyn were told they couldn't go, she's feeling a little guilty. "What do you think?"

I am not going to be the one to disappoint them. "Sure, if they don't mind staying out of the action." Tabitha probably won't mind if we leave them at the mansion when we are looking for the Phoenix. She likes company most of the time. As long as they are polite and good eaters.

"We will do whatever you say," Jenna promises, crossing her heart. I believe her.

"I still think I should come," Alonzo grumbles, but he knows he has lost by the firm set of his boss's jaw.

Ignoring him, Kallen says to the others, "We should be going now. We are losing valuable time."

"What should we bring?" Eliana asks.

I hadn't thought about that. I was kind of on a grab and go mission here, completely forgetting that we don't know how long they will be gone. Fortunately, Kallen helps me out. "We honestly do not know how long this will take. You should bring enough clothes for several days and toiletries."

"Can you give me an estimate of how long to expect them to be gone?" Liza pushes. Understandable. She does have to report their leave of absence, after all.

Unfortunately, though, we can't give her a good estimate. Kallen shakes his head and explains, "Time moves differently between realms. Depending on where we must go to find the Phoenix, it may be as if no time has passed here, or days or weeks may pass. I am afraid I cannot give you a better answer than that."

Liza opens her mouth to argue, looks at me, then closes it again. She gives us a curt nod before turning to Eliana and Josh. "I expect you back as soon as possible. Upon your return, do not speak to anyone before speaking to me so I can tell you what outrageous lies I came up with to explain your absence." She gives Kallen a quick glance over her shoulder before continuing. "If it does turn out to be a long time, my lies will become quite elaborate, and we need to all be on the same page."

Josh nods. "Understood."

Liza motions to the two in the room who are not going with us to follow her to the door. "Alonzo, Jadyn, let's gather the team and give them a heads up."

Jadyn comes over and gives Kallen and me both a big hug before following Liza. "Let's try to get together sometime when there isn't a crisis," she says with a smile over her shoulder.

"Definitely," I agree.

Tugging on Alonzo's arm, the petite Skin Walker practically drags him to the door. She is stronger than she looks. I wonder if that's a Skin Walker thing, or if she just works out a lot. Probably a combination of both. "Come on, big guy, let's go." Alonzo grunts and reluctantly goes with her. He does not throw us a smile over his shoulder. His look is definitely more of a glower with more than a hint of animosity. I really need to work on my ability to make new friends.

"What, no 'nice to meet you'?" I snark as he goes by. Okay, that probably didn't help with the gaining new friends thing. All I get in return is a growl from deep in his throat before Alonzo disappears out the door. Nope, I did not make a new friend in him today.

Next to me, Sam nudges my arm and says, "Don't worry about it. The guy's a moron."

Hmm, not that I disagree, but I suspect that Sam makes as many new friends as I do considering his tendency to speak whatever is on his mind like I do. He has friend in me, though. There, I feel better. I have made a new friend today. Glancing at Jenna, I suspect I have made two. "I get that impression," I agree with a smile.

"He's not that bad," Jenna insists. I have heard from Eliana that Jenna tries to like everyone, so I'm not going to put a lot of stock in her half-hearted recommendation. I simply smile and nod.

The four of them disappear upstairs to pack, leaving Kallen and me to wait in the living room. Wrapping an arm around Kallen's waist, I ask, "Do you think Isla saw us bringing all four of them back with us in her vision?"

"Probably," Kallen acknowledges. Pulling me into a hug, my gorgeous husband teases, "So, about this whole missing Ray thing…"

I lean up and kiss him. "You don't even sound jealous," I murmur against his lips. "You'll have to try harder if you are going to get a rise out of me."

Kallen chuckles. "I will remember that." He kisses me again. We do have several minutes to kill while the others pack, after all. Yes, this is way better than television.

Fortunately, or unfortunately considering how much I enjoy kissing my husband, it does not take the others long to pack. In less than ten minutes, all four are back in the living room and ready to go. Still, Jenna feels the need to apologize for the length of time it took. "Sorry, we had to make a few calls to let our families know we would be gone."

Out of curiosity, I ask, "What did you tell them?"

With a sheepish grin, she says, "Since Sam's and my family don't know about Eliana, we told them that we won a vacation." Not the most believable lie, but it will have to do.

"Our parents know, so we told them the truth," Eliana admits. She amends, "Most of it, anyway. I left out the part about the universe possibly ending. I just told them that you needed our help in your realm."

"We can tell them about the universe after we save it," Josh says with a wink.

I nod in understanding. "No sense in getting them all upset since we are hopefully going to prevent it." Hopefully. I can't lie and say definitely. I simply don't have enough details yet.

Glancing around the room at their bags, Kallen says, "If you forgot anything, we can provide it in our realm. So, if you are ready, we really should be going."

Eliana nods. "All set."

Gathering everyone to one side of the room, I reach out and open a passageway to the Fae realm. "That is amazing," Jenna whispers behind me, making me smile with pride over something that has become routine for me.

When it is ready, I gesture to Kallen to go first just in case the others are nervous. Which I am certain they are since they are entering a passageway basically to the unknown. I remember being nervous my first time, too, and I'm the one who created the thing. Eliana and Josh follow after Kallen. Jenna and Sam are obviously the most anxious, but they do not let that stop them. They hurry through before they change their minds. I follow and close the passageway behind me after a brief hesitation in case any of them change their minds. They don't.

With a grin, I spread my hands wide and say, "Welcome to the Fairy realm."

## 6   Chapter

"Wow, it looks…um…just like our realm," Jenna says, a hint of disappointment in her voice.

I laugh and admit, "You know, I was a little disappointed the first time I came here, too.  It was nothing like the Fairy realms in movies and books back home."  This earns me a scowl from my dear husband.  I shrug in a 'I can't help it if it's true' kind of way.

"Is that an ocean?" Sam asks, looking out over the sand and water.

"Yes," Kallen nods.  "We are approximately where Australia would be in your realm."

Sam nods.  "I've always wanted to go to Australia."

"I don't believe we are actually in Australia," Josh points out.

"If you are done with your geography lesson, maybe you could concentrate on, you know, saving the universe," a voice snarks from the area of my ankle.

Jenna lets out a little shriek and takes several steps back. "Is that a Tasmanian devil? Aren't they dangerous?" Wow, she certainly knows the animal kingdom.

I snort down at the little beast. "The only thing this one is a danger to is a slab of bacon."

Giving Jenna a better reply to her question, Kallen says, "In general, yes. This one happens to be Xandra's Familiar and is not a threat to you."

"You have a Familiar?" Jenna says in awe, forgetting her fear. "Can it perform magic like you can?"

I shake my head. "Mostly, he's just annoying." Feeling guilty that I am being mean, I add, "But, he has saved my life on several occasions. He can also channel my magic, which is really dangerous for anyone else to do."

"Nice of you to remember that," Taz snarls. "Don't count on it happening again."

"Oh, you love me and you know it," I tease him.

If Tasmanian devils could make rude gestures, Taz would be making one about now. He is forced to settle for walking away with his tail pointed straight up in the air. I do not want to know what he is muttering under his breath at the moment.

"Are you having a conversation with it?" Josh asks.

"Those snarls and growls you hear from the beast apparently sound like words to Xandra," Kallen explains.

Josh grimaces. "That must get annoying if only she can understand him."

"It does," Kallen acknowledges.

"The wanker is just jealous because you like me better," Taz snarks from the terrace steps. I roll my eyes but don't say anything. I don't want to have to explain what he just said.

"I did not realize you were bringing back a group," Kegan calls from the doorway to the mansion. He has Keelan cradled in his arms again, dressed appropriately for the night chill in a tiny hat and warm pajamas. It is still the middle of the night in the Fairy realm.

"We decided to make it a party," I tell him, ushering everyone toward the house. "Where is Isla?" I ask.

"Waiting impatiently in the kitchen with Tabitha and Garren." With a grin, Kegan adds, "Tabitha is making an early breakfast." Confirming that Isla did know we were going to bring back a group of people. She must have passed that information along to Tabitha.

"I hope you're hungry," I tell everyone.

"Sam is always hungry," Jenna says with a fond smile in his direction.

"I hope she's not going to any trouble just for us," Eliana says, a trace of guilt in her voice.

I shake my head. "Most likely, she is annoyed at being woken up in the middle of the night yet again, and she is taking it out on her pots and pans."

"If that's all it takes to get 4 a.m. bacon, I'm waking her up every night," Taz declares.

I scowl down at him. "Let me know how that works out for you." Tabitha likes her sleep. My irritating little Familiar would soon find himself without any bacon at all. Which just might kill him. I hear it is possible to die of a broken heart.

We make our way through the house to the kitchen with Kallen and me in the lead and the rest following behind. Kegan takes up the rear with Keelan, making cooing noises and funny faces. Apparently, he has given up hope of getting the child back to sleep anytime soon. Keelan is going to be one cranky baby tomorrow, I bet.

We should probably give our guests a tour of the mansion since they will be staying for however long, but for now, they will need to content themselves with curious glances into rooms as we pass them. We need to get started on a plan. When we finally reach the kitchen, we find Tabitha cooking waffles and bacon. Taz hurries to her side just in case she 'accidently' drops something. I note Felix is already there. Taz is definitely a bad influence on my other Familiar who has gained several pounds since moving in with us. He actually needed them, though, unlike Taz.

Isla and Garren are at the huge island counter drinking coffee. Garren looks ready to fall back to sleep despite the caffeine he is guzzling. His eyes are barely open. I wonder if he looks back fondly at the time he spent in his cave in the Dragon realm where he could get as much sleep as he wanted. All he had to do was put up with Dragon fire and Goblin stench. He certainly doesn't get all the sleep he wants here. On the other hand, we are fire and stench free. I glance at Keelan. Mostly stench free. The boy has his moments.

Both Garren and Isla rise when we enter the room. "Grandmother, I would like to introduce you to our friends from the Cowan realm," Kallen says, introducing the highest ranking person in the room first. I leave him in charge of that kind of etiquette because I would never remember all the rules. Kallen points to each person as he says, "This is Eliana, Josh, Jenna and Sam. Everyone, this is Isla, my grandmother and High Chancellor of the Fairy realm." Pointing to the other Fairies in the room, he introduces them next. "This is Tabitha; my cousin Kegan and his son, Keelan; and Garren, Isla's husband." Garren seems slightly offended to be introduced last. Maybe Kallen isn't as good at this as I thought. Or, he did it on purpose. He does like to needle Garren on occasion. Lots of occasions.

After a round of 'nice to meet you's', Isla indicates the stools around the counter. "Please, have a seat. There is much to discuss."

"I assume Dagda is on his way?" I say as I climb onto a stool.

Isla nods. "Yes."

Eliana's eyes widen a little. "Isn't he the King of the realm?"

"He is," I confirm. "And my biological father," I fill in for Jenna and Sam. Thinking of parents, I ask, "Are Mom, Dad, and Zac still sleeping?"

"Yes, I thought it unnecessary to wake the whole house," Isla says. "Best we have a plan in place before filling them in." Good point. I wish I hadn't been woken to end of the universe news with no plan in place.

"We would have a plan if a certain Archangel we know wasn't so damned tight-lipped," Garren grumbles under his breath.

I can't help but defend my friend. "You know Raziel can't say anything. He'd lose his wings. Not to mention violate our free will." Sometimes, I admit silently to myself, free will may be overrated. At least, when it comes to saving the universe.

"Thank you, you are a dear friend," Raziel says from the doorway, almost startling me off my stool. Adriel is with him. From her scowl, she is not any happier than Tabitha or Garren to be woken up in the middle of the night, and she can get downright crabby about things. Most Angels of Death can.

"If it makes you feel any better, I cannot pry any information out of him, either," Adriel grumps, reaching for a mug from the cupboard. She pours herself a cup of coffee.

Watching her reminds me of my manners. "Would anyone else like coffee?" I ask, rising from my stool to get more cups. "By the way, this is Raziel and Adriel. They're Fallen Angels." I don't usually introduce people by what type of supernatural being they are, but Garren already mentioned that Raziel is an Archangel.

Raziel smiles and holds out his hand to Eliana. "Eliana, it is very nice to meet the Cowan who carries within her the essence of two gods." He also shakes hands with Josh, Sam and Jenna, referring to all of them by name without being introduced.

"Show off," Kallen mutters under his breath.

"Leave him be. It is the only fun he has with his knowledge," Adriel says, taking a seat at the counter. She may be grumpy about Raziel not sharing information with her, but she loves him too much to let anyone else disparage him.

Biting her bottom lip, Jenna glances back and forth between the Fallen Angels. Finally, she blurts out, "Is it rude to ask what kind of Angels you are?"

"Yes," Adriel drawls, not at her friendliest in the middle of the night. Who am I kidding? I love her, but she could never really be described as friendly any time of day. "But, we will tell you, regardless."

"Be nice," I admonish to my friend.

I get a look that tells me exactly what I can do with my admonishment before Adriel continues. "Raziel is an

Archangel, and he is the only one among us who is omniscient. I am an Angel of Death."

The tension in the room among our guests just ratcheted up about a hundred notches. "Angels of Death do not kill people," I hurry to explain. "She simply strips the souls of those who die of all the bad stuff on them, and then she decides if there is enough left of their souls to move on or not." Okay, that comforted no one in the room. It did earn me another dirty look from Adriel for making her sound rather heartless. To be fair, she does have to leave emotion out of the equation when she is making those decisions.

"You have nothing to fear from Adriel," Raziel assures everyone with a beautiful, Angelic smile.

"Unless you get close to her before she brushes her teeth. Who knew Angels could melt eye membranes with their morning breath," Taz snarks. A tiny snort of laughter escapes me and I have to cover it with a cough. Out of the corner of my eye, I see Raziel trying not to laugh, as well. He may not understand Taz, exactly, but he does know everything. I give the Archangel a pointed look and he returns it with a half-shrug as if to say, 'It's true.' I will not be divulging the details of this conversation to Adriel, even if she is looking at us suspiciously at the moment.

The kitchen door bangs open, signaling that Dagda has finally arrived. "Just once, once is all I ask, could you please have an emergency that does not involve dragging me out of bed in the middle of the night?" He stops short, and quits complaining, when he sees that we have company. Instead of introducing himself, he demands, "Why are there three Cowans and…" he stares at Eliana as if trying to figure out her magic, "and whoever she is in this kitchen?"

"Nice to see you, too," I snark. "Thank you for going out of your way to make our guests feel welcome."

Realizing how rude he is being, Dagda clears his throat and assumes a more regal posture and tone. "My apologies." That would be convincing if he actually meant it. I never have to wonder where my occasional bouts of rudeness stem from. It's an inherited gene. "I believe introductions are in order," Dagda not-so-subtly hints.

Seeing that I am growing annoyed with my father, Isla does the honor before I can choke him to death with his own rudeness. When she is done, she fills Dagda in on the little problem of the Phoenix. When she is finished with that, my father is several shades paler than he was when he entered. At least he's no longer being rude. Shock has swallowed his rudeness whole.

His lack of sleep now forgotten, Dagda takes a seat at the counter and sighs. "How, exactly, do you propose we find a being who could be disguised as anyone in any realm?"

Way to be encouraging. "That's why Eliana is here," I explain tightly, not any less annoyed with him for his pessimism than I was with his rudeness. "We are hoping that the essence of Ra within her will be able to help us."

Dagda gives my friend a much more appreciative appraisal than he did when he first came in. "Do you truly carry the essence of a minor god within you?"

Eliana chafes a bit at him referring to Ra as a minor god, but she does not contradict him. "Yes," she replies. "Two, actually."

Dagda nods. "Then we may actually have a chance." Glad he has finally boarded the optimism train. You should never start out on a save the universe journey with a poor attitude. Yet, I still find I am a bit insulted he didn't think we had a chance with just me on our side.

"Could you explain a bit more about the Phoenix?" Josh asks the room in general. "Honestly, those of us who are not magical are trying to reconcile the magic and the science without much luck." I smile at his honesty, and the fact that he is not intimidated by the King of the Fairies.

Dagda nods and proceeds to give us a better understanding of what the Phoenix does than either Kallen or Isla did. "Of course. To put it simply, the Phoenix is the glue that holds the realms together. That is why she must constantly travel between them. She serves as a sort of conduit, a magnetic force in the ripples of the realms. Through her, the pieces of the universe are held eternally together. Within her, she carries Cosmic Fire, which is needed to anchor each realm in place while orbiting the sun. Cosmic Fire cannot be controlled, though. Just as the cores of the suns and the stars in the universe will grow hotter over time until they eventually go supernova, so does the Cosmic Fire within the Phoenix. It is only by dousing the flames every five hundred of the Phoenix's years until they are just smoldering ash, can the Phoenix keep from going supernova herself. If that happened, because she is the glue holding everything together, it would start a chain reaction with every star and sun in the universe. The Phoenix prevents this through her deaths. But, since she is immortal and can never truly die, her essence, if you will," he says with a nod toward Eliana, "never truly dies. She reforms from the smoldering ash, and the Cosmic

Fire within her begins to grow again. This is why her death and rebirth is vital to the universe."

"That makes sense," I nod, finally getting it. I scowl at Kallen and Isla for not giving me such an in depth explanation earlier. Unfortunately, neither of them knows why I am scowling at them. Apparently, they thought they explained it just as well.

"So, when she reforms from the smoldering ash, the Phoenix does not reform from all of it? She leaves some of her ashes behind?" Eliana asks. "Xandra mentioned that Ra stored them for her."

Dagda nods. "From what I understand, the leftover ash is the remnants of the darkness her soul may have picked up in that lifetime." He looks to Adriel for confirmation.

The Angel of Death nods. "Her darkness is burned away by her Cosmic Fire."

Dagda continues, "As she is an immortal being, the ashes are still a part of her and cannot be destroyed. The ashes are sought after because some believe they carry some of the power of the Phoenix, as well. That is why they are hidden away."

"Do they?" I ask. "And would the power gained from them be dark power?"

"No one really knows for certain, but as they are burned by Cosmic Fire, it seems doubtful," Isla says, but she is looking at Eliana, not me. Isla believes someone knows for certain. Namely Ra.

Eliana avoids the question in Isla's eyes. "How long has it been since the last time the Phoenix was reborn? Are her five hundred years up, or do we have a little time?" Eliana asks. Excellent question. If the Phoenix is already past her expiration date, we're screwed.

"In Cowan years, it has been several thousand years," Kallen says, not really answering Eliana's question.

Josh frowns. "I thought she had to die every five hundred years."

"Five hundred of *her* years," Kallen reminds him. "The Phoenix experiences time differently than the realms do." He nods at Raziel and Adriel. "Much as the Angels do. They are outside of time as we experience it."

"We know her time is near, but we do not know the exact dates," Isla says. "For example, it could be days or weeks for the Fae, or decades or even centuries for the Cowans."

"This isn't confusing at all," Sam grumbles, earning him an elbow to the ribs from Jenna.

"I agree," I grin. I definitely like Sam. He's a mutterer like I am.

"That makes sense why Ra was the last one to help her hide her ashes," Josh says, staying on track with the conversation, unlike Sam and me. "He was still around then."

"Are you able to communicate with Ra now?" Dagda asks Eliana. I have explained the basics of Eliana's coexistence with the Egyptian god in the past, but as Dagda knows from my own magic, things can change and grow over time. Maybe Eliana does have a better communication method with the god now.

No such luck. "Ra communicates with me, but it is often through dreams. It is rare for him to communicate directly," Eliana admits. She hurries to add, "I have no doubt that he will help us if he can, though."

"Maybe you should take a nap," Kegan suggests. When I give him a sour look, he shrugs. "How else is she going to dream?" He does have a point, though I doubt it's quite that simple.

Proving he is not the only one thinking along these lines, Isla says in a not so subtle hint, "We have prepared rooms for you all."

With a grimace, Eliana says, "Honestly, I don't think I could sleep right now." Nor do I believe the god within her can be manipulated like that. From what I understand, he communicates on his timetable, not Eliana's. Much like the Angels do with me. Damn higher beings and their annoying ways.

"We did just tell you the universe might be ending," I say sympathetically to my friend. "Information like that tends to disrupt normal sleep patterns." I wouldn't be able to go back to sleep right now with that hanging over my head, either. Giving Kegan another sour look, which I also pass along to Isla, I say, "Maybe we should come up with a plan that doesn't involve Eliana napping."

Steering the conversation in a more helpful direction, Josh says, "You knew that Ra kept the ashes. Did the lore happen to give any idea as to where?"

"If we knew where, we would already be looking there," Kegan snarks under his breath. Across the table, Sam snickers. Hmm, he and Kegan just may be kindred spirits. I'm not sure that's a good thing.

Being the laid back guy he is, Josh isn't ruffled by the snark. "Often, there are references to ancient cities or locations in what is believed to be mythology. We already know that much of what is considered myth by humans is actually true. If there was a place mentioned, we would have a starting point if we can match it to an approximate modern day location."

Dagda nods. "True, but unfortunately, we already know that the location has long since been taken over by Cowans. This happened thousands of years before the Fairies left your realm. Virtually all ancient aspects have been destroyed."

"We know this?" I ask, surprised that I wasn't informed we had this much information. I shoot another glare toward Isla and Kallen for keeping me in the dark. They both ignore me yet again. They are so good at that. Too good for my taste.

Again, Dagda nods. "Heliopolis."

Eliana groans. "He's right. Heliopolis has been occupied for at least five or six thousand years. There is nothing left from the time Ra may have walked the land."

"If there was a hiding place there, it has been found," Josh says, as disheartened as Eliana.

I'm not convinced. "Not if it's warded like the temple of Isis we found. It would have been impossible to gain access without magic."

Brightening, Eliana says, "If that's true, it could still be there. Also, we don't know the boundaries of ancient Heliopolis. Wherever the temple, or whatever it was, is located may be deep in the desert, away from the human population."

"Which makes it that much more difficult to find," Sam points out.

"If the Phoenix ashes were thought to be powerful, wouldn't magical beings have been searching for them of the centuries?" Jenna asks. "Would the wards have held against every magical creature looking for them?"

"If Ra put them in place, I suspect they would have. Maybe once we get close, Ra will guide us," Eliana says excitedly, not losing momentum over Jenna's doubts. She is obviously growing to like this plan.

"What do you hope to find?" Jenna pushes. When all eyes turn to her, she asks, "What kind of clues are you looking for?"

"Yeah, it's not like the Phoenix would have left an itinerary for her future realm to realm travels," Sam points out.

"Or even a how-to spell for tracking her down on a specific date," Kegan adds unhelpfully. Yes, I believe the two of them are kindred spirits. From my husband's annoyed expression, he is not pleased with this revelation. One Kegan can be quite enough around here.

"No, but the Angels are pretty certain there are clues to be found," I inform both of them. My eyes can't help but travel across the table to the Angels present hoping for some sort of confirmation.

Adriel nods. "It has always been believed that Heliopolis holds secrets about the Phoenix. Unfortunately, it is warded from the Angels."

Interesting how she worded that. "Meaning the Angels don't really have a clue what's in Heliopolis, if anything?" I press.

Flushing because she may have said too much, Adriel tries to dig herself out of her 'too much information' hole by saying, "None of this was my area of expertise."

"It is a good starting point," Kallen says before I can grill Adriel any more since he knows she won't give anything else away. Continuing the conversation will do nothing but frustrate us both. "We should depart immediately," my gorgeous husband urges.

Frowning, I ask, "Are you suggesting that we just wander around the area of ancient Heliopolis until something comes to us?"

There is a snarky response dancing on my husband's tongue. I can see it there doing pliés and jazz hands. Yes, his snarky comments like to mix dance styles. Before he can speak, though, Eliana says, "The closer I am to the hiding place, the more likely Ra will lead us the rest of the way."

I study her a moment trying to figure out if this is wishful thinking, or if she knows this to be true. I decide I can't tell. With a sigh, I reluctantly concede that I don't have a better idea. "I guess that's our plan, then."

"Once you have found the temple, you are to return here with any information," Dagda instructs, using his most regal voice. He must be trying to impress our guests because he knows it will not impress me. "We will make a plan for approaching the Phoenix together."

I roll my eyes. "If I didn't know better, I would think you are implying that I'm not very diplomatic."

"I was not implying," Dagda says dryly. I give him a sour look, but I can't really disagree.

Proving that he is way more diplomatic than I am, Kallen says, "If time allows, we will do so."

Dagda doesn't like Kallen's response, but he accepts it with a curt nod. He cannot help but add, "Remember, the fate of the universe is at stake."

"No pressure, though," I mutter under my breath. Sam hides a snicker with a cough.

"You are not going anywhere until you eat," Tabitha says as she begins to load the countertop with plates of food. "You cannot save the universe on an empty stomach."

Kallen and Kegan are the first to dig in. I'm impressed how Kegan has learned to devour food left handed since he is still holding Keelan. Our guests are a little shy at first about helping themselves, but a few more encouraging words are all it takes. Soon, everyone has a plate loaded with breakfast foods, and we dig in like it could be our last meal.

We'll try really hard to make sure it's not.

# 7 Chapter

"That was delicious, thank you," Josh says to Tabitha when he has finished everything on his plate. Smart guy. The way to Tabitha's heart is praising her food. That and not saying things that will make her want to smack you in the back of the head.

Tabitha beams with pride. "You are a very nice young man. Unlike others I know," she adds, glaring at Kallen and Kegan. There is no heat behind her glare, though. She loves them both dearly.

Kegan rises from his chair and wraps his free arm around Tabitha's shoulder. He is still holding Keelan in his other arm as he is still too young for a high chair. "You know we love your cooking. Otherwise, we would not eat so much of it." His nose wrinkles and his expression turns sour. After a quick sniff of the air close to his son, he sighs. "Someone needs to be changed. Again." He gives Tabitha a hopeful look, but she just shakes her head and walks away with a wicked grin on her face. Resigned to his fate of diaper duty this time, Kegan turns toward the door. His eyes light up when he spies his wife entering the kitchen. There is new hope for begging off diaper time.

"You never came back to bed. What is going on?" Alita asks through a yawn. Glancing around the room, she notices the extra people and her face flushes. She runs a hand through her tangled hair and glances down at her rumpled pajamas. "Sorry, I did not realize we have guests."

In an attempt to ease his wife's discomfort, Kegan does some quick magic. Suddenly, Alita is dressed and her hair is as smooth and shiny as ever, easing her embarrassment at showing up so disheveled. She gives him a grateful look. Aw, Kegan really is a good husband.

Behind us, Jenna gasps in surprise. "That was amazing!"

"Thanks," Kegan says with a grin, enjoying her thrill at such little effort toward magic on his part. He turns back to his wife. "There is a problem with the Phoenix," Kegan sums up for her.

"I brought back my friends from the Cowan realm to help. We're actually on our way back there now to look for the temple that stores the Phoenix's ashes," I tell her. I do a quick round of introductions.

Reaching out for Keelan, Alita says with more confidence than the rest of us feel, "If anyone can fix this, you guys can." I give her an appreciative smile. Until she adds, "At least my son doesn't need to be involved this time." Yeah, it's probably going to be a while before any of us live that one down. Though, it's Raziel who is the target of Alita's cocked brow. The Archangel shrugs helplessly. He did what he had to do to save us all from Demons.

Our guests are oblivious to the exchange. "What should we do with the things we brought?" Josh asks, glancing at the bags lining the kitchen wall.

"Leave them here," Kallen tells him. "They will be put away."

"I will put them in the rooms I made up," Tabitha says. Suddenly, the bags are gone.

"We do get those back, right?" Sam mutters under his breath to Jenna.

"Of course," Kallen assures him. "Likely all in one piece, too." Sam's eyes go wide until he realizes Kallen is joking.

"Do you need me to come along?" Kegan asks.

"So you can get out of diaper duty? I don't think so," I tease. Honestly, there is no way I would take him away from Alita and Keelan right now to do something dangerous.

To my great surprise, Kegan actually looks relieved. Usually, he wants to come with us. Then again, he does have a family of his own, now. One of whom is a newborn babe. When the universe may be about to end, who wants to be away from his wife and child?

Alita gives me a hug. "Be careful," she whispers in my ear.

"Always," I lie with a grin. Turning to Raziel, I ask, "Any words of advice?" It never hurts to try to wheedle information out of an omniscient being, right? I don't get my hopes up that he will say something useful, though.

"Follow your instincts, they are always your best guide," he says as cryptically as ever, proving I was right in keeping my expectations low. His eyes move to Eliana, indicating he is including her in his sage advice. She seems more receptive to it than I am, only because she does not know him well enough to resent that he could be saying so much more.

"Thanks," I grump. A thought hits me and I direct my question to Adriel this time instead of Raziel. "If the universe blows up, what happens to the Angels?"

"We live outside of the constraints of the mortal universe," she informs me. Well, at least she and Raziel will survive even if the rest of us don't. They'll ascend again and get their wings back. Reading my mind, Adriel says softly, "Remember, you have wings, too."

With a surreptitious glance at my husband, I mutter, "I don't find that comforting at the moment." Besides, I still don't have a clear answer on whether or not my part time wings make me truly immortal.

Not liking the morbid direction this conversation is taking, Kallen urges, "We should go." I nod and help him usher our friends back out to the beach.

"Sorry you didn't get a better look around at the Fairy realm," I say to them when we are back on the sand.

"That's okay. It doesn't seem that much different than home," Sam says with a shrug.

"When this is over, you will need to return so we can show you that is not necessarily true," Kallen informs him. "The open use of magic here makes all the difference."

Eliana smiles. "It would be nice not to have to hide my abilities all the time."

Josh wraps an arm around her shoulders and pulls her close. "If things get too stressful in our realm, maybe we can move here."

"You're welcome any time," I tell them. "Your families, too." I sneak a peek at Dagda who is standing on the terrace to make sure he would be okay with more Cowans moving in. He inclines his head slightly in agreement. The thought of having Eliana on our side far outweighs the challenges of having more Cowans among us, apparently. Turning back to my friend, I ask, "Okay, where are we going?"

Eliana, being knowledgeable on all things Egypt, replies, "The only thing left of ancient Heliopolis is an obelisk. It's in the northeast area of Cairo."

Oh, that sucks. I grimace and tell her, "I can't open a passageway in the middle of an urban area. I think I'll open a passageway at my old house, and then we can teleport from there."

"Why not our house again?" Jenna asks, more out of curiosity than being against the idea of my house.

"Because people might be watching our house now," Josh says astutely. Liza may be his boss, but he doesn't trust her not to spy on our movements any more than I do.

"What?!" Jenna gasps.

Sam chuckles. "Like they aren't already considering the fact that the government knows about Eliana. It was a big risk for Xandra to come directly to us last night."

If I had thought it through more, I wouldn't have gone straight to them. "Sorry about that," I tell Eliana sheepishly.

Eliana shrugs. "No big deal. I don't believe anyone is bugging the inside of our house. Sam scans it regularly." She gives her friend an affectionate smile.

Shaking my head, I say, "I don't know how you can live with the government in your business like that."

With a wink, Eliana replies, "I believe the government here knows what you are doing all the time."

I laugh. "They do. It's a little different when it's family, though."

"I'm sure it is," she acknowledges. She adds, "Josh and I considered all of this when we decided to work for the government. Being able to help people with my abilities outweighs the infringement on our privacy."

"So far," Josh chimes in. "If that changes, we have a backup plan." That's good to know. I don't press for details, though. If I needed to find them, I'm certain I could.

"Where is your old house?" Jenna asks.

"In the mountains in Colorado," I tell her.

She smiles. "At least Sam and I didn't lie to our parents. We get to visit Colorado and Egypt on our 'vacation.'"

Eliana laughs. "Good point."

"Is everyone ready?" I ask. When I get a round of nods, I reach out and open a passageway. A familiar picture of my childhood living room appears before us, and I usher everyone through.

Before I can go through myself, Dagda grabs my arm and pulls me into a hug. "You are to return to us," he says quietly so only I can hear him. "The Phoenix is dangerous. She is not known to be kind or generous or forgiving. Be careful what you say and do around her, or you could get yourself and your friends hurt or killed. Furthermore, do not trust her. She will attempt to mislead you if you get too close to her secrets."

I can hear the fear in his words. Not for the universe, but for me, his daughter, and for Kallen. Hugging him back, I say softly, "It's going to be okay. We've got this." I instill more confidence in my words than I actually feel. I don't like what he said about the Phoenix being untrustworthy. Like this wasn't going to be hard enough.

Stepping back and masking his fear again, Dagda raises a brow and teases, "Perhaps you should work on your grammar while you are gone."

I roll my eyes and step through the passageway. "Always the grammar police." I close the passageway on his chuckling.

Turning to the small crowd in the living room, I tell them, "Again, I'd love to give you a tour, but that will have to wait until next time."

"Understood," Eliana nods. "How many of us can you teleport at once?"

"I could probably do everyone, but let's do two trips just to be safe. You, Kallen and I will go first. Once we determine the coast is clear, I'll come back for the others." I can tell Josh isn't thrilled with the plan, but he reluctantly nods.

"How long will it take?" Jenna asks.

"If there is no one around, I'll be back in a few seconds," I tell her. I hold my hands out to Kallen and Eliana. "You guys make yourselves comfortable," I say to Josh, Jenna and Sam. "I'll be right back." I teleport the rest of us away.

It only takes a second to figure out we are in the right place. Ugh. I forgot how hot it is in the desert. Immediately, the desire to peel off my jeans and sweater hits me when we appear in the sand miles outside of Cairo. That would probably seem inappropriate to the others, so I refrain. It's a good thing I remembered my deodorant, though. "Wow, you lived here for a year?" I complain, looking around for danger as I speak and seeing nothing but sand and harsh sunlight.

"You get used to it," Eliana assures me. Gazing over the sand as well, Eliana scowls. "There's someone coming. You should hurry and get the others before they arrive."

I don't like the worry lines forming around her eyes, but she's right. I need to get the others before we're observed. "I'll be right back." With a last look around, I teleport away. But in the split second before I leave, too late to stop what I am doing, I am convinced I hear the sound of engines and then gun shots. I really hope it was my imagination playing tricks on me. Though, desert mirages tend to involve water, not bullets.

# 8 Chapter

Back in Colorado, I am faced with a dilemma. I know Josh well enough to know that he would kill me if Eliana was in danger and I didn't bring him to her. He also has training from the government, and I didn't miss the fact that he decided to arm himself before leaving this realm earlier. On the other hand, Jenna and Sam could be major liabilities if there is danger when we return. Ultimately, I decide to leave the decision to Josh. He knows his friends better than I do.

Finding the three I left behind a moment ago standing exactly where I left them, I blurt out, "I think when I left Kallen and Eliana were under attack."

Instantly in warrior mode, Josh asks, "By who?"

"I don't know," I reply honestly. "But, I'm pretty sure I heard gun shots right when I teleported away. I couldn't reverse the process," I add, not wanting them to think I ran away from the danger. I put a hand up to stop a barrage of questions from the three of them. "First, Kallen would have put up a wall of magic as soon as he heard the weapon discharge. It would have been instinctual. And we all know Eliana would do the same in her way. I'm sure they're fine. My concern," I glance at Jenna and Sam before returning my gaze to Josh, "is how to proceed."

"Can you shield us?" Josh asks. He knows the answer to that, so I am assuming he is asking for Sam and Jenna's sakes.

"Yes."

"Then bring us all back. I don't like the idea of leaving them here."

"Um, neither do we," Sam concurs. Concern is etched on Jenna's face, but she nods, as well.

I want to argue, because bringing non-magical people into danger goes against my instincts. But, I also want to get back. I know Kallen and Eliana can take care of themselves, but that doesn't make it any easier not being there with them. Ultimately, I decide to abide by Josh's decision so I can get back there myself. "Okay, let's go."

As I prepare to teleport again, I create a wall of magic around the three of us. I have never tried to teleport a wall of magic with me before. We'll see how this works out.

It turns out that it works just fine. Good thing because bullets are flying. To our left, right where I left them, Eliana and Kallen are fending off an attack of a very human nature. Two trucks filled with armed men are shooting at them, and now at Jenna, Josh, Sam and me. The shock of us suddenly appearing doesn't slow down the attack in the slightest.

"What's going on?" I shout to Kallen.

"They arrived just as you left. They began their attack as soon as they noticed us," my husband shouts back. That was rather unfriendly of them. The bullets are ricocheting off Kallen's magic just like they are mine. He is so easily reflecting them that Eliana hasn't even bothered to use her power yet.

"I believe it was some sort of weapons deal!" Eliana calls back.

"Great," I mutter under my breath. "Seems like they work!" I return. Though, the buyer may now have less ammunition to purchase.

Eliana turns to Kallen and says something to him that those of us in my magical dome can't hear. Whatever it is, he doesn't like it. He shakes his head, but Eliana continues to speak. Eventually, Kallen nods. I am about to ask what is going on when I see for myself. Kallen lets his magic around Eliana go. Then, as if she has the ability to teleport, she is gone. Except, she's not really gone. She is just moving too fast for our eyes to track her.

In front of us, the guys in the truck begin disappearing. It takes a moment for those left to notice and start freaking out. About a hundred yards in the distance, they begin to pile up. Unarmed and unconscious. Eliana is taking them out one at a time. The freaked out guys with the guns try to find her, firing their weapons in all directions now, and doing more harm to each other than us. If it wasn't for the fact that these guys are trying to kill us, it would be rather fascinating watching their idiocy. This is like watching the bad guys in a live action, superhero comic book.

It only takes a couple of minutes for Eliana to finish up. When she has the last of them on her unconscious bad guy pile, she finally slows her pace. It still amazes me she can move that fast. I can't even keep up with Kallen on his morning jog on the beach. I really should exercise more. Not that it would ever make me as fast as Eliana, though.

After a quick scouting run around the area, Eliana finally comes back to us. She hasn't even broken a sweat. Impressive since it's at least two hundred degrees out here. Being unaccustomed to the heat may be causing me to exaggerate slightly.

With a grateful smile, Eliana says, "Thanks for keeping these guys safe while I did that."

I shrug. "What are friends for?" My eyes narrowing, I accuse, "You knew danger was coming before I left."

With a guilty shrug, Eliana says, "I had an idea."

This time it is Josh narrowing his eyes at her. "An idea?"

"Fine, I sensed they were a threat," Eliana admits. "But, we couldn't just let them get away with whatever they were doing."

With a resigned shake of his head, Josh kisses her cheek. "That's just one of the reasons I love you. You always do the right thing."

"Next time, a little heads up would be nice," I complain.

With a sheepish smile, Eliana says, "If I had told you, you would have stayed instead of going back for the others. I figured Kallen and I could handle these guys."

"Are they gun runners?" Sam asks, moving toward the trucks to investigate.

"Looks like it," Josh replies with a grimace.

Nonplussed, Kallen asks, "What is a gun runner?" How strange for him to be on the other side of the knowledge spectrum.  Secretly, I kind of like it.

Josh is the one to answer him.  "People who illegally sell weapons.  I think we interrupted a deal."

Shielding her eyes and glancing from the sun to the bad guy pile, Jenna asks, "What do we do with them?  We can't just leave them out here unconscious.  They will die."

"Which could save a lot of lives," Sam mutters which earns him a glare from his more compassionate girlfriend.

Josh shakes his head.  "Others would just take their place."

Eliana is pulling out her cell phone.  "I'll call Agent Amman."  She moves a few feet away and makes the call to the Egyptian government agent she has worked with in the past.  The one whose family we helped save the last time Kallen and I were in Egypt.  After an animated conversation that we can't hear, Eliana comes back to us. "I think I just made his month," she says with a smile.

"How long until he gets here?" Josh asks.

"He's getting in his car now and was calling for back up as soon as we hung up," Eliana tells him. "Maybe half an hour."

Frowning, Kallen asks, "How will he know where to go? We are in the middle of nowhere."

"He pinged my cell phone for a GPS location," Eliana explains. When she realizes he has no clue what that means, she adds, "My phone is emitting a signal, and he can use satellites to find it. That will give him the coordinates he needs to find this exact location."

Kallen nods in understanding. "Handy," he says. He is often amazed at how Cowans compensate for not having magic.

"Except for the fact that anyone, from any government, can do that with anyone's cell phone," Sam points out wryly.

Josh chuckles. "I doubt anyone is currently pinging your cell phone."

"No, but they could," Sam grumbles.

Jenna leans around Sam and explains, "He's a conspiracy theorist."

"Ah, got it," I reply with a grin. Though, what he is saying is true. I remember that from growing up in this realm. Privacy and cell phones do not necessarily go hand in hand.

Looking around nervously, Jenna asks us, "Can you sense anyone else?"

I look to Eliana. "You are the one who can sense non-magical beings, not us."

"Really?" Jenna asks in surprise.

"It is another being's magic we sense, not their person," Kallen explains.

"Score one for Eliana," Sam says with a prideful smile in his friend's direction.

Eliana scowls. "It's not a competition."

"But, it is still impressive," I assure her. "Trust me, there are a lot of people back home who would be jealous." One of the few things that make Cowans a threat to supernatural beings is their ability to sneak up on us.

Not wanting any more flattery sent her way, Eliana takes a moment to scan the area with her senses. Finally, she shakes her head. "No one else."

"That doesn't mean others are not on their way," Josh says. "They may have called for backup when you guys showed up."

"Good point," Eliana says with a nod. "We should probably move closer to the trucks so we're not out in the open."

"You mean so *we're* not out in the open," Sam says with a sigh as he points to himself and Jenna. "Sucks being magicless and vulnerable."

Jenna laughs. "You poor baby." She grabs his hand and pulls him toward one of the trucks.

Kallen is already there looking over the weapons the men were planning to sell. Josh joins him and begins explaining what each thing is. I find it mildly interesting, but I've seen enough movies not to be that impressed. I'm just glad these particular weapons will not make it to their intended destination. How odd that we landed in the desert right where an arms deal was supposed to go down. The odds of that must be astronomical.

Twenty minutes later, Agent Amman's SUV is coming toward us and kicking up a huge sand cloud in its wake. He parks a few yards away and jumps out of the car. A wide grin covers his face as he pulls Eliana into a hug. "I did not know if I would ever see you again since you started working for your government."

Eliana returns his grin, but says, "I'm not a prisoner, you know." Sam snorts behind her, but she ignores him.

After greeting the rest of us, Agent Amman turns his attention to the pile of unconscious bad guys. "Very tidy of you," he comments, meaning it as a compliment. Looking at his watch, he continues, "In about three minutes, there is going to be a swarm of agents here." He looks up at us. "I suggest you get going."

Josh cocks a brow. "Going with the anonymous tip lie?"

"Some of the best information comes in anonymously," Agent Amman says in confirmation.

Kallen gestures toward the pile of bad guys. "What about when they begin talking about magic?" he asks out of curiosity.

Agent Amman grins. "Do you really think these men will be taken seriously? That is, if they even decide to admit that they were bested by several young, unarmed people?"

"Not likely," Josh says. "Their street cred would be shot."

"True," Sam concurs.

"Thank you," Eliana says with a grateful smile to Agent Amman.

He shakes his head. "No need for thanks. Explaining your presence would be a political nightmare for all of us."

Grimacing, Josh agrees. "Without a doubt."

The agent doesn't need to tell us twice. We are more than ready to get out of here. After a quick round of good byes, everyone gathers around me. When they are touching me, I teleport us away. I am not planning to go far, just a couple of miles from this area so as not to be discovered by the swarm of agents coming.

As soon as we are caught in my magic, though, I feel a sharp tug. Like the magnetic pull of a compass showing me the way. Feeling no malice behind it, I do not hesitate to follow. Especially when I realize I felt a smaller one the first time I teleported. Maybe it wasn't a coincidence after all that we ended up at that particular spot in the desert right as an arms deal was going on.

# 9  Chapter

Our reappearance is a little bumpy since I am not used to teleporting so many people at once, and they are not used to being teleported. Jenna stumbles and causes Sam to fall on his butt in the hot sand. Josh holds a hand out to him and helps him up.

"Well, that was fun," Sam grumbles, brushing the burning sand from his hands and pants.

Kallen isn't paying attention to them. His eyes are focused on me. "What was that?" he asks.

So, he felt the pull, too. "I suspect Eliana has a better answer than I do," I tell him honestly.

Sure enough, Eliana's eyes are already searching for something. "Ra showed her the way," she says simply, her eyes still scanning the horizon.

"What?" Josh asks in surprise.

"Ra's magic touched Xandra's, showing her which direction to go," Eliana explains over her shoulder.

"Why didn't he do that the first time?" Sam asks reasonably.

With a shrug, Eliana says, "He did. I guess he wanted us to take care of that mess back there." Which is why Eliana was much less surprised than the rest of us that danger was afoot. With a fond smile, she says, "He does have a special place in his heart for Egypt, after all. He hates the violence and crime that plagues it." Turning her attention back to the task at hand, she says, "It's around here somewhere. The temple Ra built for the Phoenix." So, it is a temple. Good to know. Eliana begins to walk forward, but the rest of us hang back giving her space to walk freely.

Shielding her eyes from the glare of the sun on the sand, Jenna calls to her friend, "Is it buried under the sand? Because I don't see a thing."

"After thousands of years, it must be," Sam says.

"Do you sense anything?" I ask Kallen. I can't feel any magic in the area, but he is more in tune with his senses in that regard than I am.

He shakes his head. "I suspect the wards in place prevent magical detection."

"Hopefully Ra remembers exactly where it is, then," I say out of the corner of my mouth.

"Here!" Eliana calls from twenty yards away. "It's here!" I guess he remembers.

"I hope she means it is buried in the sand. Otherwise, the heat is making her hallucinate," Sam mutters to Jenna. His snark is rewarded with an elbow to the ribs, but I can't help a smile. Honestly, I was thinking the same thing.

Joining Eliana, I ask, "How do we get to it?"

"We dig," Eliana replies wryly.

"No one mentioned there would be hard physical labor," Sam grumbles.

"I suspect she means with magic," Josh points out. "We should probably stand back."

"Do you need help?" I ask Eliana.

She shakes her head. "Not for this part."

"Okay, we'll be over there, then," I tell her, taking Kallen's hand and doing as Josh suggested. He, Jenna and Sam join Kallen and me about thirty yards away.

When we are a safe distance from her, Eliana calls on her power. The air around her begins to shimmer, and the sand around her feet begins to dance. The tiny grains lift from their resting places and become a wall of sand. From where we are standing, it soon looks like a massive sandstorm about to bury us all and leave us for dead. But, I know from experience that Eliana's power will not bring harm to those she cares about. We are safe from the effects. The sand moves harmlessly to the side instead of heading toward us and returns silently to the earth a few hundred feet away in a huge pile.

Around her, giant dunes of sand continue to form as Eliana focuses on the one spot she wants to clear. With her power to move the earth, and her power over the wind, she is digging a hole of massive proportions. This is not a quick process. It takes time to dig so deeply through the sand and safely displace it. She is making sure we don't find ourselves the victims of a sand avalanche when we near whatever it is she is clearing. Which I appreciate. I would assume that being buried alive in hot sand would totally suck. At least Kallen and I could magic our way out. If Jenna or Sam got caught up in an avalanche of sand, they would suffocate if we couldn't get to them in time. Or be crushed. That much sand would have some serious weight associate with it, wouldn't it?

Eventually, the air around Eliana begins to settle. The final grains of sand move to the side. Now, she is standing on the precipice of the hole she dug and peering down at what she found. Tentatively, the rest of us move closer, eager to see what she has uncovered but not wanting to disturb her sand piles.

Honestly, I expected something bigger. My imagination is probably skewed by the size of the pyramids, not to mention the temple of Isis we discovered. Compared to those buildings, this one is tiny. But, it is still a decent sized temple, I suppose. It could probably hold fifty or so people.

"Are you teleporting us down there?" Jenna asks, glancing over the edge. The temple is a good thirty feet down.

"That would be best," Kallen says. "We do not want to disturb the sand."

Nodding, I say, "I agree."

Before I can make a move to start teleporting everyone, Josh asks, "What about traps? Any idea what we can expect to run into?"

I groan aloud. "I forgot about ancient Egyptian traps." All of their sacred buildings were equipped with them.

Eliana shrugs. "Other than leading us here, Ra hasn't communicated anything about the place."

"Helpful," Sam mutters under his breath. I appreciate his muttering. It saves me the trouble.

"The best we can do is proceed with caution, then," I say, trying to sound encouraging.

"Why don't you and I go first," Eliana suggests. "Kallen can keep an eye on things up here until we figure out how to get inside. Just in case there is more unwanted company."

"I doubt there is a chance of running into more gun runners," Josh points out, knowing full well that she could detect any incoming danger of that sort. He's not fooled. She's just trying to keep him safe.

"It should only take a minute to figure out how to get in," I tell him, giving Kallen a pleading glance. I can't blame Eliana for wanting to protect Josh and her friends whenever she can. When Kallen doesn't look convinced, either, I add, "If there is a trap, it would be silly for all of us to get caught in it. If you stay here, you could rescue us." I add my best convincing smile to my words.

My smile must work. Still not liking the idea of staying behind, Kallen reluctantly agrees to it. After all, the non-magical people would have a much more difficult time rescuing us if we needed it. "As soon as you have the temple open, you are coming back for us, correct?"

"Of course," I say, trying to sound as honest as I can. It really depends on what we find.

Kallen narrows his eyes. "I will not hesitate to slide down the sand if you do not come back."

He would, too, which would be dangerous. With a grimace, I nod in acknowledgement. "Got it."

Her voice full of excitement, Jenna urges, "Hurry back, please!"

After giving Josh an appeasing kiss on the cheek, which does not appease him at all, Eliana holds her hand out to me. I grab it and teleport us to the front of the temple. Actually, a few feet away from the front of the temple just in case there is some sort of trap at the door. Cautiously, we take a few steps forward, scanning the area for any sign of a trip switch or anything of the sort.

"Boo!"

My heart stops for a moment, and in unison, Eliana and I turn and glare up at Sam. He is laughing until Josh punches him hard in the arm. Kallen gives Josh a satisfied grin. He likes how he deals with his friend since it is exactly what Kallen would have done to Kegan in the same situation. Sam is not as appreciative of the gesture. He rubs his arm and glares at Josh.

Getting back to what we're doing, Eliana and I inch closer. The building before us is square with a flat roof. There are three steps leading up to the door, which is the only opening. There are no windows. The bricks that make up the temple look ready to crumble, but I suspect that there was magic involved in their creation. This building has withstood thousands of years of whatever the desert threw at it, and it will continue to stand for thousands more.

We make it to the door without incident only to find there is no handle. I feel around looking for a switch or lever to open it, but find nothing. "Any suggestions?" I ask.

Instead of responding, Eliana steps to the door. She reaches out and places a hand on it. A soft, greenish glow begins to emanate outward from where she is touching. Soon, the entire door is glowing. The glow turns to a brilliant flash of light, and when our retinas have recovered, we find that the door has disappeared completely.

"Um, I hope that comes back," I mutter. We need to lock the place back up when we leave. It would be rude to do otherwise. Not to mention seriously piss off the Phoenix if she found her temple without a door and her ashes missing.

"I think it does," Eliana says, but she's just as surprised as I am. We wait a minute to make sure nothing comes flying out of the temple. When nothing does, she says, "I think it's safe."

"I'll get the others," I say with a nod and teleport back to the top of the huge hole in the sand. I hold my hands out, and Kallen, Josh, Jenna and Sam eagerly grab my arms. In a blink, we are all standing in front of the now door-less temple.

"You broke it?" Sam exclaims.

"It disappeared when Eliana touched it. She's pretty sure it'll come back, though," I assure him. I really hope she's right.

"Do we go right in?" Jenna asks nervously. "Or do we throw a rock or something in first just to be safe?"

"I like the rock idea," Josh replies.

"How about a magical one," Kallen suggests since no one wants to go digging around through the sand looking for a rock. He creates a decent size stone in his hand. "Care to do the honors?" he asks Jenna.

In awe that he created a stone out of nothing, Jenna reaches for it. Once it is firmly in her hand, she turns back to the door and tosses it through. Nothing happens. We wait a few seconds in case there is a delayed reaction. Still, nothing happens. Either this place is not filled with traps, or it is just trying to lure us inside before trying to kill us. I suspect the latter.

"Does that mean it's safe?" Jenna asks.

"One way to find out," Eliana says with a sigh. She takes a step over the threshold. Fortunately, she does not burst into flames or anything equally as horrible.

The rest of us huddle in after her. Inside, we find ourselves in a narrow hall just barely wide enough for us to fit side by side in twos. The sun illuminates only a few feet in, so we can't see where the hall leads. Stating the obvious, I say quietly, "We need light." I'm not sure why I'm whispering. I doubt there is anyone else here. Then again, some traps could be noise activated.

Josh reaches out and grabs a torch from the wall. "Eliana, will you please help us out with that?" In an instant, the end of the torch is aflame. "Thanks," he says with a smile. Holding the torch in front of him, he begins to walk forward.

"Maybe any traps that are here won't go off because Ra is with us," Jenna suggests hopefully.

"Could be," Eliana replies. I don't hear much hope in her voice, though. Not very reassuring. Still, she reaches out and catches Josh's shoulder to stop his forward progress. "If that is the case, I should go first."

"It is likely that the Phoenix would have wanted the place warded against everyone. Including its maker," Josh insists.

"I was afraid someone would say that," I grumble, believing he may be right. If the ashes of the Phoenix do carry her essence, she wouldn't want anyone to have control over them. Including the person storing them for her.

"Then how do you explain us getting inside?" Jenna counters.

As if to answer her question, the door that disappeared a moment ago reappears. Firmly in place and sealed shut. Turns out there's no handle on this side, either. I really hope that Eliana's touching trick works again when we want to leave.

"Perhaps getting in was not what we needed to worry about," Kallen says quietly, voicing the fear echoing around in my head.

"Let's keep going," Josh urges. "We can worry about the door after we find what we came for." If there are any clues to find. Reaching out, Josh grabs another torch from the wall. He lights it with the one Eliana set aflame, and he hands it to Kallen. When Eliana cocks a brow in his direction, he shrugs and says, "I figured you would want your hands free."

"Good point," Eliana acknowledges. Squaring her shoulders, she begins to move forward.

Now that we can see more of the temple, we discover that the entry hall is only about ten feet long. At the end, we can go either left or right. I hate choices like that. I am always positive I am going to pick the one that lands us in a lake of lava as opposed to bringing us to the gold room or something equally as lucky. In this case, the ashes room. I never would have predicted that I would find ashes more valuable than gold. Then again, I never would have predicted most things that have happened to me. Fortune teller I am not.

"Do we split up?" Jenna asks.

Shaking his head, Kallen replies, "That would not be wise. Any traps are going to be magical. Best that we keep our power to resist them concentrated." Suddenly, I feel like laundry soap or floor cleaner. Concentrated for better results.

I do agree with him, though. Kallen didn't need to add 'because traps made by ancient gods are super powerful' to back up his words. That's just a given. Whatever we are about to face is going to suck. Majorly suck. I can feel it in my bones. My bones are rarely wrong even if my mind sucks at predicting things.

Proving me right, a giant blade swings from the ceiling. Jenna lets out a shriek as it comes straight for her. There is nowhere for her to move, so Sam valiantly steps in front of her to protect her from it. I appreciate his bravery and potential sacrificing of his own life, but the blade is stopped by both my and Kallen's magic before it comes close to doing anyone harm. No one is getting sliced in half by an ancient Egyptian blade on our watch. Not right this minute, at least. The day is still young, though. Best not to get too cocky.

The blade was not the only thing that stopped. I believe it takes a moment for Sam's heart to start beating again. He was positive he was a goner. Considering how sharp the blade looks, he would have been. With a shaky voice, he says, "Neat trick, thanks."

"So much for Ra's presence keeping us safe from traps," Jenna says wryly. She gives Eliana a guilty look. "Sorry."

Eliana shrugs. "It's true. Apparently, Josh was right. I really can't blame her. The Phoenix wanted this place to be safe for her ashes."

Turning to Sam, Jenna wraps her arms around him. "You stood in front of the blade for me."

Sam shrugs off her gratitude, but he hugs her back tightly. Staring up at the thing that almost killed him, he says, "Honestly, I think it would have gone right through me and kept going." It does look awfully sharp for a thousands of years old blade. Maybe the Phoenix takes the time to sharpen it whenever she's in town. Or magic keeps it sharp. Yeah, probably that.

"Not that holding this blade in place isn't fun," I begin, "but which way do you want to go now?" Standing in one spot for too long in here is making me nervous. The floor beneath us might give out or something.

Glancing up at the blade Kallen and I are still holding, Josh says sheepishly, "Oh, sorry." He turns to Eliana. "Are you feeling a pull in either direction?"

"Left," she replies, beginning to walk that way. She lets out a loud 'oomph' when she runs into a brick wall that wasn't there a minute ago.

"That must be the right way if the temple is trying to keep us out," I say, moving closer to the wall. I reach a hand out and pull it back when I get a sharp zap running up my arm. "Ow!" Annoyed, I pull magic, ready to zap it back. Yes, I can be childish that way, but that hurt.

Kallen puts a staying hand on my arm. "Retaliation is probably not the answer here."

Scowling up at him, I demand, "When did you become the Dalai Lama?" Behind me, Sam snickers, but Kallen is completely lost by the reference.

Ignoring my Cowan snark instead of asking for an explanation, Kallen replies, "There is writing on the wall now. I believe they are hieroglyphics."

"He's right," Eliana says in surprise. I'm surprised too since the wall was blank a moment ago. Eliana moves closer to the wall again to study the writing. Learning from my mistake, she is careful not to touch it. After a moment, she says, "It's a riddle of some sort."

Trying to keep the impatience out of his voice, Josh asks, "What does it say?"

Taking her time to make sure she is deciphering the hieroglyphics correctly, Eliana slowly reads,

> *"To pass through this wall:*
>
> *She will come with a voice that lures but breath that repels.*

*She will come with eyes that reflect the grass but ears that hear the sky.*

*She will come with hooved feet but reptilian legs.*

*She will come with the shadow of a mammoth but the stature of one who strikes fear in those with magic.*

*She will come with skin of scales but hair of silk.*

*She will come with a scent sweeter than all in the universe but will reek to heaven.*

*She will come with the need to call upon the earth but will bend the laws of natural order.*

*She will come with two hearts of mortality but the souls of the eternal."*

"I admit, I don't know enough about other realms to know if this creature exists, but it doesn't seem possible," Josh remarks when Eliana is finished reading. Taking out his phone, he begins taking pictures of the wall. Good idea considering none of us has a photographic memory, and the writing could disappear as quickly as it appeared.

"Because it is not one creature." All eyes turn to Kallen, and he continues, "I am not sure what the Phoenix wants, but I believe she is talking about different beings…"

He doesn't get to finish his sentence. A force so powerful that not even those of us with magic are able to fight it pushes us against the walls of the temple. Flames surround us, licking at us, ready to taste our flesh. The heat is like nothing I've ever felt before. Even the Demon inferno felt mild compared to this. We struggle against the magic holding us captive, but it is no use. We are pinned in place and no amount of magic Kallen or I throw at it makes a difference. Eliana attempts to use her power, as well, but she is no more successful than we are. This trap was not created by Ra. This one must have been created by the Phoenix, and she seems to really hate company. Especially the uninvited kind.

Suddenly, a voice whispers through our minds, singing neural synapses as it goes. If we survive, we are all going to have migraines. "You have overstepped, Ra. Even you do not have the right to come here. It is only our ancient friendship which prevents me from killing these mortals you brought to my sacred sanctuary."

Eliana's mouth opens, but the voice that passes her lips is not her own. It is deep and rich, and very masculine with an underlying threat. It is like velvet wrapped around lava. Soft, smooth and dangerous. "You have broken your oath to the universe, my dearest one. I have come to help you find your way."

"You speak to me of breaking oaths? You left this world, leaving these mortals to find their own way, and they found nothing but destruction and pain."

Eliana shakes her head, and Ra's voice says, "They have found much more than that. There is more good in this universe than there is evil."

The Phoenix's voice is growing agitated. "The balance has shifted."

"Perfect balance will never be maintained. It is impossible. The slightest shift can unbalance the scales. But the weight of one good deed outweighs a hundred evil ones. For this reason, the odds will always be against evil."

"You have always been a fool, my love." Ouch. The Phoenix sounds like she really means that.

Ra is not offended. "I have been called worse," he offers. "Tell me what I can do to change your current path."

"You are fond of riddles, so I have given you one. Only, you must let the mortals figure it out on their own. If they are capable." I try hard not to be offended. It doesn't work. In a message meant for the rest of us before she departs, the Phoenix warns, "Do not return without her."

The last echo of the Phoenix's voice is accompanied by a sharp increase in the heat of the inferno around us. Just as I fear our skin is going to melt off, the magic holding us becomes a fierce pressure against our bodies. It is no longer just holding us in place, it is crushing us. How the hell are we supposed to return with some magical creature if this trap kills us first? I continue to struggle against it, but my magic is still useless. I can't even turn my head to see how Kallen is faring. Great, I'm going to die without even a final look at my husband.

Fortunately, the Phoenix has other plans. That is, if I consider a massive amount of pain fortunate. With a final twist of magic, we are literally shoved through the wall of the temple like it's jelly. The magic propels us back to the top of the hole and drops us on our backs in the hot sand. We can only watch in awe as the mountains of sand Eliana so carefully dug out are pulled back to the temple, all of its walls still intact despite our burrowing through one of them, and burying it once more.

My entire body aches as I lie here. But, I'm still alive, so I'll take the massive amount of pain as a win. Besides, I don't think anything is actually broken. I move my arms and legs a little bit just to be certain I can. I notice I am not the only one doing this. Kallen reaches out and winds his fingers with mine and squeezes.

"Well, that sucked," Sam gasps through a mouthful of sand.

Yes. Yes, it did.

# 10 Chapter

"King of The Understatement," Josh grumbles to his friend from where he is lying next to Eliana.

"I would just like to say, I don't like the magical adventures you have with these guys," Sam announces, pushing himself to a sitting position and pointing at Kallen and me.

Forcing my own sore body to sit up before I get sand burns, I mutter, "So glad we brought you along."

"You prefer sociopathic gods like Set?" Josh asks Sam, reminding him of their last adventure without Kallen and me. I am so much better company than a sociopathic god. I'm certain of it.

With a half grin in Eliana's direction, Sam says, "At least I didn't get pushed through a stone wall that time." Eliana glares at him. He may have come out of that adventure unscathed, but she didn't. Jadyn filled me in on the details.

"How did that happen?" Jenna asks as she sits up. "I mean, the wall didn't even crack. It was like it absorbed us and then spit us back out."

With a shrug, I give her the only explanation I can. "Magic." If she wants a better one, I am not up for the job.

"I find I am not as big of a fan of magic as I once was," she complains. "That was terrifying."

Changing the subject, Sam asks Eliana, "So, that was Ra's voice, huh?"

Eliana nods. "Yes."

Eying Eliana curiously, Josh asks, "Is he still on the surface?"

This time, Eliana shakes her head no. "He has retreated."

"He couldn't help you fight those flames?" Josh presses. There is no criticism or judgement in his words, just curiosity.

Eliana shakes her head. "The flames I can create were no match for those. I couldn't use wind to fan them away, and even my call to the water molecules in the air went unanswered."

"I believe we just had our first taste of Cosmic Fire," Kallen says wryly. "A very small taste, thank goodness."

I'm not sure his idea of small and mine are the same. But, I guess if you look at it in terms of this incident and Cosmic Fire destroying the universe, I guess it was a small taste. "Meaning we could have been incinerated if the Phoenix so chose?" I clarify unnecessarily. If nothing else, I am much more determined to convince the Phoenix she should die and be reborn. Maybe she'll come back a little less cranky.

"Yes."

Jenna gasps. "Wait, does that mean the Phoenix is in there?"

With a grimace, Kallen says, "I believe so. At least for now."

"Which explains why the Angels couldn't find her. They can't see past the wards. It's the perfect hiding place for her," I add. Step one down, we know where the Phoenix is. At least we don't have to chase her through all the realms.

Josh bursts my 'we got this' bubble. "And we have no way to get to her, either," he points out.

"Not unless we figure out her riddle," Eliana replies with a sigh. Remembering Josh's actions before the unfortunate Phoenix event, she asks, "Did your phone survive the attack?"

Josh fishes it out of his pocket and slides his finger over the screen. He smiles broadly. "I have just become a very loyal customer of this company."

"No doubt. I thought my face was going to melt off, yet your phone survived. That is some fine manufacturing to stand against Cosmic Fire," Sam comments.

Kallen bursts their consumer dreams. "I suspect the Phoenix chose not to harm us or any of our possessions this time around. I suggest we return to the Fae realm and begin to decipher the riddle," he urges, eager to get away from here.

I agree. I am more than ready to get the hell away from here. Gazing at the spot the hole was a moment ago, I can't help but ask, "Do you think the Phoenix is okay in there?"

"She is immortal and virtually indestructible," Kallen reminds me. "I am sure she is fine." It still makes me sad to leave her all alone buried in the sand.

"She must be terribly lonely down there," Jenna adds.

"Considering the way she greets company, I suspect she likes it that way," Josh points out.

Pushing my sore body to a standing position, I debate how strong I'm feeling at the moment. Glancing around at the others, I decide I'm feeling strong enough to teleport us all back to Colorado. I don't want to leave anyone here to face the wrath of the Phoenix alone if she decides we didn't leave fast enough. "Come on, let's go."

Kallen stands and gives me an appraising look. He obviously followed my thought process. "Are you sure you are feeling up to this?" he asks.

"I'm not leaving anyone behind," I insist.

"That did not answer my question," he replies.

"I am fine."

"Are you sure? I'd hate to leave a leg or something behind," Sam says.

"You are in more danger of leaving your brain behind," Josh snarks with a grin.

"I am fine," I reiterate for everyone's benefit. "Now, can we go? The sooner we are away from this place, the better I'll feel."

Kallen nods and holds his hand out to me. The others gather around and put their hands on my arms. "Ready?" I ask when everyone is in place. When I get affirmative nods, I teleport us out of Egypt. I am thrilled when my old house appears before us. Even more thrilled to find that I was able to teleport all six of us across the world without incident. Okay, I may have been a little more worried about it than I let on. Cosmic Fire can really zap the energy out of a person.

"Let's never do that again," Sam insists.

"Which part?" Jenna asks.

"All of it."

Eliana nods. "I agree. I hate to tell you two, but I think it's time for you to return home."

# 11 Chapter

It's a good thing we are in the middle of nowhere, because the loud complaints that Jenna and Sam launch against Eliana's statement could wake an entire city. Arguments are traded back and forth between the friends, and tempers begin to rise on both sides. It is Kallen who finally offers a compromise. "May I suggest something?" he asks. When both sides quiet down to just muttering, he continues. "Jenna and Sam could accompany us back to the Fae realm, where they can remain while the rest of us do what we must to solve the riddle. They can stay at our home when we need to travel."

"I love that idea," Jenna says with a grin. Turning her attention to Eliana, she adds, "I know you are worried about trying to keep us safe, but we don't have to go with you for the dangerous parts. If Kallen's family doesn't mind, it would be a great opportunity for Sam and I to learn more about the supernatural world. Something that will help you and Josh in your jobs."

Eliana considers her for a long time, weighing her friends' curiosity over their safety. Finally, she asks Kallen and me, "Are you sure your family will not mind?"

I shake my head. "They won't mind at all."

"I understand Jenna enjoys research. Another set of eyes to dig through books from the archives is always helpful," Kallen adds. Aw, I love my husband. He can be really sweet when he wants to be. Across from him, Jenna glows with both pride and embarrassment that he knows this about her.

Josh turns to Sam. "Are you okay with being left behind if we feel that it's too dangerous to bring you along?"

"Left behind at a mansion on the beach? I think I can handle it," Sam says dryly.

"Is it settled then?" I ask Eliana, wanting her to have the last say on whether Sam and Jenna accompany us. She is the one who will feel the guiltiest if anything happens to them. Not that I wouldn't feel awful, as well, but ultimately, she feels most responsible for their wellbeing.

Eliana nods. "It's settled."

"Okay, then. Let's go inside so I can bring us back to the Fairy realm."

A twig snaps in the trees behind us, and all of us whip around. There, a lone backpacker stands with wide eyes. I suspect she's been there for a while. Long enough to have seen way more than she should have seen. "I, uh, I didn't know anyone still lived here," she says. "I, uh, come up here sometimes when I want to be alone." Clearing her throat, she asks, "Where did you guys just come from?"

"You didn't sense her?" Sam asks Eliana out of the corner of his mouth.

Eliana gives him a sour look. "I was a little busy arguing with you, and she's not a threat." Eliana can sense humans who are threats much more readily than non-threats.

"The fact that she saw us appear out of nowhere makes her somewhat of a threat," I point out quietly. To the backpacker, I say louder, "This is private property. You need to hike somewhere else in the future."

"Of c-course," she says, backing away.

Eliana moves forward at super speed and lightly grasps the woman's arm. "Wait, I want to talk to you for a minute," she says, keeping her voice soft and neutral.

"About what?" the backpacker asks, fear in her eyes.

Sliding her hand down to make contact with the skin on the back of the woman's hand, Eliana says in a soothing voice, "You did not see anything odd here today. You came up here like usual, and there was no one around. You don't like the feel of this place, though. It gives you the creeps. There are also wild animals living in the garage, and one of them may be rabid. You are afraid of being bitten. You are going to stay away from here from now on."

As she speaks, the woman's eyes gloss over and her expression goes slack. When Eliana is done speaking and drops the backpacker's hand, the woman's eyes clear again. Without even seeming to see us, she turns around and walks back the way she came. I watch in awe as she retreats into the woods.

When I am certain the woman is out of earshot, I say, "That's new."

Eliana's expression is sheepish. "Yeah, I don't like doing it."

"Mind control is a slippery slope," Kallen comments with a disapproving frown.

"It's more persuasion than mind control," Josh clarifies, eager to defend Eliana.

"If it keeps her from coming back, I'm all for it," I say with a pointed look in Kallen's direction. His lips press into a thin line, but he doesn't say anything. I know where his mind is going, though. Mind control is dark magic. "It's not the same," I insist. "This is a god asserting the power of persuasion, not becoming a puppet master." At least, I hope that's true. I just can't imagine Eliana doing anything with dark magic.

"The effects will wear off in a few days," Eliana hurries to say. "But, hopefully, the woman will still be too freaked out to come back."

Kallen seems to feel better knowing the effects do wear off. Permanently altering a mind without permission is a serious no-no in the Fae realm. With a relieved nod, he says, "We should go inside before anyone else sees us."

"Yeah, and I need to call Aunt Barb and find out the last time she was here," I grumble under my breath. She agreed to take care of the house for us, and I thought she was using the garage for some of her research projects again. Maybe her new boyfriend is monopolizing too much of her time for her to make it up here. If that's the case, Mom, Dad and I need to come up with a better plan for securing the area if we want to keep it as a safe retreat in the Cowan realm.

Inside the house, the others huddle together in the living room to give me enough space to make a passageway to the Fairy realm. Once I am done, I usher them through to the beach on the other side. With a promise to myself to return soon and figure things out with the house, I step through and close the passageway. Unless the universe ends. Then, there really won't be a need.

The sun has risen in the Fairy realm. Fortunately, it is not quite as hot as it was in Egypt, though it is considerably warmer than it was in Colorado. On the terrace, Kegan and Alita are sitting with Keelan. "Are you waiting for us?" I ask. "Or just out here enjoying the sunshine?"

"A little of both," Alita admits. "It is a beautiful day."

"Hopefully, you've found a way to make sure there are many more beautiful days in our future," Kegan says pointedly.

Climbing the terrace steps, I tell him, "We're one step closer."

"Really?" Alita asks in surprise. "What did you find out?"

Not wanting to tell the story more than once, I ask in lieu of answering her, "Is everyone else inside?"

Kegan shakes his head. "Grandmother is in her office, but Garren is in the garden 'helping' Tabitha."

Just as he says this, we hear loud, angry voices coming from that direction. "Sounds like he's being a lot of help," I mutter.

"They have been at it for a while now," Alita says with an amused smile. "He has been lucky to survive the morning."

"Honestly, I am surprised he made it this long," Kegan grins. "I will let them know you are back." He hands Keelan to Alita, jumps over the terrace wall and rounds the house toward the garden and the loud voices. Hopefully, he won't get caught in the crossfire if magic starts to fly.

"I can never figure out if Garren is brave or stupid," I muse to Kallen.

"You know my thoughts on the matter," he says with a grin. Definitely the latter.

Rising from her chair with her son in tow, Alita says, "I will get Isla."

"No need," Isla says from the terrace door. "I heard voices and assumed you were back. How did it go?"

"We have a riddle to solve," Kallen tells her.

With a sigh, Isla shakes her head. "Ancient Egyptians and their riddles." Realizing she may have just insulted Eliana and Ra, she adds, "My apologies."

Eliana shakes her head. "No need. They can be frustrating."

Stepping aside, Isla waves her hand toward the interior of the house. "Come inside. We had better get Dagda back here before you begin your tale."

With a laughing Kegan trailing behind, Garren comes around the house covered in potting soil and muttering about old Fairies set in their ways. He stops when he sees us. "What did you find out?" he demands gruffly.

Isla arches a brow at his dirty clothes, hands and face. "That it is foolish to tread in someone else's garden," she suggests. Her husband glowers at her as he starts walking again, but then he glances down at himself. Realizing how dirty he actually is, he uses magic to erase the mess from existence.

"Are you coming inside or not?" a testy voice demands from deeper inside the house. Tabitha, who must have entered the house through the kitchen, sounds like she's ready to kill the first one to step through the door. Fortunately for the rest of us, she's not likely to follow through on that unless it's Garren.

Eliana raises a brow in my direction, wondering if it is safe to enter. I smile broadly but keep my voice quiet as I say. "Don't worry about them. Tabitha and Garren always argue. Tabitha is all bark but no bite." Reconsidering, I add, "Just stay out of smacking range." Leaving my explanation at that, I follow Isla and Garren inside.

"She is mostly kidding," Alita assures our guests before following me inside. I doubt her words are as reassuring as she meant them to be.

Regardless, our guests do follow us. Of course, I lead them to the kitchen. "This is where we always meet," I tell them, waving toward the counter. "Have a seat. Is anyone thirsty?" The desert made me parched. I am not the only one, apparently. There is a round of requests for water.

Shooing me out of the way, Tabitha insists, "I can do better than water." It takes her just a moment to produce a pitcher of fresh lemonade for us.

"So, are you going to tell us why you are covered in sand?" Kegan asks, grabbing an apple from the fruit bowl in the middle of the large island counter. He gestures to it letting our guests know to help themselves if they are hungry. Josh reaches for a banana and Jenna takes an orange. "It looks like you've been rolling around in it," Kegan says around a bite of his apple.

"We were," I inform him, finishing my lemonade and pouring another glassful before passing the pitcher around the table once more. When it runs dry before making another full lap, Tabitha is nice enough to make us more. "Thank you," I grin, draining my second glass. Who knew the desert and Cosmic Fire could make you so thirsty?

"In an effort to save time, perhaps you should go to the palace and retrieve the King," Garren suggests testily.

Is he trying to get me in trouble? Narrowing my eyes at him, I say, "You know he hates it when I pop in when he's in a meeting, right?"

"Are any of his meetings more important than the end of the universe?" Kegan counters. He does have a point.

"This is perhaps one of the times he will consider an exception to the rule," Isla drawls.

Giving in to the peer pressure, I sigh. "Fine, I'll go get him. I'll be right back." I lean over and give Kallen a quick kiss before disappearing.

I teleport right outside of Dagda's office and knock on the door. Who says I can't learn to be polite and unobtrusive? I am therefore surprised when the door whips open a second later and an annoyed Fairy King is growling, "What are you doing out there?"

I go with, "Um, respecting your boundaries like you've asked me to a thousand times?"

I get a roll of the eyes for my attempts at politeness. "Next time just come in here like you usually do. Did you find the temple?"

Trying not to be annoyed that he did an about face on the whole intrusion thing, I say, "Actually, I came to get you so we could tell everyone what we found at the same time. That way we only have to tell it once." Repeating ourselves would just take time away from figuring out the riddle.

Dagda scowls, but he doesn't argue. "Tana should be in her office. We will swing by there to get her first." Tana has an office? If I knew that, I forgot. Meaning, I have no idea where it is. So, I let Dagda lead the way out of his office and down a short hall.

Poking his head inside her door, Dagda interrupts the meeting Tana is having with someone about the refugee camp. "We have someplace we need to be," he informs her.

Chafing at his brisk tone, she asks, "Can it wait?" Then she sees me. Rising from her desk, she grimaces and says to the Fairy in front of her, "We need to reschedule." Glad to know I'm the face of 'we need to handle a disaster right now, not later'.

Ushering the Fairy out of her office and down the hall, Tana turns back to us. "Did you discover the temple?" I guess Dagda filled her in on what is going on.

"We did. I came to bring you guys back to Isla's so we can explain what we found." Tana nods and steps closer. She and Dagda each take one of my hands and I teleport us back to Isla's.

"I will never get used to her just appearing like that," Sam whispers to Jenna when we arrive.

"Me, either," Jenna whispers back.

Eager to hear our story, Isla ignores them and says briskly, "Now that we are all assembled, proceed."

Glancing around the room, I realize she does mean everyone. Since I left, Mom, Dad, Adriel and Raziel have joined the group. Well, not everyone is here. I assume Zac has been sent to his lessons at the palace since he is too young to participate in an end of the universe discussion.

I quickly introduce Mom and Dad to Eliana and her friends. Then, smiling at the Archangel across the counter, I ask sweetly, "Are you going to give us clues if we ask nicely?"

His smile equally as sweet, he replies, "No, but I have every confidence that you will figure this out."

"Gee, thanks," I grumble. Though, I do take comfort in his words and expression. I would like to think if the universe was about to end, he wouldn't be smiling. Then again, he does have a really good poker face.

In an uncharacteristic show of impatience, Alita insists, "You are killing us with curiosity." Being a mother has given her more gumption. I like it.

Putting her out of her misery, I say, "Fine. We did find the temple, but the Phoenix gave us a riddle to figure out." I go on to explain exactly what happened while we were in Egypt. Even about the gun runners.

When I am finished, Dagda asks Josh, "You have a device that is both a phone and a camera?"

My mouth drops open. "That is what you took away from all I said?"

Dagda shrugs. "I am always interested in Cowan technology."

With a chuckle, Josh takes his phone out of his pocket, unlocks it and slides it across the counter to the Fairy King. "It does come in handy," he says.

Dagda picks the phone up and examines it for a minute. Finally, he admits, "I do not know how to make this work without magic."

Josh moves next to him and brings up his photos. He finds the best one of the wall and makes it as large as his phone will allow. He hands it back to Dagda, and those who were not with us on our journey crowd around him to look at it.

Seeking out Eliana, Isla asks, "You can read this?"

Eliana nods. "Yes." She repeats what she read to us earlier.

"To pass through this wall:

> She will come with a voice that lures but breath that repels.

> She will come with eyes that reflect the grass but ears that hear the sky.

*She will come with hooved feet but reptilian legs.*

*She will come with the shadow of a mammoth but the stature of one who strikes fear in those with magic.*

*She will come with skin of scales but hair of silk.*

*She will come with a scent sweeter than all in the universe but will reek to heaven.*

*She will come with the need to call upon the earth but will bend the laws of natural order.*

*She will come with two hearts of mortality but the souls of the eternal."*

Scowling, Eliana pauses and looks up at us. "There is a line here that wasn't there when I was reading it before."

"Sneaky immortals," I mutter.

"What does it say?" Josh asks.

Doing a quick mental translation, Eliana reads, *"She will come with peace in her heart."*

When Eliana is finished reading, I ask Isla, "Any clue what this all means? Kallen believes the riddle is referencing different beings, not just one." I smile proudly at my husband.

Isla nods. "I believe he is right."

Dagda shakes his head. "Then we are doomed."

Whoa, not the response I was looking for. "Why?!" I exclaim.

He gestures to the picture on the phone. "The Phoenix is asking for the impossible. To bring all of these beings together in peace? A couple of them, I don't even know who she means. The rest, half of them are always one step away from war."

He does have a point, but I'm going to ignore it. Instead, I say, "We have brought them together before, we can do it again." At least, most of them. "We should figure out which beings they are before we worry about the how of it all."

"Eliana, will you please write down a translation for us to study?" Isla asks, creating a piece of paper and a pencil in front of Eliana's spot at the counter.

Eliana nods and begins writing. When she is done, she slides the paper to the center of the counter for us all to see. In silence, we each pour over the words Eliana wrote until they are etched in our minds.

Finally, Kallen breaks the silence. "The first, of course, is a Siren."

"Like lure your ship and crew to death kind of Siren?" Sam asks. Jenna nudges him for interrupting.

I smile at them both. "It's okay if you have questions. The answer is, sort of. You don't have to be in a boat. Sirens would coax men to walk into water and kill themselves."

Jenna's eyes grow round. "Why?"

I give Dagda a surreptitious glance, which he tries to ignore. The telltale pink in his cheeks makes me smile, though. "Well, first it was to punish abusive men. Then, the Queen got her heart broken, and she decided that all men were evil."

"You said 'would.' Do they not do it anymore?" Eliana asks.

Shaking my head, I say, "A bunch of higher beings decided that they were abusing their powers. Now, they can't make even a frog jump in the water unless it wants to do so."

"Assuming we are to gather these beings and bring them to the Phoenix, would we technically be bringing someone whose voice lures if the power of the Sirens was stripped away?" Eliana asks.

"Excellent point," Isla replies grimly.

"The Sirens do still have a little magic left," I point out. "Enough to try to help women in danger." Before their race was cleansed, the Sirens would gain power with each soul they drowned. That is no longer true.

"We will worry about it when the time comes," Dagda interrupts. "Let us move on to the next being."

"With breath that repels. I've met a lot of beings with bad breath, but I think it was a personal hygiene issue," I muse aloud. Both Sam and Kegan snicker.

"I believe the Phoenix is referencing something other than halitosis," Isla remarks dryly.

"A more literal interpretation," Kallen says, "is breath that actually repels, as in fire." Oh, that makes much more sense. Bad breath seemed like an odd request.

I groan at the thought, though. "I am not the Dragons' favorite person."

"Are you any realm's favorite person?" Kegan chides. I scowl at him. If he wasn't holding his son right now, I would magic his stool out from under him.

"Moving on," Alita says with a sour look in her husband's direction. "All Fairies have green eyes, so that must be what the line about reflecting the grass means, right?"

Isla nods. "I believe you are correct."

"The Fairies will obviously be cooperative. The next on the list must be an Elf," Dagda states.

"I don't know, he has some pretty pointy ears himself," Taz mutters from my ankle where he plopped his plump little body a moment ago. I try not to giggle.

"Since the Elves are eager to get on Xandra's good side, I do not believe an invitation to accompany us would be declined," Kallen says wryly.

I groan aloud. I haven't spoken to any of the Elves since the whole baby incident, though Dagda has a team who meets regularly with them to try to work out a treaty. I am not looking forward to seeing the Elf Queen again. Not wanting to think any more about that at the moment, I say, "The only ones with hooved feet are the Centaurs, right?" I watch as Jenna and Sam's eyes grow round. With a smile, I tell them, "Yes, they are real." Did they think we were making them up when we mentioned them in the Cowan realm to Liza?

"Are they truly half horse, half person?" Josh asks sheepishly, embarrassed by his curiosity.

I take pity on him. "Yes. And trust me, I asked all the same questions that are going through your heads right now when I first found out about these other beings."

"What about the Fauns?" Alita asks, blowing a hole in my 'only Centaurs' theory. I try not to give her a sour look. I fail.

Kallen scours the riddle. "I do not see anything else that could indicate a Faun."

"Maybe it's supposed to mean both?" I ask no one in particular.

"For now we will assume it does mean both." Pressing the conversation forward, Dagda says, "I am confused why Dragons are mentioned again."

"What?" I ask in surprise. I look down at the part of the riddle he is referencing. "Huh, they are the only ones with reptilian legs, aren't they?" I don't make a proclamation this time just in case I'm wrong. But, I can't help but smile when I say, "Maybe my chronic halitosis theory was right, after all, for the breath that repels."

"I do not believe so," Kallen says dryly. "I still believe that refers to the Dragons. This line is something different."

Her creased brow proving that she is stumped along with the rest of us, Isla says, "Let us come back to that one."

"Okay, does anyone know what a mammoth is?" Alita asks.

"You've never heard of a mammoth?" Sam asks in surprise.

"Even though the realms look similar, they are not the same," I remind him.

"Right," he says with pink cheeks.

"If I am not mistaken, a mammoth is a large, woolly elephant, correct?" Kallen asks me.

I nod. "Basically. And they are extinct."

"Is there a creature in another realm that looks like a large, woolly elephant?" Eliana asks doubtfully.

"I don't think it's being literal," Isla replies. "The word mammoth is also a synonym for large."

"Like a Giant?" Kegan suggests.

"Yes."

"How big are Giants?" Sam asks. Good for him for asking the questions his friends are dying to ask.

"They generally range from eight to twelve feet tall," Kallen tells him.

"Wow," Jenna murmurs.

"Then how tall does one have to be to strike fear in the hearts of those with magic?" Josh asks. "Twenty or thirty feet?"

I grimace. "Actually, more like ten to twelve inches."

"How can that be?" Eliana asks in surprise.

"Because if it's who I think it is, they eat magic." When all I get is confused stares in my direction from our friends, I explain further. "Pixies are nasty little creatures who have no magic of their own, but they have the ability to 'eat' or absorb the magic of anyone around them, rendering their magic useless. They're supposed to be tucked away in their own little realm not bothering anyone, but Hades was pissed at me and let a couple loose here. They live at the palace now." In luxury. They are kept in a sealed off area and are not allowed to roam free, but they are so spoiled that they don't seem to mind.

"You pissed off Hades?" Sam exclaims. A slow grin forms on his face. "I knew I liked you. What did you do?"

"Perhaps that is a story for another time," Eliana says pointedly, trying to get her friend back on track. Sam nods reluctantly. He will definitely be pressing for details later.

"The next two are easy," Alita says. "Mermaid and Sasquatch. No one has silkier hair than a Sasquatch." She absently runs her fingers through her own short, silky black locks. Kegan leans over and whispers something in her ear, making her smile and blush.

"What about the next one? I mean, I know who reeks, but who smells sweeter than anyone else in the universe?" I ask.

"Let us come back to that one, as well," Isla says. "It appears that the Phoenix would like us to gather a member of all known races. We can narrow the list of options down when we have the obvious ones out of the way."

"Good point," I nod. "Any guesses for the last four?"

"A Witch must call upon the earth for her magic," Kallen points out.

"Don't all magical beings bend the laws of nature?" Eliana asks in regards to the next line.

"They do," Isla acknowledges.

"Okay, let's come back to that one, too," I say. "The last one must be Eliana." The two hearts thing could mean hers and Ra's.

Eliana frowns. "It could also mean you, couldn't it?"

"I don't have two hearts," I point out.

"Each of the other lines represent two different beings," Kallen counters. "I suspect this line means the both of you."

With an apologetic glance in my friend's direction, I say, "I guess we're in this together."

With a smile, Eliana shrugs. "I'm okay with that."

Clearing her throat to get our attention, Isla presses on. "To sum up, we have Siren, Dragon, Fairy, Elf, Centaur, Giant, Pixie, Mermaid, Sasquatch, Goblin, and Witch. That leaves several beings unaccounted for."

Kegan glances at Adriel and Raziel, who are notably quiet as we try to figure this out. "Should Angel be on the list?"

"They can't answer you," I remind him when both Fallen Angels remain tight lipped. "The Phoenix said that we lowly mortals must figure this out on our own, remember?"

"Sorry," Adriel mouths. I know she is dying to help. Amazing how the potential end of the universe can make even the most cryptic of communicators eager to blab. Or maybe it's just because the Phoenix said she couldn't help. Adriel really hates to be told what to do. Or not to do in this case.

"It is probably safe to assume that Angel should be on our list," Isla says.

With a grin, I snark, "Okay, we'll put them under reptilian legs." Adriel glowers in my direction, but remains tight lipped.

"What about Skin Walkers?" Eliana asks, thinking of Jadyn. "Shouldn't they be represented."

"You're right," I nod. "Hmm, could they be the reptilian legs? I mean, they can be lizards if they want to be."

"It makes more sense to put them under the 'bending the laws of nature' category," Kallen counters.

Reluctantly, because I hate to admit when I'm wrong, I mumble, "I guess."

"Are Angels the ones who smell sweet?" Alita asks.

There is a snort from around the area of my ankle. "If that's true, you certainly didn't get that gene," Taz snarks. I kick at him, but he moves out of the way too darn fast.

Choosing not to share my rude little Familiar's comment, I turn my eyes to my Fallen Angel friends. "You guys do smell good." I grin at Adriel as color floods her cheeks. She still remains silent, though. They are taking the 'no help from higher beings' thing seriously. Or, Raziel has told her what is going to happen and she doesn't want to give anything away. Now, I study her more closely, looking for clues. I get a scowl from Adriel for my efforts. "Just trying to figure out how much you know," I admit, continuing to study her.

"You really know what's going to happen next and you aren't going to say anything?" Sam asks Raziel curiously.

Raziel gives an uncomfortable shrug. "It is forbidden."

Sam shakes his head. "That's harsh. The fate of the universe is on the line."

"This is not the first time, nor will it be the last, that the fate of the universe is on the line. Raziel did not make the rules. He is a victim of them as much as anyone else," Adriel says in her love's defense. "It kills him to watch you guys struggle with your decisions and not give you any clues, or just flat out tell you what to do." She is growing angrier with every word, her voice growing cooler and her eyes sparking. Sam is shrinking farther and farther into his stool. Angry Angels of Death can be pretty darn intimidating, even when they come in petite blonde packages.

Sam holds his hands out in front of him, palms up. "Sorry, I didn't mean any offense." Adriel obviously doesn't believe him, but she doesn't say any more. She does continue to glare, making Sam squirm on his seat.

"Moving on," I hurry to say before Adriel decides she wants her old job back with Sam being the first soul she gets to strip. "We still have a lizard leg to figure out. What being are we missing?" I glance around the room, but no one jumps in with a suggestion. "Anyone?" I press.

"We seem to have covered all of the realms," Kallen says.

"What about Cowans?" Kegan asks.

"I do not remember Cowans having reptilian legs," Kallen replies dryly.

Kegan rolls his eyes. "I mean, we haven't put them on the list."

Because my maturity level is a roller coaster ride, I roll my eyes, too. "I think Eliana covers that."

Not liking to be wrong any more than I do, Kegan reluctantly admits, "I guess."

I feel Raziel's stare boring into me and turn to face him. His eyes are flashing with a mixture of frustration and, wait, is that humor? If I didn't know better, I would think he is trying to communicate something to me. I rack my brain trying to figure out what he wants me to understand. All the while, he continues to stare at me as if trying to will the information into my brain.

Maybe he is because an idea slowly creeps into my mind. A terrible, nonsensical idea. A completely inane one. I shake my head. Raziel nods his ever so slightly. Or, I just imagine that he does, I'm not really sure which. Could it be? But why? How? Finally, I just blurt it out. "A dinosaur? Really?"

All eyes turn to me in surprise. "What?" Dagda asks, certain he did not hear me correctly.

Forcing the silly words from my mouth, I say, "The only realm I know of that we left out is the dinosaur realm where Raziel used to go when he wanted peace and quiet from his thoughts."

Kegan starts laughing so hard, he wakes up Keelan who was napping in his arms. Rocking his son gently, he says in a quieter voice, "Yes, you are supposed to grab a brachiosaurus and bring it to Egypt." Across the table from him, Sam snickers. In my peripheral vision, I even see my husband trying to hold in a chuckle.

Placing my hands on my hips, I snap, "Then what other creature besides a Dragon has reptilian legs? Are you guys holding out on me about another race of beings?"

His brow wrinkled in thought, Dagda responds almost absently, "You are now aware of all of the realms we know about."

Hmm. Interesting choice of words. "Meaning there could be other ones you don't know about?"

My biological father shrugs. "It is a possibility. We certainly were not aware of the realm of Pixies until just recently."

That's true. Great, I'm not sure what's worse. Facing the idea of bringing a dinosaur to the Cowan realm, or trying to find a new realm before our time runs out. My eyes fly back to Raziel. He was trying to tell me something a minute ago. Meeting his stare again, I find even more humor there than a moment ago. With a sigh, I announce, "Nope, it's the dinosaur realm."

"How can you be certain?" Isla asks.

"A little Angel told me so," I mutter.

Isla's eyes fly to Raziel, but he has a perfectly innocent expression on his face. Too innocent. Innocent enough to convince her that I'm right. With a shake of her head, she says, "The Phoenix has set out an impossible task knowing you could not possibly complete it."

"It would have been difficult enough assembling a member of each race to travel peacefully to the Cowan realm, but capturing and taming a dinosaur to bring along?" Dagda shakes his head in disgust at the impossible task.

Sam, obviously the most outspoken of the Cowan group, asks, "Are you serious? There's really a realm that still has dinosaurs?"

I nod. "Yeah. Raziel even has a pet pterodactyl there." My eyes open wide, and I whip around to face the Fallen Angel again. "Do you think your pterodactyl is tame enough to bring with us?"

A large grin forms on Raziel's face. "I believe the Phoenix is unaware that I have made such a friend."

So, the impossible task is not so impossible after all. Who knew Raziel's ability to communicate with dinosaurs would come in handy? And a pterodactyl would be much less obvious than a brachiosaurus in the Cowan realm. Even if it flew away. Imagine what excitement it would cause in the field of paleontology if it was found. I can almost feel the scientists salivating. Which is disgusting now that I think about a bunch of scientists salivating on me.

"Would that constitute interfering if you helped retrieve the dinosaur?" Kallen asks Raziel. Good question.

Raziel shrugs. "I believe I am allowed to do a favor for a friend. After all, it was not my idea." A hint of a smile touches his lips. It most certainly was his idea. I won't tell the Phoenix if he doesn't, though.

"I hate to bring this up," Sam says hesitantly. "But, what if the Phoenix truly thought she was setting forth an impossible task. If you are able to assemble this group and return to her, do you think she will still honor her word and not just kill you on the spot?" A good, even if depressing and terrifying, point.

Isla nods. "Yes, she is bound by truth and her word as are the other immortal beings."

With a grimace, I mutter, "It is amazing how the truth can be twisted, though." Kallen reaches out and gives my hand a squeeze, but he doesn't disagree with me.

Nor is he a bucket of sunshine with his next words. "Now that we have solved the riddle, I think we need to think about the bigger picture. Assembling this group simply gets us an audience with the Phoenix, it does not mean she will agree to be reborn," Kallen points out.

I scowl at him. "Thanks for raining on our already miserable parade." I get a helpless shrug from my gorgeous husband. I hate it when a situation is so dire all he can do is shrug helplessly.

"He does have a point," Dagda argues. "The Phoenix laid out an impossible task to get just an audience with her. What do you think she will demand to rethink her decision?"

"On the other hand, seeing the impossible performed could give her hope," Eliana challenges. I have always liked Eliana for good reason. She tries to see the best in people. Or in immortal birds, whatever the case may be at the time.

"True," I agree, trying to gather some hope inside me again. "Let's go with that theory for now."

Rising from the table in unison, Kallen and Josh both say as if they were twins separated at birth, "We should get going." Eliana and I look at each other and laugh.

"Um, do either of you know where we're going?" I can't help but ask the pair of dark haired, handsome and incredibly well built guys. Damn, Eliana and I certainly lucked out in the boyfriend/husband looks department. Not that looks is all that matters. They are also supportive, intelligent, and funny. Why am I justifying this to myself? I know why I love my husband, but it certainly doesn't hurt that he's gorgeous.

"We should start with our allies," Kallen responds. "The Mermaids, the Giants." The last word sticks to his tongue like a stray dog hair. He doesn't care for the leader of the Giants much. Mostly because the guy wanted Dagda to force me to marry him instead of Kallen. Obviously, that didn't work out for the Giant Chieftain.

"Ugh, can't we do the Giants last?" I ask hopefully. I don't care much for Quinn, either. He's arrogant and obnoxious. And he tends to leer.

"Kallen is right," Isla says, crushing my dreams. Now that I think about it, she often excels at dream crushing. Mine, at least. I wonder if she took a class in it. After all, she did see me coming in her visions. She could have prepared with a 'How to Crush the Hopes and Dreams of Xandra' class. She does like to plan ahead. Hmm, I should probably be listening to her instead of thinking about this, though. "The more beings you already have standing with you when you go to the more resistant of the groups, the better," Isla continues.

I know if I don't agree, she will only come up with ten more good reasons why we should do it this way. "Fine," I sigh from the very depths of my soul. Deep down in that soul of mine, I know she and Kallen are both right. I do not, however, need to pretend I am happy about it. Huh, I wonder if my maturity is stuck at this level.

Eliana leans toward me and asks quietly, "Are the Giants really that bad?"

"No, not most of them," I reluctantly admit. "They're a bit chauvinistic, but mostly Kallen and I just don't care for one of their leaders." Eliana nods in understanding and lets the subject drop for now despite the fact that she probably has a zillion questions like I do whenever I encounter a new race. She is so much politer than I am.

Catching Eliana's attention, Isla warns, "Some of these groups are distrustful of strangers. They may want to test you."

"I understand," my brave friend nods. I give her an encouraging smile. I know she is more than up for whatever challenges are thrown at her. Even if she wasn't, Kallen and I would never let anything happen to either her or Josh if we can help it.

"Okay then, who's ready for a breathing under water spell?" I ask. Oops, I didn't mean to imply everyone can go. Before they even have a chance to respond in the affirmative, I turn to Jenna and Sam. "I'm afraid we need to leave you guys here for now. Isla's right. Some of the beings we're going to meet are not going to be very nice." The Merpeople closed their realm off from the Cowan realm a long time ago. Not so much because they hate them, but because the oceans in the Cowan realm were becoming too dangerous and polluted. Something that disgusts the Merpeople down to their marrow. If they have marrow. Maybe they do in the upper parts of their body. Anyway, they're not exactly fans of Cowans, either. Bringing one Cowan with us is probably pushing it.

Though disappointment washes over both their faces, Sam and Jenna nod in agreement. "We get it," Sam says, trying really hard to mean it. With a hopeful glint in his eye, he adds, "I was kind of looking forward to seeing the dinosaur realm, though."

Strangely enough, that one is probably the safest one to bring a non-magical person. At least, with Kallen, Eliana and me there to protect him from a stray T-Rex, it is. Giving him a broad smile, I make Sam's day. "We'll go there last, and you can come along."

"Really?" he asks excitedly.

"Really," I promise.

"Before you rush off, I believe there is one thing you have not discussed," Tana drawls. She has been surprisingly quiet throughout this conversation. Honestly, I kind of forgot she was here.

"What's that?" I ask impatiently, eager to get going now that we know what we have to do.

Glancing down at the handwritten riddle before her, Tana points out, "The Phoenix is very specific about the pronoun *she* uses."

Oh, good lord, she's right. The rest of us in the kitchen exchange worried glances. Well, that just complicates the hell out of our plan.

# 12 Chapter

"You are right, my dear," Dagda concurs, shaking his head in defeat. "As if this was not going to be difficult enough."

"Do you mean we must bring back all females?" Eliana asks for clarification.

I groan and tell her, "Yes, which could be a problem."

With a frown, my friend asks, "Why?"

"Because some of the realms are not exactly up to date on female rights. The Centaurs just recently had a rebellion of their females because they had no recognized rights whatsoever," Kegan explains.

"It won't be a problem in all the realms," I hurry to add, not wanting Eliana and her friends to think that all supernatural beings are behind in their equal rights status. "Only a couple of them."

"The Giants will not like it," Kallen says thoughtfully. "Nor will the Centaurs or the Sasquatch. Or the Dragons." So much for my 'only a couple of them' theory. Man, I really hope Raziel's pterodactyl is female. I'm pretty sure he would have mentioned it if it wasn't. At least the dinosaurs probably don't care if we take a male or female with us. Their minds are still stuck at 'is it food or not food?'

"Isn't that about half of the beings we need?" Josh asks in amazement.

Squaring my shoulders, I set my determination level to maximum. "Too bad. They are just going to have to deal with it."

Kallen chuckles and wraps his arm around my shoulders. "I know that look in your eyes. Yes, I believe you will make them 'deal with it.'"

I am pretty sure that was not a compliment. I scowl up at him. "You make it seem like I'm a tyrant."

"You are," Kegan smirks across the counter.

Smiling sweetly at Alita, I ask her ever so politely, "Would you mind taking your son from your husband for a moment?"

Laughing, Alita shakes her head. "No way. I want my husband in one piece. Even if he does not always know when to keep his mouth shut." She gives Kegan a warning glance, which he wisely heeds. Being a father has made him at least a smidgen smarter.

"Um, what would you like us to do while you are gone?" Jenna asks. "We would love to help any way we can."

The sincerity in her voice is heart-warming. "Jenna is really good at research," I tell Isla. "Maybe she can work with the scribe to find out more about the Phoenix and possible reasons she would not want to die. The Phoenix, I mean, not Jenna," I hurriedly add as color rushes to my cheeks. Sometimes it seems like English is my second language. "The more information we have when we confront her, the better."

"You would like to give a Cowan access to the archives?" Tana asks in surprise.

Sure, now she joins the conversation with a vengeance. Where was here voice when we were trying to make a plan? "Yes," I reply icily, growing more annoyed by the second. We are going to be dealing with enough prejudice in the other realms, I did not expect it in our own kitchen.

"I believe Tana's reluctance stems from a fear of Cowans discovering too much about how to harm supernatural beings, rather than where your mind has gone," Dagda says dryly. "That is a lot of power to simply hand over."

Oh, that makes much more sense. My face pinks up a bit again for making an incorrect assumption. Clearing my throat, I push past my embarrassment. "Jenna and Sam have been very loyal in regards to keeping Eliana's secret. They have also come face to face with several supernatural beings other than Eliana who were pretty evil, and they had no information on how to deal with them. They could use a bit more information than they have at their disposal back home to help keep their realm safe. I don't think either of them would use the information they gather to do anyone who is good any harm."

Jenna shakes her head adamantly. "We would not." Sam seconds that.

Dagda narrows his eyes and studies the Cowans before him. After a long, too long in my opinion, appraisal, he finally says, "I will trust you based on Xandra's assessment. Do not disappoint either of us." The last words have more than a hint of menace in them.

"We won't," Jenna promises. Her voice is a little shaky, but she is sincere. She even crosses her heart like she did back in her living room when we first met her, which is too cute. Dagda has no idea why she does this, though, and just gives her an odd look. That gesture isn't used in the Fairy realm.

Dagda glances over her head at me and raises his brows. "She's telling the truth," I assure him. When Eliana and her friends turn their questioning gazes to me, I explain, "I'm a walking lie detector. I feel like bugs are crawling all over me if someone tells a lie."

With a grimace, Kallen remarks, "Be prepared to have that feeling often as we travel between realms." Unfortunately, he's right. The Sasquatch are notorious liars. A few other beings aren't the most trustworthy, either. The Pixies are the worst. They like to lie just to make me feel like I have bugs crawling on me. Miserable little creatures, they are.

"That would be a handy skill to have," Josh observes.

"Yeah, until people start lying and I have to try not to dance around like an idiot," I snark. Giving him an apologetic smile, say, "Sorry, it's not my favorite ability." Useful, but far from my favorite.

Josh laughs. "I understand."

"Okay, so now we know we need to bring back only females. Does anyone have anything else to add to the list before we go?" I ask the room in general. My eyes linger on Raziel hoping for another clue, but he is staying tight lipped and keeping his eyes as expressionless as possible at the moment. He is done giving clues for the day. I'll have to check back tomorrow. Maybe his guilt will get the better of him over night. Probably not.

"I believe you have all the information we can decipher at this time," Isla hedges, leaving room for the possibility of other issues arising. Like they always do.

Figuring that is the best response I am going to get, I turn to Kallen, Eliana and Josh. "Okay then, I hope you don't mind swimming in the ocean. We're going to see the Mermaids first."

"I love the water," Eliana says with an eager smile. She may not show it as much as Sam and Jenna do, but she is just as curious and excited as they are. If the situation wasn't so dire, this could actually be fun introducing Eliana to these other realms and doing some sight-seeing. I suspect we are not going to have much fun on any of these trips, though. And the only sights we are going to see will be angry and/or scared realm leaders. What fun.

"Good. Oh, and just so you're prepared, most of the Mermaids don't wear shirts." With that little tidbit out there, I make my way past a now blushing Josh and head out to the beach to make yet another tear in the fabric of the realms. Everyone in the kitchen rises from their stools and follows me out.

Now that I think about it, I stand in the same approximate area on the beach every time I do this. I really hope I'm not creating a frayed spot here. I would hate to have a permanent opening into another realm right in front of the terrace. Not only would that ruin the view, it could be rather dangerous depending on which realm it happens to be. Hmm. Maybe I should move a few yards down from my usual departure spot just in case. I get an odd look from Kallen when I suddenly change spots, but I can explain my theory to him later. If there is a later.

## 13 Chapter

I need to rack my brain for a minute until I am finally able to recall the spell the Mermaids use to make it so that other beings can breathe underwater when visiting their realm. Gathering Eliana, Josh and Kallen close, I have everyone join hands. I pull magic and recite aloud, *"Bodies of land, born for soil and sand, foreign to the sea, yet protected we will be."* I can't believe I had trouble remembering something so simple. I will put it down to the stress of the universe possibly ending.

"Ah!" Josh exclaims, shaking himself as my magic burns through him. He keeps a firm grip on my hand, though. He is one strong Cowan, that's for sure.

With a wry smile, I admit, "My magic doesn't come with a friends and family disclaimer like Eliana's does. My magic hurts everyone equally." In the future, I should probably make sure Eliana and Kallen serve as buffers between Josh and me. He may be strong, but there also may be a limit as to how much of my magic burning through him Josh can handle in a single day. Eliana would be more than a little pissed if I accidently maimed her boyfriend. On the positive side, she could probably heal him. She still wouldn't like it.

"It wasn't so bad," Josh lies. He glances down at himself while touching his neck, I suspect he is looking for gills, and asks doubtfully, "Was that it? We can breathe underwater now?"

I nod. "Yup. You can now breath like a fish."

"I am afraid that does not make the sea warmer, nor easier to swim in without the proper attire," Kallen says wryly. He has already changed into a wetsuit. Damn, does he ever look good in a wetsuit. He notices me checking him out and gives me a wink. My cheeks flush a little, but I still like what I see. Shifting gears, Kallen gets back to business. To Josh, he says, "I will magic you a suit like this one if that is okay with you."

"Cool since I forgot to bring mine," Josh says with a grin, relieved to find out he isn't going to have to swim in his jeans. We did forget to tell them to they would need wetsuits. I wonder if he really has one at home.

Considering they live by one of the Great Lakes, I bet he does.

"Are you going to do mine?" Eliana asks me.

A round of "No!" echoes around us from various mouths on the beach. I turn and glare at each and every one of them.

Ignoring my glare, Isla steps forward. "It would be better if I did it. We do not want the whole realm to be wearing a black bikini."

Eliana raises her brows in my direction and I sigh. "Just something no one is ever going to let me live down." I reluctantly add, "But, Isla is right. She should create your suit. Subtle is something my magic still hasn't learned, so the whole realm could end up wearing a wetsuit."

Isla creates a black wetsuit for Eliana that matches the ones Kallen made. I ask Kallen to make me the same thing because despite my love for black bikinis, I don't need a bunch of Mermen ogling me. Not that they won't in a skin tight wetsuit, but I feel better without all that flesh showing. Plus, the water can get a bit chilly the deeper we go.

When we are finally ready, I step to the edge of the water and put a foot in. It's warmer than I thought it would be. The flipper on my foot helps. I walk forward awkwardly a few feet, flippers were not meant for wading, until the water is up to my knees. I wave to the others to join me. "Come on, we're wasting daylight." Not that there is any daylight under the sea. When they have joined me in the water, I open a passageway to the Mermaid realm. "We're going to jump from ocean to ocean," I explain. Extending an arm, I point through the passageway. "Oh, and those islands in the distance? Those are actually giant turtles. Whatever you do, don't disturb them. They wake up really cranky and will try to eat you." I turn my head to hide my grin. It's fun watching other people get shocked like I always do when going to a new place. They are not really in danger from the turtles, though, since we are so far away. They are also not being dropped on top of them and almost being eaten like Kallen and I were the first time we came to this realm together, so I don't feel too guilty for teasing them a little.

Reaching through the passageway, I feel the water in the Mermaid realm. It's warmer than ours. I am about to dive in when I am picked up and tossed through the passageway by my grinning husband. He dives in after me. Normally, I would come up sputtering. But, since I did the breathing underwater spell, I simply glower at him and slap at his arm without surfacing. Kallen swims out of the way before I can reach him, though. I shake my head and laugh. At least he's still trying to have a little fun regardless of how dire the situation is.

Eliana and Josh are much kinder to each other. They both dive in on their own. It takes a minute for them to actually believe they can breathe underwater, and their cheeks are puffy with their held breath. Kallen and I wait patiently for them to give in to the magic. Finally, they let out the breaths they are holding. When they realize they really can breathe underwater, and I am reasonably convinced that they are not going to freak out, I surface and close the passageway.

Turning to Kallen, I say, "I didn't want to get too close to the palace. You know how testy the guards get when we just pop in."

"Good thinking," Kallen nods. I love how his hair, which is due for a trim, floats all over in the water. I should have put mine in a braid, though. It's going to be a tangled mess by the time we are through here.

"How far away are we?" Eliana asks, glancing around trying to see something in the dark water.

"About a five-minute swim," I tell her. "The village is that way." I point in the right direction, and we can just barely make out softly glowing lights.

"Our presence has probably already been noted," Kallen tells us. "Expect to be greeted by guards before we reach the village."

Eliana and Josh look a little nervous, but they nod and begin to swim. Leading the way, Kallen directs us toward the village. He is a faster swimmer than I am, but he tries to match my pace instead of forcing me to match his. Eliana does the same since it would be easy for her to just zoom through the water. Josh is a strong swimmer and has no problem keeping up. In fact, I'm slowing him down, too. These people are only reinforcing my need for more exercise. I really should stop teleporting so often. It's making me lazy. And slow.

Kallen was right about our presence being detected. About two minutes into our swim, we are approached by two Mermen. I try not to laugh when Eliana and Josh catch their first glimpse of them. Hearing that Merpeople are real, and actually seeing them are two different things. To make the picture even sweeter, the Mermen are carrying tridents, the Merpeople weapon of choice. Those and attack octopi. Hopefully, we won't run into any of those. They are a little more difficult to reason with.

The Mermen stop when they are ten yards away. "Halt! What business have you here?"

They don't recognize me? I thought all the Merpeople except the Queen know and hate me. Maybe not. I start to feel all warm and fuzzy inside until the other Merman snarls, "She is the Witch Fairy." Did he have to say it with such disdain in his voice? My 'Maybe the Universe Does Hate Me' complex grows larger every day.

"So, you're popular here," Eliana murmurs softly. Okay, add another notch up the complex ladder.

"I kind of blew up the Queen's palace the first time I came," I admit. "The old Queen, the one they think I killed," I clarify. Then, I have to expound upon that because even though it does explain the magnitude of the hatred swimming toward me from the Mermen, I don't want my friend thinking that I actually did kill the Queen. "My doppelganger from another universe is the one who killed that Queen. A lot of the Merpeople still believe I did it, though." I don't understand why. The evil doppelganger from another universe alibi is very plausible.

Eliana cocks a brow. "Some of this would have been nice to know before we arrived."

"Sorry," I say sheepishly. I am so used to everyone I travel with knowing my history, I didn't even think to fill her in before we came. "I'll try to be better with the details on our future trips," I assure her. I'm not sure we have enough time for me to lay out all the details of my unfavorable interactions with other beings, though. It could take weeks. I am going to pretend that does not say anything about my personality.

While Eliana and I are having our hushed conversation, Kallen is addressing the Mermen. "We have urgent business with the Queen."

"I have not been informed that the Queen is expecting you," one of the Mermen sneers. He's really good at the sneering thing. I could take lessons from him. I wonder what he charges per hour.

"Look," I begin in my best conciliatory tone. "I know you guys don't like me. But can we cut through the crap? The fate of the universe depends on us talking to Queen Arie." That came out harsher than I meant it to. I may not truly understand the meaning of the word conciliatory.

So, it's not surprising that I get bland, doubtful expressions in response to my words. "You always seem to have an emergency, Witch Fairy."

Putting my hands on my hips, I remind them, "Um, it wasn't me who let the Sirens loose, now was it? But, I'm the one who fixed it for you." Technically, not true. It was a bunch of higher beings who fixed it, not me. I simply asked them for their help. Not going to point that out right now, though.

The cocky expressions leave the Mermen's face. They huddle together and have a hushed conversation, glancing our way often. I really wish they would speak louder. I am not above eavesdropping. After a moment, the Mermen finally turn back to us, resignation in their eyes. They know I'm going to make it to the village with or without their help. I try hard to keep the smug smile off my face.

"We will bring you to the Queen, but the Cowans must return to their realm," one of the Mermen insists.

I shake my head. "Sorry, they're with me."

Tridents suddenly pointing toward us, one of the Mermen growls, "We may not be able to stop you, but they will not make it to the village."

Well, I've had enough of these two and their machismo. It's bad enough when I have to breath in excess testosterone in the air, I certainly don't want to swallow it in the water. I might end up with hair on my chest or something. So, I make their tridents disappear, taking away their advantage over Josh. He can probably take both of them in a fair fight. "Either accompany us, or get out of the way," I snarl back. Kallen has moved closer to me, ready for a fight. Eliana and Josh have taken up defensive positions, as well. They look so prepared that I can't help but wonder if they have had any special training involving fighting under water. I'll have to ask later if that's in the Homeland Security playbook.

The Mermen want to fight. It's in their eyes and their body posture. But, they are not stupid. They know they are outnumbered and out powered. Without another word, the Mermen turn their backs to us and use their fish tails to zoom through the water ahead of us toward the village. We follow at a slower pace. And yes, it's me setting that slower pace. It's not like there were a lot of opportunities for me to improve my swimming skills in the mountains in Colorado. The fact that I currently live next door to the ocean is completely beside the point.

In front of me, Eliana suddenly comes to an abrupt stop and whips around. I am barely able to keep from swimming into her. Twisting my own body, I turn to see what she is staring so intently at. It takes a moment for me to see and feel it. A Merman is coming toward us. Fast. And his trident is at the ready.

Pulling on her power, Eliana calls to the water around her. A funnel begins to form between us and the Merman. It grows until it is a force so strong, the Merman gets sucked into it. He begins spinning around and around in the water, unable to free himself from the clutches of the underwater hurricane.

Behind us, I feel Kallen draw magic. Turning, I see him holding off the two Mermen who want to defend their own. "How does this Cowan have the power to control our sea?" one of the Mermen demands.

"Because she is not altogether Cowan," I smirk over my shoulder. Gesturing toward the Merman still flailing about in Eliana's trap, I ask, "Who is he, and why was he about to attack us?"

It takes a moment for the Mermen to answer. I'm not sure if that's because they are having a hard time figuring out who it is since the guy is spinning around and around, or if they just don't want to tell us. I suspect it is a bit of both. Finally, one of them admits, "I believe it is Soola. He was a nephew of the previous Queen."

Ah. That makes sense. "If Eliana lets him go, will you keep him from attacking us? We really don't want to hurt him."

There is some muttering on the part of the two Mermen, but they finally agree. I nod to Eliana and she stops the water from spinning. We don't even have to put up any defenses to ward off another attack. The Merman she had in her water hold is so dizzy, all he can do at the moment is relieve his stomach of all its contents. Gross. He definitely had shrimp for lunch. Seaweed, too. And, now the undigested bits are rapidly floating toward us making our little group scatter. Personally, I find it is a great motivator to swim faster than I was before. The other two Mermen also follow us out of the path of the vomit.

"Go with them," one Merman says to the other, his face a bit green now, and it's not because of the seawater. "I will take care of Soola." He must really like the guy, because the guard looks about ready to lose his own lunch. His cohort nods, and we all gladly swim far away from the area.

The rest of our swim to our destination is uneventful. We swim through the village as Merpeople gather to see what the commotion is about. I note that both Kallen and Josh valiantly keep their eyes averted from any of the topless Mermaids. Smart guys. Then again, Mermen do have impressive torsos. Eliana and I keep our eyes glued straight ahead, as well. Fair is fair, after all. I assume they are all in such great shape because they have to swim everywhere they go, which is great cardio. Not to mention their low fat diet of fish and seaweed.

Finally, we arrive at the Queen's rebuilt palace. We are allowed in, and Arie and Kai are waiting for us in their throne room. Only one of them is pleased to see us. Glancing around, I say in lieu of a greeting, "This place looks great." They have completely restored the palace to its previous state of grandeur. Well, as grand as an underwater palace can be, anyway. They are pretty limited in their ability to accessorize due to the corrosiveness of salt water. There is a lot of brightly colored coral on the walls and their thrones are carved from pearly white shells. There are several rocks around the room that I assume are meant to be chairs. At least, until I look closer at them. Turns out, they're sea turtles. Now I don't know if they are pets or furniture. It's probably best to just float in the water rather than sit.

"Thank you," Arie says drolly. She may be more pleased than her husband to see us, but she wants to get to the point of our visit. Her no nonsense personality is one of the reasons I like her. Which is evident in her next words. "Now, please tell us what horrible event has transpired to bring you here today." Staring curiously at Eliana, she adds, "I would also like to know more about this Cowan who can control the sea." News travels fast in the Mermaid realm. Or, Arie could feel Eliana's power all the way from here. Probably option number two.

"These are our friends, Eliana and Josh." Turning to them, I say, "This is Queen Arie and her husband Kai."

Kai scowls at me for not introducing him with a title, but I ignore him. Mostly because I don't remember exactly what his title is. Kallen really is much better at this stuff than I am. Speaking primarily to Arie, I explain, "Let's just say that Eliana isn't entirely Cowan."

"So I gathered," Arie replies dryly.

"The reason we have come," Kallen butts in to get the conversation moving in the right direction, "is that the Phoenix is refusing to die."

Rude of him to butt in, but it gets the desired effect. Arie stares at him in wide-eyed horror. Next to her, though, Kai starts laughing. "Impossible," he claims when he can catch his breath.

Giving her husband a warning glance, Arie turns back to us. "Explain," she demands. She is not as disbelieving as Kai is.

Kallen does the honors, explaining in detail about the Phoenix and her riddle. When he is finished, he says, "We need a Mermaid to accompany us when we return to the Phoenix."

"You want a Mermaid to accompany you to the desert in the Cowan realm?" Kai asks in disbelief. It is obvious he is questioning our sanity at the moment. He can get in line. I am constantly questioning my sanity. "She would die," he points out as if we don't know most Mermaids and hot, dry places don't mix.

I have been mentally debating our options all the way here. Really, we only have one unless we want to lug a giant fish tank full of seawater with us. Biting my lower lip, I blurt out, "Not if she has the ability to grow legs." The MerQueen is the only one who has a magic amulet that will give her legs when she needs them. It can give her consort legs, too, but we don't need Kai with us. He would just be a giant pain in the butt the entire time.

Rage jumps onto Kai's face like it's a rabid squirrel looking for a fight. Leaving his throne and rising to his full height in front of us, he growls, "I will not send my wife on a fool's errand with you." If we weren't underwater, I am certain we would see spittle shooting from between his lips as his anger affects his speech patterns. Which means it's still probably there mixing into the water, and floating toward us, we just can't see it. Gross.

Kai should not have said that he won't *let* his wife accompany us. Arie's face sets in hard lines, and she reminds him, "I am Queen. I decide where I go and what I do." Kai's face flushes a deep red, but he doesn't contradict her in front of us. They are definitely going to have more words on this subject after we leave, though. That is obvious.

"So, you'll do it?" I ask despite the death glare Kai is sending my way. I've already faced the fact that he and I will never be friends, and this is just one in a long line of death glares he has sent my way.

Without a glance in her husband's direction, Arie says evenly, "I do not see that I have a choice. I will need to make arrangements for my departure, but I could meet you in your realm on the morrow."

A grateful grin spreads across my face. "Thank you, Arie." I've always thought Arie was one of the most reasonable rulers of the realms. And, she doesn't try to steal my husband, literally, like the previous MerQueen did. That's always a plus.

Another thought hits me before we turn to go so the couple before us can continue their argument in private. "Um, think you could convince one of the Siren women to come, as well?"

With a nod, Arie replies, "As we have sheltered the rebels for centuries, I believe one will accept my invitation." At this point, she might agree to anything just to get us out of here. Her and Kai's relationship has become tempestuous since she became Queen, and she doesn't want us to witness more of their coming fight. Neither do we, so we are more than ready to get out here.

I am truly grateful, though, that Arie will talk to the Sirens as that saves us a trip to wherever the Sirens live. I've never actually been there, but I know it's quite far from here. They didn't want to risk the Mermen being influenced by the Sirens. Also, as Arie pointed out, they are much more likely to agree to her invitation than mine since I am the one who asked the higher beings to pass judgement over their race and take their power away. Some people get sensitive over such things. Go figure. "Thank you!" I say with a sincere smile and turn toward the exit.

"Xandra, you have not explained who your friend is," Arie calls after me. She really must be curious if she wants us to linger a bit longer to explain.

I glance toward Eliana who nods slightly. Turning back to Queen Arie, I tell her, "Eliana has the essences of two Egyptian gods within her. Ra and Isis."

After the initial shock wears off, Arie nods in understanding, and says more to herself than us, "That explains her command over the sea."

"All of the elements," I amend just for clarification. I don't want her to be caught off guard when she witnesses Eliana's other abilities. "We're off now. You were our first stop. We have a bunch more realms to go to before we're done." Some that will make the greeting we received in this realm seem warm and welcoming.

"Good luck," Arie calls as we head for the door. She knows we are going to need it.

## 14 Chapter

Eager to avoid another confrontation with any more guards, we don't waste time on conversation. We just concentrate on getting to the surface. In my case, I am mostly saving my breath so I can swim faster.

When we finally reach air, Eliana asks, "Where to next?"

I am definitely not going anywhere else wearing a wet suit. "First, we go home and change into dry clothes." Reaching out, I open a passageway back to a familiar ocean and beach. We cross over into the Fairy realm and wade to shore. Once we are on the sand, Kallen changes us all back into the clothes we had on before. I smile up at him. "Thank you." Our hair is dry, too. A little crusty from the sea salt, but dry. Considering we are in a time crunch, we'll have to ignore the crust.

"How did it go?" Dagda asks from the terrace where he has apparently been pacing impatiently while we were gone.

"Why are you still here?" I ask. I thought he would return to the palace. He is King, after all. I'm sure he has plenty of things there to keep him busy.

"Nice to see you, too," Dagda drawls. Then, he explains, "I thought it best to be here to greet anyone you bring back." Glancing over our shoulders, he asks, "Did Arie reject your plea?"

I shake my head. "No, actually she's coming herself since she is the only one besides Kai who can grow legs. She'll be here after she convinces one of the Sirens to join her."

Dagda nods in approval. "Very efficient having her retrieve the Siren."

"Thanks." No need to tell him it was an afterthought on our way out.

"She can really grow legs?" Eliana asks.

I nod. "It's a special spell meant only for the Queen and her Consort."

Dagda interrupts our conversation, reminding us we are in a time crunch. "I have sent word to the other realms to expect you."

"Did you tell them why?" I ask hopefully, though I know the answer.

"I believe that is best explained in person. We do not want to start panic in every realm prematurely," Dagda grimaces. No, he wants to wait until I am actually there for the panic to start. I'm not seeing how this is a better plan.

Self-pity aside, he probably does have a point, but I still hate that our little group has to be the bearer of bad news to everyone. That happens way more often than I feel it should. Oops. Guess I had a little more self-pity left in me, after all. "Fine," I mutter.

Changing the subject before I can change my mind, Dagda asks, "Are you off to the Giants next?"

With a sigh, I mumble, "Unfortunately."

Eliana smiles. "The more you complain about them, the more curious I am to see if they are really as bad as you believe they are."

"Just wait. You'll be complaining soon, too," I promise. Eliana just laughs.

The more I think about it, the more I want to get it over with. Holding my hands out, I explain to Eliana and Josh, "The Giants actually live in this realm. We're going to teleport." I should probably ask if they need a bathroom break since the toilets in the Giant realm are about the size of a hot tub back home. I almost fell in once. Thank goodness I have magic. But, I assume they would both speak up if that was the case.

Surprised to hear the Giants reside in this realm, Josh asks, "Isn't it weird to live with beings so big?"

"Actually, the Giants live apart from the Fairies," Kallen tells him. "It is safer for everyone that way."

"Yeah, no Fairy children get crushed, and since Giants don't have magic, they don't like living among the Fairies. But, they all get along well enough," I explain, not wanting them to think it's a prejudice thing. "It works out well for everyone."

"Got it," Josh nods. He, Eliana and Kallen all touch my arms, ready to teleport now. The excited expressions on Eliana's and Josh's faces are definitely not mirrored on mine and Kallen's. I try to remember far, far back to my excitement about meeting Giants for the first time. That seems like a lifetime ago.

In a blink, we are on the southern end of the continent. Even though Dagda said he sent word, I still teleport us a little way away from the Giant villages. It's not good to surprise Giants. They tend to react violently, and I don't want Josh to accidently get hurt.

"How far away are we?" Eliana asks, glancing around at the lack of a Giant village before us.

"Just around that bend," Kallen tells her, pointing in the right direction.

Even though I dislike him so much, I brought us closer to Quinn's village. Ellu, the other Chieftain, is still wary of me after watching my doppelganger kill his second-in-command. Quinn is a lot more likely to be happy to see us. Too happy if history repeats itself. I'm sure he will piss Kallen off before our visit is over despite the fact that we are married now.

At the edge of the Giant village, we find Orwick and several of his comrades waiting for us. I smile pleasantly at the tall, blonde Giant. "Hello, Orwick. Always a pleasure."

Orwick grunts in response. He knows how insincere I am despite my pleasant smile. Personally, I think the guy is an ass, and he knows it. I can only imagine the labels he has for me. "Quinn is expecting you," Orwick grumbles.

He obviously wishes his boss was waiting to execute us instead of greet us cordially. Sucks for him.

"Friendly," Eliana mutters next to me.

"Yeah, we have history," I admit.

Eliana shakes her head. "You should come to our realm more often. It seems to be the only place you make friends." I keep my mouth closed. I don't want to tell her about how many Witches I have pissed off there.

Coming to my defense, Kallen tells her, "It is difficult to make friends when forcing much needed change upon other beings." Change that may not always be my right to force upon them, even if the powers that be want me to do it. I sometimes have a hard time seeing how they justify it against the whole freewill thing.

"I can imagine. I'm glad I don't have your job," Eliana says ruefully.

"Too bad, I was going to offer it to you when we were finished with all of this," I tease.

"Liza would probably find a way to tear a hole in the realms to drag her back," Josh jokes. I suspect he might be right, though. That woman is determined. Not to mention, I suspect Liza would be in big trouble with the government if she lost track of Eliana. So, she would be very motivated to find her.

"Are you planning to stand here all day gossiping?" Orwick snipes.

"Why, do you have some good gossip to share?" I ask sweetly.

Orwick rises to his full height and puffs out his chest. "Be careful, Witch."

"Witch Fairy, thank you very much," I remind him. Too much of a mouthful to tag Angel onto it.

Another Giant steps forward, ready to intercept when Orwick takes a step toward me. "Who are they?" the Giant asks to draw Orwick's attention away from my attempted murder.

"Friends from the Cowan realm," I tell him. Next to me, I notice Kallen's lips press into a tight line. Obviously, that was not the right thing to say.

Proving this, Orwick takes a menacing step toward Eliana and Josh. "We do not allow Cowans in our village," he snarls.

"I really wouldn't get in her face if I were you," I inform him.

My warning is met with a smirk. "A puny Cowan is a threat to me?" While he is speaking, he reaches out and grabs Josh by the shirt and lifts him from the ground.

Shaking his head, Josh says, "You misheard Xandra. I am not the threat." He gestures toward Eliana, who is growing angrier by the second. "She is."

Orwick drops Josh to the ground and moves closer to Eliana. "Right," he sneers. He jabs Eliana in the chest with his index finger. "You are even punier. Not much of a threat in my book."

With a sigh, I remind the big oaf, "I did warn you." To Eliana, whose expression proves that Orwick's is not the only mind with murder on it, I say, "He's only going to let up if you show him your strength."

Unfortunately for Orwick, Eliana is pissed enough to do exactly that. Grabbing the Giant by the forearm before he can poke her again, Eliana whirls him around and hurls him a good twenty yards. Considering Orwick is at least five hundred pounds of pure muscle, I know I am certainly impressed. From the looks on their faces, Orwick's friends are, as well.

"She is no Cowan," one of the Giants accuses.

Shrugging, I remind him, "I said they were friends from the Cowan realm. I never claimed they were Cowans."

Picking himself up and brushing off the dust from the road, Orwick stalks back to us. He circles Eliana. He is embarrassed now and itching for a fight. Kallen and I pull magic just in case we need to interfere, but we keep it to ourselves for now. I know Eliana. She can handle the likes of Orwick.

"You caught me unaware. It will not happen again," Orwick promises as he continues to stalk his prey. Little does he know he is really the prey in this situation.

With a wicked smile, Eliana calls down a bolt of lightning from the lone cloud in the sky. It catches Orwick in the heel and he howls in pain. Taking advantage of the distraction, Eliana grabs the Giant again. This time, she throws him twice as high and twice as far. His buddies snicker as they watch him fly through the air. Giants are not a sympathetic bunch, even to their own kind. Nor do they feel the need to come to the defense of someone who cannot hold his own in a fight. Orwick's credibility as a tough guy is taking a real beating at the moment. Probably even more so than his body is.

When Orwick picks himself up, it's obvious he has a shoulder injury from landing so hard on it. The determination to prove himself to his comrades has not left his eyes, though. With a sigh, I tell him, "You know, she could do this all day without even working up a sweat. In fact, her sweat glands would consider this vacation time and not even bother to get out of bed. So, unless you want to end up with more than your fair share of broken bones, I suggest you just bring us to Quinn."

One of the other Giants agrees. "As entertaining as this is, Orwick, Quinn is anxiously awaiting their arrival. Come." He turns toward the village fully expecting us to follow. Like obedient dogs. I'm tempted to throw him twenty or thirty yards. Kallen rests a staying hand on my shoulder, and I remember why we are here. I reign my annoyance in, limiting myself to just thoughts of what I want to do to the Giant, not actually doing it.

Before following the Giant, though, I turn an assessing eye toward Orwick. I don't trust him not to try to attack Eliana from behind. He's never struck me as the most honorable of guys. Also, Giants like to fight dirty. "You first," I tell him.

Orwick stomps past us, making the ground quake slightly with his weight and anger. He gives Eliana a wide birth, which makes his buddies chuckle. Orwick does a fairly good job of ignoring them for the moment. He doesn't punch any of them, which I am positive he wants to do, he only glowers and mutters under his breath about pay back later.

We follow the Giants into the village. Orwick gets some strange looks over his disheveled appearance. No one dares say anything to him about it, though. Even his buddies stop giving him a hard time other than the occasional snicker. Eliana may have beaten him, but I doubt the others could take Orwick in a fight. He's Quinn's second-in-command for a reason.

Eliana and Josh are in awe as we weave through the busy street. Both being agile, they easily slide in and out between the Giants without being stepped on or jostled too much. Neither gentle nor nurturing by nature, Giants are not especially careful when there are smaller people in their midst. They expect us to get out of their way. As if to prove this, Josh just misses getting slammed in the head with a Giant finger when a woman stops to point out something to her friend, even though she obviously saw him walking by her. I am impressed by Josh's reaction time. For a non-magical person, he has skill.

Finally, we come to Quinn's house. I force back the bile that wants to rise in my throat at the thought of seeing the Giant again. It's hard not to be disgusted by someone who wanted my father to force me to marry him. Little did he know at the time that my father can't force me to do anything, even if he wanted to try. Guessing at where my thoughts have gone, Kallen reaches out and takes my hand in his and gives it a gentle squeeze. I smile up at him as we enter the house. I definitely have the right husband.

"Princess!" an overly jolly voice booms from across the room.

Pasting my best princess smile on my face, I try not to roll my eyes as I say, "Hello, Quinn."

After a nod to Kallen, Quinn's eyes take in Josh and Eliana. Actually, his eyes flicker over Josh and zoom in on Eliana. "Who is your beautiful friend?" he asks with more interest in his voice than I care for. A quick glance at Josh tells me that he's not caring too much for it, either.

"She is a friend from the Cowan realm," I tell Quinn.

"She is no Cowan," Orwick accuses as he stomps across the room. He really has that stomping thing down.

Quinn looks his second-in-command over. "What the hell happened to you?"

Gesturing toward Eliana with his thumb, one of the other Giants says, "He was tossed around like a baby doll by this one."

Quinn lets out a loud guffaw. "This little thing? She must be a powerful Fairy then."

I can understand why Quinn mistakes Eliana for a Fairy. She does have dark hair and green eyes. But, I am going to disillusion him. "She's not a Fairy. She did it with her strength, not her magic."

This makes Quinn stop laughing. Narrowing his eyes, he studies Eliana more closely. After a moment, he insists, "Explain."

"Like Xandra, Eliana is an enigma," Kallen says in lieu of an explanation. "But, that is not why we have come. The Phoenix is refusing to die."

Quinn looks at my husband as if he just sprouted a head coming out of his butt. One with googly eyes and a full beard. Quinn waves off Kallen's words as nonsense. "What an absurd claim. Now, tell me about this young Cowan."

"Not a Cowan," Orwick hisses under his breath. Quinn ignores him as he continues to ogle every inch of Eliana.

"It's true," I insist, trying to drag the Giant's eyes in my direction before Josh does something he may regret. Or Eliana decides to kill the Chieftain for being so freakin' rude. "We need to bring a member of each race with us to meet her. Otherwise, she won't even talk to us."

Finally, the truth of our words sinks in. Scowling, Quinn begins to pace the room, his curiosity about Eliana temporarily displaced. "This cannot be," he argues again, but there is doubt in his expression now.

"I assure you, it is true," Kallen reiterates.

Coming to a halt, Quinn says, "I will accompany you, if only to prove this whole thing to be an outrageous lie."

"We need a female," I blurt out.

Raising his eyebrows to his hairline, Quinn laughs again. "You expect me to trust the fate of the universe to a female?" And there is why I dislike him so much.

"It's really not up to you," I inform him. "The Phoenix insists I only bring females with me." We are not one hundred percent certain of this, but I am not going to tell Quinn that because I hate him and his misogynistic attitude.

Also annoyed by his misogyny, Eliana insists, "We were there, it's true."

This brings Quinn's attention back to her. And peeks his curiosity again. Among other things. Things I refuse to think about. After an assessing leer, he says, "Before I decide anything, I want a demonstration of your power."

"No," Eliana tells him. "I am not a circus act."

Scowling, Quinn asks, "What is a circus and how does it act?"

"Other beings don't always get Cowan references," I murmur to Eliana. I'm kind of glad someone else is feeling my pain that way. I spend a lot of time explaining my references to those around me.

With a nod, Eliana turns back to Quinn. "What I meant is, I am not here to put on a show for you." She quirks a brow in my direction and I nod. Quinn should understand what a show is.

Crossing his arms over his chest, Quinn counters with, "You want me to entrust you with one of our females, yet I do not even know if you could adequately protect her."

I snort. Loudly. Partly in insult, but mostly to mock him. "Have you looked at your second-in-command? And you really believe that Kallen and I aren't enough protection?" I'd be more insulted if I didn't know that he was just trying to get Eliana to play her hand. No, wait, I'm still pretty insulted.

Quinn narrows his eyes and ignores my question about Kallen and me, focusing all of his attention and interest on Eliana. "I was not there. I did not witness your version of events."

I am about to tell him that it was his own men who told him that Orwick was tossed around by Eliana, but Kallen beats me to it. "Do you doubt the word of your own warrior?" he asks without the smirk I would have had on my face asking the same question. That's probably for the best.

"Perhaps Orwick is not as strong as he once was," Quinn quips with a shrug and a grin at his second-in-command.

Orwick stiffens at the accusation. In a stilted voice, he grinds out, "Perhaps my Chieftain should test his own strength against the girl's."

"Perhaps they'll both choke on their own testosterone," I mutter to no one in particular. Josh covers a chuckle with a cough into his hand.

This does not go unnoticed by Quinn. "You laugh at us?" the Giant growls.

Quinn's sudden mood swing has both Kallen and me on high alert. Giants can be touchy beings, and they do not take insults lightly. But, it is Eliana who moves into his path as he approaches Josh. It dawns on me too late that Quinn had correctly surmised that threatening Josh would be the fastest way to get Eliana to comply with a show of strength. I open my mouth to warn her she is playing right into his hand, but it's too late.

Reaching out to push Eliana out of the way, Quinn suddenly finds his arm held in a vice grip. One made of delicate looking fingers on a hand that barely circles half of his forearm. It is still enough of a grip, however, for Eliana to stop the Giant in his tracks.

Scowling down at her, Quinn tries to shake Eliana loose. She doesn't budge. Bringing his other hand up, he tries to pry her fingers off his arm. With her other hand, Eliana twists the Giant's wrist until he is gritting his teeth in pain. Off to the side, Orwick grins in satisfaction. For once, I am in agreement with the big, blonde oaf. Quinn had this coming.

The shift in Quinn is tangible. He is no longer playing a game. His pride is taking a beating in front of his men, and he doesn't like it. Flexing every muscle in his impressive Giant body, he lifts his arms up, bringing Eliana several inches off the ground when she refuses to let go. Unfortunately, she cannot control gravity. When the Chieftain prepares to throw her to the side of the room, I pull magic. But, Kallen shakes his head to keep me from using it. He's right, of course. This is Eliana's fight, not mine.

When will I learn that I don't have to worry about my friend when it comes to protecting herself? Quinn is taken by surprise when his clothes are suddenly on fire. With a bellow that threatens to bring the roof crashing down, he lowers his arms and tries to beat at the flames, forgetting that Eliana still has a tight grip on his arms. His eyes fly to her in alarm when he cannot pull free.

"Let me get those for you," Eliana says with an evil grin. I like her evil grin. It has the right amount of sass and menace. I wonder if she can show me how to do that.

Pulling my mind back to the situation at hand, I try not to laugh at Eliana's next surprise for the Giant. Just as suddenly as the flames came, a small thunderstorm develops. Directly over Quinn. Eliana drops his arms and steps back as the Giant is pelted by hail. A lightning bolt snaps at Quinn's heels and he jumps. Orwick's grin grows even wider. He is enjoying the show even more than I am.

Clearly worried that she has made things worse, Josh murmurs to Eliana under his breath, "You could have simply put the fire out." There are times when he is a lot like Kallen. My husband would have said the exact same thing.

I disagree, though. Shaking my head, I say loudly and with a large dose of amusement in my voice, "No, this is so much better."

Just as I thought he would, Kallen sides with Josh. They are such a pair of buzz kills, sometimes. "We do have urgent business," my gorgeous husband reminds us evenly.

Yes, we do. With an acknowledging nod, Eliana pulls her power back. But, she is not stupid. She stands ready in case the Giant decides to retaliate. So, she is surprised when Quinn suddenly lets out a loud guffaw. An actual guffaw. Something he apparently does very well. Somehow, that makes him even more annoying. I didn't think it was possible. He's always surprising me that way.

Turning to me, Quinn declares, "I like her better than you."

Putting a hand over my heart, I reply dryly, "How will I ever recover?"

My sarcasm just makes the Giant Chieftain chuckle. Turning his attention back to Eliana, he asks, "What are you?"

Rolling my eyes, I tell my friend, "You'll grow to hate that question as much as I do."

With a scowl, Eliana replies, "I already do."

"Enough with the games," Kallen grinds out. "Will you let one of your females accompany us or not?"

Pursing his lips, Quinn considers. Finally, he says, "I will. But, I will come along, as well."

Lucky us. Stifling an annoyed groan, I remind him, "The Phoenix only wanted us to bring females." Again, not one hundred percent certain of that, but it's worth a shot. I really don't want him to come along.

Quinn is not going to budge on this. I can see it in the set of his jaw and the determination in his eyes. "This is the only way." Of course it is.

In an effort to move things along, Kallen doesn't continue to argue. "So be it then. When will you be ready to leave?" With a surreptitious glance in my direction, he adds, "We will need to teleport back as soon as possible. We have other realms to visit before the day is done."

And they will all be as much fun as this visit was. If not worse. Again, lucky us.

## 15 Chapter

Quinn and the female of his choice are ready to leave within an hour. A painful hour of hanging out in Quinn's house as preparations are made. At least the Giants are too busy to really pay attention to us except for the odd curious stare here and there toward Eliana. Apparently, word travels fast around here, and her getting the best of Orwick and Quinn has made the rounds.

Orwick, thankfully, will not be joining us. He is not happy about being left behind, even if he's still annoyed with Quinn over the mocking he received. It is the job of the second-in-command to have the Chieftain's back. We insist that it will be difficult enough to hide Quinn and whichever female he chooses to accompany us when in the Cowan realm. We leave out the fact that it will be even harder to hide some of the other beings we are bringing with us such as Dragons and dinosaurs. An exceptionally tall person would certainly be an oddity, but wouldn't totally freak out a Cowan like the others would.

In the end, Orwick is left behind, much to my relief. I'm under enough stress. I didn't want to have to deal with both annoying male Giants.

The female Giant Quinn chooses is the daughter of one of his closest advisors. Eistla is tall, even for a female Giant. She must be at least ten and a half feet. But, she is shy. So shy, she doesn't speak. Not even a hello when she is introduced to us. She simply nods or shakes her head when asked a question. Maybe she can't speak? If not, I hope that isn't a problem for the Phoenix. I do note, though, that Eistla keeps sending longing glances Quinn's way. It dawns on me that her shyness may have more to do with her feelings for him rather than being around us. Quinn doesn't seem to notice her or her longing looks. If there's love on her side, it's obviously unrequited. Lucky for her. I can't imagine Quinn would make a very good husband. Or a faithful one.

When we are finally ready to go, I insist on teleporting Eliana and Josh first. I don't want to leave them alone with the Giants for even a minute. Who knows what

Orwick would try. Next, I take Kallen and Quinn. Eistla is nervous about teleporting, so I save her for last.

Dagda is again waiting for us on the terrace. I guess he's cleared his schedule for the day. Tana is with him, and she graciously greets the two Giants. Eistla gives her a shy smile, but still remains mute. I wonder if I can do the voice thing in reverse? I'm always taking voices away, but can I make someone talk? The more silent Eistla is, the more tempted I am to try. It's nerve racking.

Near the terrace, someone has created a tent suitable for the dimensions of a Giant. The flaps are pulled back and the furnishings inside are lavish. I am going to assume Tabitha was in charge of this. The large platter of food on table in the center of the tent is my first clue.

While Tana leads the Giants into the tent to see to their comfort, a job I am relieved is not mine because the best I would have offered them is a patch of sand on the beach, Dagda comes to speak with us. "Any trouble?" he asks. He knows the Giant Chieftain, and me, too well to believe things went smoothly.

With a grimace, I tell him, "Other than Quinn forcing Eliana to show her power after she had to beat up Orwick, no."

Instead of being angry at this news, Dagda turns surprisingly sympathetic eyes toward my friend. "I am afraid he will not be the only one to do so," he warns.

Eliana nods. "I understand."

With a prideful grin, Josh adds, "Eliana is up for any challenge offered." Her cheeks turn a bright pink at his overt confidence in her abilities, but Eliana doesn't contradict him. She can't because it's true.

With a warning glint in his eye now, Dagda offers some sage advice. "Until you know your antagonizers and what they are capable of doing, tread carefully."

If only I had listened to that advice over the years. Actually, I still have trouble heeding that advice. With a knowing smile touching his lips, Kallen slips my hand into his and gives it a squeeze. He is aware of where my thoughts have gone. The pointed look my biological father gives me tells me that he knows, as well. He is simply hoping Eliana has better sense than I do sometimes.

"I will," Eliana tells Dagda with a solemn nod. I believe her. She's a lot smarter than I am that way. At least, I hope she is.

"Hey, you're back," Sam calls from the door to the house. "Did you come back with Giants?" he asks hopefully.

I nod and point toward the tent. "Yes, we did."

Jenna has joined him. "Don't be rude," she grumbles. "We don't want to act like naïve Cowans." I smile at her use of the word. She is blending in well.

Ignoring the chastisement, Sam's curious gaze remains on the tent. He is dying to get a closer look. Taking pity on him, Kallen asks, "Would you like to meet them?"

Even Jenna's eyes light up at the thought. "Yes," they both say in unison. The two of them quickly make their way down the terrace steps and over to the tent entrance with my husband.

I let Kallen make the introductions. The less time I spend in Quinn's company the better. I note that Eliana doesn't join her friends, either. Josh does, though. I think more for their added protection than for a great desire to spend more time with the Giants. I can't blame him for being distrustful after his own experience with them.

"Where should we go next?" I ask Dagda. He likes it when I ask his opinion. And since I don't want to go to any of the other realms, I will leave the choice to him. Just this once.

"I received a curt, impatient reply from the Dragons. They do not want to be kept in suspense as to the reason for your visit."

I cock my head to the side. "Are the Dragons ever *not* curt and impatient?"

With a sigh, my father admits, "No."

As much as I do not like being at the mercy of the Dragon's impatience, if we want their cooperation we really shouldn't keep them waiting too long. Look at me showing off a tiny bit of diplomacy. "Okay, we'll go there next."

"How big are these Dragons?" Eliana asks, a note of nervousness in her voice.

I reach out and pat her arm. "Don't worry, you won't have to fight one." I hope.

My father is not as hopeful. "Do not hesitate to use your own fire if they demand a show of strength," Dagda tells her, completely contradicting what I just said. I scowl at him, but he ignores me like usual. Why do I even bother to scowl? It never accomplishes what I want it to, it's just going to put permanent creases in my forehead. "Do not show any signs of weakness," Dagda continues.

Squaring her shoulders, Eliana resigns herself to the fact that she might have to fight a Dragon. "How far does their fire breath reach?" she asks me, remembering my little speech in her living room.

"You'll want to stay at least eight to ten feet away from them."

With a surprising amount of amusement in his voice considering the situation, Dagda points toward the Giant tent where Sam and Jenna are obviously enjoying themselves. I guess Quinn can be charming if he actually tries. "I believe your friends will be well entertained while you are gone," Dagda says with a fond smile. Aw, he actually likes my friends. He really has come a long way in his attitude about Cowans. He's still not a fan of Witch's in general, but my grandfather really hasn't done anything to help with that.

Focusing our attention in the same direction, Eliana and I listen in on the conversation happening in the tent. Sam and Jenna are not shy around the Giants. In fact, they are eagerly asking questions, trying to learn more about the race. Since Quinn's favorite subject is himself, he is not bothered by the questions, even if they are coming from Cowans.

Leaving them in Tana's hands, who is more than capable of stopping a Giant from harming them, Kallen and Josh rejoin us. Josh sends a couple of nervous glances over his shoulder, but he ultimately trusts Kallen's judgement that his friends are safe. Shaking his head, Josh says to

Eliana, "They are going to drive the Giants crazy before we get back."

"No, they won't," I assure him. "Quinn loves to talk about himself."

Josh chuckles. "So I gathered." Sobering, he asks, "Where are we off to next?"

"Dragons," Eliana says without much enthusiasm in her voice.

Picking up on her mood, Josh reaches out and takes her hand. "We got this," he assures her quietly.

Biting my lip, I blurt out, "In a show of full disclosure, I once melted all of the bones in one of the Dragon's bodies before healing him. Then I forced them to stop eating Goblins. So, I am not a favorite of the Dragons."

Eliana's and Josh's mouths drop open. "Why would you do that?" Eliana chokes out. I assume she means the melting bones thing.

Trying not to squirm in discomfort, I explain, "It was a fight to the death." When they grow even more horrified, I rush to add, "I didn't kill him, though. I would never. But, if I didn't prove that I could…" I let my words trail off. Next to me, Kallen puts an arm around my shoulders and gives me a reassuring squeeze. He knows that I still feel horrible about what I had to do.

Swallowing back her shock, Eliana admits with a heavy heart, "I understand. I have gone too far with hurting people when I was backed into a corner or crazy with anger and grief, too. I have had several instances where if Josh wasn't with me, I may have done something I would have regretted." She smiles at her love and Josh winks back.

"Now that you have bonded over nearly killing others, perhaps you two should bring those psycho skills to the Dragon realm before the Phoenix goes supernova," a voice snarks from the terrace.

"You know, I hear bacon is going to be in short supply in the near future," I snark back, earning me some weird looks from my companions since this is way off topic from what we were discussing. I point at Taz. "I was talking to him."

"Blasphemy!" Taz accuses. "Besides, you are not my bacon supplier."

He's right. Tabitha is. And he makes sure he sucks up to her regularly to keep the supply coming. "No, but I know where she keeps it. It would be really easy to make it all disappear."

"You wouldn't dare!"

"Hey," a voice exclaims from behind my Familiar. "He is not the only one who likes bacon around here." Kegan looks almost as horrified as Taz sounds.

I roll my eyes, but don't say anything to relieve either of their bacon worries. Turning to Kallen, I ask, "Any chance you want to go to the Dragon realm without me? It might go better."

My husband gives me an evil grin. He's even better at them than Eliana. "And miss your fascinating interactions with them? Never."

"Gee, thanks," I grumble. "Fine, let's go then."

"Do try not to start a war," Dagda tells me. Only half-joking. Actually, I don't think he's joking at all.

"I'll do my best," I reply dryly. Resigned to get this over with, I ask, "I suppose they are expecting me to open a passageway into their great hall?"

Dagda nods. "Yes."

Great. I hate going straight into their great hall. That puts us in the crosshairs of the King's guards. With a grimace, I say unnecessarily to Kallen, "Be ready with your magic. You know how testy they get around me and my mouth."

Eliana gives me a sympathetic pat on the back. "You do have a tendency to speak your mind. But, if they don't like it, that's their problem. Don't change to please them or anyone else."

So many reasons why she is my friend. "Trust me, I won't," I promise.

"Because there's no cure for your kind of crazy," a snarky voice declares from my ankle.

"Remember, you were made from my psyche," I remind him.

Taz shrugs his little Tasmanian devil shoulders. "I only acquired your good qualities. Both of them."

I am so tempted to kick him, but I don't want my friends to think I abuse animals. If only other people could understand him. Then they would know the abuse is deserved. "Isn't it about time for your fourth or fifth lunch?" I ask dryly.

"Do you really think you are going to the Dragon realm without me?" Taz counters.

I suppress a smile. He's worried about me. "I had planned on it."

Taz sniffs. "And have you come back all singed and smelling like smoke when you can't control yourself and get attacked? I don't think so. I sleep in the same room as you and the stench would keep me up all night."

I laugh. "Good to know your concern is all about yourself. Fine, you can come." I half expect Kallen to object, but he seems to like the idea. Probably because I can channel even more magic when my Familiar is around. Something I might need to do if attacked by a roomful of Dragons. "Is Felix coming, too?"

"No, he is going to keep an eye on things here. There may be trouble when more beings start to show up," Taz replies. Good point.

With a long, beleaguered sigh, I remember how boring I thought life was when I was growing up. It certainly has proved me wrong. I open a passageway to the Dragon realm while promising myself I will quit being so whiny to everyone about these trips. It may help my stress levels, but I'm sure it's not helping theirs.

## 16 Chapter

We are not greeted by flames, which is a relief. Peering around the Dragon's great hall before stepping through the passageway, we find only King Myles, Ryu, and five guards. My eyes travel to each of the latter in turn so I know where they are in the room, and I take in King Myles last. I avoid making eye contact with Ryu to avoid any chance of offense. The Dragon King seems to have aged since I last saw him. He looks like he's about to turn into dust any minute. I wonder if they force the King's out of society when they get too old like they do the rest of their race? It would serve him right if they do. Ageism is never acceptable, and he has condoned it throughout his reign.

"Come through. We do not have all day," the old King orders. He coughs out the last word and a puff of smoke escapes his nostrils. He's right. He should consider every moment precious, for it could likely be his last.

The four of us enter the Dragon realm, and I close the passage behind us before addressing the King. Pasting my most sincere smile in place, I manage to sound polite as I say, "King Myles, it is always a pleasure."

"You do not like me any more than I like you, so spare me the false pleasantries."

Eliana's and Josh's eyes widen at the King's bluntness, but I appreciate it. "Of course," I agree.

"Why are you here, Witch Fairy?" Ryu asks. His red and silver scales shine in the torch light. I think he may have gotten bigger since the last time we saw him. He has definitely put on some muscle. Do Dragons work out? An image of a Dragon at a gym pops into my head doing things like running on an enormous treadmill and lifting weights. I try not to laugh aloud. Ryu does not miss my sudden amusement, though. Believing I am laughing at him, which technically, I guess I am, he lets out a roar and a blast of fire. So much for trying not to offend him.

Kallen and I don't even have time to react before Ryu's flames are forced back by a blast of blue and orange fire stronger and fiercer than his own. It happens so fast, Ryu doesn't have time to duck before he is hit square in the face with his own fire breath. He paws at his face scales and eyes making sure he is not aflame, then he rubs his face against the cool marble floor of the great hall to find some relief from the scorching blast. I don't believe he's seriously injured, Dragon scales are pretty fire resistant, he's probably just scalded a bit.

Ryu's lack of serious injury doesn't seem important to the others in the room. Around us, the Dragon guards move into attack positions. Amused, I mutter to Eliana, "Glad to see you are as good at making friends as I am."

"Couldn't help it. Instinct," she shrugs.

"Halt!" King Myles croaks out to his guards before things turn into a fire and magic melee. Lumbering from behind the enormous table where he holds court, he approaches. I have to give Eliana and Josh credit. They don't even flinch as the massive, scaled beast stalks forward. I get nervous when King Myles passes the eight feet mark and is within striking distance. I want to pull magic, but Kallen shakes his head in warning. "Wait," he mouths.

Good call on his part. King Myles is not being aggressive. He doesn't attack with either force or flame. What he does is stick out his snout and take a long, deep sniff of Eliana. Which she tolerates with an impressive amount of calm. Still no flinching on her part. Cocking his head to the side, the Dragon King does it again. This time, he inhales so hard that he has a coughing fit. He turns his head so the smoke from his nostrils doesn't get in our faces. That's surprisingly considerate of him. What the hell is going on?

"My King?" Ryu, who has stopped rubbing his face on the floor, presses when King Myles sniffs Eliana for the third time.

Throughout his rude sniffing party, Eliana maintains her perfect aura of calm. If she's afraid, she is not showing even an iota of it. There are worry lines around Josh's eyes, but I'm not sure if they are concern for Eliana, or the Dragon King if he pisses the former off. Probably both.

I can't help it; the words just fall out of my mouth. "Smells good, doesn't she?" I muse. "I think it's her shampoo."

This goads King Myles out of his silence. Addressing Eliana, he bows his head low and says, "Greetings, my lord. Have you come to take back your gift?"

With the amount of times my jaw hits the floor in a day, it's a wonder the bones haven't shattered. Or at the very least, the hinges haven't completely worn out. Sooner as opposed to later I will probably need a good oral surgeon to repair it. This time, it's so bad that I wish I had brought a hoist with us, because I can't seem to pick it back up on my own. I try again. Nope, without some serious hydraulics, my bottom jaw is going to stay on the floor.

Eliana turns huge, round eyes toward me. "What is he talking about?" she asks. She clearly believes the Dragon King has lost his mind. So do I.

Since I don't have a clue what is going on, I turn to Kallen. The surprise and confusion on his face tell me that he isn't going to be any help. Glancing around the room, the other Dragons are as shocked as we are. So, I ask the source of all this confusion. With a great force of will, I hoist my jaw from the floor and force my mouth to form words. "What are you talking about?" I ask King Myles. I do not ask him if his grip on reality is slipping, and I am quite proud of myself for that. Though, I admit, the question may have been implied in my tone.

As I said, the shock and confusion is not limited to our side. "You bow before a Cowan?" Ryu demands in unmasked disdain toward his King. "Have you gone mad?"

I have often wondered why Myles is still King since the Dragons do not show deference for the elderly. Now I know. Right before our eyes, the Dragon King seems to shed the shroud of age. His body is no longer stooped.

He no longer seems brittle. He expands before our eyes into a ferocious beast with sharp teeth and claws and a wicked temper. A tangible rush of strength and power pours out of him. It is as if someone breathed new life into his soul. A dangerous, new life. The Dragon King's eyes flash bright with intent, and a stream of fire so hot and long even the Phoenix would be impressed, shoots from his mouth. Kallen and I pull magic to protect the four of us, but the flames are not directed toward us. We are just trying to fend off the heat. It's brutal. Not Cosmic Fire brutal, but it's still pretty bad.

"It's part of the magic of the Dragon Kings," Kallen explains in a hushed voice. "It is bestowed upon them in a ceremony when they are anointed. It is rarely used as it consumes so much energy and can create an imbalance."

"Let your magic go," Eliana whispers to us. Trusting her, Kallen and I do as she asks. Eliana steps forward and while barely avoiding his flames, places her hand on the Dragon King's chest. How is the skin not melting off her face right now? Her voice echoing loudly around the room, Eliana orders, "I command you to stop!"

Before the flame of the Dragon King kills its target, it fizzles out in a cloud of smoke. Seriously, what the hell is going on here?

## 17 Chapter

"Um, Eliana," Josh says nervously. He doesn't like her being so close to the Dragon King. Neither do I. She's within the incineration zone, and I don't know who's a quicker draw on their fire power – her or King Myles.

Across the room, Ryu is frozen in shock. The fact that his King was about to turn him to ash is having trouble penetrating what I imagine is his tiny little Dragon brain. Hm. I wonder how close Dragon brains are to lizard brains? Obviously, Dragons are more evolved, but I bet not by much. I should probably focus on the problem at hand, though, and not Dragon brains.

"He does not know," Eliana says soothingly to King Myles. Her hand is still over where I assume the Dragon's heart lives. If the old geezer has one. I, for one, am not convinced. It is clear, however, that Eliana has figured out the mystery of the Dragon King's insane behavior. I certainly hope she is planning to share with the rest of us.

"My King," another Dragon says tentatively. "Is all well here?" Brave guy after what the King just tried to do to Ryu for asking him basically the same question. Well, Ryu was much more of a jerk about it.

King Myles is still in mega-King mode, but the façade is cracking around the edges. His scales are losing their luster as each second passes, and his eyes are dulling again. "Fools," he hisses. "Do you not recognize the one who gave us fire?"

Just when I finally get my jaw working correctly again, he says something like that. I think the bone actually cracked when it hit the floor this time. I definitely am going to need that oral surgeon. And I have certainly lost the power of speech. I glance at my husband who usually comes through when this happens to me. He is going to be no help, though. Even Kallen can't seem to make his tongue work properly.

It is Josh who finally finds his voice. "Eliana, what is he talking about?"

When Eliana turns back to us, her eyes are glowing an eerie red. That's new. But, her voice is calm and even when she responds to her love. "Ra gave them fire," she explains.

Kallen's brows knit together. "I have not heard that legend before now."

"It is not legend," King Myles snaps. "It is fact."

He's so old, he may have been there when it happened. He's already pretty crabby, so I don't push my luck and ask him. Instead, I say, "Why would Ra give you fire?" I realize too late that this question was probably just as rude.

Eliana is the one to respond. Ra must be communicating the information to her, because I am certain she was just as ignorant as the rest of us two minutes ago. "They were his protectors," she explains.

I'm still confused. "Ra lived here at some point?"

Shaking her head, Eliana continues, "No, they migrated here after Ra left the Cowan realm."

Cocking my head to the side, I ask suspiciously, "Was it his idea that they eat Goblins?"

Eliana's eyes open wide. "What? No!" That's a relief. But still, what I thought I knew about Dragon history is all shot to heck now. Surmising this, Eliana adds, "There were Dragons here already. The ones from our realm came here to find sanctuary among them. As they found mates, the ability to breath fire was passed down to their young."

I gaze up at Kallen. "You didn't know any of this?" My dumbfounded husband shakes his head.

One of the other Dragons shuffles forward. The one who dared to ask the King a question after his blowup. "Our origin has been a tightly kept secret." Obviously. He moves within striking range and I tense. But, the Dragon is just trying to get a whiff of Eliana. His nostrils flare as he breathes in so hard her hair moves toward his snout. Eew, I hope he doesn't get Dragon snot in her hair. I bet Dragon snot is really hard to get out. Stepping back, the Dragon says in awe, "How is this possible?"

"I carry Ra's essence within me," Eliana explains.

Ryu has finally gotten over his shock, and he finds his voice again. His disbelieving voice. "A Cowan carrying the essence of a god?" he sniffs. "Impossible."

If Eliana wasn't here, Ryu would be toast. Literally. It's obvious his King wants to roast him with his fire breath. "Insolence," he hisses. "Leave."

Several of the other Dragons move toward Ryu, ready to make him comply with the King's command. If it comes down to a fight, my money is actually on Ryu. He's huge compared to these other guys and known to be the King's best warrior. He doesn't put up a fight, though. He doesn't believe any of this, and he is relieved to get out of here, away from the King he believes has lost his mind. Ryu doesn't waste any time finding the exit, and he leaves without even a good bye glare in our direction. Rude.

Now that that drama is over, King Myles turns his adoring attention back to Eliana. It's kind of creepy seeing him like this. "My lord, have we displeased you in some way?" he asks, speaking to the god within her, not Eliana herself. I wonder if she finds that offensive.

"I can't imagine Ra is happy you've been eating sentient Goblins," I mutter even though he wasn't speaking to me. The Dragon King ignores me. It's amazing how often I am ignored in a day. I tried to keep track once, but it got too annoying and I gave up before I hurt someone. Kallen isn't ignoring me. He narrows his eyes in my direction, but Josh's mouth curves up slightly. Turns out they are not always on the same page.

Eliana plays it cooler than me. "We have come seeking your help," she says, trying to steer the direction of the conversation back to why we are here. As much as that needs to happen, I can't help feeling disappointed. I really want to hear about the Dragon and Ra history now.

Since Dragons don't have lips, they can't really smile. But, King Myles is doing something funky with his scaly mouth that I believe is supposed to be one. "Anything, my lord." The suck up. Oops, pretty sure I said that aloud.

Speaking quickly so that the King doesn't have time to react to my impertinence, Eliana explains about the Phoenix. When she is finished, the Dragon King sits back on his haunches. He is back to looking old and withered again, the stress of Eliana's tale erasing any trace of the mighty King he was a few minutes ago. In fact, he looks even older, and I didn't think that was possible. I see what Kallen means about the Dragon King magic using too much energy. It obviously ages the Kings when they use it. Maybe King Myles isn't nearly as old as I think he is. He could be at least a millennia younger than I thought.

There is murmuring among the other Dragons. Back and forth about whether Eliana's Phoenix story could be true or not. They are quieted by a withering look from their King. "We do not doubt the word of Ra." I open my mouth to point out that Eliana is not technically Ra, but snap it closed when I realize how stupid that would be. Kallen's lips twitch in amusement, and I give him a sour look. He knows me too darn well, sometimes.

"Of course," the bravest of the Dragon guard replies. Since he actually sniffed Eliana, he seems to believe the story.

"We shall help any way we can," the Dragon King assures Eliana.

Clearing his throat, Kallen brings King Myles' attention to him. "We will also need the assistance of the Goblins."

The King asks Eliana, "Is this true?" When Eliana nods, he barks, "Bring the Goblin King!"

"Um, I hope he's a guest and not a prisoner," I blurt out.

"I am no prisoner," a squeaky little voice says from the far door. It seems the Goblin King was eavesdropping. "I come and go as I please. The Goblins will stand with you. I will raise an army and we will be ready to depart on the morrow."

I suppress a grin. Goblins want so much to be fiercer than they really are. "I appreciate your generous offer, and your enthusiasm, but we really only need one female warrior." She doesn't really need to be a warrior, but I figure it will make him feel important if I put it that way.

Sure enough, the Goblin King puffs out his little chest. "I will have the best and brightest here within the hour."

Next to me, Eliana and Josh's noses begin to twitch. It doesn't take long for the stench of a Goblin to fill a room. "You'll get used to it," I whisper lie. Eliana gives me a doubtful look. She doesn't need my ability to detect lies to know she will never get used to this smell. Still, I give her my most innocent smile.

In an effort to speed things along now that the room is filling with noxious Goblin fumes, Eliana, who is not breathing through her nose anymore, asks the Dragon King, "Will you send a female Dragon, as well?"

I can tell the Dragon King is torn when he shoots a surreptitious glance toward Kallen and me. He hates having to help us. If we had asked him to send a female Dragon to help, he definitely would have said no. I can see it in his ancient eyes that are even cloudier now that he used his King magic. He can't refuse Ra, though. I could help it, but I don't. I send a simpering grin his way. He narrows his lizard eyes, but still he replies, "Of course, my lord."

"Great, can you have them both in the Fae realm tomorrow?" I ask, having a hard time not plugging my nose when the Goblin King moves farther into the room. We need to go. Soon. Before all of my nose hairs melt and dribble down to my lips. I can't imagine that melted nose hair tastes good.

"Please," Eliana adds when the King seems irked that I am being so pushy.

Cocking his Dragon head to the side, King Myles says the only thing he can say to Ra. "It shall be done."

"Fantastic," I exclaim, already opening a passageway. "Thanks for your help." As soon as the passage is open Josh, Eliana and Kallen do not hesitate. With a final breath-holding wave, I step through myself and close the passageway behind us. With a great deal of relief, I blow out the Goblin infested air in my lungs and take in a breath of fresh sea air. Eew! Apparently, there's still Goblin residue in my sinuses, and I just refilled my lungs with it. I swear, once it gets in your nose, the Goblin stench becomes solid and glue-like. I'll probably be smelling it for days. Wait, I will actually be smelling it for days because a Goblin is coming with us. I seriously need to look up a spell to save all of our noses.

## 18 CHAPTER

I'm obviously not the only one experiencing sinus issues. Rubbing at his nose, Josh complains, "Does the smell ever go away?"

"It is quite permeating," Kallen agrees, but reassures him, "It will take a few minutes, but your sinus passages will clear."

"Hard to believe the Dragons find that appetizing, huh?" I ask, wishing I had a tissue so I could at least try to blow the Goblin stench out of my nose. I know from experience, though, that it wouldn't work. Time and fresh air are the only cure.

Eliana shoots me a horrified glance. "They truly eat those little people?"

I nod but add, "To be fair, when they started eating them, the Goblins weren't really more than forest creatures. They have evolved and become more sentient over time."

"Xandra got the Dragons to agree to eat imported cows smeared with Goblin sweat instead," Kallen says proudly. Considering his words, nauseated would probably be a better reaction than pride.

Which is the expression on Eliana's face at the moment. I definitely prefer Kallen's pride to her nausea. "That is nasty," Eliana declares.

I agree, it is. "True, but it was still a good compromise."

"You're looking a little green," Jenna says over my shoulder to Eliana and Josh. "Didn't things go well?"

Josh stops wiping at his nose to reply. "It was definitely interesting." His eyes swing to Eliana before going back to their friend. She gives him a slight nod, and he fills Jenna in on the secret that even the Fairies didn't know before now. "It seems Ra was the one who gave the Dragons their fire breath."

"What?" Jenna gasps. "Really?"

Eliana nods. "Ra confirmed it."

With a grin, Josh adds, "So, now they worship Eliana."

Her face turning red, Eliana shakes her head. "No, they worship Ra."

"Who is now manifested as you," I counter. "Don't knock it. The Dragons can be real jerks. It's awesome that you can get them to do anything you want."

"What is this?" Dagda calls from the terrace. He caught the tail end of the conversation. "Who can get the Dragons to do anything?" His voice is dripping with disbelief.

Kallen joins him on the terrace and explains what happened. By the time he is finished, Sam, Isla, Tabitha and Garren have joined us, and everyone turns surprised eyes toward Eliana. My biological father is the first to see the potential this revelation could have for the Fairies.

Dagda's eyes quickly become calculating. "When the Phoenix problem is resolved, I would like to sit down and discuss how we could convince you to join us in this realm."

Eliana smiles politely. "I appreciate the offer, but just as Xandra has a job to do, so do I. Ra chose me to protect the Cowan realm."

Disappointment clouds Dagda's eyes now, but I can tell he will not give up. He does drop the subject for now, though. Turning to me, he says, "The Centaurs and

Sasquatch grew tired of waiting and sent envoys. I explained the situation and they have both agreed to help."

"I got to see a real Centaur," Sam stage whispers to Josh. "So cool."

Relieved we don't have to travel to either of those realms, I tick off on my fingers who we have on our side now. "Okay, we have an Angel, a Giantess, a Mermaid, a Siren providing they agree, a Dragon, a Goblin, a Centaur, I assume a Faun, and a Sasquatch. That leaves an Elf, a Pixie and a dinosaur." If anyone had asked me before my seventeenth birthday if I would ever utter something like that, I would have thought they were crazy. It still seems a little crazy to me.

A harried looking Sindri, Dagda's assistant, steps onto the terrace. "I have had word from our ambassador in the Elf realm. The Elf Queens have offered whatever assistance you may need." Of course they have. They are being total suck ups right now.

"Great, thank you, Sindri." I try to thank him whenever I have the chance because Dagda rarely acknowledges how hard his assistant works.

"We will retrieve Raziel's dinosaur last, so we will not need to go to that realm until tomorrow morning," Kallen says. Good plan. We don't want to get it only to lose it in the Fairy realm. I wonder if the thing can be leash trained for our trip to the Phoenix's lair. I'll have to ask Raziel. Not that walking a pterodactyl on a leash would be any stranger to a Cowan than seeing one flying in the air. But hey, with a Centaur and a Dragon walking next to it, who would actually notice the winged dinosaur?

"Okay, we just need a Pixie then." My words come out almost giddy because I am so happy not to have to keep realm hopping. We might actually get a little time to relax before facing the Phoenix and her Cosmic Fire again. I don't know why I would tempt the universe with a thought like that, though. Now, something is bound to go wrong tonight. I try to push my pessimistic thought aside and focus on what my father is saying. He seems to be speaking to me.

"I have developed a report with the Pixies," Dagda says, shooting me a look. "I will be able to convince them to help."

Scowling, I mutter, "It's not my fault they like to argue with me."

My unhelpful husband suggests, "You could try not taking the bait they offer."

With a shrug and a grin, I reply, "Where's the fun in that?"

"What should we do now, then?" Eliana asks.

"I suggest you relax. You may have quite a fight on your hands tomorrow," Dagda replies.

"You suggest we relax and then stress us out in the same breath," I complain.

Unsympathetic to my whining, Dagda intones, "I cannot change the truth."

"The four of you should freshen up. I believe Tabitha has lunch ready," Isla says.

With a grin, Kallen wraps an arm around his grandmother's shoulders. "Are you implying we are not the freshest smelling?" he teases.

Lifting his arm from her as if it's contaminated, Isla grimaces. "The Goblins do leave their mark."

"They cannot help the way they smell," Tabitha huffs. I will never understand why she has a special place in her heart for the Goblins, but she does.

"No, they cannot," Isla agrees to avoid an argument. Her nose is still wrinkled from smelling Kallen's arm, so she doesn't sound very convincing. "But the rest of us can."

There's no arguing with that logic, so Tabitha doesn't. "Show our guests to their rooms," she instructs Kallen and me as she turns toward the house. "Lunch will be in fifteen minutes."

"Can you make it half an hour?" I beg. "Our skin is going to need some extra scrubbing."

Tabitha shoots me a dirty look, but says, "Twenty minutes."

I'll take it. "Thank you!" I call after her. Kallen and I lead the way inside the house with Eliana, Josh, Sam and Jenna trailing after us.

When we are upstairs, I let Kallen lead the way because I am not sure which guest rooms were prepared. He must have checked with Tabitha earlier, because he goes straight to a door toward the end of the hall on the third floor. "Sam and Jenna, you will be in here." Moving on to the next room, he tells Eliana and Josh, "This will be your room."

"Wow!" Jenna exclaims when she peeks inside the room. "Impressive."

Kallen smiles with pride. "Tabitha makes sure all of our guests are comfortable."

"Meet us at the stairs in fifteen minutes?" I ask the four of them. When they agree, I hold my hand out to Kallen and we make our way to our own room.

Inside our bedroom, I lean back against the closed door. "I'm already exhausted and we've barely just begun," I complain. Pushing off the door, I shake the whininess out of my voice. "Sorry, I promised myself I'd stop being such a whiner."

Wrapping his arms around me, Kallen grins, "I would appreciate that."

Giving him a playful swat, I threaten, "Maybe we need separate bedrooms."

Chuckling, Kallen leans down and kisses me. A long, sultry kiss. When he finally lets me up for air, he murmurs against my lips, "Should I move back to my old room now?"

"Never," I smile and kiss him again. After a moment, I pull back. "You do stink, though. So do I. We really need a shower before our fifteen minutes are up." When his eyes light up, I add, "Just a shower. We don't have time for anything else."

The disappointment in his eyes mirrors mine, but he knows I'm right. "Fine," he grumbles.

With a simpering grin, I tease, "Who's whining now?" With a playful growl, my gorgeous husband chases me into the bathroom and we take a quick, but not as innocent as I first suggested, shower.

## 19 Chapter

As I towel dry my hair, I say to Kallen, "I'm surprised Isla was okay with them sharing rooms since they aren't married."

Kallen shrugs. "She understands that things are different in the Cowan realm."

"I was from the Cowan realm," I point out. "Why was it different for me? We had to practically threaten mutiny to sleep in the same room and had to follow the marriage rule."

Quirking a brow, my gorgeous husband asks, "Are you saying you did not want to get married?"

"No, of course not," I assure him. "I just think it's a double standard." Then again, none of them are planning to sleep with one of Isla's grandsons. I suspect that is the greatest difference.

With a playful grin, Kallen walks to the door. "You are right. I will go insist that the four of them receive separate rooms."

"Don't you dare," I laugh. I drop the towel on the floor and Kallen makes it disappear. Magic makes staying tidy so much easier. I run a quick brush through my hair before declaring, "I'm ready."

Kallen leans down and brushes a kiss over my cheek. "You are beautiful," he murmurs.

His breath tickles against my skin. "Mmm," I sigh. "Keep that up and we won't leave this room."

With a soft chuckle, Kallen leans back and purrs, "You, my love, are a temptress."

I am about to wrap my arms around his neck and forget about the rest of the realm when we hear voices in the hall. The others are out there waiting for us. "We need to go," I sigh in disappointment and tug him toward the door.

In the hall, we find our friends freshly showered and smelling of the lavender, honey and lemon soap Tabitha makes. A huge improvement from Goblin funk. "Hungry?" I ask, leading everyone toward the stairs.

"Always," Sam grins.

"Good, because there is always plenty of food."

Isla and Garren are already seated at the table when we arrive. "Dagda has returned to the palace," Isla says in lieu of a greeting. "He will return in the morning unless he is needed before then."

"I am certain something will come up in the middle of the night," Garren grumbles next to her. Isla scowls at him, but since he is busy buttering a roll, he doesn't notice. Besides, he's right. It's happened too many times in the past to deny the likelihood.

"Let us hope not," Kegan says from the dining room door. He has Keelan in his arms. "I am sleep deprived enough already." Out of everyone in the room, he gives me a pointed look. Okay, the middle of the night things usually do have something to do with me.

"Stop complaining," Alita tells him. Her wide yawn afterward proves she is just as sleep deprived as her husband.

"Have a seat anywhere," I tell our guests who are hanging back by the door. "We don't have special places." Except Isla, who always sits at the head of the table.

"Where are Mom and Dad?" I ask Isla.

"Your mother wanted to do some research on the Phoenix," she informs me. "She is working with the scribe in the archives. Your father went with her to check on Zac."

I smile. "Dad was probably trying to stay out of the way." He often doesn't know what to do with himself when we have a magical crisis. It must be hard for him being the only non-magical being among us. I glance at three of the new faces at the table. He's not the only non-magical being anymore. I really hope those of us with magic can keep them all safe.

"I told him it was unnecessary," Tabitha says as she bustles into the room with a platter piled high with sandwiches. "He always makes himself useful." I appreciate her being supportive of my dad. Everyone has made him feel welcome. Even Dagda has made a real effort. Especially since Dad has gained the ability to hold a fishing pole.

"I see the Angels have made themselves scarce," Kallen notes. "Where did they go?"

"I believe Raziel was collecting supplies you will need when travelling to the dinosaur realm," Garren tells me.

"Supplies? Like what?" I ask, reaching for a sandwich. I really hope one of those things is a pterodactyl leash.

Garren shrugs. "I have no idea." Helpful as always.

Conversation ends until we have all loaded our plates. As we dig in, Eliana turns to me and asks, "How soon can we return to the Cowan realm?"

My hands freeze in place with my sandwich halfway to my mouth. Panic begins to build up inside me. She wants to go home? What happened to make her change her mind? "Um, I thought you were going to help us with the Phoenix?"

Shaking her head and smiling, Eliana clarifies, "I am not giving up. I just assumed that we needed to get Jadyn. Or are we doing that tomorrow, too?" Ah. Our female Skin Walker. I almost forgot. So much for being done with realm hopping for the day.

"There are other Skin Walkers we could ask for help," Isla points out. "There is a small colony in this realm."

I shake my head. "We know Jadyn and trust her. I don't want to take the chance of bringing in a Skin Walker who likes to be a trickster." Something that once got the Skin

Walkers kicked out of the Cowan realm. Those who didn't leave were forced into hiding.

"I agree," Kallen concurs. "We do not need to add any more uncertainty to the mix than we will already have." Meaning, who knows how all these beings are going to get along. We need them all to behave. That may be asking for too much from some of them. The Elves come to mind. And the Sasquatch.

Sam lets out a low whistle. "Liza is going to be mad."

Josh grimaces. "Yes, she is."

"It can't be helped," Eliana tells them both. "She will just have to deal with it."

"I'll let you explain that to her," Josh replies with a wink and a grin.

"Thanks," Eliana says dryly.

Biting my bottom lip, I debate whether or not to ask the question on the tip of my tongue. Who am I kidding? Of course I ask it. "Will your families be safe if you go against her wishes?"

This gets Isla's attention. "This person has threatened your families?" There is a hard glint in her eyes that makes me glad that I'm not Liza. Then again, meeting Liza made me glad that I'm not Liza.

"Not her personally," Eliana rushes to say. My eyebrows rise at that, and she adds, "I mean, she wouldn't hurt our families. But, she has made it clear that the government would not be happy if we suddenly disappeared."

Everyone jumps when a glass is slammed down on the table. "How can you work for those barbarians?" Tabitha demands.

"It's not as bad as it sounds," Josh attempts, but he knows his argument isn't going to convince anyone.

"Because we want to help as many people as we can, and working with the government gives us the opportunity to do that." Her voice developing a hint of steel, Eliana adds, "And there is no way I would let them harm anyone in our families."

"Your families are welcome here," Isla reminds her, "if you feel they may be in danger."

Eliana shakes her head. "No, Liza will find a way to explain our absence. I'm not worried."

Wanting to get off the subject I started so Eliana is no longer on the defensive, I announce, "We'll go get Jadyn after lunch. Then we'll have the rest of the day to relax." I doubt we'll get much relaxing done with the threat of the universe ending hanging over us, though. Things like that are not conducive to relaxing.

The others take my cue and the rest of our lunch conversation veers away from this topic. Most of it involves the back and forth of questions to appease everyone's curiosity. Isla has a lot of questions for Eliana, as the former has never met anyone with the essence of a god, or two, inside of her before. Sam and Jenna have the most questions, though. Garren, who loves to hear himself talk, takes it upon himself to answer most of them. Kallen rolls his eyes as the older Fairy drones on and on, but our guests seem fascinated by the information he imparts. Finally, Garren has an interested audience. How nice for him.

When the last bit of food is seized and eaten, it's time to go back to the Cowan realm. Managing to get Eliana away from the others briefly, I ask quietly, "Are you sure about this?" I really don't want to invite another Skin Walker to go with us, but if it will make Eliana's life easier, I will.

Eliana gives me a reassuring smile. "It'll be fine." She seems to actually believe it, at least my internal lie detector indicates she believes it. So, I decide I will, too.

"Are we ready?" Kallen asks with a raised brow. He knows what I was asking Eliana. He would have pulled her aside himself if I hadn't.

I nod. "Yup." My gorgeous husband scowls at me. He hates that word. Actually, most Cowan slang bothers him. I try not to let his bother bother me, though. I gotta be me. Another phrase he hates. The grammar, not the essence of it. He agrees with the latter.

Turning to Jenna and Sam, I ask, "Are you guys okay hanging out here, or do you want to go home?"

"Here!" they both respond in unison.

With a grin, Josh punches Sam in the arm. "Try not to get too spoiled."

"With food like Tabitha makes, how could I not?" Sam replies with a toothy grin in Tabitha's direction. The older Fairy actual blushes a little bit.

"Not to mention all the things we are learning from her," Jenna points out, not wanting Tabitha to think that they only like her for her food. Tabitha blushes even deeper. She must really like these guys because only people who have wheedled their way into her heart can make her blush. The old softie.

"Come on, let's go before Tabitha becomes the color of one her tomatoes," I laugh. I hurry out of the kitchen before I get a smack to the back of the head. My intent was to be funny, not stupid.

## 20 CHAPTER

After opening yet another passage to Colorado, I then teleport the four of us to Eliana and Josh's living room. Since I am not familiar with the layout, Kallen ends up stumbling over the edge of the coach. Fortunately, he catches himself before he cracks his head on the end table. "Sorry," I mouth.

"My car's in the garage," Josh says, grabbing his keys from a hook by the door.

"It would be faster to teleport," I point out.

With a chuckle, Josh replies, "Yes, but that might cause several of our coworkers to have mild strokes."

"It's true," Eliana confirms. "Especially Roxy." Josh nods in agreement. "I'll call Jadyn and give her a heads up that we're coming to get her." Eliana puts her phone to her ear after pressing a few numbers. A look of surprise washes over her face. "Liza?" Eliana pulls her phone away from her ear and stares at the screen to be sure she called the right number. Putting the phone on speaker so we can all hear, she asks, "Why are you answering Jadyn's phone? You're on speaker, by the way."

"Who else is there?" Liza demands curtly.

"Josh, Xandra and Kallen."

"You're done saving the universe?" Liza asks evenly.

"Um, not quite," Eliana tells her. "We actually need Jadyn's help."

"Well, she's a little busy being a cat at the moment."

"What? Why?"

"Recon."

"Is this a new case?" Josh asks.

"Yes. We got a tip about a trafficking route. We're checking it out," Liza confirms.

"What kind of trafficking?" I ask.

I can hear Liza's scowl through the phone. "Human." Before I can express my disgust, Liza growls, "Hold on." We hear a hushed conversation on her end between several people, but we can't quite make out what they are saying. Liza must be covering the phone with her hand. Okay, even I know that cell phones have mute buttons. Then again, she is in a pretty stressful situation at the moment. Or she may not know how to work Jadyn's phone.

Finally returning her attention to us, Liza says into the phone, "We could really use your help."

Eliana is torn. She knows how important it is for us to get back to the Phoenix problem, but this is her job. Her calling, really. Her mind is made up when Liza adds, "They have at least ten girls and we're not sure how many boys. We believe they are all minors."

Kallen has a confused look on his face. "What is human trafficking?" he asks. Ah, the innocence of other realms. Actually, other realms have their own different forms of atrocities. They're not really innocent.

"People are kidnapped and sold for various purposes," Josh explains with a grimace.

He doesn't need to explain further. Kallen catches on pretty quickly to what some of those purposes could be. "Children?" he gasps. His face hardening, my fearsome husband growls, "We will help." I love him so much right now. The universe may be hanging in the balance, but he will still take the time to save innocent children. We all will.

"Where are you?" Josh asks Liza. He curses under his breath when she gives her location. Glancing at us, he explains, "That's a good hour and a half drive from here."

I shake my head. "Too long. Liza, can you give a location on a map where I can safely teleport us?"

Liza takes a moment to confer with someone, then comes back on the line. "I'm texting you the coordinates now."

"Thanks, we'll be right there," I assure her.

Eliana disconnects from Liza and pulls up her messages. She hands the phone to me. I did something similar to this in the mountains, but I was familiar with that area. With a sigh, I mutter, "I hope she directed us to an open space." I'd hate to land someone in the middle of a tree.

"Are you certain you can do this?" Kallen asks with way too much concern in his voice.

"Yes," I snap because I'm trying to convince myself as well as him.

"This is farm country, so there should be plenty of open space," Eliana assures me. Her worry meter is much lower than my husband's. I appreciate that. Then again,

Kallen has seen more of what can happen if my magic goes wonky. Some of his concern is justified.

Thinking about the girls who need saving, I hold my arms out for the others to grab onto. Staring at the phone, I concentrate on the map, visualizing the space in my mind. In a flash, we are there.

"Yah! What the hell?" someone cries out. The woman then slaps a hand over her mouth because she is supposed to be in recon mode.

"Sorry, Roxy," Eliana says to the shaken woman. "We needed to get here quickly."

Shaking herself, the tall, dark skinned woman says in an awed voice, "Liza told us about it, but I didn't believe it."

With a grin, Josh teases, "How can you still be a non-believer with all you've seen?"

"True," Roxy agrees. "You still scared the hell out of me just popping in out of thin air like that."

Conversation comes to a halt when we notice a black cat bounding toward us through a field. Obviously, it's Jadyn. Clawing to a halt in front of us, she pants in a little cat voice, "They are getting ready to move. Something spooked them." Considering she is a talking black cat, which anyone who is the least bit superstitious would probably consider a double whammy in the bad luck department, I have to stop myself from asking if it was her.

But, she reads my mind. Or the expression on my face. "No, it was not me," she says dryly. Even in a cat voice she can convey dry. Impressive.

Behind us, Liza steps out of a surveillance van with Alonzo. She heard what Jadyn said. Not surprising since Jadyn seems to have a little microphone attached to a collar around her neck. Clever.

"Are you positive?" Liza demands. When Jadyn nods her little cat head, Liza asks, "How long do we have?" I wonder how long it took her to get comfortable having conversations with animals? It had to be a shock to her system initially.

"They're mobilizing now, so a matter of minutes," Jadyn tells her.

Liza lets out an impressive string of curses that even Dagda would be proud of. I'll have to share a few of her phrases with him. He needs to update his repertoire. It's dated. Turning to Eliana, Liza asks, "Suggestions?"

Eliana looks at me, then turns back to her boss. "Since time is of the essence for all of us, you guys stay here."

Alonzo shakes his head. "You need backup."

"She has backup," Kallen growls.

Before the two of them can determine who really does have the most testosterone in their veins, my money is on Kallen, Eliana shuts Alonzo down. "We need to stop them before they move out. If we ambush them with weapons and technology, we put the kids in danger. We," she nods at Kallen and me, "can do things differently. You guys will need plausible deniability on this one."

"Damn," Roxy hisses. "I would hate to be those bastards if these two can do even half of what you can do."

"We have different but just as powerful skills," Kallen assures her.

Growing impatient with having to convince the others, I step toward my friend. "Let's do this."

"Do you want me to come along?" Josh asks. I know what he is really asking. Will Eliana need him to calm her down when she confronts the bad guys capable of trafficking children so she doesn't rip their bodies in two with her bare hands and burn the stubs to ash.

Eliana seriously considers his question. For about half a second. "Yes."

Good call, because that ripping the bad guys in two and burning them to ash thing sounds really good to me, too. Unlike Eliana, I would need to use some heavy duty magic for both, but I'm sure I could come up with a spell that would do the trick. From the disgusted look on my husband's face, I don't think he'd try to stop me this time. In fact, he might beat me to it. I sure hope Josh is thinking clearer than the rest of us. We may all need to be talked down.

## 21 Chapter

"The first thing we need to do is make sure the kids are safe." Eliana's words are spoken evenly, but the fire in her eyes tells me that she is anything but calm on the inside.

"Agreed," Josh nods. "Jadyn, can you get closer and let us know if all of the children are out of the house?"

Jadyn was not about to be left behind when the four of us moved closer to the old farmhouse where the bad guys are holding the kids. Not when she has such useful talents. What Cowan would expect he was being spied on by a cat? "No problem," Jadyn says. "I'm heading for the third window from the front on this side of the house. It gives me the best view of the room where they are being held. When I start twitching my tail, that means all of them are out." Jadyn trots off toward the house like she is just a curious cat. When she gets close to the van, one of the guys dragging a child around the age of twelve out of the house kicks at her. Obviously, not a cat lover. Jadyn arches her back and hisses like a real cat would. She's good at this. She turns with her tail in the air and heads for the window.

The traffickers must be pretty efficient because Jadyn's tail starts twitching back and forth rapidly as soon as she lands on the window sill. I shudder in disgust as I think of how they became so efficient. Lots of practice. My disgust gets pushed aside now by my fury.

Watching the scene before us, Kallen's expression is hard but there's a touch of proud there as the twelve-year-old struggles against her captor. "She's a fighter."

He's right. Twisting in the guy's arms, the girl is able to bring her knee up. Right into his groin. We can hear his groan of pain from here. Unfortunately, it's not enough to bring the guy down. His face twists into a cruel mask and he brings his arm back, ready to strike the girl.

Well, that's not going to happen. "We got this," I tell Eliana before she runs out of our hiding place and blows our cover. Magic is already shooting forth from both Kallen and me. Mine creates a protective shield around the girl. Kallen's hits the trafficker. Hard. With several strikes of magic, Kallen hits the guy in the face, the gut, and the groin. Blood spurts from his nose. Fortunately, my magical shield prevents it from spraying all over the girl, who is staring wide-eyed at her captor. The guy doubles over after the gut and groin shots, but Kallen is not finished with him. The guy screams loudly as his wrist and fingers bend back so far, even a contortionist would cringe. There's no doubt that they are broken. He screams even louder when the same thing happens to his other hand.

I glance up at my husband. Unapologetic, he growls, "He will not be striking children ever again." Not with those hands, he won't. It would hurt him a heck of a lot more than whoever he hit.

It doesn't take long for the bad guy's partners to come running from the house. They take up defensive positions around the van and scan the area. The four of us duck farther back in the clump of trees we are hiding in. We don't want them discovering us quite yet. They are too close to the kids and could try to use them as shields. Or just kill them to keep them from talking. My temper flares even higher at that thought. Kallen glances down at me as he feels my magic spike with my temper. The thought of trying to calm me down doesn't even cross his mind.

After a brief conversation with his comrades, it becomes apparent that the injured man believes it was the girl in front of him who caused his injuries. His three partners laugh at first and shake their heads. After a heated argument, which includes a lot of yelling and swearing that we can clearly hear, the injured man finally convinces his buddies that it must have been the girl because there is no one else around.

"This could work in our favor," I murmur to the others.

Surprised, Josh asks, "How?"

Eliana knows where I am going with this. Her grin is definitely on the malicious side. I like it. "Who better to kick their ass than the kids they kidnapped."

Kallen's brow furrows, and he nods toward the girl. "Will that not further traumatize the child?"

"To believe she rescued herself?" I shake my head. "If anything, it will help her heal." I hope. I'm not a psychologist, but it should work that way, damn it.

My gorgeous husband is not convinced. His dark eyebrows furrow even closer together. If he's not careful, the little hairs are going to get tangled and his face will be stuck like that. Unless we shave his eyebrows. I imagine him with no eyebrows and shudder. That is not a good look on anyone. "How will she explain her actions to the authorities?" Kallen asks, dragging me from my eye brow thoughts.

"Adrenaline rush," Josh pipes in. "Happens all the time with humans in a traumatic situation."

With a shrug, Kallen finally relents. "What is your plan?" he asks me.

Um. I thought up the first part. I was hoping the others could help with the rest. Realizing this, probably from the 'I have no plan' look on my face, Eliana grins and says, "Release your magic and watch this."

Before my upper and lower eyelids can meet in a blink, Eliana is gone. I hurry to release my magical wall surrounding the girl, hoping I am doing the right thing. Staring across the field to where the traffickers are glaring warily at the girl in question, we watch in amazement. We can't actually see her doing it, but Eliana is suddenly moving the girl. The surprise on the girl's face would be humorous if the situation was different. Way different. Moving her with such speed that the bad guys can't see Eliana, my friend stretches out the girl's arm and suddenly one of the uninjured men is holding his nose. I really hope Eliana used her own fist to do that.

By the way the girl looks around, I know that Eliana has left her. After all, if she stops moving the guys will see her. I hurry and put my magic wall back up just in time to prevent the man who just got punched from being able to hit the girl back. I'm pretty sure he breaks his hand when his fist meets my magic. We can hear the bones crack, and he lets out a high-pitched shriek of pain. So much for his macho image. The fact that he was going to hit the young girl hard enough to break his own hand just pisses all of us off even more.

The guy begins to curse and dance around, holding his hand. I feel Kallen's magic rush by and suddenly, the man who just broke his hand is lying on the ground because his legs are swept out from under him. His buddies look from him to the girl and back again. They didn't see her move, but they are beginning to believe she is doing all of this. The last uninjured man takes a cautious step toward the girl.

The guy on the ground tries to get up. "I don't think so," Eliana mutters. She rejoined us when Kallen and I started using our magic so she didn't interfere in what we were doing. She stares intently at the man on the ground. Suddenly, the guy's pocket is on fire. I give Eliana a questioning look, and with a satisfied grin, she whispers, "Lighters have been known to self-combust every now and then." I give her a doubtful look but let it go. Whatever she wants to do to these guys is fine by me. The uninjured man rushes to his comrade to try to put out the flames. He is unsuccessful since they are magical. Only Eliana can douse them.

While our attention is focused on that guy, we miss something important. My right ear drum, unaccustomed to the sound of a gun going off so close to it, begins to howl in pain. I put my hand over it and stare open-mouthed at Josh, who just blew our cover. My eyes follow the direction of his, and I understand why. A man we hadn't seen before is lying near the door to the house cradling his arm, which is spurting blood. If he was smarter, he's be putting pressure on that wound instead of cradling his arm. Apparently, he's not. A gun is lying several feet away from him. Josh must have shot his gun arm to keep him from firing at the girl.

"I was coming to warn you about him," an out-of-breath Jadyn pants. When the commotion started, she snuck inside the house to search it.

No one has a chance to respond. The other men are reaching for their guns. At least, those without broken hands are. The still uninjured one makes a move to grab the girl to either kill her, or use her as a human shield. Probably shield now, kill her later. Eliana is gone in a blur. The girl is whisked out of the man's grasp, but not before she kicks him in the groin. I know it was Eliana's foot that did it because the guy flies back about fifteen feet. He's lucky my friend was holding back. I'm sure it was to keep the little girl from getting whiplash when she was moved so suddenly, not any regard for the bad guy's injuries. I'm also sure that he will never be able to father children after that blow. Good. The realm doesn't need any more people like him in it.

In our ears, we hear Liza's voice. She gave us all coms before we made our way over here. "We're moving in. The four of you stand down. Josh, wipe your prints."

We would do as Liza tells us, but these human trafficking sleaze balls just don't know when to quit. Apparently, their injuries aren't great enough. The two who can shoot have their guns trained on the girl, and there is no doubt in any of our minds that they are going to fire on her.

Kallen wraps the girl in magic, and she is now safe from their bullets. But, that's not enough for me. I will not let that little girl suffer the trauma of being shot at on top of what else has happened to her. After all, she doesn't know that she's surrounded by a bullet-proof wall of magic. Without any thought as to what is going to happen, I ram my magic into the ends of the trafficker's guns as they pull back the triggers.

Apparently, what happens when magic is rammed into a firing gun is that the gas in the gun barrels explodes. This would probably have only hurt their hands if my magic didn't force the explosion back toward them. I can't see through the flames to see if they still have faces or not. A big part of me just doesn't care. I never thought I would feel that way about another person. But, I've never come across human traffickers before, either.

"Eliana, we want information from them," Josh says urgently.

I open my mouth to argue against saving them, but close it again. Yes, these men are trafficking children for illicit purposes. Even burning to death is too good for them. But, Josh is right. They may have vital information that could save many other children from this same fate. Not to mention, later on I would probably feel guilty about burning someone to death. Even if they are akin to monsters.

She doesn't want to do it. That is obvious from her tight lipped expression. But, with only the slightest hesitation, Eliana nods curtly. Her power reaches out to the men, and the flames are extinguished. They are badly injured, but they are also cursing loudly. So, obviously they can still talk which is all we need. Liza and her team should be able to get some information from them. Preferably before getting them medical attention.

"I guess the order 'stand down' has a different meaning for you than it does for me," Liza drawls from behind us. She has her gun drawn and trained on the men lying on the ground. The rest of her team moves around us. A couple of them secure the bad guys while the others make sure the children are okay.

"They were going to shoot her," Josh explains. He turns his gun around and offers it to Liza.

Liza shakes her head. "Alonzo needs to get his prints on it."

Before we left them, Alonzo and Josh traded guns just in case something like this happened. That way, Liza wouldn't have to explain why Josh's firearm discharged when technically, he's not supposed to be here. The report is going to read that Alonzo fired the shot.

"Good to see my aim has improved," Alonzo grins as he approaches us after handcuffing the bad guys. Sobering, he says, "Walk me through it." He and Josh move a few feet away to go over the details of the shooting. When they are done, Alonzo takes the wiped gun and fires it into the empty field away from the house.

"He needs gun powder residue on his hand," Liza explains to Kallen and me.

"Got it," I nod. I vaguely remember that from watching crime shows on television years ago.

Kallen leans down to say quietly in my ear, "We really need to be going now."

We do. Getting Eliana and Jadyn's attention, I tap my wrist where a watch would be. I'm not wearing one, but they get the idea. Liza notices my action, as well.

"Go," Liza tells us. "You should be gone before back up arrives anyway." She glances over at Josh and Alonzo. "Are you two all set?"

Josh rejoins us. "All set," he confirms.

"Try to get them back sooner as opposed to later," Liza drawls. "Obviously, we need them."

Not as much as the universe does at the moment, despite what just happened here. I realize I muttered this aloud when Liza's eyes narrow. She may be growling at me, too. This is a definitely a good time to leave. Holding my arms out for everyone to grab onto, I teleport Kallen, Josh, Eliana and Jadyn away with me. Liza is still growling as we disappear. The woman does not like me.

## 22 CHAPTER

"I don't think your boss likes me very much," I mutter sheepishly when we arrive in Colorado.

Jadyn laughs. "You may want to curb your muttering habit. You'd probably make more friends."

"Yeah, I hear that a lot," I admit.

Pulling me into a one-armed hug, Kallen kisses the top of my head. "You are perfect just the way you are." Uh huh. Until the next time I mutter something he doesn't like.

I'm going to take the compliment right now, though. I smile up at him. "Thank you." Standing on my toes, I give him a long, lingering kiss.

Clearing her throat and rolling her eyes, Jadyn reminds us, "We're in a hurry, remember?" Eliana giggles behind her.

I'm tempted to stick my tongue out at both of them, but I refrain. Instead, I herd us all inside my old house so I can create a passageway between realms. Relieved to be leaving a realm where child trafficking is a thing, I step through the passageway to the place that now feels like home to me.

We are greeted by a very grumpy Fairy King. "What took so long?" Dagda demands, even though barely any time would have passed in this realm while we were gone.

"Hello to you, too," I grumble. "I thought you were gone for the day?"

Taking a more diplomatic approach, Kallen tells Dagda, "We were side tracked by a Cowan issue that had to be dealt with or children would have been severely harmed."

That wipes the scowl from Dagda's face. "What happened?" he asks, more curious than angry now.

Kallen begins telling him the story. Since I lived it, I don't feel the need to listen. Instead, I lead the others into the house, ignoring the Giantess trying to get my attention as we go by. My adrenaline is still running a little high and I am definitely not as good as Kallen at diplomacy on the best of days. Best to leave whatever issue the Giants are having to someone who will care. I mean, who can better assist them.

In the kitchen, Tabitha is bustling around getting food ready for the growing crowd at the mansion. She turns from the stove where something that smells delicious is cooking and takes us in. Her eyes zoom in on Jadyn. "I'm fresh out of cat treats, so if you're hungry, I suggest you change." Jadyn may be able to fool Cowans, but Tabitha can see her soul. She knows exactly who the cat is.

As we watch, Jadyn transforms from cat to her normal self. At least, I'm pretty sure this is her normal self. I've never asked if the way she normally appears to us is the way she was born, or just another shapeshift. Who knows, she could be a giant blob until she decides what shape to take. It just seems rude to ask.

"I tried cat treats once," Jadyn grins. "They paled in comparison to whatever is in that pan."

Tabitha narrows her eyes. "I am happy to hear it," she drawls.

Jadyn laughs and gives the older Fairy a hug. One that Tabitha is not too annoyed to return. "It is good to see you."

"You, too," Tabitha agrees, her annoyance completely gone now. If it wasn't, Jadyn would have received a good smack to the back of her head for her pertness.

The kitchen door opens and Garren walks in. To no one in particular, he says, "I set up a tent about a hundred yards down the beach for the goblins. We shouldn't be able to smell them even if the wind changes direction later."

"Won't they think that's rude?" Eliana asks me quietly.

I shake my head. "They're aware that every other race in the universe besides the Dragons think they stink."

As if on cue, the stench of goblin swamps the kitchen. My gag reflex is not the only one activating. Eliana and Josh slap hands over their noses and mouths. "I thought they weren't coming until tomorrow," I complain.

"The goblins came ahead to make sure proper accommodations are made for the Dragons," Isla informs me as she enters the kitchen. I notice she is not breathing through her nose. "Garren, will you please reassure them that everything is prepared and escort them to the tent you set up. And strongly encourage them to stay there," Isla adds, ignoring the glare from Tabitha. Again, why Tabitha has a soft spot for the stinky little guys none of us will ever understand.

Garren nods and gives his wife a kiss on the cheek. Shaking his head, he tells her, "You know, at one time I had gotten used to their scent. Either that time has passed, or they smell worse than they once did."

"They have stopped wearing any type of camouflaging scent so they can collect their sweat to rub on the cows," I remind him. They used to try to hide from the dragons by covering their scent with other less appealing ones. Less appealing to Dragons, anyway. I note that both Eliana and Josh simultaneously look grossed out and intrigued by what I said. The distinct green tint to their skin tells me which one is winning out.

Once Garren is gone, Isla questions us about our trip back to the Cowan realm. I let Josh explain to her what happened. When he is finished, Isla asks, "What will happen to these men once they have been questioned?"

"They will go to prison," Eliana tells her. Clearly, other possible ideas for punishment are running through her mind, though.

Isla shakes her head. "They deserve much worse."

I agree. But, we aren't the ones who can or should decide those things even though I almost did. I push that thought to the back of my mind. I was right, I would feel guilty now if I had done what I was thinking at the time.

Wanting to change the subject, I ask, "Do you know what the Giants want to talk to me about?"

A tiny smile tugs at Isla's lips. "Oh, yes." Back at the stove, Tabitha snickers.

I groan loudly. "I'm not going to like this, am I?"

Isla's eyes slip from me to Eliana and on to Josh. "It is not you, Xandra, who will not appreciate the Chieftain's request."

A splash of red covers Eliana's cheeks. "I know I am not going to like this."

Isla, in a rare show of mirth, laughs. "No, you will not." She finally explains. "It seems the Giants found out about the reverence the Dragons showed you. Now, Quinn is more determined than ever to win Eliana's hand in marriage. Much to Eistla's chagrin," Isla adds. It appears I was right about Eistla's unrequited love for Quinn.

Eliana gasps in outrage, too angry to speak. So, I do it for her. Cocking my head to the side, I ask, "What do you mean, win her hand?"

"He wants to battle Josh for it," Tabitha chuckles.

"I assume he was told that is not going to happen. That would not be a fair fight," I insist

Josh scowls, offended by the implication that he is not able to take on the Giant. "I will fight him."

Eliana glares at her love. "No, you will not. Whether you would win or not is not the issue. I am not a toy to be fought over." Turning back to Isla, she asks, "Would it be harmful to Fairy/Giant relations if I throw the Chieftain in the ocean? Far, far out into the ocean."

Isla doesn't get a chance to respond. Dagda and Kallen enter the kitchen just as Eliana finishes speaking. "As much as I would like to see that," Dagda says sincerely, "I am afraid that would not help with the problem at hand. I have spoken to Quinn, though, and reminded him that Fairies do not barter or battle for wives. Either a woman chooses us or she does not. We must accept the latter with grace and dignity."

Tabitha snorts. "Like you would have accepted a refusal from Tana with grace and dignity."

Standing a little taller, Dagda refuses to acknowledge she is right. "Fortunately, I was not tested in such a way."

"Except when she left you for all those years," I remind him. "From what I hear, you did not handle it with grace and dignity."

Dagda would probably have more to say on the subject, primarily words that would make my ears bleed, but we are interrupted yet again by the stench of goblin. It chokes the words right out of my father's throat. This time, it is growing stronger by the second. One of them is in the house and is coming toward the kitchen. Lord, it would suck to always have your stench announce your arrival. Though, I see it would be useful in preventing friction between Dagda and me. Nothing stops an argument faster than a stench that brings to mind a thousand decaying rat carcasses covered in feces and then smeared in orange marmalade. I have no idea where the citrusy undertone is coming from. Nor do my offended senses care. I just want to get out of here before the stench gets worse.

"I think I'll show our guests around." Grabbing Kallen's hand, I say over my quickly retreating shoulder to my friends, "Let's go find Sam and Jenna." There is no hesitation in either Eliana's or Josh's forward momentum. In fact, Kallen and I must pick up our pace so they don't knock us down in their attempt to get out of the room. Jadyn attempts to follow, but Isla stops her with a question. She gives us a longing glance before turning her attention back to Isla and Dagda. I feel badly for her, but not badly enough to let my senses get any more bombarded with Goblin funk than they already have today.

After leaving the kitchen, we can't find our friends, and it takes us a little while to discover where Sam and Jenna have disappeared to. Kegan, who we find reading to Keelan in the library, finally informs us that Tana and Alita brought them to the palace. "Are you heading there?" he asks, setting down the book on a side table and scooping up his son. "We'll join you. The goblin stench is starting to make its way up here. Keelan is already teething. He does not need another reason to be grumpy." The words are said with a loving glance in his son's direction. Kegan doesn't mind if his son is a bit grumpy from time to time. In fact, he's remarkably laid back about most things that come up with the baby. Much more so than Kallen and I were with the Elf baby. Then again, Kegan wasn't particularly calm around the Elf baby, either. Maybe it will be different for Kallen and me, too, when it's our own child. I sure hope so.

Tapping my chin, I pretend to mull over our options. "Hmm, stay here with the Goblins or go to the palace?"

"It would be cool to see a real palace," Eliana muses.

"Then off to the palace we go," I say with a grin. I hold my arms out, ready to teleport everyone.

Kallen gives me a pointed look. "Perhaps our guests would like to ride to the palace." He has that 'why don't you conserve your magic' look on his face. I narrow my eyes in his direction but don't say anything.

"Ride? Do you mean on horses?" Josh asks.

Kallen chuckles. "No, we have vehicles here just as you do in your realm."

Oh, I get it. Kallen also wants to show them some differences between living in a magical vs. a non-magical realm. "Do you think Isla will mind if we take the carriage?" I ask.

"Carriage? Really?" Eliana asks, obviously amused by the old-fashioned mode of transportation.

"Yeah, the Fairies aren't big on air pollution," I tell her, not ready to spoil the secret as to how the carriages move.

"Carriages, palaces, this is really starting to sound like a Fairy tale," Josh teases.

Eliana rolls her eyes. "Like they haven't heard that before."

"A few times," Kallen assures her, but he doesn't mind the teasing. "Shall we?" He gestures toward the library door.

We take the back stairs, hoping to avoid as much of the Goblin stench as possible. We avoid the kitchen area altogether, assuming that the Goblin was in search of

Tabitha. The Goblins love their one true defender. Circling the house, we make our way to the garage, which is large enough to fit several cars, or carriages, as the case may be.

Kallen slips in to speak to the driver who is on duty. Isla doesn't keep a full time driver, but when things get crazy, she doesn't want to hassle with driving the carriage herself, so she has one on call. This counts as one of those crazy times. After a moment, the large garage door opens, and the carriage pulls out into the driveway.

To say Eliana and Josh are shocked is an understatement. "Um, how is this possible?" Josh asks.

Silly question. "Magic, of course," I tell him. "I told you, Fairies don't like air pollution."

"Bad for the lungs," Kegan agrees as he climbs into the carriage with his son. Poking his head back out, he asks our friends, "Are you coming?"

"You're sure this is safe, right?" Eliana asks hesitantly.

Nodding toward the driver, Kallen reassures her, "He's the best driver around. I believe he's only crashed ten carriages. Twenty at most."

I swat at my teasing husband's arm. "Not funny." Turning to Eliana, I tell her, "His magic is more than sufficient to keep the carriage afloat and on course to the palace. There's nothing to worry about. It will be a nice, relaxing ride." Fairy carriages do not have wheels, and they are not pulled by horses. They hover above the ground, which provides for the smoothest ride, and run solely on magic.

More reassured by my words than Kallen's, Eliana and Josh climb into the carriage. Running a hand over the brand new and super soft royal blue leather, Eliana is impressed. "Wow, this is nice. Much more comfortable than car seats."

"Grandmother just had the carriage redone," Kallen tells her. His eyes travel in my direction and I groan. I know what's coming next. "It was a necessity after I tried again to give Xandra a driving lesson." The corners of his mouth are trying hard to curve up into a grin despite my glowering in his direction. Yup, there it is.

"Didn't go well?" Josh asks.

With an exasperated sigh, I admit, "I used a bit too much magic." Under my breath, I add, "It's a good thing I can teleport."

"The carriage got stuck at the top of a tree," Kallen feels the need to explain. You wouldn't think he'd be able to speak through all the laughing he's doing. Pointing out the window, he indicates a particular tree about a hundred yards away. "That one."

Shocked and impressed, Josh exclaims, "That has to be at least forty feet high!"

"Forty-five," Kallen nods. "It got tangled in the upper branches with several of the stronger ones breaking through the windows. The old leather was completely destroyed."

"It was due for an overhaul anyway," I grumble.

"Yes, I believe those were the exact words Grandmother used when she had to retrieve the carriage from the top of the tree. Right after, 'Xandra is never to drive the carriage again.'"

Surprised and curious, Eliana asks him, "Were you not able to do it? Get it down, I mean." She knows how strong Kallen's magic is.

"He was laughing too hard," I inform her.

"I was watching from our bedroom balcony. It really was funny," Kegan pipes in. "Of course, I made sure Alita and Keelan were well away from the site of inevitable disaster beforehand. Alita brought him to visit her mother about a mile down the beach. You can't be too careful when Xandra tries to do delicate magic."

"You know, you won't be holding your son forever," I tell him in my sweetest, I'm going to get you later, voice.

Kegan waves me off. "You're too busy for revenge right now. So, I have to get all my fun in while I can." Unfortunately, he has a point. Then again, it's said that revenge is a dish best served cold. If the universe survives, I'll have to find out if that's true.

"Even in our realm, the first time you try driving it can be difficult," Eliana says in an attempt to soothe my injured pride.

With a sigh, I admit, "It was not my first time. Or my second. Or my third."

Not sure what to say about that, Eliana decides to change the subject. I like her even more for it. "How far away is the palace?" she asks.

Kallen points to the window next her. "When we go around this next bend, it will come into sight."

Josh and Eliana turn their heads eagerly to get their first glimpse of the palace. Kallen takes advantage of their distraction and attempts to kiss away the teasing he has been doing. Okay, I admit it. I am defenseless against his kisses. After just a moment, I don't even remember he was teasing me. All I can think about is the feel of his full lips pressed against mine, and the love he is pouring into this kiss.

"You know," Kegan says dryly, "there are some things I would prefer Keelan not learn about until he is much older."

Oh, yeah. I forgot he was here. Instead of admitting that, I stick my tongue out at him. "Consider this step one of my revenge."

Kegan shrugs. "It's a lot less painful than having my stool pulled out from under me."

Eliana turns her head back toward me and giggles. "Did you really do that?"

"Regularly," I tell her with a grin.

Shaking her head, she replies, "It's a wonder you have any friends at all."

"Trust me, my cousin deserved everything he was served," Kallen assures her.

"There it is!" Josh exclaims, pointing out the window. Eliana turns around again to enjoy the view instead of listening to Kegan's response to Kallen. Huh, I guess he's not too worried about the words Keelan may be learning.

I try to remember the excitement of seeing the palace for the first time, but my memory is marred by the fact that Dagda and I were still basically enemies then. At least, he seemed like he was my enemy at the time. I'm certainly glad that turned out to be incorrect. I enjoy watching the excitement on my friends' faces, though.

When we pull up in front of the palace, the doorman rushes forward to open the carriage door, assuming that Isla is inside. He tries to hide his disappointment when he finds us instead. I shake my head. Someday, maybe Dagda will hire a doorman who is actually nice to me.

Once inside, we stop on the balcony that looks over the great hall so Eliana and Josh can take it all in. Turning to me, Eliana asks, "You will live here one day?"

I nod. "If Dagda had his way, Kallen and I already would. We prefer Isla's house for now, though."

"Not ready for all the politics?" Josh asks with a knowing grin.

"Exactly." Turning toward one of the sets of stairs leading down to the Great Hall, I say over my shoulder, "Come on, let's go find the others."

Clearing his throat, Kallen stops my forward movement. "Xandra, did you forget the new rule Dagda passed?"

Rolling my eyes, I sigh loudly. "I'm only allowed in the archives if the realm is in imminent danger and there is no other possible solution that either he or Isla can come up with." Glancing up at Eliana and Josh, I add, "Long story."

"Stories," Kegan mutters and I glare at him.

"Geez, you destroy a room a few times and no one lets you forget it," I mutter under my breath.

"It looks like the point is moot," Kallen says with a relieved smile. Across the hall, Sam, Jenna and Alita emerge from a hallway. When they spot us, Jenna waves.

We meet them in the middle of the Great Hall, and Jenna is all smiles. "Isn't this place amazing? I can't believe the river runs right through the palace."

Noticing the books Sam has tucked under his arms, Eliana asks, "Did you guys find something?"

Nodding excitedly, Jenna replies, "We think we did."

I wish there was a little more certainty in her voice, but I don't want to burst her excitement bubble by saying so. "What did you find?"

Glancing around the busy hall that always has Fairies coming and going, Sam asks in a hushed voice, "Should we take this conversation someplace a little more private?"

"Isn't he cute when he's in spy mode?" Jenna asks with a giggle, which earns her a hard stare from her boyfriend. She ignores it.

Despite Jenna's teasing, Kallen nods. "We should indeed." I'm not sure if he's just indulging Sam, or if he really thinks we should take the conversation somewhere more private. Probably a little of both. After all, we don't know who Dagda has told about the possible end of the universe. Causing mass panic amongst his staff is something I am actively trying to avoid.

Leading the way to a small conference room, Kallen opens the door and ushers us all in. Sam sets the books he is carrying down on the table in the middle of the room, and Jenna begins flipping pages in the first book. When she finds the one she is looking for in that one, she leaves it open and moves on to the next one. When that is open to the right page, she glances up at the rest of us. "Did any of you know that the Phoenix has an enemy?"

Frowning, Kallen says, "It is no secret that many covet the power of the Phoenix."

Jenna shakes her head. "No, that's not what I'm saying. She has a true enemy. Someone she has been fighting for a long time."

"Do you think that has something to do with why the Phoenix is willing to destroy the universe?" I ask.

"Maybe she's tired of running," Eliana suggests.

Again, Jenna shakes her head. "No, I don't think that's why she's doing it."

I bite my lips so I don't say, 'why did you bring it up then?'. So, my words sound muffled when I say them anyway. Kallen scowls at my rudeness, but hey, it was a fair question.

Jenna is not offended. She actually smiles and says, "I'm glad you asked." With a dramatic flourish of her hand, she points at the second book. "That's why."

The rest of us who were not in the archives when the discovery was made crowd together to read the passage Jenna is indicating. When we are done, we read it again. After that, we read it one more time. Finally, Kegan is the first to speak. "I do not get it." Neither do I.

## 23 CHAPTER

"Neither did I, at first," Jenna says with a grin.

"Care to explain for those of us who are a little slower on the uptake?" Eliana urges, trying to keep the impatience out of her voice.

Jenna finally understands that none of us are enjoying the suspense. She gets to the point. "This," she says, indicating the second book, "is a copy of a firsthand account of a Fairy who met the Phoenix. The scribe said the original was a crumbling scroll so the previous scribe preserved the information here."

"That's probably enough backstory about the how of it," Sam interrupts. Glad he said it before me, because he gets a nasty glare thrown at him by Jenna. She still likes me as far as I can tell. I don't want to spoil that with my rude comments.

Despite her annoyance with Sam, Jenna does move on. "Anyway, if you read closely what the Fairy described, I think the enemy of the Phoenix is herself."

Dragging my doubting eyes away from Jenna and back to the book, I reread the words printed there. *'Darkness followed the Phoenix wherever she went. An inescapable force constantly reminding her of her past with all if its losses and mistakes. Never did she dwell on moments of happiness though I know they existed. No matter how hard she tried, the Phoenix could not keep the darkness at bay. I fear for her soul.'*

Kallen is the first to speak. "You believe this darkness has become too much for her to bear?"

Jenna nods excitedly. "Yes, I do." Probably not the best thing in the universe to be excited about. I assume she is excited about her discovery, not our possible demise.

"So, what, she's tired of continuing on while everyone she loves during her lives die?" I ask. I'm not sure I buy it. "Do you really think she would doom the entire universe to run away from her memories?" She was created to be a superior being with a whole lot of responsibility. Eternal responsibility. I would certainly hope she was made of stronger stuff than that. Then again, depression can be a deadly force. Maybe Jenna is right. Maybe we need to look into finding an antidepressant strong enough to withstand Cosmic Fire. I doubt Prozac is up for the job.

"Can you imagine how many she has lost by now?" Jenna asks. As if reading my thoughts from a second ago, she adds, "Who could handle that degree of grief and depression forever?"

In a neutral voice, Kallen acknowledges, "You make a good point." Though he has on his best poker face, I am convinced that he is not convinced by Jenna's theory. I believe he's with me on the 'made to be able to handle it or why else does she exist' theory.

"Okay," Kegan begins hesitantly, "say this is true. What do we do about it?" His eyes flick to me and I see that he is willing to accept this explanation. "You could use that memory spell on her that you used on the Elf warriors. Get rid of the memories that she doesn't want anymore."

I shake my head emphatically. "No way am I going to poke around inside the brain of the one being responsible for keeping the universe alive." Besides, how the heck would I even know what memories to get rid of? Would she make me a list? Considering the fact that she has been around since the beginning of time, I don't think even my magic is strong enough to erase that many memories. Not to mention the amount of time it would take. I doubt I could beat the Cosmic Fire clock.

"I concur. That would be a bad idea," Kallen agrees instantly. I take a moment to decide if I should be insulted by his ready agreement. Ultimately, I decide I should not be insulted by the truth. This time, anyway. There are times that I find the truth very insulting.

Jenna shrugs. "I'm not sure what you should do with this information. But, other than histories of her origin story and purpose, there's really not much else in the archives that references the Phoenix. The scribe is going to keep looking for anything else that could be useful, of course, but she thought we were lucky to find these two things."

I glance up at Kallen. "Should we bring this to Isla?"

He nods. "We need to share all the information we find. Grandmother may even recognize who wrote this."

Sam is shocked by his words. "She may have been alive when this was written?"

Kegan laughs. "Grandmother is old, but not quite that old. He meant that she may recognize the name."

Sam's cheeks turn a light shade of pink. "That makes more sense."

"Fairy lives are centuries longer than Cowan lives, though," I tell him. "It was a reasonable question."

"You may not want to repeat that in front of Grandmother," Kegan smirks.

I toss a sour look his way. I was trying to make Sam feel better, and he just ruined it. Parenthood has not done much to reduce the number of times in a day he is a jerk. "Alita," I say with my most saccharine sweet smile. "I promise when I make you a single parent that Kallen and I will always be there for you and Keelan."

"Uh, thank you," Alita says, trying to determine just how serious I am. Ultimately, she turns to her husband and shakes her head solemnly. "I guess I will never be able to hold our son again."

This wipes the smirk from Kegan's face. "Why not?"

"Because as soon as you set him down, I may lose you forever." She tries not to giggle as she says these words to her husband. I guess she decided that I wasn't serious, after all. Darn. I need to get better at being threatening.

Kegan just rolls his eyes. "With all the craziness in her life, Xandra will never get around to me." Hmm. He may have a point. I need to be sure to pencil revenge in somewhere on my schedule. Kallen will probably help me remember since it involves Kegan.

Shaking her head with an amused smile on her lips, Eliana says, "Perhaps we should get back to discussing what to do with this information."

Kallen appreciates having another level head in the room. "Yes, we should," he agrees. "We will return to the house and share this information with Grandmother." To Jenna, Sam and Alita, he adds, "Good work finding this." Even if he doesn't necessarily agree with Jenna's assessment of the information, he does appreciate their hard work.

I slip my hand into Kallen's and give it a loving squeeze. Then, his words sink in and I groan. "Can't you just send a message?" I ask hopefully. Yes, I said I was going to be less whiny. Goblin stank could make anyone go back on her word, though.

Understanding where my mind has gone, Kallen chuckles. "We cannot avoid home for the duration of time there are Goblins in attendance."

"Why not?" I demand, growing to like the idea. "We do have a bedroom here, and there are plenty of guest rooms for everyone else."

Jenna wrinkles her pretty, freckled nose. "Are they really that bad?" she asks.

"Worse," Eliana nods.

"They are pretty bad," Josh agrees. "You'll want to breathe through your mouth, not your nose."

"You don't have a spell to make gas masks?" Sam asks.

I consider the possibility until Kallen spoils it for us all. "That may not be culturally sensitive," he says dryly. No, probably not.

"By this time, Grandmother has insisted that they remain closer to their lodging than the house," Kegan points out. Which is most likely true, despite Tabitha's love for the small beings.

"I'm starting to feel very guilty for leaving Jadyn there," Eliana remarks, making my own guilt on the matter surface.

"Alright, grab those books and let's go," I say with as much enthusiasm as I can muster. Which means I sound more like I'm going to get several toenails pulled off and then glued back on with a salt based paste.

We don't go straight to the carriage, however. Despite his insistence that we return home, Kallen suggests a quick tour of the castle for our friends. After all, this may be the only time our friends travel to this realm; they really should see everything while they are here. I get suspicious that Kallen is avoiding the Goblins, too, but just doesn't want to admit it as his tour becomes very thorough. Did our friends really need to see every spot he and Kegan hid when they were in trouble as children? The only thing hiding in most of these dark, small spaces now is spiders. Big, hairy brown spiders that I am positive are poisonous even though both Kallen and Kegan assure me they are not. Still, Dagda should really do something about them. He doesn't want to end up with a palace full of spiders. If it does happen, I hope it's before Kallen and I take up residence.

It is two hours later when we finally make our way to the carriage and back home. Jadyn is drinking a cup of tea with Tabitha in the kitchen when we arrive. "Nice of you to finally rejoin us," she drawls.

All my guilt comes rushing back. "Sorry about that."

"That would be much more convincing if you sounded like you meant it," Jadyn replies. She smiles at the older Fairy whose company she has been enjoying. "It's a good thing Tabitha has plenty of amusing stories to share about all of you."

I give Tabitha, who is smiling innocently, a sour look. "How nice of you to be so entertaining."

"One of us needed to entertain our guest," she says smugly.

Inhaling deeply, Kegan asks, "How did you get the Goblin stench out of here. You cannot even tell the little beasts are around."

Since he is not holding his son, Tabitha reaches behind him and smacks the back of his head. "Do not be rude," she admonishes.

Rubbing the spot that may develop a goose egg, Kegan grouses, "I thought you would stop doing that when I became a father."

Tabitha snorts. "I will stop doing that when you no longer deserve it."

"Then your last act upon your deathbed will be one last slap to his head," Kallen smirks. Kegan reaches around his wife and punches him in the arm, making my charming husband laugh.

His laugh is short-lived, though. Beside me, Kallen tenses. "The Elves are here."

"Yes, they arrived a few minutes ago. The Elf Queen was looking for the two of you," Jadyn informs us.

I roll my eyes. "Of course she was."

With a sideways glance at Sam and Jenna, Jadyn asks, "Have you prepared them for the effects of glamour?"

No, we have not. With everything else going on, I completely forgot to warn them. Turning to the Cowans in the room, I explain, "The stories about glamour are true. The Elves can make you feel like joining them is the most wonderful idea in the world. Try to keep in mind that they would make you slaves, and you'd spend the rest of a very long life serving them and believing you are happy to do it."

"No way," Sam scoffs.

"It does seem unlikely that anyone or anything could convince Sam to be that nice," Josh smirks. "Even magic."

By his initial expression, it is obvious that Sam knows he's being insulted. But surprisingly, he doesn't argue. His eyes are suddenly glued to the door. His face becomes slightly slack and a dopey smile unfolds on his lips. Uh oh.

"I assure you, if I desired your company, you would come willingly to serve me," a soft, sexy voice says behind me.

I don't need to turn around to know who it is. I felt her coming. And her glamour. "Knock it off," I growl. Spinning around, I inform the Elf Queen, "These Cowans are off limits. If you use even the tiniest amount of glamour on them again, I will strip you of the ability permanently." I'm not certain I could actually do that to such a powerful being as the Queen, but she doesn't know that.

She isn't willing to risk her magic. With the slightest of pouts on her face, she withdraws her glamour. "I was only having a little fun with your friend. I would not have permanently altered his state of mind."

Jenna gasps. "Permanently altered his state of mind?"

Her voice dripping with distaste, Eliana steps closer to her friends and tells Addylyn, "You will not have fun at my friends' expense. If it happens again, Xandra will not be the only one coming after you."

Instead of becoming defensive after being threatened by a total stranger, Addylyn studies Eliana more closely. "You are not a Cowan." It sounds more like an accusation than a statement of fact.

"You are incorrect," Eliana says evenly, offering no other explanation.

"Addylyn," a sharp, male voice says from behind her. "You promised to behave." A large Elf warrior steps out of the shadows and into the kitchen.

The pout is back on the Elf Queen's face as she turns to her husband. "Are you following me?"

"Yes," her estranged husband says.

Stepping around Addylyn, Kallen holds his hand out to the Elf warrior. "It is nice to see you again." Oh, he's smooth. Nice way to prevent a marital spat in the middle of the kitchen.

The Elf warrior returns the greeting, ignoring the glower his wife is sending his way for admitting to following her. "Yes, always a pleasure. Please forgive the intrusion, and know that your friends are safe from any more glamour from the Queen."

Addylyn opens her mouth to admonish him for speaking of her like she is an unruly child, until she remembers that she is trying to win him back. She decides to focus on something else. Pasting a pleasant smile on her face, she returns her attention to Eliana. "You may be Cowan, but there is more to you than that. Are you a hybrid as our dear Xandra is?"

I roll my eyes. "I am not your dear Xandra," I grumble. "I also don't like being referred to as a *hybrid*." It makes me feel like some sort of pea plant or something.

"After all we have been through, you will always be dear to me," Addylyn counters, her smile never faltering.

Not wanting to get into all of that, I decide to abate her curiosity. That will be the quickest way to get rid of her.

With a quick glance at Eliana, who nods slightly, I explain, "Eliana holds within her the essence of two gods." With a smile of my own, I add, "So, you should take her words seriously."

"Interesting," is Addylyn's only reply. I don't like the calculating gleam in her eye. She is trying to figure out how she can use this information to her advantage.

I am not the only one who picks up on this. Her husband clears his throat. "We will leave you know." He turns to leave, and to my great surprise, Addylyn follows him out. She gives Eliana one last glance over her shoulder before disappearing through the doorway.

When they are finally gone, I sigh loudly. "You're going to want to watch out for her," I inform my friend. "She's sneaky. And a little twisted in the head."

"So I gathered," Eliana nods.

"Despite her husband's promise, I believe it best all of you avoid the Elves," Kallen says, directing his statement mainly at the full Cowans in the room.

"No problem there," Sam says, shaking his head as if to clear it. "I have no desire to become anyone's slave." He is definitely a believer in glamour now.

Wrapping her arm around his, Jenna teases, "Except mine." Sam raises a brow but doesn't argue. He has it bad for her.

Tabitha rises from the counter and brings her empty cup to the sink. "Perhaps it is best if you make yourselves scarce for now. The more you interact with our guests, the more trouble you are likely to stir up."

"Hey!" I exclaim defensively. "Addylyn started it by using her glamour." Granted, my mouth does get me in trouble on a regular basis with other beings, but this time was not my fault.

"And the Sasquatch will likely go out of their way to antagonize you, as will the Centaurs, because they like to get a rise out of you. Which they always do," Tabitha points out.

"She does have a point," Kallen, my traitor husband, concurs.

"Fine," I grumble, but there is a distinct lack of disappointment or angst in my voice. Get out of babysitting our *guests*? This is exactly what I was hoping for. I try to hide my glee as I head out of the kitchen toward the stairs with the others trailing behind me.

## 24 Chapter

"Well, I am now officially over my excitement about meeting all these other magical beings," Jenna grumbles as we enter the second floor sitting room. She is worrying her lip and giving sidelong glances to Sam. She's more concerned about the Elves and their glamour than she let on downstairs.

"Do not let a bad experience spoil your excitement," Kallen insists. "Not all races are like the Elves."

With a deep breath, Jenna nods. "True, all the Fairies we've met have been very nice." Now is probably not the best time to tell her that many of the Fairies do not like Cowans.

Flopping down in an armchair, Sam asks, "What do we do now? Hide in here all night?"

"We could take a walk on the beach," I suggest.

"Are you fans of card games?" Alita asks.

Before anyone gets a chance to respond, angry voices can be heard from outside. We can't understand the words, but the tone is very clear. There's about to be violence.

"Stay here," I tell the others.

"You are not going alone," Kallen insists.

"I'll come, too," Eliana also insists.

Knowing I won't be able to talk either of them out of it, I nod and hold my hands out to them. To the others, I say again, "Stay here." When Eliana and Kallen grab my hands, I teleport us to the large living room near the terrace. I didn't want to put us in the middle of things without being able to assess the situation first.

As I expected, the trouble is between a Centaur and a Sasquatch. They two races may be trying to work out their problems at the government level, but there is still a great deal of prejudice on both sides amongst individuals. Quinn is standing between them, but with his propensity for violence, I doubt he's going to make the situation any better. In fact, he's probably giving them pointers on how best to kill each other.

Peering out the terrace door, Eliana asks, "What is that?"

Since Centaurs are a known image in her realm, I assume she means the other being. "A Sasquatch," I tell her over my shoulder as I step onto the terrace.

"The Centaurs and the Sasquatch are often at odds with each other," Kallen explains as he and Eliana follow me out.

I roll my eyes at his euphemism for 'they wish the other would die horrific, incredibly painful, deaths and disappear from the universe completely.' Well, if they don't knock it off and get along, they may both get their wish. "What's going on?" I ask Isla, who is currently trying to talk some sense into the Centaur involved.

"I will tell you what is going on. That beast insulted my husband," the Centaur claims. She has a spear in her hand, and it's aimed at the Sasquatch's heart.

"After she tried to stomp on my foot with her *hooves*," the Sasquatch argues, a sword at the ready. She, at least I assume it is a she since Sasquatch are androgynous and I can't really tell, says the word hooves like she actually means cockroach infested, fungus laden, snotty nose hair covered, flat, dead rat in the middle of the road. She can really pack an insult into the tone of her voice.

"Oh, then by all means, go ahead and kill each other," I say dryly.

Isla gives me a dirty look for my sarcasm. "Not helpful."

"But, Isla, she," I point at the Sasquatch, "was *almost* stepped on! And her," I point at the Centaur now, "husband who she just revolted against because of his sexist ways was *insulted*! Killing each other and completely destroying our chance to save the universe seems completely acceptable." Behind me, Kallen clears his throat to cover his chuckle. Sometimes he enjoys my sarcasm.

Because she is a good friend, Eliana joins in with a helpful gesture. "If you want to hurry things along, I could help with that." She creates two balls of fire that dance in front of her. "Who first?" she asks me.

I tap my chin. "Hmm, which thing happened first again? Was it the almost stepping on or the insulting of the sexist husband?"

"The almost stepping on," Kallen says helpfully. He is actually enjoying this exchange instead of admonishing me with a glower like Isla currently is. His grandmother shifts her glower in his direction now.

Spoiling the fun, Quinn drops to one knee in front of Eliana. "You are incredible. Tell me what I must do to win your heart."

Eliana rolls her eyes and says in a most sincere way, "Get up or I'll use these on you." Quinn laughs heartily, but he does rise to his feet. He's not a complete idiot. Close, but not quite complete. Like a jigsaw puzzle with a piece missing in one corner.

Taking a step back so her silky white hair doesn't accidently catch on fire, the Sasquatch demands, "Who is this fire-wielding demon?"

I can't help but snort. "I've seen Demons recently. She looks nothing like a Demon."

"Good to know," Eliana smiles.

"Your point has been well taken. There is no need for such a display of power," the Centaur insists. She has lowered her spear, but she has not put it in its holder I note. Centaurs do like to be prepared when the Sasquatch are around.

The tingle I get down my spine tells me she is lying. Just as Eliana sensed, only a show of power greater than their own will stop these two races once they start fighting. "Uh huh," I mutter. Aloud, I introduce them to Eliana and give them the briefest of explanations about who she is.

When I am finished, there is a suspicious gleam in the Sasquatch's eye. "To have such power in a realm that does not appreciate magic. Such a waste."

Behind me, the Centaur snorts. "Surely, you do not believe she would come to your barren realm."

"I am quite happy in my own realm, thank you," Eliana informs the Sasquatch as she lets the fire balls in front of her dissolve.

A crowd has gathered around us. The Elves, Goblins, and Fauns came to see what the commotion was. Two Dragons are making their way down the beach and are within earshot. This seems like the perfect time to make an announcement. "Just to be clear," I yell so no one can claim later that they did not hear me. "Eliana has every intention of returning to the Cowan realm after this is over. Nothing you say or do will convince her otherwise." I give Eliana a sideways glance and she nods in agreement. I address the crowd again. "If there is any more violence or threats of violence, you will be forcibly sent back to your realm to tell your people that you are the cause of the demise of the universe. Zero tolerance from here on out." There is a lot of murmuring in the crowd. I'm pretty sure a few insults are quietly lobbed my way, but I can't quite make them out. No one openly goes against what I said, though.

The sound of rattling plates gets all of our attention. A large number of Fairies from the palace are coming around the house carrying trays of food. I guess Dagda recruited his kitchen staff to help feed all of our guests. I bet that's a relief for Tabitha, even if she will grouse about it to everyone who can hear her.

As the Fairies set up the food on buffet tables they create on the beach, Isla thanks everyone for coming to help and welcomes them to dinner. She stays behind to field questions and calm nerves while the rest of us retreat back into the house.

"That's a lot of hair," Sam remarks from his position at the window in the large living room. I didn't really think they would stay put upstairs. They are way too curious for that. "How do they keep it so clean and white?"

"That is a long story," I inform him. "And the basis for their long running conflict with the Centaurs."

Obviously, I did nothing to appease Sam's curiosity. I only compounded it. "I will explain it to you over our dinner," Kallen promises.

When he mentions our dinner, I realize there are delicious aromas wafting in from the kitchen. Tabitha has been busy. Over the sound of my rumbling tummy, I say to our guests, "I believe Tabitha has prepared some of our favorite Fairy dishes. I hope you're hungry."

"No one is eating a thing until you wash up," Tabitha calls from the dining room. That Fairy has excellent hearing.

The next hour and a half is spent over dinner. True to his word, Kallen gives our friends a quick history lesson in regards to the feuds and bad blood between the various races currently occupying the lavish tents set up on the beach. After dinner, we end up spending a quiet evening in the library. Most of us play cards or curl up with a good book. Jenna searches the shelves for anything possibly relating to the Phoenix.

Kegan and Alita turn in early, shortly after Keelan falls asleep in his father's arms. "Maybe we can actually get some sleep tonight," Kegan whispers to his wife on the way out. Funny, that look in his eye does not suggest that he has sleep on his mind. Alita's cheeks turn a little pink, but her step quickens. Good for them.

Not long after, the rest of us decide to call it a night, as well. We have a long day ahead of us. A day that could be one of our last. Yes, Kegan and Alita definitely have the right idea about how to spend the rest of this night. Sleep is not the comfort I am looking for if my days are limited.

## 25 CHAPTER

Not long after Kallen and I fall into a sated sleep, I begin to dream. This is not a typical dream. I was drawn here by a mind other than my own. I suspect I know whose.

*In my dream, there is a familiar presence in the distance and I go to her, picking my way carefully through the rushes. Desperately hoping there are no crocodiles hiding among them. Eliana smiles when I finally reach her. "I wondered if Ra would call to you, as well."*

*I glance around at our surroundings. We are on the edge of what I assume is the Nile. "Why are we here?"*

*Eliana shrugs. "I do not know. Ra will show us in his own time."* I try not to grimace. My patience is not as well matured as Eliana's.

*We do not have to wait long, though. Voices travel toward us over the sound of the river's current. The deep, velvety, very masculine voice of Ra reaches us first. "I knew I would find you here. I was disappointed to wake and find you gone. Are you well?"*

*The next voice we hear is also familiar. Familiar because it once pounded through our heads while our bodies were practically on fire. The Phoenix. My first reflex is to cringe and wait for the gust of Cosmic Fire. When it doesn't come, I relax and strain my ears so I can listen carefully to her words. Whatever she is saying must be important if Ra wants both Eliana and me to hear them.*

*Funny, when she's not trying to almost kill us, the Phoenix's voice is actually pretty. Pretty like an Angel's. I suppose if one is going to make eternal beings, it would be rather cruel to give them voices that are grating and annoying. Who would want to listen to that forever? "I woke this morning to that familiar humming," the Phoenix is telling Ra. "The sound that my mind creates when I have been dreaming the taboo."*

*We can barely see the two of them through the rushes. Eliana is a bit taller than me, so she has a slightly better view. I can just make out Ra moving closer to the Phoenix and wrapping his arms around her. "Tell me," he encourages.*

*Even though her face is turned away from us, I can hear the sad smile in the Phoenix's voice when she replies. "You do not want to hear of the dreams that make me crazy."*

*"Was I in this dream?" Ra asks, pushing for more despite her words.*

*"In a way. I dreamt of love."*

*Ra's smile is so brilliant, I can see it clearly through the rushes. "That sounds like a wonderful dream. Why would that make you crazy?"*

*The Phoenix sighs. "When you have loved as many times as I have, love and pain become blurred."*

*All teasing gone from his voice now, Ra turns her to face him. "Talk to me. Tell me of these dreams of love that haunt you."*

*My jaw drops open when I see the Phoenix. She looks like an Egyptian goddess. She has long, straight black hair, her skin is a soft tan, and her bone structure is somehow both strong and delicate. Her beauty outshines that of Cleopatra or Nefertiti. I guess she really can take whatever form she wants, and I suspect she always makes certain she is considered beautiful by each realm's standard.*

*Just when I am convinced that the Phoenix is not going to respond to Ra's pleas, she begins to speak. "These dreams bring themselves into my waking thoughts. They affect how my day will progress, and with the gentlest of nudges, they merge into my perception of reality. Past offenses of lovers long dead become the trespasses of my current lover.*

*"I try to remember that it is my own imagination to blame. I tell myself this is not real. He would not betray me as others have." I expect Ra to give her assurances at this point, but he doesn't speak. He doesn't want to interrupt her flow of words, recognizing she needs to get them out or she may never speak them to him. "Yes, we have had issues with trust, mostly on my part, and sometimes it feels as if I will never be able to move past them. But, you are a good man. I believe in you more than I have anyone else in my many lives, and I will not let my subconscious make me believe that this is all hopeless."*

*The Phoenix turns in Ra's arms so she is once again facing the Nile. "But, how to turn off the hum after it has submersed itself into my conscious mind. How do I push the anxiety and the fear away? I try to picture my mind rolling those feelings into the shape of small pebbles and watch as I skip them across a muddy river of empty souls who ruined their own chances of finding true love. The souls who were not willing to take another chance when necessary, when the one they love disappointed them in some small way. One is not enough. One chance. Who could possibly live up to those standards? I know I cannot. I ask for chance after chance. I move between the realms with the ease and grace of a chameleon camouflaging itself from its predators. I ask for trust, but in return must constantly veer from the straight line of truth."*

"Not with me," Ra reminds her gently.

*As if she didn't hear him, the Phoenix continues.* "Who has never strayed from the tight line of the truth, I ask myself. Truth is relative. We all have our own version. I try to make my mind see the reason in this, but despite my own lies, I am still devastated by the lies of others. Even after all this time. I am not the chameleon then. I am the wounded prey. I am the victim seeking revenge. I have done unspeakable things with my power to those who have betrayed me."

*After feeling a tiny bit of her Cosmic Fire, I imagine a heap of scorched bodies left in her wake. I can't help but shudder at the thought. Beside me, Eliana grimaces. Her thought process is obviously similar to mine.*

"How did I get here?" *the Phoenix asks herself more so than Ra.* "This is not who I am or how I want to feel. I *cannot move forward as long as I hold onto the past. 'Stop!' I scream inside my head. I tell myself over and over that I do not really feel this way, but I continue to be bombarded with these thoughts. The louder I scream for them to stop, the louder they scream back. 'We are right.' 'Do not trust.' 'Run, hide, stay inside your own soul. Do not let yourself be hurt again.'"*

*After a brief pause to wipe away a tear, the Phoenix continues. "But, what is life without the risk of pain? I have lived enough lives to know the loneliness following such a path. I cannot be so perverse as to say that I do not want love. I am not a fool. 'Take the risk yet again,' I tell myself. Each time I know I am gambling with my own sanity, but damn it, I will try. I dig deep inside myself for the courage and the strength to remain on the shore of that river of empty souls, to not let the erosion of the soft dirt beneath my feet carry me away with the current. I take a step back – not to safety, but from it – to learn how to love the scars that make love stronger. The scars of battles won and battles lost. I feel the intensity of the peace making process within me, and sometimes it burns."*

"I'm pretty sure that's her Cosmic Fire she's feeling," I mutter, then clamp a hand over my mouth. Eliana just *smiles at my inability to keep my thoughts in my head instead of on display for all to enjoy.*

*Finally, Ra responds to all the Phoenix has shared. He says simply, "Open your heart to me and I will soothe the humming that haunts you. I will cherish your soul and never let the emptiness you fear take hold of you."*

*He is kissing her now. Passionately. So passionately, I am starting to feel like this dream has shifted genre from drama to porn. "Um, do we need to stay for this?" I whisper to Eliana.*

She opens her mouth to respond, but I never get to hear what she says. My eyes are suddenly wide open and I can no longer hear the rushing current of the Nile or feel the soft rushes against my skin. Instead, I am being shaken by strong arms attached to my very concerned husband.

"Okay, I'm awake," I insist, pushing his hands away that are clutching at me a bit too tightly.

Relief washes over Kallen's face. "I have been trying to wake you for ten minutes," he informs me.

Ah, that explains the intense shaking. I run my tongue around my mouth to make sure he didn't rattle any of my teeth loose. When I am reassured that my smile will not resemble that of a cartoon hillbilly, I explain, "Ra pulled Eliana and me into a dream again."

Kallen's dark brows rise almost to his hairline. "Why?" He moves back so I can sit up.

Running a hand through my snarled hair, I shrug. "I'm not quite sure what the point was. He had Eliana and me eavesdrop on a conversation he had with the Phoenix when they were together. Well, not really a conversation," I correct. "More like a monologue on her part. She was talking about how she didn't trust love."

A soft knock on the door gets our attention. After making sure we are both appropriately dressed, Kallen climbs off the bed and opens the door. He invites Eliana and Josh in and closes the door after them. Josh takes a seat in one of the chairs across the room from our bed, but Eliana prefers to pace. "I'm not sure what we were supposed to gain from that conversation," she admits.

I shake my head. "Me, neither." I move to the edge of the bed and sit cross legged. "Maybe the Phoenix has given up on love altogether?"

"That seems likely," Eliana agrees. "But, would that make her want to destroy the universe? Seems a bit like overkill."

True, then again, how many times can one heart be broken before it can't take anymore? Even if it sits in the body of an immortal destined to travel the realms forever. "Revenge?" I suggest. "Maybe her last lover was a giant ass and she's mad enough at him to kill everyone and everything?" I think about Kallen betraying me. I just might get that angry. Fortunately, though, I wouldn't have the power to destroy the entire universe. Even more fortunate is the fact that Kallen would never do something so awful to make me feel that way. As if he can tell where my mind has gone, Kallen winks at me and smiles.

Josh interrupts our back and forth. "Would one of you mind telling Kallen and me exactly what happened in the dream?"

Eliana stops pacing. "Sorry," she says with a chagrined smile. She tells the guys what we heard. She has a great memory because it's almost word for word. Maybe Ra is helping her out with that?

When she is finished, Josh's brow dips in thought. "From what you've said, your ideas do seem the most likely. Hopelessness or revenge are likely motivators in her current actions."

"Maybe Jenna was right," Eliana says. "Maybe the most dangerous enemy of the Phoenix is herself."

I think back to the last words the Phoenix spoke and shake my head. "I don't know. She was pretty determined to change her way of thinking." With a frustrated sigh, I complain, "I wish we had more information about her lives. How many has she lived since that conversation with Ra? How many new loves has she had? Where has she been?"

"Can't you find that stuff out from the Angels?" Josh asks.

I snort. "Not likely. Other than cryptic messages here and there, they're not very forthcoming with useful information."

Eliana flops down in the chair next to Josh. "I don't understand how you can live with an omniscient being and not want to kill him on a daily basis for not telling you what he knows."

"Who says we do not?" Kallen mutters.

I glower up at him. "It's not Raziel's fault," I defend, even if I often feel that very thing.

Glancing at the clock on the bedside table, I curse under my breath. "If we're going to go to the dinosaur realm, we need to hurry. The Mermaids and Sirens should be here any minute." After dinner last night, we debated going there to get it over with. Ultimately, we decided we were too tired to go to yet another realm. Especially one that involved capturing a prehistoric creature. So, we put it off until this morning like we originally planned.

Eliana and Josh rise from their chairs and Josh grins. "Guess I better drag Sam out of bed, then. He'll be pissed if he misses his chance to see real dinosaurs. You know," he adds with a wicked glint in his eyes, "his entire bedroom was dinosaur themed when we were little. I'm pretty sure he still has some toy dinosaurs in a box in his closet."

Eliana laughs. "I believe it." The two of them go off in search of their friends.

After they close the door behind them, Kallen asks, "Do you really think this is about a broken heart?"

Again, I shake my head. "I really don't. I mean, yeah, the speech Ra wanted us to hear makes it seem like that, but I just don't think so. There's something we're missing. Call it a gut feeling."

"Perhaps Ra is only speculating," Kallen suggests. "Offering possibilities."

I shrug. "Could be. But, unless he decides to explain himself, which I seriously doubt will happen," ancient gods are just as cryptic as Angels according to Eliana, "then we'll never really know for certain." The price of getting the occasional help from immortal beings is having to guess how, exactly, they are trying to help you. I'm not always certain it's worth it.

## 26 Chapter

Sam and Jenna are already in the driveway when we get down there. We want to avoid the beach and our multiple guests. Despite Josh's claim that they would have to drag him out of bed, Sam is wide awake and he is wearing the broadest grin I have ever seen in my entire life. My stomach growls loudly as we approach them, but we are all opting to postpone breakfast until we get back for fear of making Sam's head explode with impatience. I give the house, and the kitchen, a longing glance over my shoulder before creating a passageway to the dinosaur realm.

"Why are we in a house?" Sam asks, not bothering to hide the disappointment in his voice as he steps through the passageway. "There were no houses when the dinosaurs roamed the earth."

"Technically, we're in a cave if that makes you feel better," I tell him. "This is where Raziel stays when he comes here."

"Oh," Sam replies, his illusions of the dinosaur realm still tainted by the homey cave with its comfortable furniture. Glancing around, he asks, "Does he keep the pterodactyl in a cage or something?"

I suspect if that was true, Sam's head really would explode. In disappointment. "No," I chuckle. "I just thought it would be safer to bring us here rather than take the chance of landing in the path of a T-Rex or a raptor."

His eyes gleaming again, Sam asks, "Are there really raptors here?"

Since I have not taken an inventory of the dinosaurs running free in this realm, I can only shrug and say, "Probably." I want to keep his hopes up.

"What are we waiting for, then?" Sam demands, searching for the exit.

Jenna swats his arm. "Stop being so impatient. We should come up with a plan before we go out there. I, for one, do not want to end up being an afternoon snack for a T-Rex. I'm scrawny and would probably get stuck in its teeth for weeks."

Eliana laughs at the idea. "I promise you will not become a dinosaur tooth pick."

"She was describing herself more as an annoying popcorn kernel than a toothpick," Sam points out.

Eliana rolls her eyes. "Fine, I won't let her become an annoying popcorn kernel, either."

"That's very kind of you either way," Jenna says dryly. "I still think we need a plan. Has anyone even brought what we need to catch the pterodactyl?"

I can't help a smile. "Um, I think we have that covered." I glance up at Kallen and suddenly he's holding a leather harness attached to a long rope. "You might want to put a muzzle on that," I note. I don't know for certain if pterodactyls bite, but I assume they do. Kallen nods and adds an additional piece of leather at the front of the harness.

"Okay, you have that covered. Do you know how to find the thing?" Jenna asks.

I turn back to the passageway that I haven't closed yet. "You're late," I call to the two Fallen Angels who have just exited through the kitchen door of Isla's house.

"Sorry," Adriel says through a yawn. "I overslept." The two of them pick up their pace and hurry through the passageway.

"Jenna was just asking if we knew where to find your friend," I say to Raziel.

"Oh, she never strays far from here," Raziel replies. I note he has some leaves and fruit in his pocket. Treats for the pterodactyl maybe?

"Do you come here that often?" Eliana asks.

"I used to," Raziel nods, then his eyes find Adriel. "I find I no longer crave the solitude." Adriel's cheeks pinken slightly, but she smiles up at him.

Sam clears his throat, interrupting the tender moment. "So, we should probably hurry, right?"

Josh punches his friend in the arm. "Way to kill a moment," he mumbles.

"He is right. You do need to hurry," Raziel nods.

I want to ask if he means in general, or if things are about to blow up, literally, in the very near future. I don't waste my breath because I know he won't be able to tell me. Instead, I usher my friends toward the exit. Since the cave isn't very big, it doesn't take long to be standing in front of the shimmering curtain of magic that keeps the dinosaurs out of Raziel's cave.

Sam starts to walk forward, but I grab his arm and pull him to a stop. "I wouldn't do that," I warn. I glance at Raziel who moves forward. It only takes a few seconds for him to lift the magic. Letting go of Sam's arm, I smile. "Now you can leave without being incinerated." I try not to laugh when his face blanches. The worst he would have received was a feeling of being zapped with a stun gun, but it's much more fun letting him believe otherwise.

Taking a step back, Sam says to Josh, "You go ahead. I'll be right behind you."

Josh shakes his head. "Such a coward," he mocks and strides through the exit. When he doesn't immediately burst into flames, Sam follows him out, the rest of us on his heels.

The last time I was in this realm, it was winter time and I nearly froze to death. This time, it's winter and I fear we may freeze to death. Fortunately, my gorgeous husband is a quick draw when it comes to magic. Each of us is suddenly wearing a warm parka and snow boots.

"How do you know what size?" Jenna asks, lifting her foot to inspect her new boots.

Kallen smiles. "The magic knows." Content with his answer, Jenna nods and puts her foot back down in the foot-deep snow.

"Aren't dinosaurs coldblooded?" Sam asks. "I thought they would prefer a warmer climate."

"That's still up for debate. Also, there were polar dinosaurs back home. Paleontologists have found dinosaur fossils in northern Alaska and remains of Antarctic dinosaurs from the late Cretaceous period," Josh informs him. When we all stare at his impressive dinosaur knowledge, his cheeks turn a little pinker than the cold should be making them. "I may have been a dinosaur geek as a kid, too."

Wrapping an arm around his waist, Eliana teases, "I think you still are."

A loud, ear-piercing shriek fills the air. Shielding my eyes from the glare of the sun on the snow, I search the skies. "Is that your friend?" I ask Raziel.

He chuckles. "That would be a pteranodon. Same family, but they are much bigger."

I roll my eyes and mutter, "Some of us haven't been alive long enough to be able to tell the difference between dinosaurs by the *sound* they make."

"Jealous?" Adriel fires back.

Before I can respond, the ground beneath us begins to shake rhythmically. "Um, is that an earthquake, or is something very large walking toward us?" Jenna asks nervously.

"The latter," Raziel says. "But it should not bother us." He points toward the top of a group of trees. "It is an herbivore." Sure enough, a dinosaur with a long neck is munching on the few leaves still left on the tree. There are several oohs and aahs from our group as we take in the sight.

Allowing the ogling to go on for only a moment, Kallen clears his throat. "As interesting as this is, we do need to find one dinosaur in particular."

"Technically, a pterodactyl isn't a dinosaur," Sam points out.

From the expression on his face, Kallen already knew this. "For our purposes, we believe it will be close enough." I hope he's right.

"There is a clearing not far from here where she likes to nest," Raziel says, pointing toward a break in the trees.

He begins trudging through the snow and the rest of us follow behind. There is little conversation as we walk.

Mostly due to the fact that the wind has picked up and is howling through our ears. We wouldn't be able to hear each other if we did speak. After about five minutes and half a frost-bitten foot, we arrive at our destination. Sure enough, there is a small clearing. An empty one.

"Um, you don't happen to have a special whistle or something to call the thing, do you?" I ask Raziel.

A tree directly across the clearing from us snaps in two with a loud crack. Even over the howling wind, the sound echoes its way to us. Followed by the sight of what snapped the tree in half. I admit, I am not a dinosaur expert. But, really, does it matter which set of giant teeth is eating you alive? I doubt knowing whether it is a T-Rex or one of its cousins would make a difference in pain levels and certainty of death.

"That is so cool!" Sam exclaims, almost giddy in his excitement.

"We'll see if you still feel that way when you become its lunch," Josh mutters.

"From the way it's eying us, I'm pretty sure it's not an herbivore," Jenna adds.

"Definitely not," I agree. The thing has teeth meant for ripping meat apart, not picking leaves from trees. If I didn't have magic, I'd be in fear for my life about now.

Hell, even with magic, coming face to face with a creature that's twice the size of a Dragon is pretty darn scary.

The shaking of the ground beneath our feet a few minutes ago was nothing compared to the shaking we feel now. We also have to shield our faces from the onslaught of snow blowing toward us. It seems a charging dinosaur is better than a snowplow when it comes to clearing a path in the snow.

"Are we just going to stand here and let it eat us?" Sam gulps. "Or do you guys have a plan."

"We have a plan," I assure him. Then I glance up at Kallen. "Right?"

Kallen reaches over and grabs my hand. "A wall of magic is all we need." I'd feel better if there was more confidence in his voice, but he's probably right. We can stop almost anything with a wall of magic.

"That will not be necessary," Raziel assures us. Before any of us can pull him back, he runs out into the clearing directly in the path of the dinosaur. We all watch in horror, waiting for the gruesome trampling and eating to occur. Not that we would be able to see it in any detail with all the snow flying around. Thank goodness.

On instinct, Kallen and I pull magic and prepare to thrust it toward the dinosaur before any of the gruesome images in my mind become real. But, Adriel calls out to us. "No, let him be. He knows what he is doing."

I glance back at her, scraping my bottom jaw on my shoulder. "Are you serious?" Adriel nods and she looks pretty darn confident. So, Kallen and I don't throw our magic at the dinosaur. Neither do we let it go. Best to be prepared since Adriel's judgement may be blinded by unconditional love.

But, she is not wrong. The rest of us watch in amazement, and Adriel simply watches, as the giant creature stops in its tracks. I'm not a physics expert, but it seems something that large would need a bit more braking room than the several yards in which it came to a full stop. Obviously, there is magic involved. I try to use my internal magic detector to pick up on it and am surprised to not feel a thing. I glance up at Kallen who looks just as confused as I am. So, I direct my question to the only one not surprised by what just happened. "How the hell did he do that?"

Adriel shrugs. "The dinosaurs love him."

I narrow my eyes at her. "Really? That's the answer you're going with?"

With a smug grin, she replies, "Yup." My eyes narrow even farther as she is probably making fun of my frequent use of Cowan slang now.

"I think she's right. Look," Eliana exclaims, drawing my attention back to the scene before us.

I shake my head. This cannot be happening. The giant dinosaur cannot be nuzzling its nose against Raziel's hand like it's just a giant puppy.

"There's another one," Josh points out. "A little one by the bushes. It's going to join them." Sure enough, a small raptor like thing approaches Raziel, who holds a hand out for it to sniff.

"If he loses a finger, I am not reattaching it," I grumble.

"You would, too," Adriel says dryly. She's right. I would reattach any limb or digit someone I care about may have lost. Even if they were doing something incredibly stupid when they lost it. Like petting carnivorous dinosaurs. I'm a good friend like that.

Proving that his patience can be as short of mine, Kallen calls out when a third dinosaur joins the mix, "We really do not have time for a reunion with all of your reptilian friends."

Raziel glances back at us sheepishly. "Of course, sorry. They bring me peace, and I lose track of time here." Since dinosaurs have limited mental capacity, they do not constantly badger him for information.

"Dinosaurs bring him peace?" Sam asks in surprise.

I just shrug. "To each their own." I figure Raziel's reason for liking it here is personal. I'll let him share if he wants to do so.

"I guess," Sam agrees. Then he asks, "Do you think they will let us pet them?"

"Absolutely not," Adriel drawls, bursting his dinosaur dream bubble.

A shadow falls over us for a second before moving on toward Raziel. A high pitched shriek not much different than the one we heard earlier pierces the air, though different enough to know that it is not the pteranodon again. "That's a pterodactyl, right?" I ask Josh and Sam.

"Pretty sure," Josh says, then admits "but seeing them in real life is definitely different than seeing drawings in books. I can't be certain." Understandable.

The question is answered when the giant bird creature lands next to Raziel and nuzzles at the pocket holding leaves and fruit. Raziel turns and nods at us. Yes, this is the one. "Great," I sigh. "That thing has a wingspan at least twenty feet wide."

"Probably only fifteen or so," Kallen corrects.

I glower up at him. "Yes, that five feet makes a huge difference when it comes to concealing it in the Cowan realm," I snark.

He raises a brow. "It could have been worse. Some have a wingspan as great as forty feet." I guess I should be grateful we didn't end up with one of those.

After whispering in the pterodactyl's ear, Raziel creates his own harness with a leash. It's much less restricting than the one Kallen made, which makes me nervous. Raziel slowly puts the harness over the creature's neck and moves around to fasten it behind its back and wings. When it is secure, he leads the thing back to us. The other dinosaurs give him what can only be called forlorn looks before turning back toward the direction they came. I didn't even know dinosaurs could feel forlorn let alone express it on their reptilian faces. I suspect these dinosaurs are not quite the same as the ones we had back in the Cowan realm.

Jenna takes several steps back as Raziel approaches. "Does it bite?" she asks him.

"Only other dinosaurs and fish," the Fallen Angel replies with a smile.

Jenna is not convinced. "You're sure it doesn't want to find out what people taste like?"

"Being eaten by a dinosaur is not in your future," Raziel assures her with a wink. I raise a surprised eyebrow in his direction and he shrugs. "I am not affecting her freewill by telling her thus."

"Uh huh. So, if I list off possible ways I could die, will you tell me yes or no?"

"No."

"That's what I thought." Turning my attention to the more immediate matter, I ask, "Is it going to follow you through the passageway?"

"More importantly, is it going to obey your commands, or will it try to escape once in a new realm?" Kallen asks. I'm not sure that's more important. I would say our questions are equal. I try to convey that idea with my sour look in his direction.

"Rest assured, she will cooperate," Raziel says, absently petting the pterodactyl's wing.

"Good enough for me," I say. "I'm too cold to walk back to the cave, so I'm going to open up a passageway here." Without waiting for a response, I do so.

From out of nowhere, the stupid little raptor like dinosaur comes tearing through the snow. It leaps through the passageway like it just found the world's largest free buffet of gourmet food. Which it may have. I've personally never tasted Fairy, but anything would have to better than other dinosaurs.

"That can't be good," Sam says. Unnecessarily, in my opinion.

Through the passageway, I find Isla glowering at us. "I certainly hope you plan to catch that."

Fortunately, Kallen is already on it. With a lasso of magic, he impressively ropes the small dinosaur and drags it back through the sand to its own realm. I smile up at him, promising with my eyes to make it up to him later. He winks at me and nods.

"That was awesome, man!" Sam exclaims.

With a proud smile, I agree. "Yes, he is." Sam rolls his eyes as he meant the action, not necessarily the Fairy like I do.

"You two are almost as bad as them," Sam complains, jabbing his thumb toward Eliana and Josh. This earns him a solid punch in the arm from Josh.

"Perhaps you should come through before another mishap occurs," Isla drawls.

She's correct. We step through the passageway from the frigid cold to the warm, salty air of the beach. Kallen pulls his magic back and the parka's and boots disappear. Raziel is the last to come through, and he was right. The pterodactyl follows him without any fuss at all. It's probably too much to hope for that the rest of its time with us will be this easy, though.

Darn it. I keep telling myself I won't challenge the universe like that. When will I ever learn? I am just going to ahead and assume it will be never.

## 27 CHAPTER

"What the hell is that?!" a deep voice booms from the Giants' tent.

Startled, the pterodactyl stretches out its wings, knocking Sam and Jenna to the ground in the process, and lets out a loud shriek. It pushes off the ground and prepares to take flight. Kallen and I both pull magic to keep it grounded, but Raziel already has the situation under control. He lays soothing hands on the prehistoric creature and is able to calm it.

Since he has that under control, I have plenty of time to turn and glower at the Giant Chieftain. Between gritted teeth, I grind out, "If you scare it away, I am going to send you to its realm to get another one. And trust me when I say, she's just a baby compared to the other creatures who live there."

Since the pterodactyl stands about as tall as Quinn and has a much greater wingspan, the Giant blanches. Something he quickly tries to cover up with bravado. Puffing out his chest, he says, "I will gladly hunt more creatures such as this one."

I roll my eyes and mutter under my breath, "I would love to introduce him to a T-rex." Beside me, Josh covers his snicker with a cough.

Kallen has helped Sam and Jenna back to their feet. They don't look injured, thank god. Still, I ask, "Are you two okay?"

Jenna nods but she's rubbing the arm that was hit with the pterodactyl's wing. "I might be a bit bruised tomorrow, but I'm okay."

"Same," Sam says.

"No, you won't," I assure them. I move closer, careful to make a wide path around the now calm pterodactyl, and put my hands on both of them. I use my magic to heal any part of their bodies that may have been injured.

Jenna smiles widely. "Thanks." I suspect her arm hurt a lot more than she wanted to let on.

"I am going to bring her around back," Raziel says. He begins to lead the pterodactyl toward the back of the house.

"Now will you explain what manner of creature that is?" Quinn asks.

I glance toward the pterodactyl to make sure Quinn's voice hasn't startled it again. He was quieter this time, but maybe the creature didn't react to his volume last time, but his stupidity. Hmm, if the thing really does have an internal stupidity meter, it might be worth keeping around after all this is over. Then again, stupid tends to out itself sooner as opposed to later in most people all on its own.

"It is a dinosaur," I explain. I give Sam a warning look when he opens his mouth to say that is not technically true. He closes his lips and bites his tongue. Something I suspect doesn't happen often.

"I thought all the dinosaurs were extinct in the Cowan world," an Elf I don't recognize asks.

"We did not retrieve this one from the Cowan realm," Kallen tells her.

"Then where did it come from?" a Sasquatch asks. It might be one I know. The Sasquatch are very similar in appearance with their androgynous faces and hair covered bodies. I am not always discerning enough to pick up on the subtle differences in the shades of white of their hair.

I open my mouth to respond, but Kallen grabs my hand. "We need to prepare for departure as it seems everyone has assembled." He nods a greeting to Arie and Kai, but ignores the Siren standing with them. I guess he still holds a grudge against the Sirens for allowing their leader to kidnap him and try to enslave him for all eternity. He's funny that way.

Kallen tugs on my hand and I follow him up the terrace steps and inside the house. Our friends follow after. Once we are far enough from the beach that no one out there will hear me, I pull my husband to a stop and demand, "What was that all about?"

With a raised brow, Kallen responds, "Do you really want the Sasquatch or the Giants to go looking for the dinosaur realm?"

I am not the only one confused. "Why would that be a problem?" Josh asks. "Could they even access it without Xandra's power?" He knows I am the only one who can tear holes in the fabric of the realms.

Then it hits me and I stare up at Kallen in disgust. "You think they would try to weaponize *dinosaurs*?"

He shrugs. "Let a giant carnivore loose on an unsuspecting population and suddenly you have a new realm to live in."

"Who could be that horrible?" Jenna exclaims. Her eyes travel toward the beach and there's a little more fear in her expression than there was a minute ago.

"No one, if we can help it," I mutter, determined as Kallen now to keep the dinosaur realm a secret.

"To answer your other question," Kallen says to Josh, "there are access points between all realms. You simply need to find them."

"No one has found the dinosaur realm before now?" Sam asks in surprise.

Kallen shrugs. "If they have, they have not returned to tell about it."

Understanding the implications of that statement, Jenna shakes her head and says, "Eew."

"You have returned," a tired Dagda says through a yawn. He's standing in the doorway to the kitchen with a cup of steaming coffee in his hand.

"Didn't get much sleep last night?" I ask.

He shakes his head. "I spent the evening fielding requests and demands from our guests. I had to send more guards to keep the Sasquatch and the Centaurs apart."

A little bit of guilt tries to climb up my spine. We were right here last night and could have handled all of that. Then I think about how Kallen and I spent the evening, and I am suddenly feeling more glad than guilty that we were not interrupted.

Following at least part of my train of thought, Dagda says, "I thought it best to let you rest. You may have quite a fight ahead of you today."

"Maybe the Phoenix will be so impressed we gathered everyone she insisted upon that she will say, 'Okay, I'm ready to die again now.'" My words obviously fall upon unanimously unbelieving ears from the looks everyone in the room is giving me. "It could happen," I say defensively. This was as unconvincing as my first sentence. "Fine," I grumble. "It's going to suck."

Clearing his throat, Dagda says, "I should prepare the others for departure." He strides forward, gives me a quick hug and a kiss on the top of my head, then disappears out the terrace door. His uncharacteristic behavior does nothing to soothe my nerves, but I smile. I like having two fathers who care about me.

When Dagda is out of sight, Jenna asks Eliana, "Are you sure you don't want us to come along?"

Eliana shakes her head. "I would feel much better knowing that you are safe."

"Technically, no one is safe," Sam points out. "If the Phoenix refuses to die, we are all goners."

"Helpful of you to point that out," Josh snarks.

Sam glares at him. "My point is, what difference does it make if we are in danger here or with you?"

There is sympathy in her eyes as Eliana answers him. She understands his desire to fight for his future, but he simply doesn't have the power necessary to be of actual help to us. "Because Xandra and I already have a crowd of people to keep safe. We have no idea what is going to happen, and if there is to be a fight, we already have our hands full."

I know that Sam is about to argue something along the lines of 'what difference does two more make' when Jenna elbows him in the ribs. "We understand. After all," she gives Sam a pointed look, "we did promise to not argue about going along for the dangerous stuff if you let us come here with you."

A sheepish expression washes over Sam's face when he is reminded of this. "Yeah, I guess we did."

"We'll stay here and see if we can figure anything else out about the Phoenix," Jenna adds.

I smile appreciatively at her for ending the argument with such efficiency. She is used to handling Sam and his curiosity. I don't blame him for being curious, but what Eliana didn't say was that she will protect those outside to the absolute best of her ability. But, if one of them dies on her watch, she would not be devastated like she would be losing one of these two. It sounds harsh even thinking it, but it doesn't make it any less true. Nor does it mean she won't fight as hard for the strangers on the beach. I get it. I would feel the same way if Alita wanted to come with us.

Glancing down at the jeans and long sleeve sweater I donned this morning to travel to the frigid dinosaur world, I say, "We should change into something a little more suited for the desert. Then we'll head out."

"After breakfast," Kallen insists much to Josh's relief.

Oh, yeah. I got so wrapped up in dinosaurs that I forgot we left for their realm before breakfast. As if on cue, the smell of bacon wafts into the room. A blur of black shoots past us toward the kitchen. He goes by so fast,

I'm not even certain which direction he came from. I shake my head. The only thing that gets my Familiar moving that fast is bacon.

"After breakfast," I agree and the rest of us follow Taz into the kitchen at a little less hectic of a pace.

## 28 Chapter

"So," Sam begins around a mouthful of pancakes, "how are you planning to get everyone to the Cowan realm?"

I've been wondering that myself. Opening a hole between the realms in the middle of the desert is risky. Keeping it open long enough for everyone to get through it is riskier. The chance of an Egyptian government satellite picking up images of Dragons, Goblins, Giants, Centaurs, Sasquatch, Fauns and dinosaurs? That's the biggest risk of all. At least the rest of them could pass for Cowans. The Elves might have to hide their pointy ears, though.

Surely, someone would be sent out to investigate once the images were seen. What if they showed up in the middle of whatever is going to happen? But, there is no way I can bring everyone through my old house in

Colorado and then teleport them all to Egypt. I considered asking the Angels for help until I remembered that we weren't supposed to receive any help from immortal beings. The Phoenix's rules suck in this sick game of 'Try to Save the Universe'.

Reading my mind, Kallen puts a comforting hand at the small of my back. "I cannot think of another way, either." Sam gives him a quizzical look and Kallen explains. "Xandra will have to simply open a passageway between realms in the middle of the desert and hope that we avoid any type of surveillance the Cowans may be using."

"Considering where the Phoenix temple is located, I doubt there is much surveillance out there," Josh says. He takes a swig of his orange juice in an effort to hide the doubt in his expression.

"If it was farther away from the Heliopolis area, I would agree," Eliana sighs. "Since it's not, we would be taking quite a risk."

"Why don't you get ahold of Agent Amman and see if he can do something to prevent anyone from getting satellite images?" Sam asks before shoveling more pancake into his mouth. He obviously appreciates Tabitha's culinary skills.

"I don't think that's his department," Eliana replies. "Besides, it's not only the Egyptian government's satellite that could be an issue."

"Not to mention, I don't think anyone would be able to keep it quiet. Dragons? Centaurs? Big foot?" Josh shakes his head. "It would be on the front page of every newspaper in the world."

I sigh. "Then, we hope we get lucky." Please, universe, do not take that as a challenge. Pushing my nearly empty plate away, I stand up. "We really need to get going."

Eliana stands and circles the island counter. She pulls Sam and Jenna into a big hug. "I'll see you soon," she promises.

I am impressed by how believable her words are. Either Eliana is way more confident than I am, or she is a better liar. Since I am not feeling like bugs are crawling on me, I guess it's the former. I can't help but smile. I am so glad she's on my team.

Josh gives Jenna a hug, but Sam just gets a fist bump. "Don't get killed," Sam tells him.

"I'll do my best," Josh replies dryly. I would wonder about the closeness of their friendship if the concern and fear wasn't so apparent in Sam's eyes. He meant his words.

He is ordering his friend to come back alive. Since the only way Josh can die is if Eliana dies, and the only way Eliana is going to die is if I die, and the only way I'll die is if Kallen dies, or vice versa, I'm going to do my damnedest to make certain Josh follows his friend's order.

Jenna and Sam leave the remnants of their breakfast and follow us out to the terrace. Dagda has the band of misfits we will be travelling with assembled in a line in the sand. There is a bit of jostling for first in line, but Dagda works it out. When he wants to be, he is a master negotiator. That's never really helped him in our relationship, but it's good to see that others listen to him.

"They got bacon in this realm of yours?" a voice asks from my ankles.

"Not in the middle of the desert," I inform my Familiar.

"Get your mind off food," Felix growls next to him.

"You know," I say to them both, "I'm only supposed to bring females with me."

"Then put me in a dress and call me Franny, but you are not going without me," Taz insists.

"Nor me," Felix concurs.

"Besides, what do you call the two wankers standing next to you?" Taz points out, indicating Kallen and Josh. "Are you implying they are not male?"

"Good point," I mumble. Josh and Kallen would absolutely refuse to be left behind, so Eliana and I haven't even bothered to try.

"Xandra," Dagda calls from the beach. "It's time."

Kallen glances down at me, his lips pressed into a firm line. When we discussed this at dinner last night, he was not in favor of me using so much magic before we even leave the realm. I tried to reassure him it wouldn't be that big of a spell, but when I couldn't stop squirming in my chair, he knew I was lying. Eventually, the merits of the plan outweighed his concern enough for him to quit arguing about it. They did not erase his worry, though.

Pulling magic through me, I close my eyes and quietly begin to recite the spell that pops into my head. *"Worry and fear for those who are dear, an admirable trait when none know their fate. A riddle spun, the answer undone. A request made and must be obeyed. Except these four, we take no more. Those left behind in fear and grief, sleep is all I can offer as relief."*

Before the meaning of my spell can become clear in their minds, all of the males on the beach slump to the sand.

Including Dagda. He thought it only fair that he be included. I think it's because he's planning to claim plausible deniability, but I didn't delve too deeply into his reasons. He's the one who will be left behind with all the angry males who had planned to accompany the females from their realm. Over the last couple of days, Taz and Felix had overheard more than one conversation about said males trying to take matters into their own hands when confronted with the obstinate Phoenix. This whole situation is a big enough mess. I have no intention of letting anyone make it worse.

"Time to go," I inform the shocked females as I descend the terrace steps.

Well, not all of them are shocked. Ari shakes her head as I walk by her. "I warned Kai you would not allow him to accompany me."

I give her a sheepish grin. "So, let's get out of here before he wakes up and tries to kill me instead of the Phoenix."

Ari cocks a brow. "I don't even want to know how you knew that was his intention." Her eyes glance down toward my ankles and the light of knowledge shines from her eyes. "I guess we all need Familiars," she mutters. With a last glance at her husband sleeping soundly in the sand, Ari follows me on the two legs she has now instead of a fish tail. Kallen gives her a hand when she finds the sand a little difficult to manage at first. When she is stable, he drops her arm and comes to stand next to me as I prepare to make a passageway to the Cowan realm.

Isla catches my eye from where she is standing several yards away. We had not discussed it at any point before now, but everything about her radiates that she is ready for a fight. Her stance, her expression, the magic swirling around her. She's coming with us.

A grin forms on my lips and I give her a slight nod of approval. I knew in my heart, if not in my mind, that she would not be able to stay away. I glance up at Kallen and whisper, "I hope I am still as brave as she is when I reach her age."

Kallen leans down and gives me a quick kiss. "Neither age nor time could possibly diminish your courage with any significance. You simply have too much of it."

Yes, and let's hope that it doesn't become the death of me. Or the rest of the universe.

## 29 Chapter

*Ra, I could really use your help.* I utter this silent plea in my mind. Since I don't have an internal GPS system, and the Sahara Desert is vast, I need a little help making it back to the exact spot of the Phoenix's temple. As if answering my silent prayer, Eliana moves closer and stretches her hand out. I put mine in it before closing my eyes and reaching out to open a passageway. A clear image appears in my mind of the temple, and I know I have picked the right spot. I open my eyes and Eliana nods. She can sense the temple.

Eliana is the first to go through. She walks several hundred feet away from the passageway and begins to excavate the temple as she did before. Kallen, Josh and I usher the beings the Phoenix requested through. I suspect Raziel may have used a small amount of magic on the pterodactyl, because it is now obeying Josh as it had the Fallen Angel. If he did, I hope it's not enough for the Phoenix to sense. She was adamant about no help from other immortals. Since Raziel is omniscient, I am going to assume it is not. Though, I'm still surprised. It feels a little bit like cheating, something I didn't think the Fallen Archangel would do.

Most of the beings come through without incident. It is not until the Sasquatch tries to cut in front of the Centaur that we have a problem. Suddenly, a spear is drawn and it is met by a sword. I move closer to them and hiss, "Do you really think the Phoenix is not watching? The whole point of this was to get along in her presence." To add more of an impact to my little reminder, I make both of their weapons disappear. Pointing at the Sasquatch, I growl, "Get back in line." She hesitates for a moment, but after glancing between me and Kallen, she decides it is not worth the fight. Or the embarrassing loss.

The Dragon comes through last and she is carrying the cage with one of the Pixie's. The tiny green monster sticks its tongue out at me as the Dragon plods by, then shouts over its shoulder, "What is the Phoenix going to think of me being in a cage?"

"That we're not stupid," I inform the female Pixie.

The Pixie laughs and nods. "Probably." After glancing around, she says, "You're not planning to leave me in this god forsaken place, are you?"

Considering all the ancient Egyptian gods abandoned this area many millennia ago, I guess she's right. It is god forsaken. "Depends," I shrug indifferently.

The Pixie narrows her eyes, then says to the Dragon, "Bring me closer to her." The Dragon ignores her. Whether that is because she wants me to be at full power, or whether she didn't actually hear the tiny creature, I'm not certain. Either way, she keeps plodding away while I close the passageway.

"I could bite her for you," Felix offers.

"Tempting," I mutter, but I shake my head. That would not seem very peaceful if the Phoenix really is watching us.

Everyone else is focused on Eliana now. Especially the Dragon, who is staring at her in awe. From what I can tell, she has almost reached the temple. I take a moment to gaze at our eclectic group. A tiny bit of fear passes through me as my eyes go from being to being. I really hope I haven't brought them all here to be sacrifices to Cosmic Fire.

My adrenaline begins to kick in when the roof of the temple becomes visible. I feel Kallen stiffen beside me, preparing himself mentally and physically for whatever comes next. I reach over and curl my fingers around his. He gives me a tight smile, then goes back to watching Eliana's progress.

When the temple is fully visible, I address the crowd. "Eliana and I are going to go in. You will stay here with Kallen and Josh." I give the Sasquatch and the Centaur the evil eye. "Calmly and quietly." Both give me curt nods in acknowledgement of the underlying threat in my voice. Satisfied, I give Kallen a quick kiss, then move to Eliana's side. "Ready?" I ask my friend.

"As ready as I'll ever be," she responds.

Since I can't ask for more, I reach out and take her hand. In a blink, we are standing in front of the temple in the middle of the hole Eliana dug. Before either of us can lose our nerve, we approach the door. This time, it opens on its own. I suspect that means it will close again on its own once we're inside. With a final glance over my shoulder at Kallen, I step into the gloom of the temple. I was right, the door slams shut behind us. Neither Eliana nor I are startled by it this time.

Eliana creates a small orb of light so we can see the walls. We grab two of the torches, which she lights, and make our way to the end of the hall where it splits off into two different directions. "Left or right?" I ask Eliana. Last time, it was to the left, but who knows, the Phoenix may have gotten bored on that side and moved to the right.

Eliana's forehead scrunches in concentration. After a few minutes of wondering if she actually heard me, I open my mouth to ask my question again. Before words come out, Eliana turns to me and says, "I can't sense her at all."

"What?!"

"There seems to be no one here except us."

This can't be good. Not good at all. "Was it all a ruse? Did she send us on a wild goose chase to give herself a chance to escape?" I wonder aloud.

Tensing beside me, Eliana says quietly, "I take that back, we are not alone."

I feel it now, too. A presence. A dark presence. One so dark, I feel like it's oozing tar all over my senses. I can feel the weight of it on my skin. My skin that suddenly feels like it's on fire. So much so, I glance down at myself to make certain I'm not actually being covered in hot tar. To my surprise, I'm not. I glance at Eliana who is doing her own body check. "What is going on?" I whisper.

"I have no idea," she whispers back.

I am getting a strange feeling of déjà vu and I don't like it. It seems like I've felt a presence like this before. Not necessarily one that has made me feel like I'm on fire, but the darkness. Slowly, the feeling of déjà vu morphs into an actual memory. "Shadows," I murmur.

"What?" Eliana asks.

"The presence, or whatever it is, it feels like the darkness from the Shadow realm."

Nonplussed, Eliana says, "I'm afraid you will need to be more specific. What is the Shadow realm again, and what kind of darkness is there?"

I grimace. For once, I wish I was the most ignorant person in the room. It would save a lot of time if Eliana already knew this stuff. I suppose Kallen feels like that a lot with me. "Hell, basically," I tell her. "The condensed version is that all the bad stuff the Angels of Death scrape off souls gets put in that realm. Eventually, the scraped bits join other scraped bits and become, well, sentient Shadow creatures."

"Can Shadows leave the Shadow realm?" Eliana asks, obviously hoping the answer is no. I can't blame her. Who wants to hear that pure evil has a get out of jail free card?

As we speak, the dark presence is moving ever closer to us and overwhelming our senses. Now, it feels like the hot tar has been set on fire. "No," I whisper back. "Not usually," I amend, thinking back to my little brother being possessed by Shadows before I rescued him from the Shadow realm.

Eliana scowls at me for my wishy-washy response. "Any way to know for certain?"

I don't have a good answer for her. "The Angels usually keep them locked up pretty tight. I can't see them letting any escape." I grimace. Without my help, anyway. Then, I remember that there is an Angel of Death right outside who might be able to answer the question for us. If only the door wasn't locked up tight. "We need Adriel. She's the only one who would know for certain." At Eliana's surprised expression, I add, "Kind of her job, remember?"

"Oh, yeah." Eliana glances back down the hall toward the door. "I don't think that's a possibility."

Unfortunately, neither do I. So, the only option left is to try to deal with this ourselves. Considering the fact that it is getting closer, I am going to assume that this Shadow, or whatever it is, has had enough time to become at least somewhat sentient. "Keep the torch close," I whisper to Eliana. "They don't like light." Then, I remember that she could encircle both of us with fire on a whim if necessary and smile sheepishly at her. "Guess you have the light thing covered, huh?"

"I do," she agrees, forcing a smile on her face. "I just hope it's enough."

Me, too. I guess it's time for us to engage, then. "Hello?" I call out. "Phoenix? Are you in here?" Yes, I sound like an idiot. It would have sounded worse if I had said, 'Hey, Boogeyman Shadow Thing, what's going on?'

No response. I raise a brow at Eliana, hoping she'll give it a shot. I am surprised to find her eyes glowing red. Even more surprising? She's sporting a goddess as a robe. At least, I assume that the shimmering image over her is Isis. Now is probably not a good time to ask. I even bite down on my tongue before it gets any stupid ideas.

"Show yourself, you foul fiend, so I can rid this plane of your existence!" Isis demands. Well, that would piss off anyone, even if they were not a foul fiend. Wow, someone less diplomatic than me. I am amazed.

"Maybe we shouldn't go right to threats," I suggest between gritted teeth.

I can sense Eliana's internal struggle. She is trying to pull the goddess back, to regain control. I wish I could help her, but I suspect my magic would only make things worse for her. It takes a moment before the shimmering image of Isis is gone, but Eliana's eyes are still glowing red. She nods at me to let me know she is back in control, but I am definitely asking her about the eye thing later. If there is a later.

Turning my attention back to the thing that may decide that, I say loudly, "We have brought the Phoenix those she asked to see."

"LIES!" a voice hisses through our minds, much like the Phoenix spoke to us before. Only this thing has its volume turned all the way up and the word is now echoing back and forth in my brain. I feel like a church bell. If I open my mouth, I'm positive I would sound like one as the echoes escaped through my lips. I put my hands over my ears as if that will help. It doesn't. I don't feel quite as stupid when I see Eliana doing the same thing. She doesn't get any relief, either.

"Could you tone it down a bit? We're trying to have a conversation here, which is a lot easier if our ears aren't bleeding," I grumble.

"Just like a mortal to confuse telling lies with conversing," the voice hisses. This time, it is several decibels lower, but you could still hang me in a belfry and call people to church on Sunday.

"Seriously, stop doing that!" I exclaim. "Can't you speak in a normal voice? Or did you lose that ability when you lost your body?"

"I still have a body," the voice hisses. This time, it's voice is considerably lower. I think I insulted it by saying it had no control. Good to know I can get under its skin. Wait, it still has a body? "You're not a Shadow?" I ask in confusion.

"Not for much longer," the voice growls.

"Okay, so you are a Shadow. Now I'm even more confused. How can you have a body if you're a Shadow?" I am beginning to suspect how, but I don't want to give it ideas if I'm wrong.

Apparently deciding it does not need to answer that question, the Shadow hisses, "Why have you really returned?"

I glance at Eliana in confusion before saying, "I told you. We brought everyone the Phoenix requested we bring."

"Impossible!" the Shadow shouts at full volume again.

"Ow!" I shout back as loudly as I can. "Fine, if you want to speak at this volume, we'll both do it." Childish, but I'm trying to prove a point. Except, Shadows don't really have ears that can bleed. Damn. When the stone walls vibrate a little at the loudness of my voice, Eliana gives me a pointed look. The Shadow is being loud in our heads. The echoes in there are much less likely to affect the integrity of the temple. I grimace in acknowledgement and return my voice to normal. "Look, I thought it was impossible, too, at first. But, I've done a lot of work with those from other realms, and I've gotten many of them to trust me. Not to mention, no one wants the universe to end. So, they all agreed to come along. Peacefully and voluntarily," I add, just so it's clear I didn't force anyone to come.

The roar that the Shadow lets out is deafening. Literally. My ears are ringing, and I actually feel my ear drums shatter. I think I'm going to vomit from the pain. To make matters worse, I lose my balance when I am suddenly propelled backwards. Just as I couldn't fight the force of the Phoenix before, I can't fight off the hold the Shadow has on me. So, the only thing left to do is put my hands on my head and prepare for my fingers to shatter when I am rammed into the door. I'm hoping they will provide enough cushion to save my skull from shattering, as well. I am so worried about that, I hardly even notice the burning sensation and scrapes on my back as I'm shoved along the sandy floor. My skin was smooth enough, it really didn't need a sandpaper treatment. Poor Eliana is sliding right along next to me. I really wish I could have spared her from all of this.

"Door!" Eliana shouts and reaches for my hand.

Understanding, I grab her hand in mine and I pull hard on the magic trapped in the earth. The murky, polluted Cowan realm magic. I hope it's enough. Pulling on Eliana's power as well as my own, I ram it all toward the door. The explosion of sand and stone would probably have been terrible if I wasn't already deaf.

"It worked," I mutter in both shock and relief. That is the last thing I am able to say before I am buried upside down in the sand all the way to my waist and my mouth and nose fill with sand. At least we're no longer being sanded like an old table that needs refurbishing. Often, it's the little things in life that make it bearable.

# 30 Chapter

I'm not really claustrophobic, but I think panicking when your mouth and nose are filled with sand and you are buried upside down all the way up to your waist is normal. I can only imagine what we look like with only our legs dangling out of the sand. So, I do what I do best. I throw magic at the problem. Unfortunately, my magic and Eliana's magic are not working well together in the excavation process. I can even feel Kallen's magic in the mix as he tries to help. As one of our magic digs a hole, someone else's fills it up as it digs a different hole. Including the holes now being physically dug by my ever faithful Familiars. I can hear Taz cursing as his efforts become ever more futile. If we keep this up, Eliana and I are going to suffocate sooner rather than later. I decide I need to push my panic aside and let Eliana do the heavy lifting here. She will be much more efficient. And timely.

As soon as I let my magic go, I feel Kallen's pull back. He must have realized the same thing I did. Taz and Felix also back off. Now that it has no competition, Eliana's power takes over and within seconds, I can feel the hot desert sun beating down on my face. I open my eyes, which is a mistake because there is still some sand on them, and wince as the particles fall onto my eyeballs. Turning to the side, I cough out as much sand as I can from my lungs and attempt to blow it out of my nose. Gross and vulgar, yes, but I'll take breathing over being decorous any day. I use my magic to heal my ear drums and to rid my body of any stray sand granules I couldn't cough or blow out. Including the ones that got stuck in very uncomfortable places as I was dragged through the sand. Any thoughts Kallen may have of ever making love on the beach again have been rendered moot by this experience.

By the time I am done, Kallen is by my side. He and Josh slid down the sand dune, risking a sand avalanche to get to us. I can't be mad because I would have done the same thing if the situation was reversed. Josh makes his way to Eliana and pulls her into his arms. Since she is conversing quietly with him, I am assuming she healed her own ears and doesn't need any help from me. So, I fall into Kallen's open arms and let him hug me tight.

"What the hell happened in there?" he breathes into my ear through my sandy hair. I didn't worry about getting the sand out of my hair, other places were a bit more urgent, so there's a lot of it. I feel him using his tongues to get stray granules he came into contact with off his lips. Normally, I'd be concerned he was getting spittle in my hair, but right now I really don't care.

"There's a Shadow in there," I respond into his muscular chest.

Kallen leans back so he can see my face. "What?"

"You heard me correctly. There's a Shadow in there." I glance up the sand dune Eliana created when excavating the temple. "We need to talk to Adriel." I hate to break up the passionate kiss Josh is giving Eliana at the moment, but I do. Clearing my throat to get their attention, I say, "I'm going to teleport us to the top." The two reluctantly split apart and reach out for the hand I've extended. Taz and Felix make sure they are touching me, as well. In a blink, we are all back where we started. This day is not going at all as we planned, I sigh to myself. Then again, can wishful thinking and 'we'll just have to wing it' really be considered a plan? We really need to work on our strategy skills.

"What happened down there?" several voices demand at once. Some concerned for our safety, but most concerned for their own.

"Are your great abilities not enough?" the Sasquatch snarks. Would it be wrong to punch her? Or to shave her bald? I'm certain the latter would be a much greater punishment in her mind.

The idea is gaining momentum in my mind when Kallen steps between us. "If you believe this to be an easy task, you are welcome to try to resolve it on your own," he drawls.

"Perhaps I shall," the Sasquatch responds obstinately.

I roll my eyes. "Be quiet before I insist you follow through on those words." Since her claim was only a show of bravado with no real substance behind it, the Sasquatch clamps her mouth closed. Convinced she is going to keep it that way, I hurry over to Adriel and tug on her arm until she follows me away from the prying ears of the crowd. I gesture for Eliana, Josh, Isla and Kallen to join us, as well. I feel bad leaving Ari and Jadyn out, but I don't want to be accused of playing favorites. When we are a short distance away, I ask Adriel, "How could a Shadow have gotten here?"

"What?!" Adriel squeaks. She honestly squeaks. I didn't even know she could make a sound like that. I don't think she did, either. Embarrassed by her initial reaction, her voice is back to normal when she says, "You must be mistaken."

"Since I have been up close and personal with the Shadows, I'm pretty sure I can identify one. Not to mention, it said it was a Shadow," I insist.

"It also said it has a body," Eliana points out. "That was not true."

I try not to give her the sour look my face is trying hard to morph into. That was not a helpful reminder if we want the others to believe me. "Regardless, it was a Shadow," I insist. Returning my attention to Adriel, I ask again, "How could a Shadow have gotten here?"

Adriel shakes her head. "It's simply not possible. Yes, you were allowed into the Shadow realm, but you are the only one other than an Angel of Death who has been granted permission in millennia. So, unless you let more than two Shadows loose when you left, it's impossible."

I do not hold back my sour look for her. "You were right there with me when I left," I remind her.

Eliana stares at me in confusion. "Two? I thought you only let one out."

I sigh. "Technically, I did. I've told you about Nixie, haven't I? She's not really a Shadow. She's a conglomeration of goodness that was scraped away with the bad stuff. She's currently roaming the realms and having the time of her life freaking other beings out." Without a body, she's limited in the ways she can entertain herself. Since she is doing no real harm, I'm not worried about it.

"Even if you and Xandra had released another Shadow, how would it have ended up in this realm?" Kallen asks. "We would have noticed it if it had followed us here on any of our journeys, right?"

Adriel nods in defeat. "Yes, and I would have felt it had it been living for any amount of time in the Fairy realm." Her brow folds in concentration, trying to figure this out. "No Angel of Death would risk Rashnu's wrath by setting a Shadow free intentionally."

That I believe. Rashnu is one scary Angel when she wants to be. I open my mouth to ask her about unintentional acts that might let a Shadow free when I notice the lines of concentration on Kallen's brow. Where Adriel's was folded more in confusion, he is making the face he does when an idea is coming to him. I cross my fingers and hope it's a good one. "What are you thinking?" I ask my gorgeous husband. I tamp down the urge to smooth out the lines on his forehead with kisses for fear of breaking his concentration. Not to mention, this really isn't the time or place for it. He's just so darn sexy when he's concentrating. Okay, he's always sexy.

"I do not believe it was necessary for the Shadow to escape," he says. We all stare at him until he explains. "The Phoenix ash. What if, like in the Shadow realm, the ashes from her past rebirths somehow melded together to create a Shadow-like being?"

"Would someone mind explaining to me what a Shadow is?" Josh finally asks. Isla, who has been standing by quietly, which is odd for her, answers him. After he gets his explanation, Josh asks, "Wouldn't the Phoenix have taken measures to prevent that from happening?"

Maybe, maybe not. I think back to the dream that Ra shared with Eliana and me. In it, the Phoenix certainly didn't act like she had a clue that her previous bad deeds could do anything except give her bad memories and affect her love life. Was that what Ra wanted us to get out of that conversation? "What if she didn't know it could happen?" I counter.

Adriel shakes her head. "All supernatural beings know about the Shadow realm and what happens there."

"But, an Angel of Death doesn't scrape the Phoenix's soul when she is reborn, right?" I ask, letting my mind delve new possibilities.

Adriel's brow creases. "No," she says hesitantly, trying to figure out where I am going with this. "Like I said before, her darkness is burned away by her Cosmic Fire."

"What if it's not," I counter again.

Adriel puts her hands on her hips and huffs, "Are you really going to argue that *anything* could survive Cosmic Fire?"

I think about it for a moment before nodding. "I am."

Adriel may not like my idea, but Eliana is warming to it. "If the Phoenix is immune to Cosmic Fire, why would it be able to completely burn away any part of her?" she asks the Fallen Angel of Death.

Adriel opens her mouth to respond, but closes it again. After a long moment of consideration, she throws her hands up in the air in defeat. "I guess I've never thought about it that way."

"So, it's possible then that her darkness may burn to ash, but it's not destroyed," I say.

Kallen is next to embrace the idea. "If that was the case, her ashes should have been stored in different locations, not all in one place."

"He's a genius, give the wanker a cookie," Taz mutters.

I ignore him. "But, she didn't. Now, the darkness from the ashes has found a way to join together like darkness does in the Shadow realm to form a separate sentient being."

"Only, this darkness is all from the same person," Adriel points out.

Her meaning hits me and I groan. "Which means it's basically an evil twin with all of the Phoenix's knowledge and memories dating back to the beginning of time." At least, all the ones before her last rebirth.

"Most likely," Adriel agrees.

"Why now?" Josh asks and we all turn to him.

"Why now what?" I ask.

"Why are you just learning about the existence of this darkness now? Those ashes have been here for thousands of this realm's years. Do you believe that it took that long for them to mix together?"

Excellent question. Since darkness doesn't really need a physical body, it doesn't matter if the ashes were mixed together. The essence of the darkness is what would bond. Which means, the process had probably been occurring since the second time the Phoenix died and left ashes behind. So, Josh is right. Why now? I glance at Kallen and find him deep in thought.

"Perhaps they needed to build strength?" Isla says more to herself than any of us.

Adriel nods. "That could be. It takes a long time for the darkness in the Shadow realm to form sentient beings."

Even I started this ball rolling, something is still not adding up here. "Wouldn't the Phoenix have noticed the darkness Shadow thing when she visited the temple?" I certainly was able to feel the presence of the Shadows in the Shadow realm. A shiver goes down my spine just thinking about it. I glance down at the small temple and rule out the idea that it was able to hide anywhere in there to avoid detection.

"I think she did, but she may not have known what it was," Eliana says thoughtfully. Lowering her voice just in case the Shadow has excellent hearing, she continues, "In our dream, she talked about the overwhelming feelings of darkness she experienced sometimes." Her eyes light up. "And I doubt she was the only one to sense it. Remember the passage Jenna found? The one that made her believe that the Phoenix was her own worst enemy?"

Before any of us can respond, a collective gasp from the crowd behind us has us all whipping around. My eyes follow theirs and I can't hold in my own gasp. "Is that…?"

"I think it is," Kallen nods.

Wow. I have never seen anything so beautiful in all my life. Nor any anything so sad.

## 31 CHAPTER

Above the temple, giant swaths of color are swirling. Reds, oranges, and yellows dance together in perfect rhythm, all brighter than any I have ever seen before. I don't even think these color shades are on the normal color spectrum. Even the desert sun beating down cannot dim them. It looks like the sky is on fire, but the image is so beautiful, so inviting, it makes you want to twirl and dance your way toward it. And in the center of the dancing colors there is an image. A Phoenix. Not the person, the bird. This Phoenix is similar to the images I have seen in books. It is the image that popped into my mind when Isla burst into our room and started us on this journey.

What makes the image so sad is that the Phoenix is crying and thrashing about as if being tortured. Amongst all the beauty of its surroundings, it is experiencing pain and desperation. The feelings are tangible. They touch my skin in faint whispers, in almost silent pleas. Pleas for help.

Eliana and I turn to each other at the same time. "We need to go back," we say in unison. I hold my hand out to Eliana, ready to teleport back to the temple and save the Phoenix from the darkness that is torturing her.

A hand on my shoulder stops me. "We need a plan this time," Kallen insists. "This could be a trap. The way it is trying to lure us down there, I'm almost certain it's a trap. Either way, if you are going up against darkness that has the knowledge, and at least some of the power of an immortal being, you cannot 'just wing it', as you like to say."

The tug on my heart drawing me to help the Phoenix immediately is strong, but I know Kallen is right. We need a plan. "Suggestions?" I ask impatiently.

He glances over his shoulder at the beings behind us. "There is something significant about having all of these beings in one place. I think we need to spend a bit more time figuring out what that is. I believe it is key to stopping the darkness."

I frown as a thought hits me. "Eliana couldn't feel the presence of the Phoenix when we were in the temple, and neither could I. So, doesn't it make sense that the Shadow insisted we bring them here?" I certainly don't want to do anything to help that entity's evil plans along.

Eliana shakes her head. "It must have been the Phoenix. Otherwise, Ra would have alerted me."

Good point. "You don't believe he was doing that last night?" I push, not mentioning the dream outright again. We technically aren't supposed to have any help from other immortal beings.

Eliana shakes her head again. "No. The Phoenix was definitely in that temple the first time we were here. She wrote that riddle for us."

Her words do not erase the frown on my face. "Okay, then where is she now?"

"Considering the fireworks down there, I would say she's still there," Josh says.

"I didn't sense her," Eliana reminds him.

"Maybe the Shadow is somehow preventing you from sensing her," Isla suggests.

"That's possible," Eliana nods uncertainly. "It was strong enough to send us both flying from the temple."

"Good thing Sam wasn't here to see that. Neither of you would ever live it down," Josh teases. Eliana gives him a sour look and he does a good job of wiping the smile from his face. Now is not the time for teasing.

As the others have been talking, I've been staring over their shoulders at the assembly of beings standing in the sand. What could be the significance of having them all here? A terrible thought hits me. If the Shadow wants them, is it for some sort of weird blood ritual or something? A spell that requires the blood of each race? Did we bring them here to be slaughtered? I shake my head to loosen the idea's grasp on my mind. If that was the case, the Shadow would have been pleased that we brought them all, not disbelieving.

As that thought slips from the forefront, another one takes its place. One that makes more sense. Slapping my forehead, I announce, "I know why the Phoenix refuses to die."

All eyes turn to me. Kallen is the first to speak. "Why?"

"Because of the Shadow. My guess is that if she dies and leaves more ashes, the Shadow will become more powerful than the Phoenix is and would wreak havoc on the realms."

Kallen's scowl is not the response I expected. "More havoc than blowing up the entire universe?"

Oh, right. Let the universe be taken over by evil or destroy it altogether. Either way, the Phoenix would not be much of a protector. Not yet ready to give up on the idea, though, I shrug. "Maybe she sees it as the lesser of two evils."

"Do you really believe she would make that choice for the entire universe?" Eliana asks.

I shrug again. "I don't know. I mean, she didn't seem like the most compassionate being the last time we met her." When she almost burned us alive and then shoved us through a wall.

"True," Eliana admits.

"Maybe after all the lives she has lived in different realms, she feels like she knows what's best for all of us," Josh adds with distaste pouring from his words. The idea that someone could be that egotistical is disturbing.

"Wait, if that's true, she is majorly affecting our freewill." I turn to Adriel. "Can't the Angels do something to stop her because of that?"

Adriel shakes her head. "One, the Angels asked for your help because they could not even find the Phoenix. Two, the Phoenix exists outside of the scope of our authority."

Interesting. If we live through this, I am going to have a lot of questions for the Angels about why they can't do anything against the one being who holds the power to destroy everything. Well, everything except the Angels. Do they have a treaty or something?

"Xandra," Kallen says, drawing my attention back to the problem at hand. "What about light? You said you fought off Shadows with your Angel light when you were in the Shadow realm."

Before I can respond, I see something out of the corner of my eye and I turn my head back toward the temple. "Um, I don't think this Shadow has issues with light."

The others follow my line of sight until they see it, too. Adriel sucks in a breath. On her exhale, she exclaims, "Impossible."

"You know, out of all the words in the English language, I am beginning to think that one is the one most people don't understand its true definition. It seems every time someone says it to me, it never turns out to be true," I point out. As I speak, my eyes never leave the dark patch that has oozed from the temple and is slowly inching its way up the sand dune. "Do you think we should get out of here?" I ask.

"And go where?" Isla asks. "There is no place to run, and we certainly cannot teleport away and leave the others behind."

I don't know, the latter doesn't sound half-bad at the moment. At least, I wouldn't feel too guilty leaving a few of them behind. With a sigh, I let that fleeting thought go. I could not live with myself if I left any innocent beings to deal with this kind of evil, even if I don't like half of them. Not to mention the entire realm of Cowans who wouldn't stand a chance against it. "Then we fight." I turn to the only one with any real knowledge of Shadows. "Can anything else destroy them besides light?"

Adriel considers. "Possibly Rashnu, I have seen her do it once. But, that is not going to happen."

Kallen scowls. "Since light appears to be a moot point, are you saying we have no other way to fight this thing?"

I glance down to see how much progress the Shadow has made and am surprised to see that it has not made much. "I don't think it's totally immune to light. It's not moving as quickly as the Shadows in the Shadow realm can."

Josh whirls around to Eliana. "What about burying it deep under the sand? At the rate it is going, it would take centuries for it to free itself."

"Except, then it would no longer be exposed to light and could probably move faster as it finds its way to the surface," Eliana points out.

Josh's face falls. "Right."

One of Kallen's hands falls on my shoulder and the other points to the sky above the temple. I look up and find the image of the crying Phoenix gone. The colors have stopped swirling and are forming words. We do not get a riddle this time. The message is perfectly clear. *Only I can stop it.*

Okay, guess that answers the question of whether or not we can be heard up here. "If you can stop it, then why don't you?" I demand, super annoyed now.

The words change, spelling out the last thing we want to see. "It is too late."

# 32 Chapter

Hands on my hips, I announce, "Yeah, I don't buy it."

Eliana looks at me in surprise. "You don't?"

I shake my head, growing more certain by the moment. "Nope."

Kallen eyes me curiously. "Why?"

"Because I feel like I have sand beetles crawling all over me," I growl, trying very hard not to do my 'someone's telling a lie' dance. I figure flailing about like a maniac would not strike confidence in the hearts of those we brought with us.

"What is going on?" the Centaur woman asks. She trots over to us followed by the others. They are tired of waiting for us to come back to them.

Can't say that I blame them. Doesn't make it any less annoying, though. "We're trying to figure that out now."

The Centaur narrows her eyes. "We were under the impression that you had this figured out already. Why did you insist we come with you if you had no idea how to handle the situation?"

Kallen takes as much offense to her tone as I do. "Because we were led to believe by the Phoenix that she would stop this nonsense if we did as she asked. It seems she lied."

She lied. Wait a second. I can feel the Phoenix's lie right now. In fact, I feel like I have bugs crawling in all kinds of uncomfortable places because her lie is so big. But, when she spoke to us before, I didn't feel a thing. It could be because I was so focused on the Cosmic Fire threatening to consume us, but I don't think so. So, why is she lying now?

Whipping around, I move close to Adriel and speak so only she can hear me. I hope, anyway. "Would the Phoenix know who I am?"

Adriel nods. "It is likely."

"Then, she would probably know that I can detect lies, right?"

Adriel shrugs. "I do not know. Being aware of your existence and knowing the extent of your powers are not necessarily one in the same."

She has a point. Lots of beings know who I am, but most of them don't even know that I'm part Angel, let alone know that I am a walking lie detector. But, I have a feeling that the Phoenix knows more about me than I know about her. I glance at Eliana. Could Ra have communicated with the Phoenix when we were here last time without Eliana being aware of it? I have no idea how that would work, but I am not ruling out the possibility.

"What are you whispering about?" the Giant woman asks. She has joined the Centaur and is standing akimbo glowering at us. I guess her shyness is just around Quinn because she looks anything but shy at the moment.

"I demand to know what is going on," the Sasquatch says, joining the growing crowd next to us.

"Is there anything I can do to assist you?" a soft voice asks. Surprised by the sincerity of it, I scan for the source. Just behind the Centaur is a Faun. Her delicate features are twisted with worry, but there is eagerness in her expression, as well. She truly wants to help. That is so sweet.

"Xandra, we should all be involved in your discussion," Ari insists. Addylyn is standing next to her, and she nods in agreement.

"You're right," I admit. "This involves all of us. So, here's what we know." I fill them in on everything from our first visit to the temple below until now and our theory about the ashes.

"What was the riddle?" Ari asks.

Josh pulls out his phone and hands it to Eliana so she can read it to everyone.

> "To pass through this wall:
>
> She will come with a voice that lures but breath that repels.
>
> She will come with eyes that reflect the grass but ears that hear the sky.
>
> She will come with hooved feet but reptilian legs.
>
> She will come with the shadow of a mammoth but the stature of one who strikes fear in those with magic.
>
> She will come with skin of scales but hair of silk.
>
> She will come with a scent sweeter than all in the universe but will reek to heaven.

*She will come with the need to call upon the earth but will bend the laws of natural order.*

*She will come with two hearts of mortality but the souls of the eternal.*

*She will come with peace in her heart."*

When she is finished, Eliana hands Josh his phone, which he shoves back into his pocket.

Ari looks at me like I'm crazy. "Obviously, we need to enter the temple in the order laid out in the riddle." When I give her a doubtful look, she smiles. "I know your proclivity for falling into dangerous, complicated situations may make this hard to believe, but sometimes, the simplest answer is the correct one."

I am not the only one with doubts. Eliana cocks her head and asks, "What do you think that will accomplish?"

Ari shrugs. "I don't know, but obviously, passing through whatever wall you ran into before is important."

I think back to our most recent sojourn into the temple and frown. "The wall wasn't there."

"It was not there when we first entered before, either," Kallen points out. "Only when we attempted to move in that direction did it appear."

My frown turning into a scowl, I snark, "So, you think it's an invisible wall that only appears when approached?"

Kallen raises a brow at my snark. "Would that be so unusual considering the extremes ancient Egyptians went to in order to guard their secrets?"

"Not really," Eliana answers for me. "If this temple was built by Ra, it could have invisible walls." He is a god, after all.

"Okay, say you're right. How are we supposed to fit everyone inside? There was barely enough room for the four of us last time." There's no way the Dragon is going to fit in the narrow hallway. The Giant might if she crawled on her hands and knees. It's pretty iffy for the Centaur and Sasquatch, as well.

Isla, who has warmed to the idea, smiles. "Magic, of course."

"Like in Harry Potter?" Josh asks.

I smile when everyone except Eliana and I stare at him blankly. "Not a popular book in other realms," I point out. To the others, I explain, "It's a book about wizards and sometimes objects are bigger on the inside than they are on the outside."

Isla shakes her head. "I believe the temple is of the same proportions inside and out."

She obviously didn't understand what I was saying. "But, will it expand as we all enter to accommodate us?"

Isla considers this. Finally, she says, "I do not know."

"Ra created the temple," Eliana says. "I believe he controls its dimensions."

My eyes widen. "So, you can make it bigger?"

"Would that not be considered help from a higher being?" Kallen asks.

Isla shakes her head. "The Phoenix already knows that Ra has instilled certain abilities in Eliana."

"Then, I guess we give it a shot," I say with a sigh. I am still far from convinced this is going to work. Glancing down again, I ask, "What about the Shadow?"

"We ignore it for now. If anything happens, I am certain between the lot of us we can handle it," Addylyn says almost flippantly. On closer inspection, she is trying hard to conceal her own concerns about the situation. I give her a small smile for trying to be confident and encouraging for the others. She's not all bad, I guess.

"How are we to get down there?" the Dragon asks. "I do not believe I would fare well if I must slide down." An image of her doing somersaults in the sand and the cage with the Pixie going flying pops into my brain and I have to fight not to giggle.

Isla answers the question with action instead of words. Suddenly, there is a staircase wide enough for all of the larger beings to descend. The steps are a little too big for the rest of us, so Kallen makes another set next to Isla's with normal sized stairs.

Josh shakes his head. "I don't think I'll ever get used to your type of magic."

"If you were around it long enough, you would," I assure him. Then I think of Dad and how hard it is for him to be one of only a handful of beings without real magic in the Fairy realm. Josh probably wouldn't be happy if they are ever forced to leave the Cowan realm.

Eliana and I lead the way down the stairs. Kallen, Isla, Adriel and Josh are right behind us. We are the first line of defense in case of an attack. Interestingly, the Shadow retreats as we approach the temple. Not without words, though.

"Fools," it hisses. Several with us are shocked that something without a mouth can speak. I think the Giant is going to pass out. Giants hate spirits. They are one of the few things that truly scare the race of oversized beings.

It's not the Shadow itself that is getting to me right now. It's the maniacal laughing the thing is doing. A feeling of dread crawls up my spine. Are walking into some sort of trap? If so, Ari better not ever give me a hard time about the damage I caused in the Mermaid realm since this was her idea. Then again, if it is a trap, the universe will probably end and she won't be able to say anything at all.

## 33 Chapter

At the bottom of the stairs, Josh hands Eliana his phone again. "Okay, everyone," she begins, "line up as requested."

She reads the first couple of lines. I expect to have to decode the riddle for everyone, but the Siren and the Dragon immediately step forward. Okay, I guess those were easy ones.

When Eliana reads the next couple of lines, I know something is going on. Isla is shocked when she finds herself moving forward. "It is like the pull of a magnet," she tells us. Beside her, Addylyn nods in agreement.

This idea is reinforced when Eliana continues reading. We expected to have to lead the pterodactyl into place, but as soon as the Faun and the Centaur are positioned, the dinosaur moves into place on its own. Josh lets go of the leash and steps back, confident that it's not going to fly away.

Next comes the Giant. When she takes her place, there is a loud 'Oomph' from low in the sand. I glance over to find the Pixie trying to move into position, but the metal bars of her cage are making that a bit difficult. All she managed to do was knock the cage over and fall face first into the hot sand. She comes up sputtering and spitting sand out of her mouth. "A little help here!" she exclaims. Kallen, the nice guy that he is, jogs over to her and lifts her cage. I guess he's not too nice because the Pixie flops onto her back on the bottom of the cage when he rights it so quickly. I don't miss the smirk on my husband's face. The Pixie has said some rather cruel things about him in the past.

After Kallen hands the Pixie to the Giant, Ari and the Sasquatch move into place. Adriel and the Goblin are next. Adriel covers her nose and mouth to try to fend off the stench, but from her expression, it is obviously not helping. The desert heat is only making the stench worse. Regular Goblin sweat is disgusting. Roasted Goblin sweat is downright nauseating. If I am not mistaken, Adriel is trying hard not to lose her breakfast.

A sudden tug inside me makes me lurch forward. Jadyn and Eliana are right there with me. Because I represent both the Witch and one with a mortal heart and eternal soul, we are all pulled together. Leaning over to Eliana, I whisper, "I don't like being in the back."

She grimaces. "Neither do I."

At the front of our parade, the Siren and the Dragon have continued to move forward. A high pitched squeal is followed by a burst of flame. I stretch up on my toes to try to see what is happening. Since I am never going to be able to see over the beings in front of me, I decide to teleport. Unfortunately, deciding to do it and actually doing it turn out to be at odds with one another. I can't teleport. I try to move to the side but find that is impossible, too.

My eyes fly to Kallen. "I'm stuck."

"I was afraid of that," he says with a grimace.

Josh, who ran ahead to see what is going on comes jogging back. "They ran into the wall and can't stop trying to move forward."

"What?!" several beings exclaim. They begin to struggle against whatever hold has been put upon us, but to no avail.

I try to fight the urge to shuffle forward, but can't. Soon, we are all piled on top of one another and being pressed against the wall like we're in a trash compactor. Panic is spreading like juice from a crushed grape.

Isla, always with the cool head, shouts above the clamor, "Everyone touch the wall!"

Eliana and I exchange a glance. "That must be it," Eliana nods.

I agree. "Do it! Touch the wall!" I reiterate.

Surprisingly, everyone obeys. Everyone except Josh and Kallen reach between the others and lay a hand, or a claw, or prehistoric fingers, against the temple wall. Eliana and I have to really squeeze in to reach it. I suspect the Phoenix put us in the back on purpose just to make it harder. I do not even want to think about the body parts my hand comes into contact with before I finally feel the brick beneath my fingers. I'm certain at least two beings thought I was making inappropriate advances.

Since Eliana is a bit taller than me, she touches the wall first. That makes me the last one to make contact. As soon as I do, I brace myself for the explosion. There's always an explosion in situations like this. Except, when there's not. In fact, imploding is the direct opposite of exploding.

With a whoosh, we are all sucked into the temple that seems to be shrinking, not expanding. I feel Kallen's arms around my waist, trying to keep me from being pulled in. Even with his strength, he can't stop it. Josh loses his grip on Eliana, as well. She and I follow the others into the imploding temple and once we are in, there is a loud pop.

Only, we aren't in the temple. At least, I don't remember there being trees, a crystal blue lake, or a bright sky with two suns and a moon visible inside the temple. Maybe we just hadn't gone far in enough before? That's probably not it.

## 34 Chapter

Stunned into silence, our group stares at our new surroundings. Gone is the desert sand and heat. They have been replaced by a refreshing breeze and lush, green grass beneath our feet. The water in the lake is so clear, you can see the smooth bottom. The afternoon light is not overwhelming like the Saharan desert sun, even though this place apparently is warmed by two suns. But, none of this is as surprising as the other sight before us. Wherever we are, we are not alone.

Excited shouts go up all around us. 'They're here!' and 'They did it!' seem to be the most popular. Smiles radiate and shining eyes take us in. In the sky, a familiar sight dazzles us. Swirling hues of red, orange and yellow. They are being spread through the sky by large birds. Birds that sharply resemble the image of a Phoenix we saw earlier. Only, none of these are sad or crying. They definitely are not being tortured. In fact, everyone here seems as happy as can be. What the hell is going on?

I'm not certain if I said that aloud, or if Eliana simply read my mind. Shaking her head, she replies, "I have no idea."

It doesn't take long to figure out that all the women here look alike. Everything about them – their hair, their skin, their eyes, their teeth, all identical. Even their bodies are the same size. No shifts in weight or height. A world of identical…what would be the word for twin multiplied by a hundred?

A voice behind us startles the heck out of me and I pull magic as I whirl around. The woman who spoke isn't even phased by it. "Xandra, Eliana, welcome."

Not surprising, she looks like all the other women here. "Welcome to where?" I ask.

The woman's smile widens. "Why, to the Phoenix realm, of course."

Seriously? Another realm no one knew about? Okay, that's not the important thing right now, but seriously, how many realms are still out there undiscovered? Considering I am tasked with trying to make them all get along, it would be nice to have a solid number to work with. "Um, everyone believes there is only one of you," I blurt out. Tact and I aren't even on speaking terms anymore. We filed for a legal separation ages ago.

The woman nods. "Yes, we know."

Tilting my head, I ask, "Is that the royal we, or are there really a ton of you?" Heck, maybe we're having a group hallucination. That would make a lot more sense.

The woman looks puzzled for a second, but then her smile returns. "Ah, a Cowan colloquialism. No, that was not a royal we. There are many of us."

Eliana is as confused as I am. "Then why does everyone believe there is only one of you?"

"Because that is what we wanted you to believe, of course," the woman replies as if that is a perfectly normal thing to say.

I am about to point out that makes her and the others liars, but I decide to pick my battles more carefully this time. "Could you please start from the beginning before my head explodes?"

"Yes, we would all like to hear this," Adriel growls. She has moved next to me with her arms crossed tightly over her chest. Anger flashes through her eyes, and she is a breath away from going all Angel of Death on the woman.

I don't believe Adriel's current Fallen status would hinder her at all right now.

Instead of being afraid, the woman claps excitedly. "I was hoping you would be the one who came. We find mortal death fascinating and have a ton of questions for you."

"After you explain what's going on," I interrupt. I take a step closer to Adriel, ready to grab her if she decides to attack the too-gleeful woman.

The woman sighs. "I suppose we must get to the problem before we can have any fun."

"Problem?" I ask. I glance around. Everyone here is so happy. How could there be a problem?

Nodding, the woman says, "Yes, problem. It's quite simple really. Our Cosmic Fire has been stolen."

I blink. I blink again. I blink yet again. I turn and watch Eliana blink. I turn back to the woman and blink again. Finally, all I can say is, "What?"

The woman nods as if she just said something perfectly reasonable. "Yes, our Cosmic Fire has been stolen."

"Do you know who took it?" Eliana asks, as dumbfounded as I am.

"Why, our sister, of course. No one else can contain it." The 'what an idiotic thing to ask' is implied in her tone.

Now, I am afraid it will be Eliana I'll need to hold back. I sidle a bit closer to my scowling friend. "Okay," I begin, glancing around at the other versions of the woman, "why don't you steal it back? There seem to be plenty of you."

"That would require us to leave this realm," the woman replies. Again, the 'what an idiotic thing to ask' is implied in her tone. She seems to be a master at that.

"If any of you leave this realm, it will be known there is more than one of you," a voice directly behind me says. I glance over my shoulder at Jadyn and sigh. I think she's right.

"Let me guess," Eliana snarks. "You want us to get it back for you."

The woman nods and smiles broadly as she looks between Eliana and me. "You two are our last hope."

I put my hands up in front of me to stop her from continuing. "If Eliana and I are your last hope, why did we have to bring the others with us?"

The woman's grin widens. "Why, it was the only way for you to enter our realm."

I wonder if they are all this annoying. "You keep saying things like you expect us to know the how's and why's. Since no one in any of the realms knew about this one, it's not possible for us to know either of those things. Please," I implore, "start at the beginning."

"Sister," another woman says, "let me handle the explanations."

A slight pout forms on the first woman's face. "I was having fun. We do not get to speak to anyone besides each other."

"It shows," I mutter, earning me a nudge in the ribs from Adriel and Jadyn. I twist my neck so I can glare at both of them.

The second woman pats the first woman's arm. "There will be plenty of time for you to speak to them later. Run along now." With a put upon sigh, the first woman walks away. The second turns to us and holds out her hand. "I was called Chol the last time I lived among the realms."

"Not Phoenix?" I ask and want to kick myself. Of course they don't go by 'Phoenix'. They would each want their own name.

Chol smiles. "No," she says simply. Not even a hint of mocking tone in her voice. I think I'm going to like Chol.

"Will you please explain what is going on?" Eliana presses.

"Of course. The Phoenix as a lone figure living and dying and being reborn is a myth. No one soul could withstand the process for eternity. Not to mention, there are multiple universes to consider. How could one of us be in them all at the same time?" She pauses as if her question is not rhetorical.

To move things along, I say, "You couldn't."

Chol smiles. "Of course not. So, we take turns in each universe. When our cycle is complete, we return here until the next time we are needed."

My curiosity getting the better of me, I ask, "How many lives have you lived?"

"Twenty-four," she says proudly.

"If you are not really being reborn when you die, why the show? Why leave the ashes behind?" I ask, growing annoyed at the magnitude of the lie set upon the universes.

Chol is not fazed by my annoyance. "The ritual is the only way for us to pass the Cosmic Fire back and forth. As for the ash, I believe you already know what that is."

"It is darkness from your souls," Eliana says.

Chol smiles at her. "Yes. We cannot tarnish our world by bringing it back here." I glance around again. No wonder everyone here is so happy. There's no darkness on any of their souls. Then I think more about what Chol just said. They don't want to taint their own realm, but they have no problem leaving the darkness behind to taint other realms. Maybe I'm not going to like Chol, after all.

Impatient to get to the point, Adriel asks, "Why would one of you have stolen the Cosmic Fire and for what purpose?"

Proving she can use the 'what an idiotic question' tone, Chol replies, "Why, to destroy the universes, of course."

Universes. I didn't even consider before the possibility that all of the universes would be destroyed. "That would wipe out all of existence," I point out. "Including this place, right?"

Chol nods. "Yes. So, you can see our problem."

I'm not certain if she means it's a problem that everyone would be goners, or that the problem revolves around her race being goners. I decide it best not to ask. I don't think I would like the answer. "Why would one of you want to do that? And is the Cosmic Fire really stolen if you gave it to her when she took on her new life?" I ask instead.

A slight frown touches Chol's face. "Perhaps stolen is the wrong word. Refuses to give it back is more appropriate. We believe Huma may have lived too many lives. We hesitated to let her go out there again, but she insisted she was fine."

"Do you have a limit as to how many lives you are supposed to live?" Eliana asks.

Chol shakes her head. "We did not, but we may need to reconsider. Huma was the first of us. She has lived the most lives, so we are just discovering there may be a limit as to what our souls can handle."

That makes sense, I guess. "Okay, I'm starting to understand. But, why did you make us gather all of these women?" I gesture toward all the females from each race we brought with us.

"As Garuda said, it was the only way for you to enter our realm." Chol smiles at our assembly. "It is a miracle you pulled it off."

"Pulled what off?" I ask.

"This realm was created without access points. The only way to pass in and out of it is during our Phoenix ritual.

But, some of us knew that we needed to have, what would the Cowans call it? Oh yes, a back-up plan. Most among us did not really believe we needed one and fought the idea. So, we eventually came to a compromise. We cast a spell across each universe that if a female from each known realm and race came together peacefully of their own free will, without assistance from any higher beings, and requested access, they would be admitted. This would open a passage to travel back and forth through until we create a new spell to close it off. Of course, we all thought that was an impossibility as no two realms could go long without conflict of some sort." Chol's smile widens as she stares at me. "Until you were prophesized. We knew you would be the one to come and save us all."

I'm back to being confused again. "I was prophesized a long time ago. When, exactly, did this Huma steal the Cosmic Fire?"

Chol appears to be doing some mental calculations. Finally, she says, "Approximately one thousand Cowan years ago."

My mouth drops open. "And you are just now asking for help?"

"Neither of you were born a thousand years ago." She does have a point.

"I believe she is saying it was not an issue until the current Phoenix neared the end of her life," Adriel explains. She looks to Chol for confirmation and Chol nods.

"No pressure," Eliana mutters. Louder, she says, "We felt a taste of what Cosmic Fire can do, and we were helpless against it."

"Not to mention, Huma seems to have a Shadow protecting her," I add.

Chol laughs. Which makes me want to slap her. I refrain, but I do have to inconspicuously stop Adriel's hand from flying forward. Man, is she ever strong. The strain of keeping her hand in place must be showing on my face even though I'm trying to hide it. "What's so funny?" I grind out between clenched teeth. Wow, Adriel really wants to punch this woman.

"That you believe the Shadow is protecting Huma." Chol laughs harder for a moment before saying, "The Shadow would not lift a finger to help us, nor can it harm us."

"Well, it can harm us," I snark. "We took a nosedive in the sand because of it."

Chol waves her hand as if to say 'that's just crazy talk'. "No, that was Huma."

Eliana shakes her head. "I couldn't sense Huma's presence."

"Oh, you could," Chol says. "You simply confused her dark aura for the Shadow."

"So, you're saying the Shadow is harmless?" I ask in disbelief.

"Perfectly harmless. It is simply a collection of memories we all chose to leave behind." She directs her next statement to Adriel. "That is why there has never been a need to send it to the Shadow realm. We don't want it to mix with those other Shadows who might use its knowledge for personal gain."

Makes sense. Sort of. I am still dumbfounded. "So, you just let it roam free?"

"Of course not, silly." Okay, now I know that a Phoenix can be as condescending as any other supernatural being. The pressure between Adriel and I is reversing. She is now keeping me from punching Chol. Oblivious to our struggle, Chol continues, "It was locked up tight in that temple Ra built for Huma." She narrows her eyes at Eliana. "Until someone set it free." A bit of color touches Eliana's cheeks, but she bites back any angry retort in favor of hearing the rest of the story.

"Why is Huma's aura so dark?" I ask, trying to move the conversation toward the finish line. I suspect if we don't finish soon, Chol will end up pummeled to the ground by one of us. My money is still on Adriel, but Eliana and I would have her back.

"We are not quite sure," Chol admits. "It could be the effect of living too many lives, or she could have intentionally made bad choices during her cycle in order to darken her aura."

"Why would she do that?" Eliana asks.

Isla, who has been remarkably quiet this entire trip, steps forward. "She intended to do this before she left this realm."

Chol sighs. "We believe so."

Again, I glance around at the beings who inhabit this realm. "Everyone here is so happy. It's hard to believe one of you would plan something like that." Turning back to Chol, I ask, "Could it be that not all of the darkness was burned from Huma's soul?"

Adriel's eyes light up with knowledge. "It is not possible to remove all of the darkness and memories from any soul. Over time, the leftover bits become more and more entwined with the soul, making them impossible to ever remove." She is an Angel of Death, she would know.

"Meaning," Isla says, "living too many lives could damage even the soul of a Phoenix."

"That is our theory, yes," Chol nods. "No universe is a perfect place," she adds as if this statement explains why no one thought of this possibility before.

The ground beneath us shakes as the Dragon in our party shuffles forward. "If we are of no use here other than door openers, can we return home? I would like to spend the remaining time of our existence with my family."

"Thanks for the vote of confidence," I mutter.

The Dragon snorts and a tiny puff of smoke leaves her not-so-delicate nose. "You are egotistical enough to believe you can conquer Cosmic Fire?"

I shrug. "I don't know if I can conquer it, but between Eliana and I, we might be able to figure out a way to steal it back." I wish I could have instilled more confidence in my words. I have to feel it to do it, though.

"I am afraid we must ask you to remain until our Cosmic Fire is returned," Chol informs the Dragon.

This time when the Dragon snorts, fire shoots from her nostrils. That probably wasn't good for her nose hairs. Do Dragons have nose hairs? I try to sneak a peek, but the light is not in my favor to get a good view. "Are we prisoners?" the Dragon demands.

"Yes," Chol says, pleasant smile still in place.

Again, I stare open mouthed at her. "You are holding us hostage?"

She laughs at me yet again. "Not you two, silly. Just the others. At least until you have returned our Cosmic Fire."

"You can't do that!" the Sasquatch exclaims and Jadyn, Ari and the Siren chime in after her.

"There must be another way out of here," the Centaur insists. "You said the spell was broken."

Chol raises her arms and waves them in different directions. "Yes, it is. The passage may only be opened and closed by a Phoenix, though. None of whom will open it for you. You are free to roam anywhere you like. You may attempt to seek another exit if you do not believe me."

I believe her. No one will find an exit from here until the Phoenix women are ready to let us go. The grumbling behind me is growing louder. Soon, there will be more than words being thrown about. "What do you want us to do?" I ask Chol. "The sooner we get out of here, the better."

"We want you to put Huma out of her misery," Chol replies.

My jaw is currently getting grass stains. When I can wrench it back into place, I ask, "You want us to kill your sister?"

Chol's expression says she is thinking I am an idiot again. She might as well wear a banner across her forehead exclaiming for all to know. "No one can kill a Phoenix," she reminds me. "I said, 'put her out of her misery.' Make her happy again, at least happy enough to agree to go through the ritual. Once she is back here, we will attempt to decondition her to the best of our ability."

"What happens if you cannot?" Isla asks.

"She will not be allowed to live through another cycle."

Suddenly, a thought hits me. "When you start a cycle, do you carry all of your good memories of previous cycles with you?" I ask Chol.

Chol shakes her head. "That is also part of the ritual. Even some of those memories are erased. It would be too much of a burden to carry so much with us for eternity. It also makes it easier to leave those we may have grown to love behind."

Now I understand what Ra was really trying to show us in the dream. The same thing the Fairy who met her said, only the Fairy didn't know how big of a discovery it was at the time. From the glee radiating off all these Phoenix women, they must each begin their cycles with light hearts and souls, free from any pain they may have felt before. Huma definitely did not have a light heart or soul when she started her cycle. So much darkness was still attached to her soul that she was probably having flashbacks from previous cycles, and mostly only remembering the bad parts since many of the good ones that would counteract them were washed away. I glance at Eliana and can tell the same idea is going through her mind at the moment. Great, how the hell are we going to help Huma overcome many lifetimes of pain and suffering before she goes supernova? I've read a few books on psychology, and not one had a section on that.

## 35 CHAPTER

Even if we don't have a clue as to how to do this, we still need to get going on it. Huma is literally a ticking time bomb. "Send us back," I insist.

Chol, who was answering some question Isla asked her, smiles at me. "You have accepted the challenge?"

I scowl at her. She said the word challenge as if this was a game of truth or dare or something. "Um, you're holding my friends hostage and the universe is going to end soon if we don't do something to stop it. What choice do we have?"

Chol's smile doesn't even falter. "We always have choices. We simply do not always choose wisely." She gives me one succinct nod as if that little nugget of wisdom should set me straight. Adriel is struggling hard now to keep my fist next to my side. "In this, you have chosen wisely," Chol finishes.

Since punching her is a bad idea, it's my turn to give her the 'what an idiotic thing to say' look. I hope I pulled it off as well as she and Baruda can. "Right, thanks for noticing," I snark. "Just send us back."

"Of course," Chol says for the millionth time. Obviously, it's one of her favorite expressions. I am so sick of hearing them pass through her lips that I may never use those words again. Well, I'll probably use the words separately, just not lumped together as a phrase. It would be hard to never use the word 'of' again. Course I could probably do without.

While I am contemplating my future vocabulary, Chol is heeding my request. Before I know what is happening, my body is sucked backwards. Eliana is next to me, her arms flailing as widely as mine. If we're not careful, we're going to smack each other in the face. The others we brought with us chase after us, either to save us or to try to come with us, I'm not certain which. Well, actually, I could probably divide them up into groups of who would be doing what. Isla, Jadyn, Adriel and even Ari and the Faun are probably trying to save us. The rest are probably just trying to save themselves. With a loud pop, the Phoenix realm disappears from our view. Our backs hit hot sand, and one sun is glaring down at us with enough strength to burn out our retinas. We are definitely back in the Cowan realm.

Josh and Kallen rush to our sides. "What happened?" they ask in unison.

It's so cute, I can't help but ask, "Were you practicing that?" I force myself to a sitting position and shake off some of the hot sand.

Seeing that I am fine, the tension on Kallen's face eases, and he drawls, "We did want the harmony to be perfect."

I nod in appreciation. "Good job."

"Seriously, what happened?" Josh presses as he pulls Eliana into a bone crushing hug. At least, it would be if he had her strength. Josh is not quite as used to his love disappearing as Kallen is, and he may be freaking out a bit.

Eliana gently disentangles herself from his bear hold. "We're fine," she insists. Lowering her voice in an attempt to keep Huma from hearing, she says, "We got pulled to the Phoenix realm."

I stare up at my gorgeous husband so I can watch the confusion and disbelief dance across his face. I don't get to see that very often. It's usually me offering the entertainment in that regard. Kallen opens his mouth to object to the idea, but I hold my hand up. "It's real," I assure him in a whisper, even though it is probably obvious to Huma where we were. "And, there's more than one Phoenix," I throw out. Might as well hit him with it all at once. I keep my eyes glued to his face. This time, I'm looking for developing fissures that would indicate his head is about to explode.

Josh isn't stunned into silence like my husband, but he does keep his voice low. "Where are the others?" he asks, oblivious to the significance of the declaration I just made.

"Still in the Phoenix realm," Eliana says with a grimace. "They're being held hostage."

Kallen's brow scrunches together. "What is the ransom?"

"That we put Huma out of her misery." I explain as I stand and brush the rest of the sand from my clothes. It's way too hot for sitting on the sun scalded particles. My skin was beginning to blister through my clothes.

It's Josh's turn to frown. "Who is Huma, and why do you have to kill her?" He glances at Eliana. "Which I assume you are not planning to do."

Eliana shakes her head and smiles. "No, we are not. Nor are the other Phoenixes asking us to do so. They simply want us to talk her out of destroying the universe and to give back the Cosmic Fire so another Phoenix can take her place." Again, nothing Huma hasn't probably already figured out, so it's okay if she hears us.

Josh nods in understanding. "Good to know. Did they give you any ideas for accomplishing this?"

I snort. "Yeah, they basically said, 'figure it out.'"

Out of the corner of my eye, I see something dark moving our way. Kallen sees it, as well. He moves to take up a defensive position between me and the Shadow. I appreciate the gesture, but he needs to know that it's unnecessary. "It can't hurt anyone," I tell him quietly and explain what Chol told us.

Kallen shakes his head and mutters, "So many damn secrets in the universe."

"The wanker is just now figuring that out?" a voice snarks from my ankle.

I glare down at my Familiars and realize they were nowhere to be found while I was getting sucked into another realm. "Where have you guys been?"

"As your dad would say, we were doing recon," Felix explains.

Nonplussed, I glance around the deserted desert. The only thing here is the temple. "Where?" I ask.

"Under that pile of sand over there," Taz snarks, pointing to some random spot with his tail. "Are you an idiot? We were doing recon inside."

"What is he saying?" Kallen asks.

I put a finger up to indicate he needs to wait a minute before I can give him a full response. He scowls at me, but clamps his mouth closed. I turn my attention back to my Familiars. "What did you find out?"

"We found out that the Phoenix has no idea what we are. She thinks we're just wild animals, so she let us wander in and go wherever we liked."

"Really?"

"She even petted us," Felix informs me, the distaste evident in his tone. He doesn't like to be touched, especially by strangers. I'm kind of surprised he didn't bite the Phoenix. At least, I hope he didn't.

Suddenly, it dawns on me that we might be able to use the Phoenix's ignorance to our advantage. Lifting my eyes so that it's not obvious I'm speaking to the two Tasmanian devils, I stare at Kallen and ask again, "What did you find out?"

Kallen looks at me like I'm insane. He opens his mouth to probably imply this orally, as well, but I shake my head slightly and glance down at Taz then back up at him. It takes a second, but I can see it in his beautiful green eyes when he finally understands. "Not much," he says.

Taz's response is a bit different. "There are two chambers. One has a bunch of empty pots that probably held her ashes. The other is where she is holed up. She seems to have super hearing, but we don't believe she can see what is going on outside the temple. If you make a plan, try to keep your mouth closed while doing it," he adds as if I didn't understand what 'she can hear but she can't see' meant. I glower down at him, but he ignores me as usual.

Eliana is about to ask what is going on, but I put my fingers to my lips. To Kallen, I mouth, 'paper and pencil.' In an instant, he creates them and hands them over. Scribbling as fast as I can, I write down what Taz told me. Eliana and Josh's eyes widen in surprise. Eliana asks for the paper and pencil and I hand it over. She writes something down and hands it to me. Her question is, 'What are you thinking.'

Excellent question. One I don't quite have an answer to yet. I shrug and give them each an imploring look, hoping they might come up with something. Three foreheads scrunch up in concentration and three mouths remain tightly closed. I sigh in frustration and turn to ask Felix and Taz if they have any ideas.

My Familiars are nowhere to be found.

# 36 Chapter – Taz and Felix

"Do you think she noticed we're gone yet?" Taz asks Felix.

"She was quite focused on what she was doing," Felix responds.

Taz rolls his eyes. "A fancy way of saying she doesn't have a freakin' clue." Felix doesn't respond, but Taz knows he's right. "What odds will you give me that she does something stupid while we're trying to execute our plan?"

Felix glares at him. "Xandra is impulsive, not stupid."

"Suck up," Taz mutters. Louder, he asks, "What was the point of going out there and telling her all that again?"

"To give her an idea that there are alternatives to whatever she is thinking of doing," Felix explains for what he feels like is the hundredth time. "While she ponders a way to use us to her benefit, we have time to do what we need to do."

"She's going to come looking for us as soon as she notices we're gone. She would never let us walk into danger alone," Taz points out.

This is not news to Felix. "Which is why we snuck off. We have probably five minutes before she figures out what we're doing. By then, we'll be in place."

Taz eyes Felix for a second as they make their way down the temple hall. "If you get her killed, I'll have to kill you."

Felix snorts. "You could try." But, he has no intention of getting this Xandra killed. Not after all she has done for him. "Xandra will be fine."

"Let's try not to get ourselves killed, either. I couldn't spend an eternity without bacon."

"That I cannot promise you," Felix informs his doppelganger as they round the corner that leads to where the Phoenix is.

When they reach her, she smiles widely. "You have returned. I heard you growling outside. It seems you don't like the intruders any more than I do." Her smile becomes sad. "It will be nice to have your company as it all ends."

Taz fights back a snort. If the crazy bird had any idea what they had planned for her, she would already have burned them alive.

## 37 CHAPTER

"Damn it!" I exclaim. My Familiars must have gone back into the temple. I point furiously at the building so the others will understand why I'm upset.

Eliana writes, "What are they doing?"

"Getting themselves killed, probably," I mutter. Kallen nudges me and points to the paper. Right. There is more danger for Felix and Taz if the Phoenix has any idea they are associated with me. Then again, why the hell does she think there are Tasmanian devils in the middle of the Sahara? It's not like they're natives here. Maybe she was never good at zoology.

I grab the paper from Eliana and write, "We need to go after them."

Josh takes the paper from me and writes, "Without a plan?"

I nod. I am going to save my Familiars, with or without a plan. Seeing the determination on my face, Eliana takes the paper back and writes, "We're coming with you." I smile at her in appreciation.

As if choreographed, we all turn toward the temple and begin walking. Once we are inside, the Phoenix will sense our presence. She always has before. So, there's no use in trying to sneak in. When we reach the door, Eliana extends her hand and her eyes glow red again. The door disappears and we enter the gloomy hall. Kallen and Josh remove the torches from the wall and Eliana lights them for us. This is becoming way too routine for my taste.

I don't need Eliana to guide us this time. My tie to my Familiars steers me in the direction we need to go. I stalk ahead of the others, ready to fight to the death to save the stupid, brave little guys. Fortunately, there are no obstacles in our way this time. No walls to block us, just an open door inviting us to step inside. I do so and stop dead. I came to rescue them and here they are curled up on Huma's lap practically purring. Even Felix! He sure seems to have gotten over his abhorrence to being touched. I hear a gasp behind me as the others see the same betrayal I am seeing.

Except, I take a look beneath the surface of the scene. Felix is not at all relaxed. If his muscles were any tighter, they'd snap like rubber bands. His expression is pained. I'm certain the others can't tell, but I know my Familiars and their expressions. And Taz? Taz has that look in his eye he gets when he's about to do something stupider than even I would dream of doing. Oh, no. My Familiars have decided to play hero, and I have no idea what their plan is. Then again, at least they have a plan. Better than I can say for the rest of us.

"Have they changed sides?" Josh murmurs.

"Seems so," I lie. I ignore the sudden feeling of bugs crawling on me.

A pitying smile plays across Huma's face. "Were these your pets? Did you plan to attack me with them?" She shakes her head. "How foolish. Ra should have told you that animals are drawn to me."

Josh's eyes narrow. "Did he…" I nudge him hard in the ribs before he can blurt out that Taz just rolled his eyes.

To cover for the tiny faux pas, Felix begins to growl at us. At least, that's what it sounds like to everyone else. "There, there, my dear, you are safe with me," the

Phoenix soothes while petting his head. If only she knew how close to vomiting Felix is at the moment. He is probably going to have a nervous breakdown from all the touching when this is over. Providing whatever plan the Tasmanian devils have works. I have my doubts. Mostly because I still don't know what it is.

I try not to laugh at the Phoenix's ignorance, because what Felix actually said was, "Keep her talking so we can explain the plan to you."

So, I do as he says. I search my mind for the question I would most like answered. "Why did you give us that riddle if you knew there was a possibility that we could do it?"

Okay, maybe that was the wrong question to ask. Her eyes flashing, the Phoenix's face twists in fury. "I did not give you the riddle. My sisters found a way to communicate it to you." Oh, that makes so much sense, I can't believe we didn't figure it out on our own.

"How?" Eliana asks.

"I do not know," Huma snarls. "They should not have been able to communicate with anyone outside of their realm."

Taz pretends he is responding to Huma's anger and begins to snarl at us. Well, at the others. To me, he says, "You know, they really shouldn't leave their past memories just lying around. She's pretty chatty."

"Writes well, too," Felix adds with a snarl.

Their words hit me hard, and I find myself struggling not to show the shock on my face. The Shadow sent us the message? Why?

"Once you had the riddle, all I could do was make sure you understood the rules." Huma focuses her glare on Eliana. "Ra was not to aide you."

"He didn't," Eliana assures her. Well, he may have a tiny little bit, but no need to put that information out there. Huma is pissed enough already.

Conversation lulls and I need to keep it going. "Aren't you worried someone is going to see the Shadow out there?" I ask.

Huma laughs, but there is no humor in it. "I am about to go supernova. What does it matter?" Good point.

"Yes, the one thing that can kill a Phoenix," Taz growls. He bares his teeth in what I think is supposed to be a grin. I stare at him like he's crazy. It's the one thing that will destroy all the universes, as well.

Obviously, I am not getting what he is trying to communicate, so he tries again. "It's a good thing you have the Sun God with you," he says pointedly and growls in Eliana's direction.

"Keep the conversation going," Felix urges. "She's about to blow."

What?! My eyes shoot back to Huma and I can see it. Around the edges of her aura, tiny little flames are beginning to appear. Eliana sucks in a breath beside me. She sees it, too.

Okay, what do you say to a supernatural being who is about to go supernova? 'Gee, it's getting hot in here' just doesn't seem like the right thing to go with. "Why kill everyone?" I blurt out. "Why does everyone else have to suffer because you are unhappy?"

The Phoenix returns her attention to me. "I am doing everyone a favor. These universes were a mistake from the very beginning. Putting flawed beings into flawed worlds to live flawed lives. What good could come from that? All that resulted was violence and pain."

"That is not true," Eliana says. "I love my life and so do my friends."

Huma waves a hand at her words. "Only because you are young. If you lived longer, you would understand."

"Liar." To my surprise, Kallen said this. I stare up at my husband. I usually blurt those kinds of things out, not him. I guess I'm rubbing off on him. He's not finished, either. "You feel those things and you want them to end. You do not care how, or that everything else will die with you. You can only think of one way out as you are otherwise immortal, and you are taking it like the coward you are." A smile spreads across my face. I love him so much.

Kallen was not the only one speaking. While he spoke, Taz filled me in on more of the plan. I consider myself quite talented to be able to listen to them both at the same time. I'll pat myself on the back later, providing it still exists.

"Say the word Benu-Phoenix to Eliana as you touch the Phoenix and then teleport," Taz ordered as I pretended not to listen to him.

I have no idea how he expects Eliana and me to get close enough to the Phoenix to touch her. She's still a powerful immortal who has the ability to wield Cosmic Fire. She'd disintegrate us before we took two steps toward her.

Unless two suicidal Familiars distract her, that is.

## 38 Chapter

Huma screams as two sets of sharp teeth pierce the tender flesh of her thighs. The tiny flames of Cosmic Fire dancing on her aura rise like solar flares, and I know my chances of saving my Familiars is slim to none. But, I'm sure as hell going to try.

Grabbing Eliana's arm, I tug her forward. She doesn't hesitate at all. Keeping my hold on her, we rush the distracted Phoenix who is about to burn my Familiars alive. Thrusting my hand forward to the first spot I see on her body that isn't currently flaring with Cosmic Fire, I make contact with her ear. I turn to Eliana and whisper, "Benu-Phoenix." Then, I teleport.

As soon as we leave the temple, I feel a tug at my core. I don't even need to glance at Eliana to know that her eyes are shining a bright red as Ra directs us to where we need to go. In an instant, we are standing before the obelisk in Heliopolis. Minus two Tasmanian devils. I wasn't certain I could teleport without them while they still had their teeth in the Phoenix's flesh, but I had never focused my magic so hard on anything before. I sigh in relief. I just hope it was soon enough to save them both.

My time to dwell on the fate of my Familiars is brief. "Create a circle!" Eliana orders.

Just as she didn't hesitate to follow me when I rushed Huma, I don't hesitate in doing as she asks. I create a circle large enough to encompass the obelisk. As soon as I do, I drop my scorched hand from Huma's ear. There may not have been Cosmic Fire flaring there, but her entire body is way above the average 98.6 degrees Fahrenheit.

There is a tug on the back of my shirt, and Eliana pulls me out of the way of the punch Huma throws. With her other hand, Eliana stops the forward momentum of Huma's fist as easily as if a she is stopping a flea. I expect the smell of burning flesh to fill the circle I created, but instead, I have to jump back when their joined hands erupt in flames. Since nothing is disintegrating, I am going to assume that Eliana created the flames herself. Maybe to protect her hand from Huma's heat? I'll ask later. She's a little busy at the moment restraining the Phoenix.

As we stand before the obelisk, it dawns on me that maybe I should have brought Taz and Felix along. After all, this was their plan. A plan which neither of them explained to me how it is supposed to end.

It turns out, I don't need to know. Her eyes still glowing a brilliant red, Eliana begins to speak. As happened before, her voice comes out velvety smooth and very masculine. "Benu-Phoenix, temple of Ra, protector and marker of the benben stone, keeper of sacred law unchangeable and unalterable. Open for thy God."

Outside the circle, crowds of people are walking along. Some stop to stare at the obelisk, still visible to them, but they keep moving. None come near it. They are being unconsciously repelled by my magic. Thank goodness, because if they could see what is really happening to the obelisk at this moment, there would be mass hysteria.

The almost seventy-foot-tall structure splits down the center, the opposite sides separating from each other. When they are about ten feet apart, meaning I need to expand my circle, something begins to rise from the ground. If my retinas weren't currently being burned, I would be able to tell what it is.

Pinches on my back announce the arrival of my wings coming to protect me from harm. I expand the right one, wrapping it around Eliana to shield her, as well. Ra may be invincible, but Eliana's mortal body is not.

"You cannot defeat me!" Huma roars. Great, now my ear drums need protection, too. I wonder how many times ear drums can rupture and be repaired before they finally give out completely. I'm hoping not to find out.

"I am not here to defeat you," Ra tells her.

If I could open my eyes at the moment, I would be staring at Eliana as if the god inside her had lost his mind. Since I can't, I have to settle for scowling in her direction with my eyes shut tight. Since hers probably are as well, the point is likely moot.

The Phoenix isn't buying Ra's words. "You have called forth the primordial stone. Tell me you do not believe it has the power to kill me. You fool! Nothing can kill me," she insists at about two hundred decibels.

"Must you keep shouting?" I ask, turning my face in the direction of her voice. Since it is behind my wing, she still can't see I'm looking at her. "It would be nice to have only one of my senses disabled at a time."

A flash of heat shoots toward me. The Phoenix may not be able to see me, but she can certainly hear me. Maybe this wasn't the right time to provoke her. Regardless of what Ra is doing, she still has control over her Cosmic Fire. My wing holds against the onslaught of heat, but there is the distinct smell of singed feathers in the air. "Hey!" I exclaim. "These are the only pair I get!"

"Huma." Ra's voice is still velvety smooth, but there is a layer of steel just below the surface. "Stop." To my great surprise, she does. The attack of Cosmic Fire ends before my blood begins to boil and melt my skin from the inside out. When this is over, I need to remember to thank him. Through Eliana, of course. Darn, I said I wasn't going to use that phrase anymore.

"What does it matter?" Huma asks. "What do any of these mortals matter? They are here only to suffer and die."

"Um, I for one get a lot more out of life than that," I inform her.

"You are not truly mortal," the Phoenix spits out. It's a phlegmy sort of spit, like she really worked up a good one to show her disgust at the possibility of my not dying with everyone else. She really knows how to make a person feel unloved. And wet.

As Huma is speaking, I sense a shift in Eliana. I somehow know that Ra is retreating and my friend is once again in control of her body. And her voice. Next to me, Eliana's voice comes out in a raw whisper. "Sunglasses would be nice." Her vocal cords must be tired after having to create Ra's much deeper voice.

Sunglasses. Huh, why didn't I think of that? Oh, yeah, because I suck at that kind of magic. Still, I concentrate on creating sunglasses good enough to keep our retinas intact. I make them the kind that wrap around the eye completely like goggles. I don't want any stray light seeping in to blind us.

"What is this?!" the Phoenix cries.

Daring to open one eye, I lower my wing. It is still amazingly bright in my circle, but I can just make out a pair of dark glasses in front of me. Apparently, I made a pair for the Phoenix, as well. A quick glance around the perimeter of my circle informs me that everyone walking by is also wearing my special brand of sunglasses. People are stopping in their tracks and trying to pull them from their faces. Hmm, that's going to be difficult for someone to explain. Makes me glad I live in the Fairy realm. Remembering that Eliana does not, I give her a sheepish smile.

My friend shrugs. "I live in the United States." So glad she can take things in stride like that.

Giving up on trying to get her sunglasses off, the Phoenix rounds on Eliana. "Ra has retreated? He finally understands this is the end, then." A smile born from true sociopathy forms on her face.

Eliana shakes her head. "No, he has simply realized that you cannot be reasoned with anymore. Not even by someone who once loved you with all of his heart."

Before the Phoenix has a chance to respond, Eliana reaches her hand toward the obelisk and the light emanating from it. Closing her eyes, she whispers, "Let me touch the sun."

Wow, and I thought some of my ideas were bad. Calling upon the sun seems like a recipe for speeding up the Phoenix's plans. I am about to tell my friend this, when a beam of light extends down into my circle from above. Pure, unfiltered sunlight. Hot, hot, hot sunlight. Hot because it is not just light. It holds within it energy from the sun itself. It is not Cosmic Fire, per se, but if I was being burned by the two, I really wouldn't be able to tell the difference. Either way, I would be dead.

"What are you doing?" Huma demands, her voice higher now. She is beginning to suspect that her plan is not going to work.

So am I. As soon as the energy from the sunlight hits the energy of whatever that is inside the obelisk, we are all knocked on our butts. Eliana is the first to rise, her hand still extended toward the ray of sunlight and a smile in place on her face. She turns to the Phoenix. "Even you cannot destroy the primordial stone. It is older and more powerful than you are."

"Neither can it kill me," Huma counters.

"True," Eliana nods. "But as long as it calls to the sun, time will not move forward."

What?! I swing my head from side to side, just now noticing that the people outside my circle have stopped moving. Some of them in mid-step. Time really has halted. Crap, what does that mean?

It is only when Eliana turns her smile on me that I realize I said that last part aloud. "It means we are in a stalemate. If time does not progress, the Cosmic Fire within the Phoenix cannot expand."

"Meaning she can't destroy the universes. Got it," I nod in approval.

"As long as time stands still, neither of you will see the ones you love," Huma snarls.

I pretend to think about that for a moment. "True," I say slowly. "But, Eliana and I will be kept company by all the wonderful memories we have shared with them. You, on the other hand, will continue to be tortured by whatever demons you are carrying around inside you. For eternity," I add. "Between the three of us, I think it'll suck more for you."

Huma screams in frustration and my wings close in around my head in an effort to protect my eardrums. Eliana almost chokes on a feather when they do the same for her. "You cannot do this!" Huma howls.

Pushing my feathers aside, Eliana's smile grows wider and cockier. "I carry the Sun God within me. He can wield the power of the sun for eternity, so yes, we can do this."

I can see it in her eyes the moment the Phoenix realizes she has been beaten. "My sisters told you what to do," she says bitterly.

I shake my head. "Nope. They pretty much just said 'figure it out or you never get to see your friends again.' Apparently, sociopathy runs in your family."

Huma glares at me. "Liar."

I shake my head yet again. "Nope. A little birdie told my Familiars." After a pause, I clarify, "Actually, a little birdie's memories, you know, all the dark ones, told my Familiars. As they pointed out, you really shouldn't let something evil like that loose after keeping it caged for millennia. It's likely to turn on you. Especially if its survival is at stake."

Huma screams in frustration once again. Damn it, immortal or not, I'm sick of it. Ramping up my magic to immortal level, I take her ear-shattering voice away.

## 39 Chapter

Talking about Taz and Felix makes my heart clutch. Are they okay? Did I get us away from them before the Phoenix killed them with her Cosmic Fire? I need to find out. Which means we can't really spend eternity here in a stalemate. An idea pops into my head and even I am impressed by its brilliance. And my modesty. "Look, this is getting old. How about if I arrange for all of your bad memories to be stripped from your soul so you don't have to feel all this pain anymore?"

Huma stares at me in bewilderment. "Only the Phoenix ritual can rid us of our memories."

I cock my head to the side. "Are you sure about that? I mean, have you ever tried another way?"

The Phoenix's forehead scrunches together in thought. "There has never been a need."

Eliana rolls her eyes. "Yet, here you are carrying around all this baggage from who knows how many lives. I think there's a need."

There is the teeny tiniest glimmer of hope in Huma's eyes. "How can this be done?"

I smile. I guess she doesn't like being a sociopath, after all. That's good to know. I can't even imagine the amount of soul pain she has been living with to drive her to this point. "If you get us back to the Phoenix realm, I'll explain."

Huma's eyes harden again. "This is a trap. Once I am back among my sisters, they will force the ritual upon me."

I can understand her concerns. Mostly because they probably will do exactly that. "Yes," I nod. "You are about to go supernova, and they are going to keep that from happening. But, I promise you will be happy in your realm once again. You won't be living with this pain any longer. Look, this is going to take trust on both of our parts. You need to trust that we can do what we say we can, and we need to trust that you won't destroy the world once Eliana lets the energy from the sun go, right?"

Her shoulders slumping in defeat, Huma asks, "Can you truly do as you say?"

"I can't personally," I admit, "but I know some people who can." I really, really hope they can. I don't say that last part aloud. Nor do I mention how painful the process will probably be on someone who is still living. If the Phoenix is in so much emotional pain she is willing to destroy universes to make it go away, then she probably won't care about the physical pain. Well, she might while it's happening, but it will be worth it in the end. "Do we have a deal?" I ask.

After a long moment of internal deliberation, Huma finally agrees. "We must hurry. I do not have long."

Eliana nods. "We know. Do you still have the ability to transport us to your realm without going supernova?" Exerting that much energy may push her over the edge.

"Yes."

I hope she's right. In a great leap of faith, Eliana pulls her hand back and releases the energy she and Ra called upon. The beam of light retracts, and the primordial stone and its own blinding light disappear into the earth once again. The obelisk slides back into place. That's convenient. I was worried we'd have to explain breaking the thing. Except for the freak sunglasses incident, we are going to leave this place the way we found it. How unusual for me.

When everything is set, Huma holds her hands out to us. As I place mine in hers, I wince. She is even hotter than she was a few minutes ago. Huma nods and simultaneously, I drop my circle and she transports us to the Phoenix realm. Nobody in the area should have seen a thing, it happened so quickly. Besides, they're all still too busy trying to get their sunglasses off to notice anything else. I pull my magic back as we leave the realm, relieving them of the problem. I try not to think about how far away people were affected by the sunglasses since I was using a lot of magic at the time. It's probably for the best not to know. Plausible deniability.

We are met by a round of applause when we arrive in the Phoenix realm. The identicals gather around us and gush over our success. If they hadn't held our friends hostage while we were gone, I would appreciate it more. "Could you just perform the ritual?" I drawl. "She's about to blow."

Turning their attention to their sister, several among them gasp. Chol steps forward. "To the temple. Hurry!" Several of the Phoenixes grab hold of Huma and practically drag her away. For happy souls, they're not very gentle with each other. As Chol turns to follow them, she says over her shoulder, "You will wait here."

"Yeah, kind of figured you weren't going to let us watch," I mutter.

When they are gone, Eliana glances around. "Where do you think they put the others?"

"Probably locked in a dungeon somewhere," I offer. "I can't sense any of them close by."

Eliana frowns. "Do you really think they have a dungeon?"

"I think they're crazy enough to have a dungeon."

"You got me there," she agrees.

"I guess I need to try to make good on my end of the deal," I say. "I'll be right back." To Eliana, I will literally be right back. No matter how long it takes me in Angel time, it will feel like no time has passed for her.

I rely on my wings to bring me where I need to go. I am not surprised to find myself in the grand garden where many of the Angels like to congregate when they have down time. Several of them wave to me and I wave back, not one hundred percent certain who they all are. I really should spend more time here and get to know more Angels. They are my kin, after all.

It takes a few minutes of wandering around, but I finally find Rashnu. She is having a discussion with another

Angel, and it does not appear to be going well. Rashnu is wearing the expression she wears right before she turns into a giant, soul-eating monster. It doesn't take long for the other Angel to back down and slink away. I hurry up and turn around, ready to come back later when Rashnu is in a much, much better mood.

It's too late. She spotted me. "Xandra," she calls. "Have you not come here with a request?"

How does she already know why I came? That question must be on my face because Rashnu smiles, all traces of the annoyance she was feeling a moment ago gone. The Angel has some serious mood swings. As long as they swing in my favor, I'm okay with that. "Word of someone promising the services of my Angels is quick to reach my ears."

Uh oh. Maybe her mood is not swinging in my favor, despite her smile. I feel a hundred different shades of red pass over my cheeks. "Sorry to do that without asking you first. Heat of the moment and all."

To my relief, Rashnu gets it. "I understand. You had to make the deal to save the universes, a task set upon you by us, the Angels. I cannot begrudge the path you needed to take to accomplish the near impossible."

Technically, she could. I am glad she is choosing not to do so. "Thanks," I say, mustering a smile even though I'm not one hundred percent convinced she's still not the tiniest bit annoyed with me. "So, is it possible?" I ask.

Rashnu nods. "It will be difficult, tedious and quite painful, but it can be done."

I consider her words. "Painful for the Phoenix, not you guys, right?"

Rashnu smiles. "I appreciate your concern. No, we will not be the ones feeling the pain. Exhaustion perhaps, but no pain."

My eyes widen a little. "You will be directly involved?"

Nodding, Rashnu explains, "It will take a great deal of power to accomplish what you have promised. More power than my Angels of Death could muster on their own."

See, she is the tiniest bit annoyed with me. "Sorry again," I hurry to say. I do not want Rashnu to stay annoyed with me.

Rashnu waves off my apology. "Someday, you will repay me. Until then, go and assure all of the Phoenixes that we will do as you said." After a slight pause, she adds, "We might as well take care of the rest of them while we are at it. We do not want another situation like this one to arise."

"Good point," I nod. With a final wave, and more than mild concern over what repaying her will consist of, I exit Angel time. I am back in the Phoenix realm standing with Eliana, who is looking at me expectantly.

"Aren't you going to talk to the Angels?" she asks.

I grin. "I already did."

Eliana shakes her head. "I will never get used to that. What did they say?"

"They'll do it."

"Good," she sighs in relief.

Behind us, in a temple about a thousand feet away, a brilliant burst of Cosmic Fire explodes into the air before being sucked back down. The blast knocks us backwards. Hard. I'm getting really tired of this happening. So is my butt.

## 40 CHAPTER

Since nothing else blows up, and the fire is sucked back into the temple, we assume that it's just part of the ritual. Even if it's not, Eliana and I aren't going to rush toward the temple to check it out. The Phoenixes are immune to the Fire, we're not. So, if there is a problem, they can deal with it.

It's another twenty minutes before Chol finally returns. Impatient to get the heck out of here and back to Kallen, who is probably having conniptions right along with Josh by now, I speak as soon as she is within hearing distance. "Where are our friends?" I demand.

Chol waves a hand in the air as if the question is irrelevant. "We sent them home as soon as you left."

"What?!" Eliana and I both exclaim at once.

Chol pulls that 'you're an idiot' face again. "Why would we want to keep them here?"

"Um, because you said you were going to hold them hostage until we stopped Huma," I remind her.

"Yes, but they were such a bother. You were already doing as we asked, so we saw no reason to burden ourselves with them any longer."

It's a good thing Eliana is strong. I didn't even realize my hand was on its way to Chol's face until Eliana grabs it. She gives her head a slight shake and I sigh. She's right. Hitting the Phoenix is probably not the right thing to do at the moment. No matter how much I really, really want to do it.

Deciding a different line of questioning would be safer, Eliana asks, "There is a new Phoenix in place now?"

Chol's smile is broad. "Indeed. She is young and has never lived outside of this realm before. Her excitement was contagious."

They have different ages? Considering all of the Phoenixes are female, and identical, I thought they were clones all created at the same time. It briefly crosses my mind to ask how they come into being, by birth or cloning, but then I decide I just don't care. "Yeah, we could feel the excitement all the way out here," I snark under my breath instead.

My sarcasm completely lost on her, Chol asks, "Really? How fascinating."

Still gripping my slapping hand, Eliana replies, "Yes, it is. If our friends have returned home and the new Phoenix is in place, are we free to leave?"

"Oh, yes. The sooner the better. We do not like outsiders in our realm."

Considering we just saved the universes, that was pretty damn rude. "We got that," I mutter. Then, I can't help but ask, "Are you bothered by the fact that everyone now knows the secret of the Phoenix?" Might as well push her buttons like she is mine.

"Don't be silly," Chol scoffs. "We sent each being back to their own realm with their memories altered. Except the Angel, of course. Her mind is off limits."

I eye her. "Which means my mind is off limits, as well."

Chol sighs in disappointment. "Yes. Yours, however," she says to Eliana, "is not."

Before either of us know what's happening, Chol zaps Eliana's forehead with a burst of Cosmic Fire. Then, she unceremoniously shoves us out of the Phoenix realm.

We find ourselves once again in the hot desert sand. On our backs. Being blinded by the sun.

"What an ungrateful…"

"Eliana!" Josh shouts before I can finish my sentence. He and Kallen are heading toward us.

Probably for the best I didn't finish since we are right in front of the Phoenix's temple. Who knows if the new one is inside and listening or not. To my great relief, Kallen is carrying Taz and Felix in his arms. I have never been so happy to see the Tasmanian devils in my life. Some of their hair is singed, and they are obviously a little weak if Kallen has to carry them, but I can sense that essentially they are fine. A little rest and a whole lot of bacon will perk them both right up.

A groggy Eliana pushes herself to a sitting position. "What happened?" she asks.

Oh, no. Her mind has been erased like the others. Panicked, I ask, "What do you remember?"

She opens her mouth to speak, but closes it again when her eyes begin to glow red. After a few seconds, she turns to me with a wicked smile. "Everything."

I grin back. "I guess Ra and Isis weren't about to let you forget, huh?"

Eliana shakes her head. "Nope."

Kallen and Josh have reached us now, and I ask them both, "Do you remember why we're here?"

Kallen's movements become a little more cautious. "Yes," he says slowly. "Do you not remember?"

"Maybe her brain got singed like your hair," Taz says to Felix.

"Bite me," Felix replies.

I laugh. "I'll explain at home," I tell all three of them. I stand up and don't even bother to brush the sand from my clothes. I also don't care about satellite images at the moment. I just want to be home. I reach out, tear open a passageway and gesture the others through. I follow them and close the passage behind us. We did it. The danger has passed and the universes are safe. For now, anyway. Who knows what tomorrow will bring.

I expected a warm welcome. Or at least a 'Thank you for saving the universes.' I did not expect Tabitha standing on the terrace with her hands on her hips growling, "It is about damn time. Where have you been?"

Nonplussed, I respond, "Um, saving the universe." Did the Phoenix's wipe *everyone's* memories? Do they have that much power?

Apparently not, because Tabitha grouses, "Isla returned over an hour ago. Why did you not return with her? And what the hell is wrong with her? She is acting like she has no idea what has been happening over the last several days."

Ah. I now understand her frustration. "That's because she doesn't," I say as I walk toward the house.

Noticing for the first time that Kallen is carrying Taz and Felix, Tabitha gasps and rushes toward us. The warm welcome that I was expecting is lavished on the little beasts. Tabitha takes them into her own arms and glares at all of us. "What did you do to the babies?"

"Babies?" I mouth to Kallen who shrugs.

Tabitha shakes her head. "You can tell me later. I am going to get them inside and something to eat. They look like they are about ready to perish."

I narrow my eyes at my Familiars. Taz, who was starting to perk up a minute ago, does suddenly look like he's on death's door. Felix, from whom I would expect better, also seems to have taken a turn for the worse. "Yeah, they're barely holding on," I snark. Then, I remember how they solved the Phoenix problem and heroically risked their lives so we could follow through with their plans. Guilt washes through me and my voice is much more sympathetic when I say, "Could you make them some extra bacon? They've earned it." I'm not even sure Tabitha heard me. She's too busy cooing to them in a soothing voice as she walks into the house.

"For a Fairy who would not let me have a pet as a child, she has certainly grown attached to those beasts," Kallen grouses.

I smile and wrap my arms around him. "Don't worry. I'm sure she'll feed you, too. After she feeds them."

Kallen snorts. "I will probably get their leftovers."

There is a squeal from the porch and Sam and Jenna come rushing out of the house. They practically tackle Eliana and Josh. "You did it!" Jenna shouts. "I mean, you're back, so you must have done it!"

Eliana laughs. "Yes, we did it," she confirms.

Jenna lets go of her and engulfs both Kallen and me in a hug. "You guys are awesome!" she declares.

"Thanks, we try," I laugh. Now her excitement is contagious.

From inside, we can hear Dagda. His voice is growing louder and more frustrated by the second. "How can you have no recollection of what has transpired over the last three days?" I suspect this is not the first time he has asked this question.

"We had better get inside," I tell the others and hurry up the terrace stairs.

In the large living room, we find Dagda pacing back and forth in front of an increasingly irate Isla. Garren is sitting on one of the couches shaking his head in dismay. "How many times do I need to explain this? My memories are gone," Isla growls. "If I knew how or why, I would be able to retrieve them."

Eliana steps around me and holds her hand out to Isla. "Maybe I can help with that," she says.

Isla stares at her curiously, then to everyone's surprise, she steps toward Eliana. Usually, she would ask a million questions and be certain she understands exactly what is about to happen. Isla never likes the uncertain. This memory loss thing must be really tearing her apart inside to jump in with both feet and little knowledge of what is to come.

Slipping her hand into Eliana's, Isla's expression changes almost instantly. Her eyes become slightly glazed and her mouth is slack. I can feel Eliana's power reaching out to her. I remember the backpacker in Colorado and how Eliana was able to temporarily erase her memory. I suspect she is doing the same thing in reverse. She is giving Isla back her memories. Retrieving them from wherever they have been locked away. Hopefully, it will not be temporary as her power of influence is.

As soon as Eliana breaks contact with Isla, the latter snaps back to herself. Her eyes grow wide and she stares at my friend. "That was amazing," she whispers almost more to herself than Eliana.

"Do you remember now?" Dagda asks impatiently.

Isla nods, still staring at Eliana. "I remember things I didn't even realize I had forgotten with time. My entire memory has been restored."

"What?" Josh asks. He stares at Eliana in awe and then grins. "I guess a new power is manifesting."

Eliana's cheeks flush slightly. "I guess so."

"Will it be permanent?" I ask. "I mean the memories, not the new power."

Eliana nods. "I believe so, but I can't be certain."

Even though I can tell Dagda is interested in Eliana's new ability, he is more interested in the state of the universe. "*Now* will someone please tell me what happened?"

"If the rest of you want food, you better get your butts in the kitchen," Tabitha calls out.

"She has been stress cooking all day," Jenna explains. "There is a ton of food in there."

She doesn't need to tell us twice. I don't move quite as quickly as I did when going after the Phoenix earlier, but it's pretty darn close. I am famished. So is my husband if his long strides and speed mean anything. A frustrated Dagda trails behind us, knowing he's not going to get any information until we get food.

In the kitchen, we find Jenna was correct. I think Tabitha made every dish she knows how to cook in the time we were gone. We all grab plates and dig in. Isla and Garren join us. After a few minutes, Mom and Dad and Zac rush in, having figured out we are home. Kegan, Alita and Keelan follow close behind. While we eat, we tell them all the tale of the Phoenix. I don't really care at this point if the Phoenixes want their realm to be a secret. I figure that if Eliana and I have to keep one of them from destroying the universes, we have earned the right to share their secret with the ones we love. Besides, we know the people in this room won't tell anyone else.

"You'll restore Jadyn's memory when you get back home, right?" I ask Eliana.

She nods then grins. "I'm sure it's driving Liza insane that Jadyn can't remember anything." Considering she is as easily frustrated as Dagda, I believe it.

"That's probably putting it mildly," Josh says with his own grin.

Adriel and Raziel eventually make their way into the kitchen, as well. I suspect they were hiding upstairs until after all the explanations were made. Adriel would not have wanted to clue anyone in to the fact that she still had her memory while Isla did not. It only would have aggravated them all more.

We convince Josh, Eliana, Jenna and Sam to stay one more night. The last two are easy. Josh and Eliana take a little more convincing as they feel guilty leaving their boss hanging. At least until Kallen explains how time moves faster here than in the Cowan realm.

After a good night's sleep, we spend the first part of the day showing them around the Fairy village. Eliana and Josh enjoy it much more than their trip to the Giant village a couple of days ago. At least here everyone is their size. After a swim in the ocean and an early dinner, it's time to bring them back to the Cowan realm.

"You promise you will come back the next time you get a vacation, right?" I ask as I give Eliana a hug good bye in her living room.

"I think your father would come here looking for us if we didn't," she laughs. Dagda spent our entire last dinner together trying to convince her to move to the Fairy realm to no avail.

"Don't worry, he can only get here if I let him through," I assure her with a smile.

"Good to know."

We say our good byes to Josh, Sam and Jenna, who also promise to visit us again in the Fairy realm. Kallen and I are about to return through the passageway I made when Eliana's phone rings. She looks at the display and frowns. Answering, she says, "Hi, I'm going to put you on speaker."

She presses a button and a man's voice comes through the phone. "We have had seismic activity but no earthquake, sunglasses appearing out of nowhere which can't be removed until they disappear on their own, claims that a solar flare hit the obelisk in Heliopolis, and a temple has been unearthed in the desert north of the city. Care to explain any of these things?"

"Agent Amman," Josh says. "Nice to hear from you. Sorry to hear about all that, but we have no idea what you're talking about."

"Uh huh," the Egyptian agent says. "Are you home and safe?" he asks.

"We are," Eliana assures him.

"That's all I really needed to know." Agent Amman ends the call. I suspect his life is going to be busy for a while, but he will never share all he knows with his government.

I smile at Eliana. "It's good to know that you have people who watch your back."

She glances over my shoulder at the crowd who came down to the beach with us to see them off. "Right back at you," she says with a grin.

With a last wave good bye, Kallen and I step back through the passageway to our own realm and I close it. Wrapping his arms around me and leaning down, my gorgeous husband whispers in my ear, "I know the perfect way to thank you for saving the universe."

I know that gleam in his eye and images pop into my head of all the ways he could thank me. I look from him to our family standing in front of us. I know exactly who I want to celebrate with. "Good night," I tell the group, and I teleport Kallen and myself straight to our bedroom. If I have my way, we won't be leaving this room for days. After all, we did save more than one universe. I wouldn't mind a thank you for each and every one of them.

Somewhere, back in the farthest reaches of my mind, a tiny little calendar begins to form. One that usually has one day a month circled in red. My mental eye takes note of the fact that it's been a while since I added a new circle. In fact, it's been way too long since I added a new circle.

Oh. My. God.

Printed in Great Britain
by Amazon